TRESE 6

High Tide at Midnight

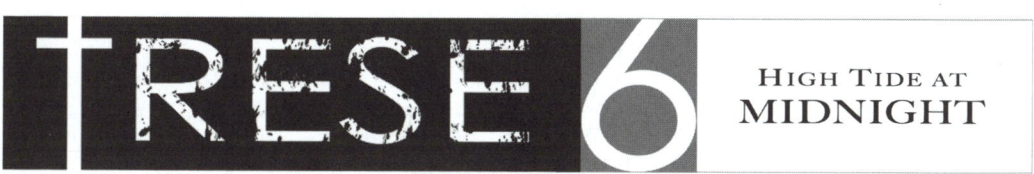

Budjette **Tan** KaJo **Baldisimo**

ABLAZE

WRITER
BUDJETTE TAN

ARTIST
KAJO BALDISIMO

FOR ABLAZE

MANAGING EDITOR
RICH YOUNG

EDITOR
KEVIN KETNER

DESIGNERS
RODOLFO MURAGUCHI
CINTHIA TAKEDA

Publisher's Cataloging-in-Publication data

Names: Tan, Budjette, author. | Baldisimo, Kajo, artist.
Title: Trese Vol 6: High Tide at Midnight
Series: Trese
Description: Portland, OR: Ablaze Publishing, 2022.
Identifiers: ISBN: 978-1-68497-129-9
Subjects: LCSH Manila (Philippines)—Fiction. | Philippines—Fiction. | Crime—Fiction. | Mystery fiction. | Noir fiction. | Graphic novels. | Detective and mystery comic books, strips, etc. | BISAC COMICS & GRAPHIC NOVELS / Crime & Mystery
Classification: LCC PN6790.P53 .T36 v.5 2022 | DDC 741.5—dc23

Trese Volume 6: High Tide At Midnight. First printing. Published by Ablaze Publishing, 11222 SE Main St. #22906 Portland, OR 97269. TRESE © 2023 Ferdinand-Benedict Garcia Tan & Jonathan A. Baldisimo. Ablaze TM & © 2023 ABLAZE, LLC. All rights reserved. Ablaze and its logo TM & © 2023 Ablaze, LLC. All Rights Reserved. All names, characters, events, and locales in this publication are entirely fictional. Any resemblance to actual persons (living or dead), events or places, without satiric intent is coincidental. No portion of this book may be reproduced by any means (digital or print) without the written permission of Ablaze Publishing except for review purposes. Printed in China. This book may be purchased for educational, business, or promotional use in bulk. For sales information, advertising opportunities and licensing email: info@ablazepublishing.com

10 9 8 7 6 5 4 3 2 1

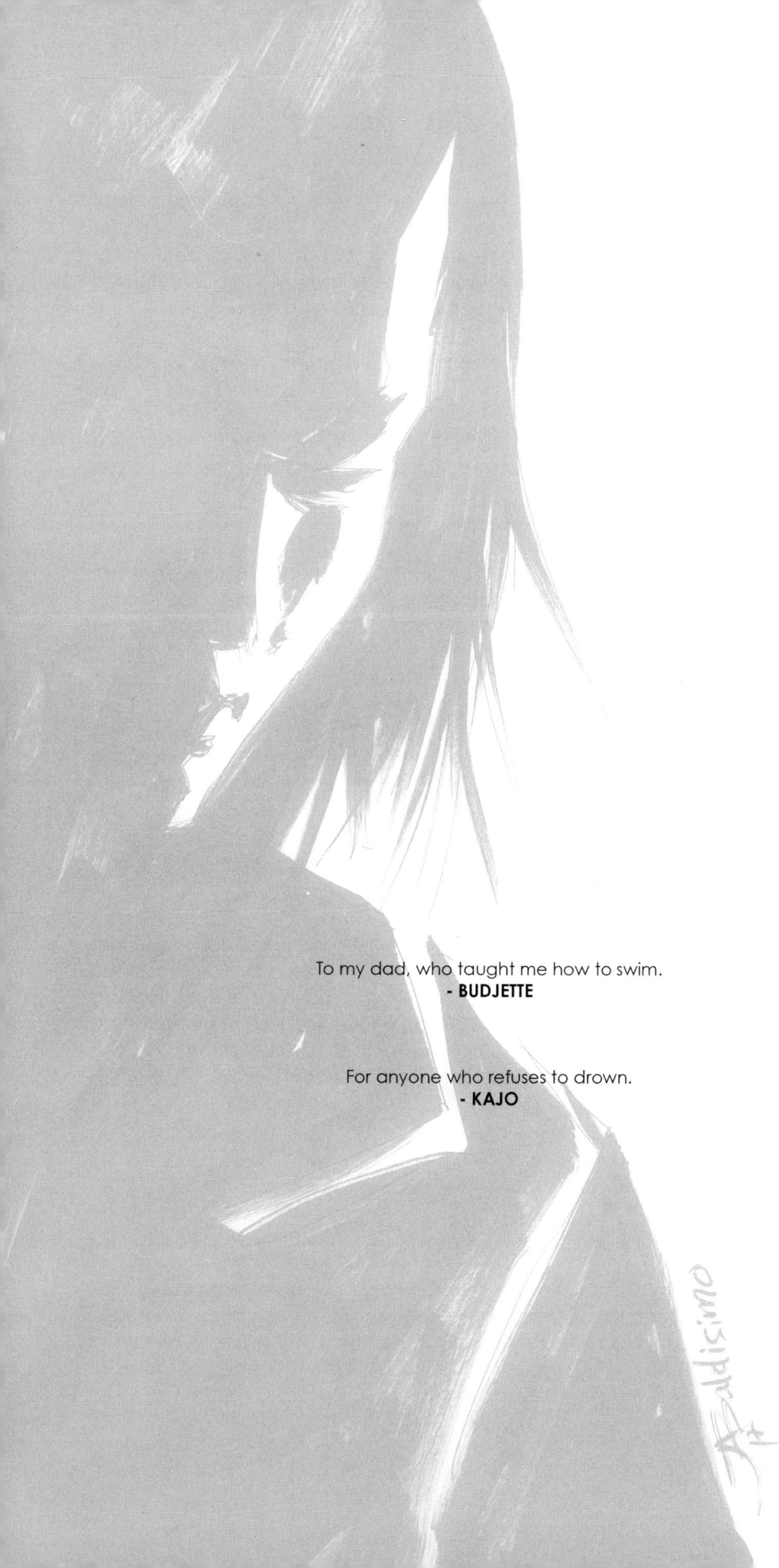

To my dad, who taught me how to swim.
- BUDJETTE

For anyone who refuses to drown.
- KAJO

INTRODUCTION

The first time I picked up a copy of Trese, I thought, "Holy crap, this is awesome!"

I first heard of Budjette in the 90s, because of Alamat. To hear of a bunch of friends making comics just because they wanted to blow my mind. I've followed Budjette's writing since then, and I remember having high expectations when the first Trese came out.

I was not disappointed.

Budjette and Kajo have captured a part of the Filipino psyche that tries to make sense of the traditional and the modern; the aswang hunter in the city, if you will.

Through Alexandra Trese, we glimpse a different Manila that overlaps with the one we know and love (or try to). The Trese series runs on the idea that many of the things we think of as normal or nature-induced actually have supernatural origins. In this volume, it's the floods that annually plague the metropolis.

Let me digress a bit. You're wondering why I was asked to write the introduction to this volume, and whether I am related to the author. No, Budjette and I are not related; we just happen to share a last name. The reason you are reading my words right now is because of a character introduced in the fifth volume: the Madame. It's the book where Trese's arch enemy is revealed, and she's the wife of a certain ex-dictator. Budjette said that he got his inspiration for the Madame from my story "The Child Abandoned," which is based on an urban legend from the 70s. I am very honored to have unwittingly contributed something to one of my favorite graphic novels.

This volume is exciting because it offers you, dear reader, broader insight into Trese's world. You meet her family. You uncover old wounds. You are taken deeper into the Manila underworld and are privy to the infernal machinations that keep our glorious city running. Here's a spoiler for you: you're going to end this book wondering what's going to happen next, and wishing that Budjette and Kajo would finish the seventh one already. I know I did.

And so I bid you turn the page. Trese's Manila--or the Madame's, depending on whose side you're on--awaits.

Yvette Tan
November 2014

Yvette Tan is an award-winning horror writer who nowadays writes more about food and travel. She's constantly on the move, writing from beaches, coffee shops, and hotels. She says that she's currently working on her third short fiction collection to follow her books Waking the Dead and Kaba, but we think she's really just snacking. Follow her at @yvette_tan on Twitter and Instagram.

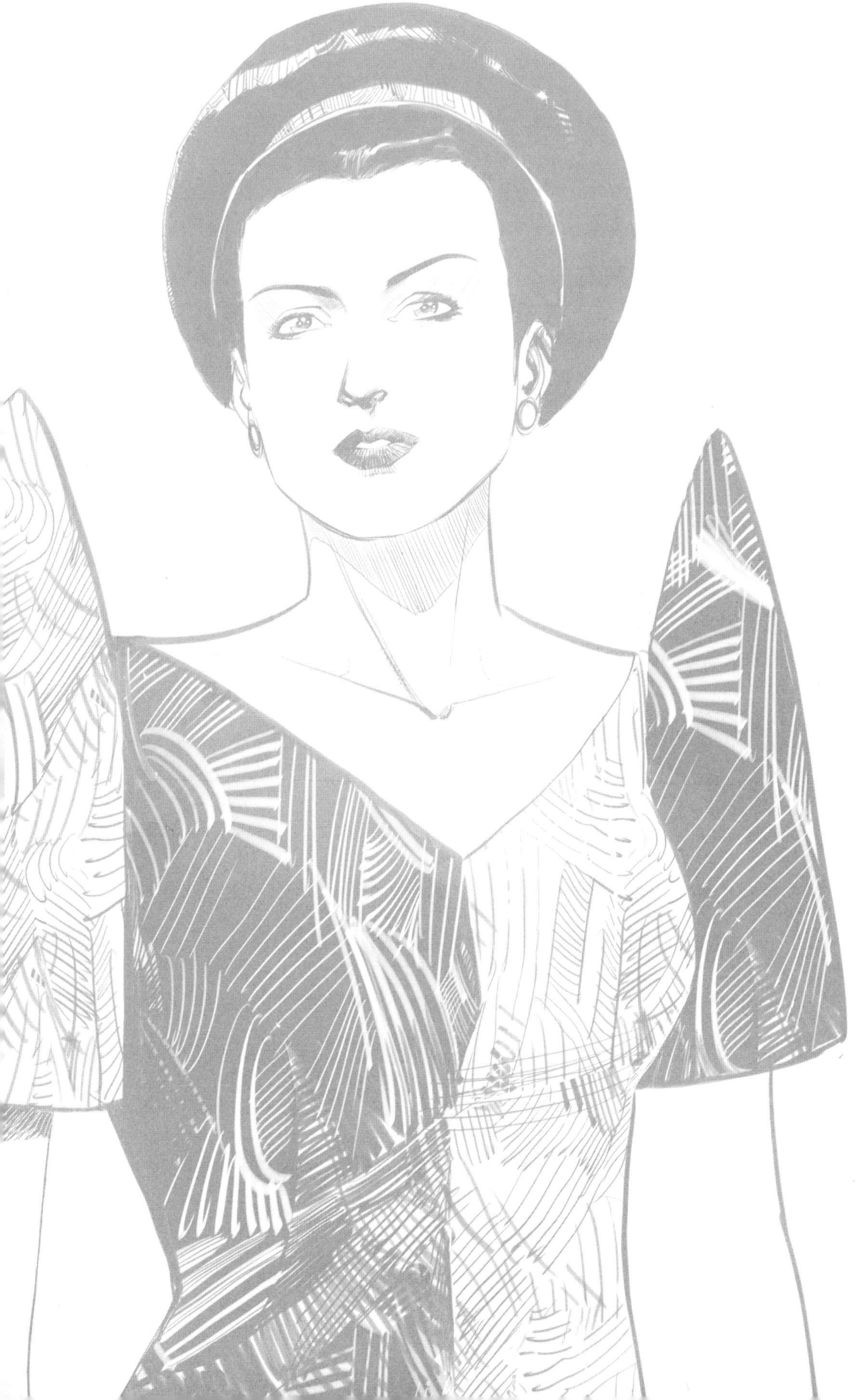

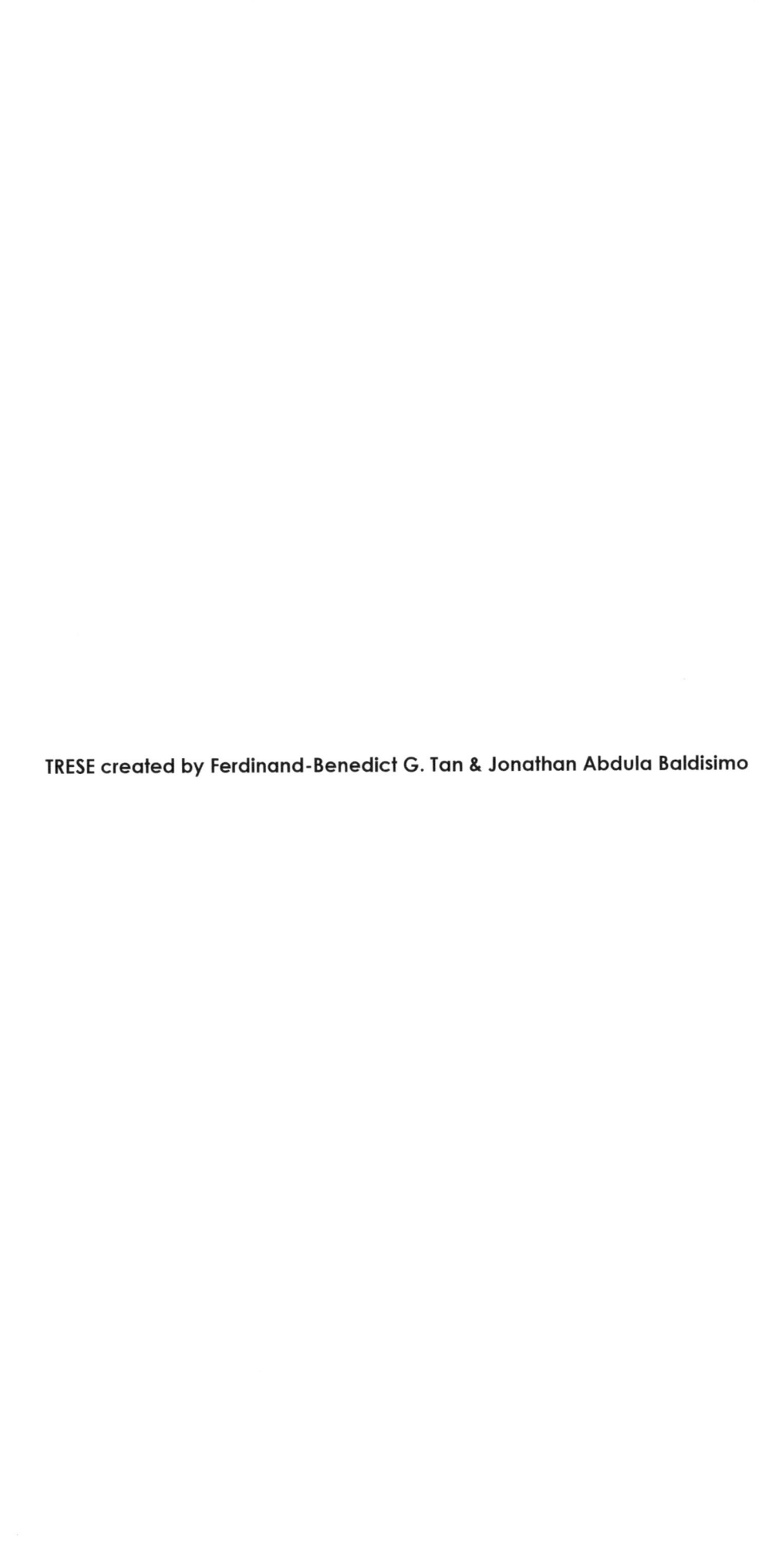

TRESE created by Ferdinand-Benedict G. Tan & Jonathan Abdula Baldisimo

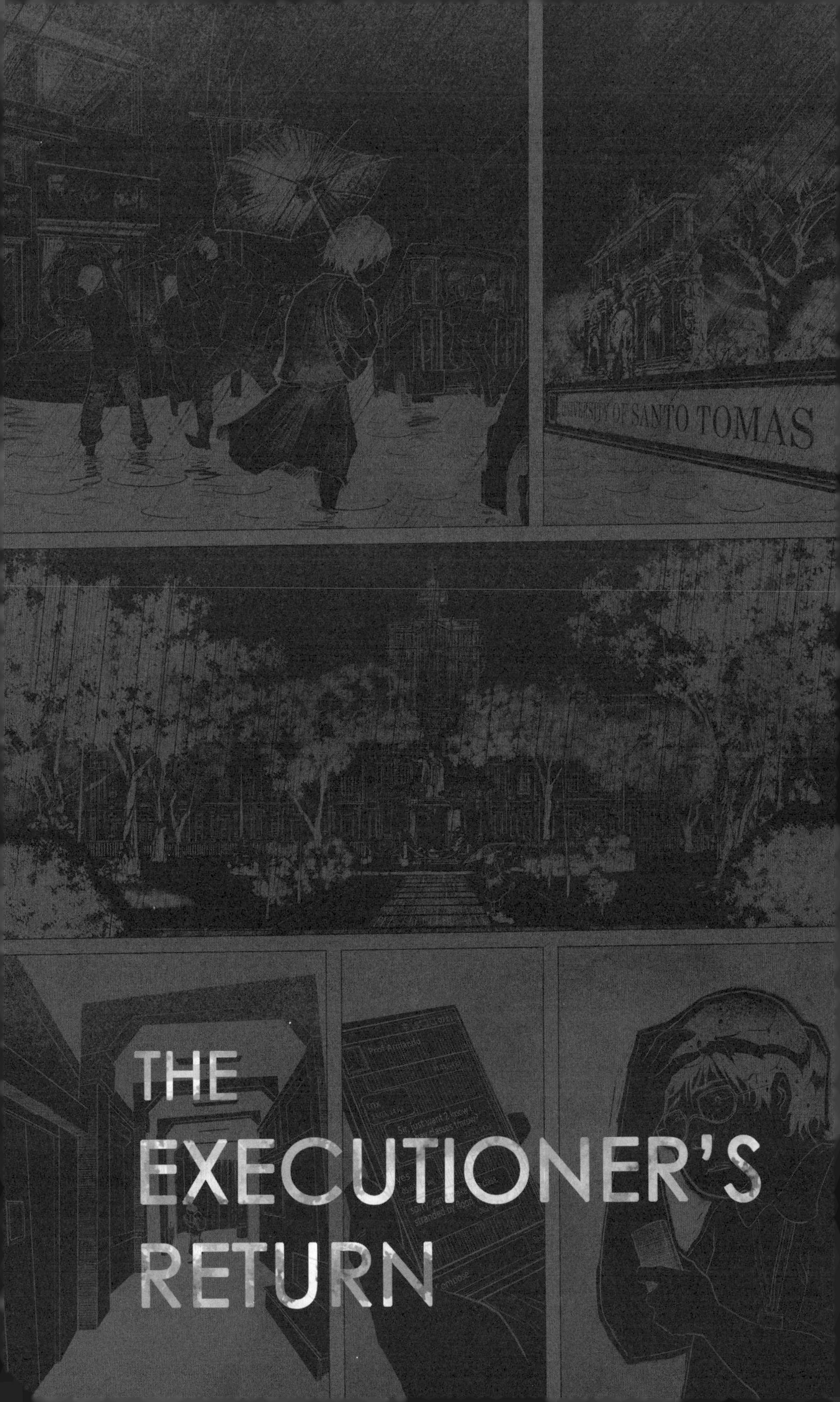
SANTO TOMAS
THE EXECUTIONER'S RETURN

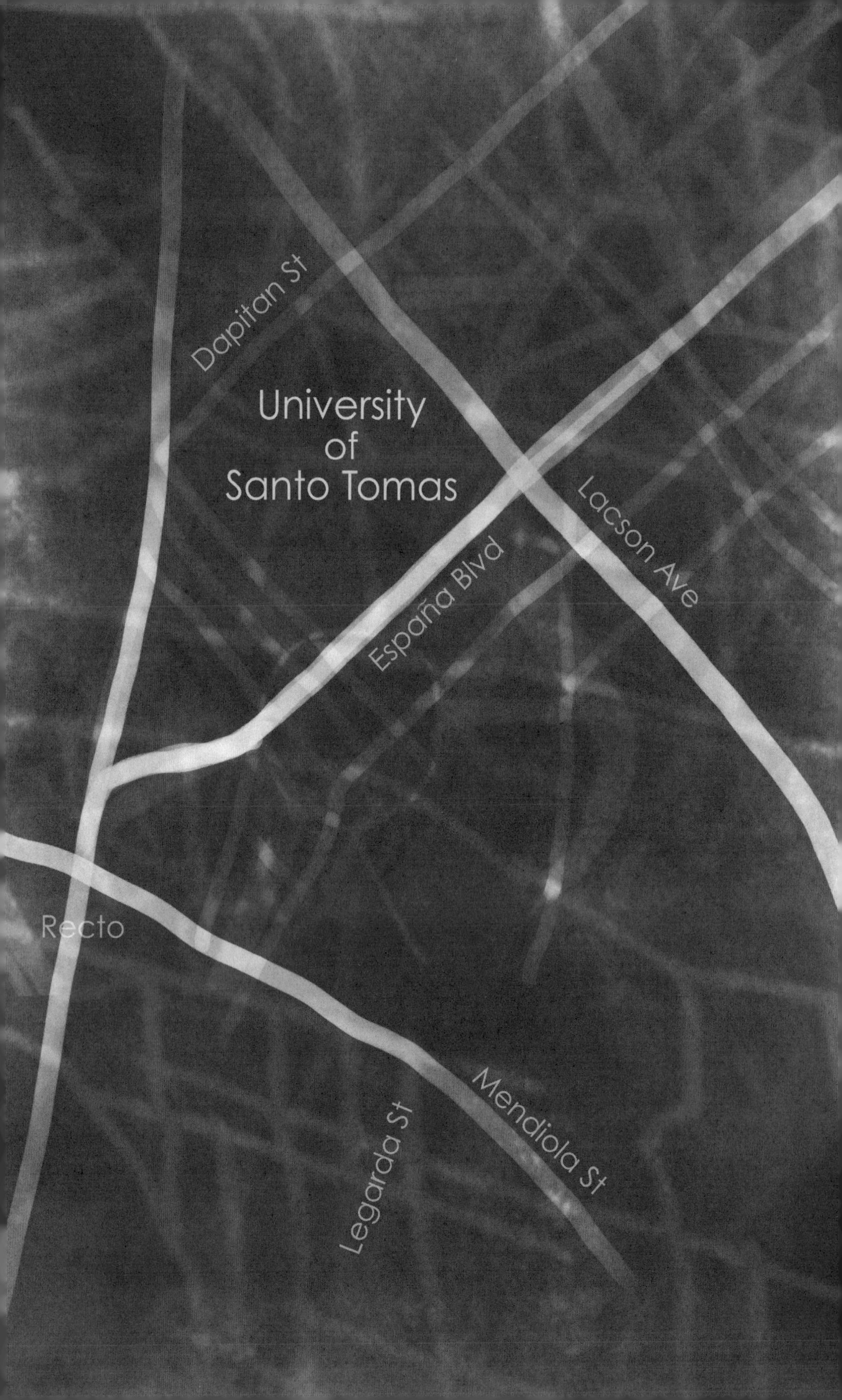
Dapitan St
University
of
Santo Tomas
Lacson Ave
España Blvd
Recto
Mendiola St
Legarda St

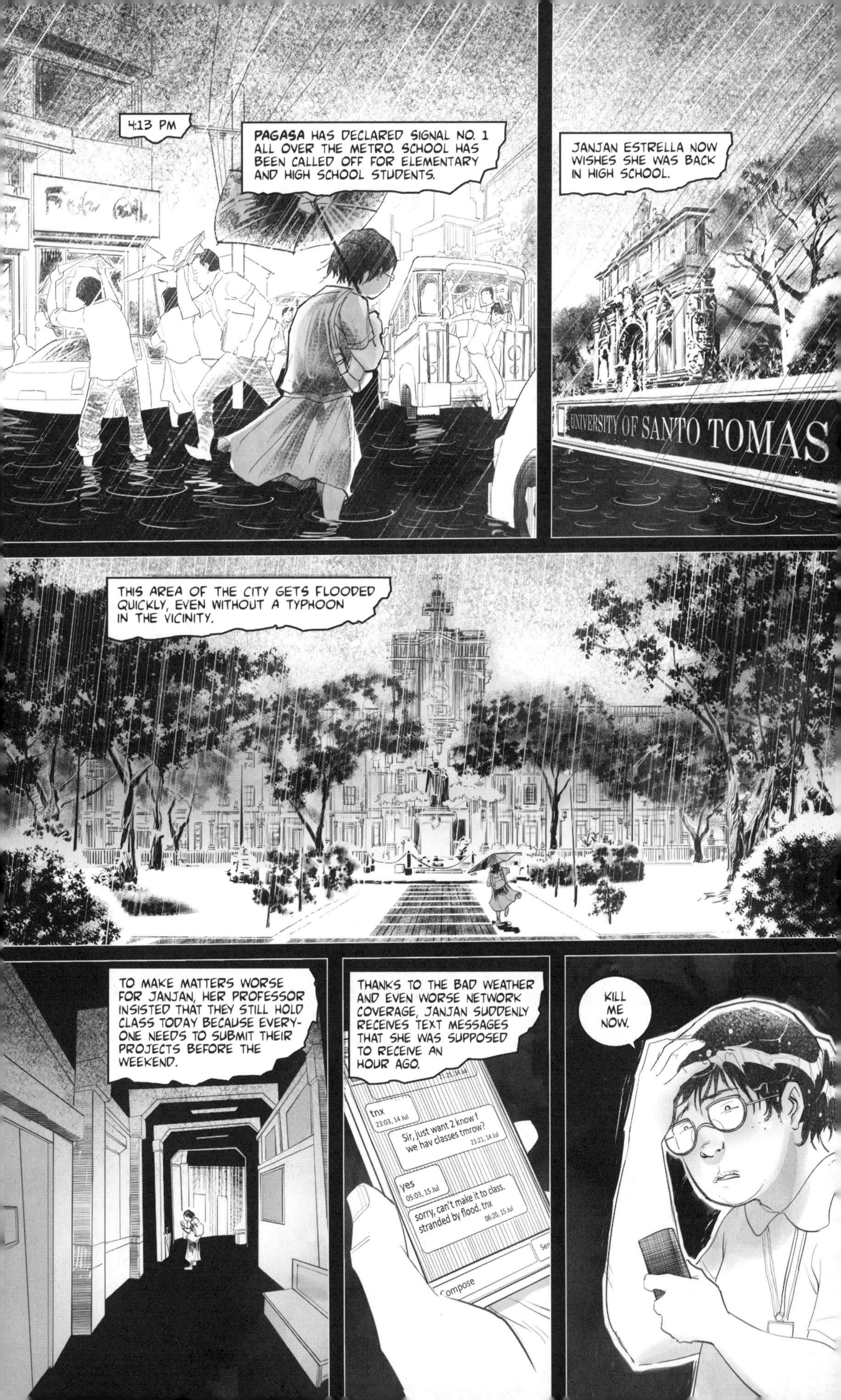
4:13 PM
PAGASA HAS DECLARED SIGNAL NO. 1 ALL OVER THE METRO. SCHOOL HAS BEEN CALLED OFF FOR ELEMENTARY AND HIGH SCHOOL STUDENTS.
JANJAN ESTRELLA NOW WISHES SHE WAS BACK IN HIGH SCHOOL.
UNIVERSITY OF SANTO TOMAS
THIS AREA OF THE CITY GETS FLOODED QUICKLY, EVEN WITHOUT A TYPHOON IN THE VICINITY.
TO MAKE MATTERS WORSE FOR JANJAN, HER PROFESSOR INSISTED THAT THEY STILL HOLD CLASS TODAY BECAUSE EVERY-ONE NEEDS TO SUBMIT THEIR PROJECTS BEFORE THE WEEKEND.
THANKS TO THE BAD WEATHER AND EVEN WORSE NETWORK COVERAGE, JANJAN SUDDENLY RECEIVES TEXT MESSAGES THAT SHE WAS SUPPOSED TO RECEIVE AN HOUR AGO.
tnx
23:03, 14 Jul
Sir, just want 2 know f we hav classes tmrow?
23:21, 14 Jul
yes
05:03, 15 Jul
sorry, can't make it to class. stranded by flood. tnx
06:20, 15 Jul
Compose
KILL ME NOW.

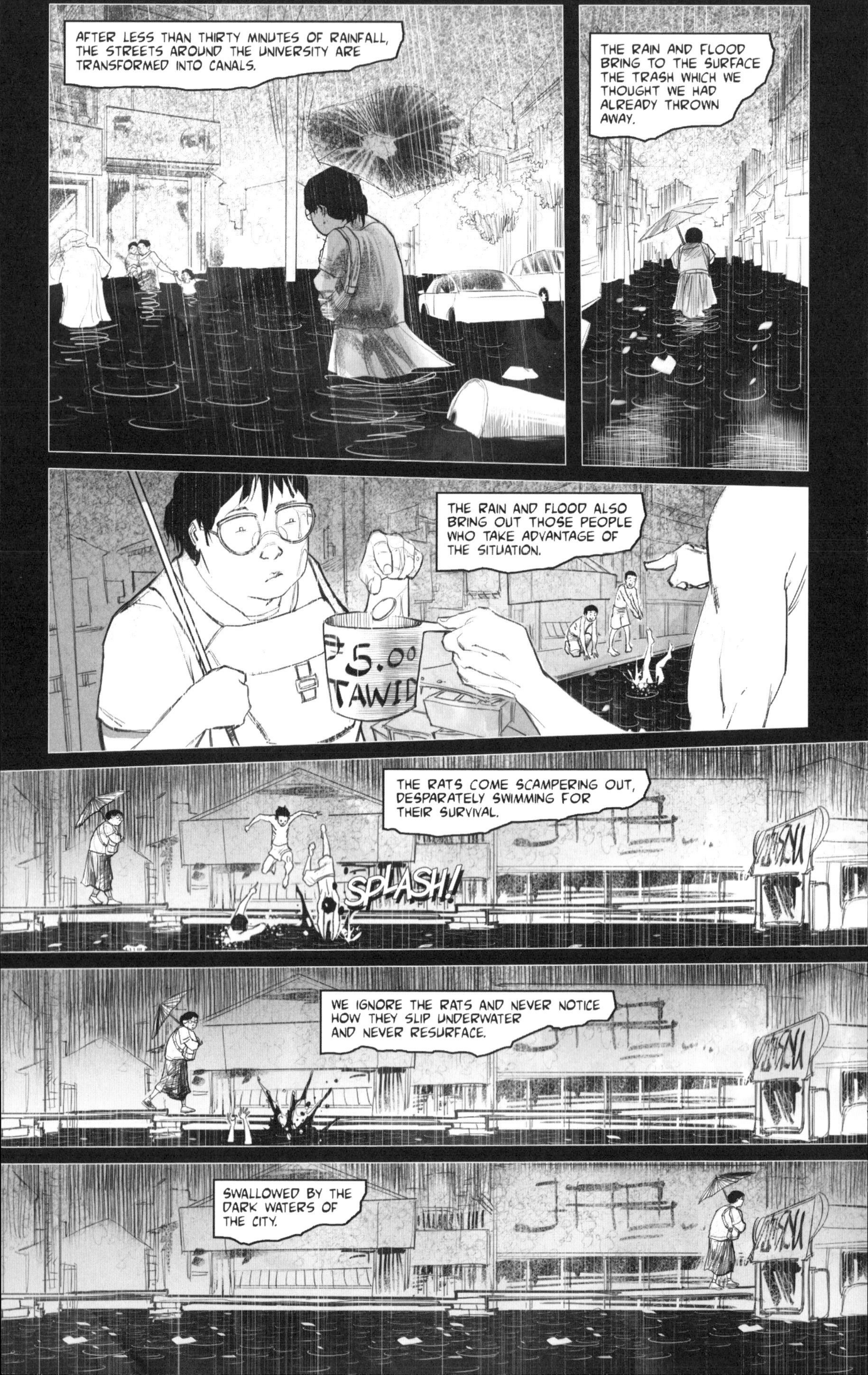
AFTER LESS THAN THIRTY MINUTES OF RAINFALL, THE STREETS AROUND THE UNIVERSITY ARE TRANSFORMED INTO CANALS.
THE RAIN AND FLOOD BRING TO THE SURFACE THE TRASH WHICH WE THOUGHT WE HAD ALREADY THROWN AWAY.
THE RAIN AND FLOOD ALSO BRING OUT THOSE PEOPLE WHO TAKE ADVANTAGE OF THE SITUATION.
₱5.00 TAWID
THE RATS COME SCAMPERING OUT, DESPARATELY SWIMMING FOR THEIR SURVIVAL.
SPLASH!
WE IGNORE THE RATS AND NEVER NOTICE HOW THEY SLIP UNDERWATER AND NEVER RESURFACE.
SWALLOWED BY THE DARK WATERS OF THE CITY.

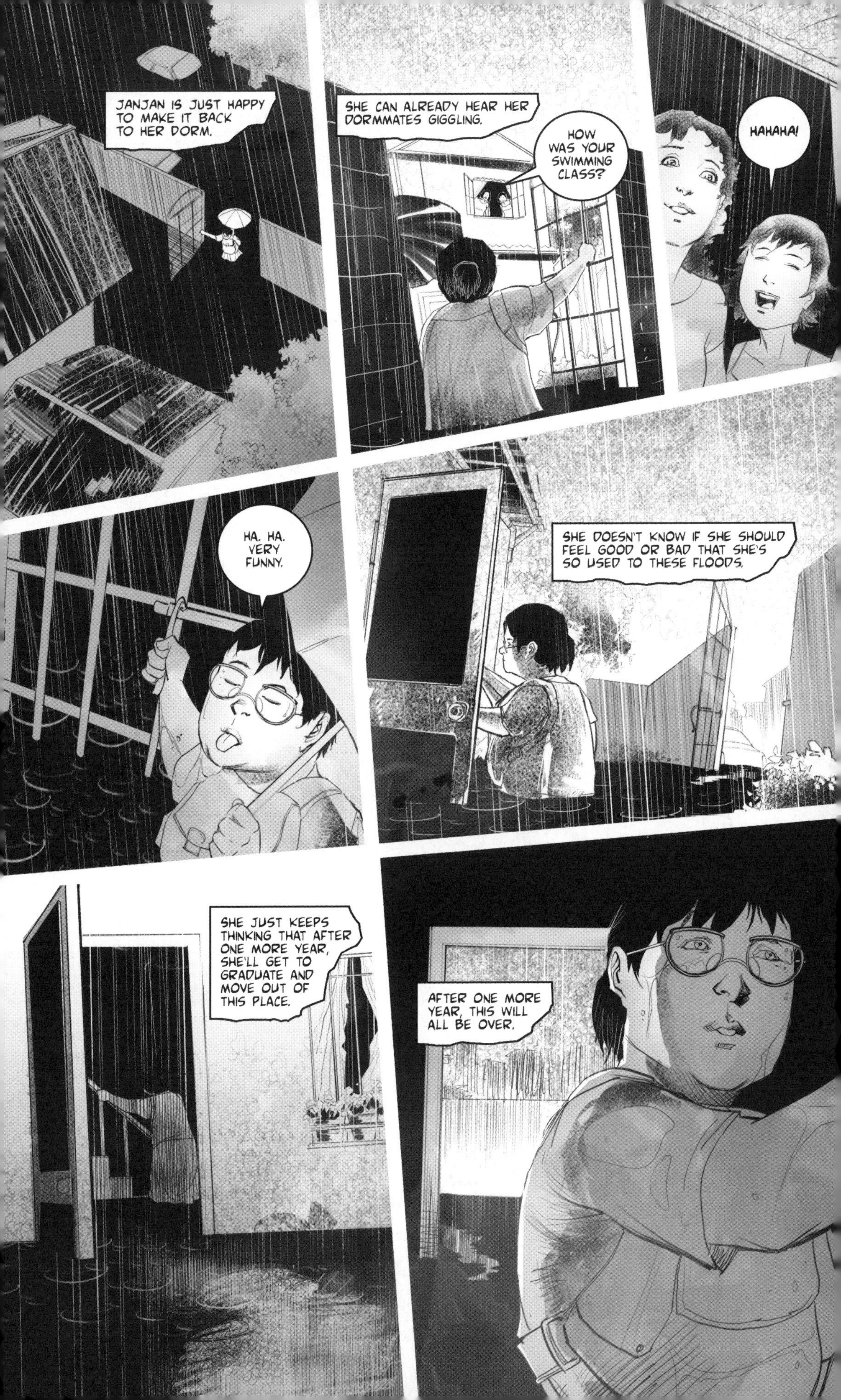
JANJAN IS JUST HAPPY TO MAKE IT BACK TO HER DORM.
SHE CAN ALREADY HEAR HER DORMMATES GIGGLING.
HOW WAS YOUR SWIMMING CLASS?
HAHAHA!
HA. HA. VERY FUNNY.
SHE DOESN'T KNOW IF SHE SHOULD FEEL GOOD OR BAD THAT SHE'S SO USED TO THESE FLOODS.
SHE JUST KEEPS THINKING THAT AFTER ONE MORE YEAR, SHE'LL GET TO GRADUATE AND MOVE OUT OF THIS PLACE.
AFTER ONE MORE YEAR, THIS WILL ALL BE OVER.

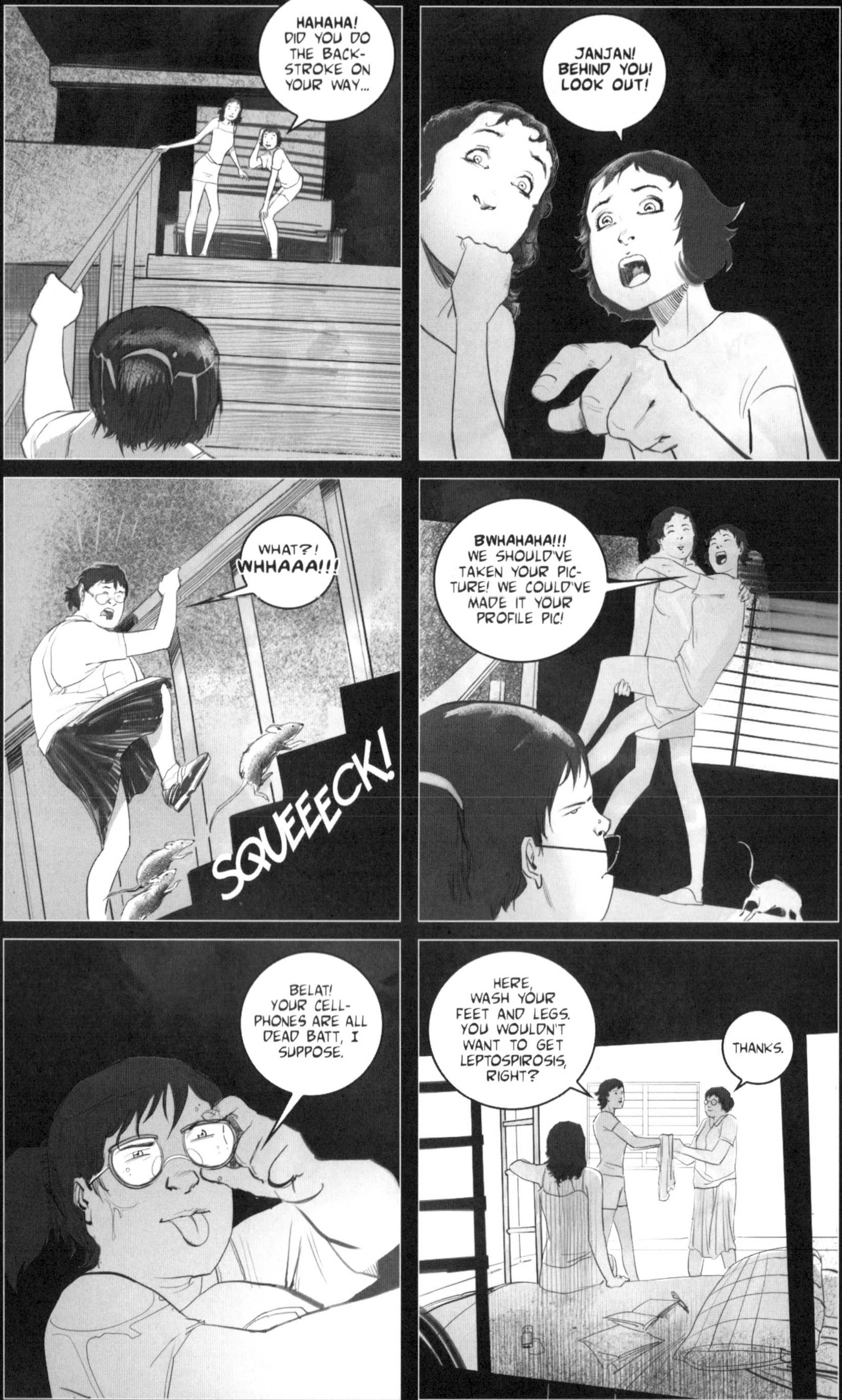
HAHAHA! DID YOU DO THE BACK-STROKE ON YOUR WAY...
JANJAN! BEHIND YOU! LOOK OUT!
WHAT?! WHHAAA!!!
SQUEEECK!
BWHAHAHA!!! WE SHOULD'VE TAKEN YOUR PIC-TURE! WE COULD'VE MADE IT YOUR PROFILE PIC!
BELAT! YOUR CELL-PHONES ARE ALL DEAD BATT, I SUPPOSE.
HERE, WASH YOUR FEET AND LEGS. YOU WOULDN'T WANT TO GET LEPTOSPIROSIS, RIGHT?
THANKS.

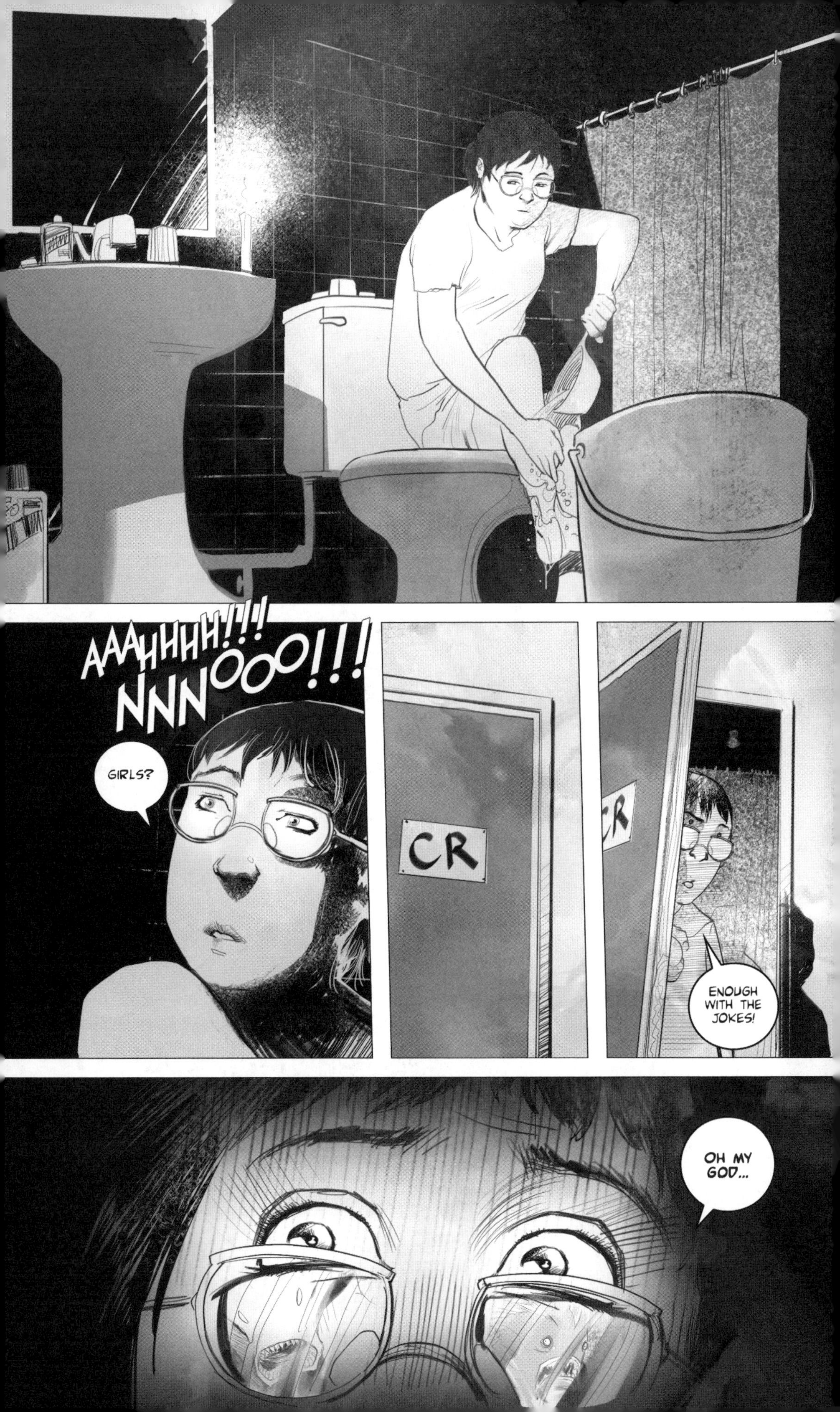
AAAHHHH!!!!
NNNOOOO!!!
GIRLS?
ENOUGH WITH THE JOKES!
OH MY GOD...

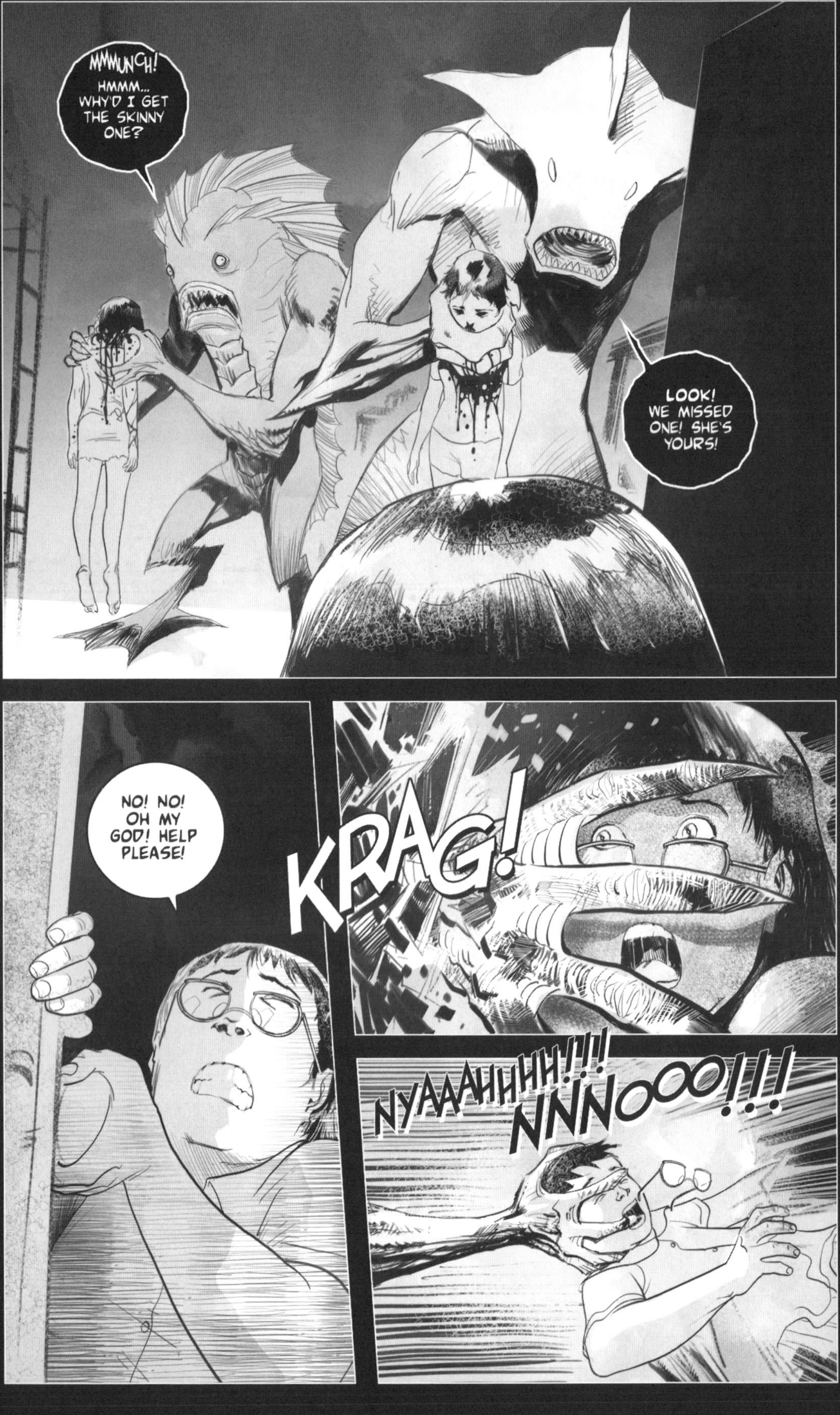
MMMUNCH! HMMM... WHY'D I GET THE SKINNY ONE?
LOOK! WE MISSED ONE! SHE'S YOURS!
NO! NO! OH MY GOD! HELP PLEASE!
KRAG!
NYAAAHHHH!!!! NNNOOOO!!!

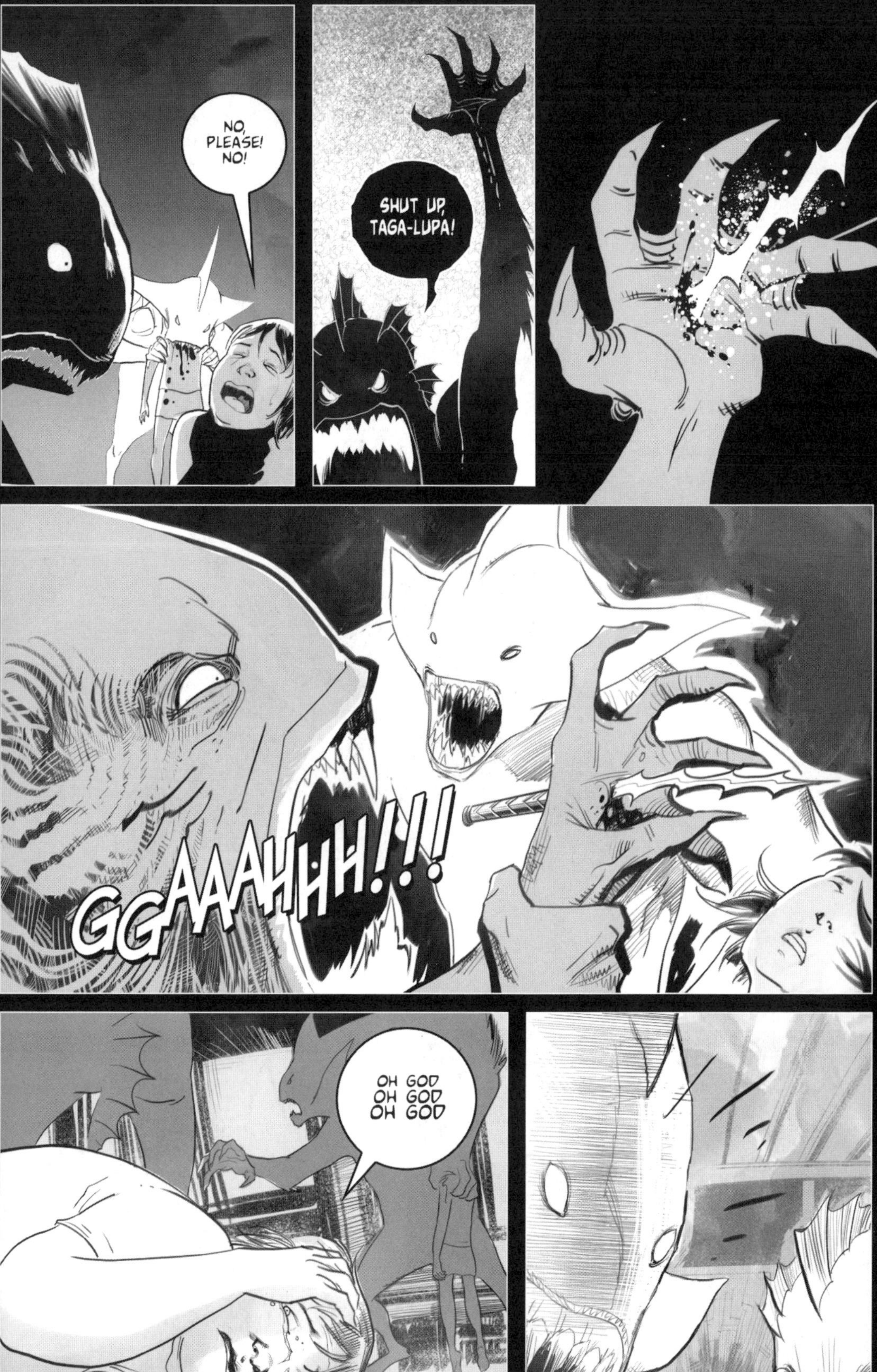
NO, PLEASE! NO!
SHUT UP, TAGA-LUPA!
GGAAAHHH!!!
OH GOD
OH GOD
OH GOD

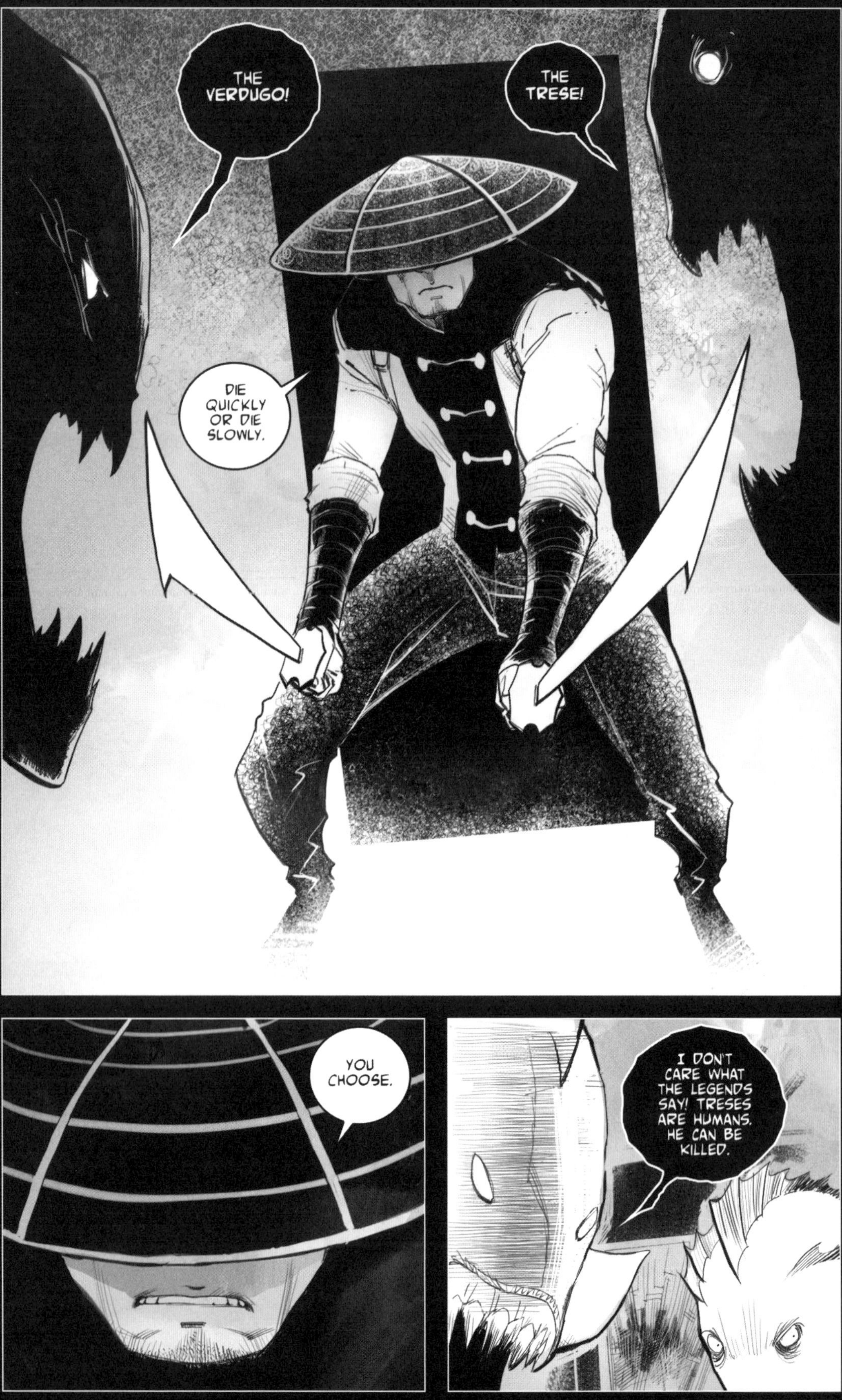

THE VERDUGO!
THE TRESE!
DIE QUICKLY OR DIE SLOWLY.
YOU CHOOSE.
I DON'T CARE WHAT THE LEGENDS SAY! TRESES ARE HUMANS. HE CAN BE KILLED.

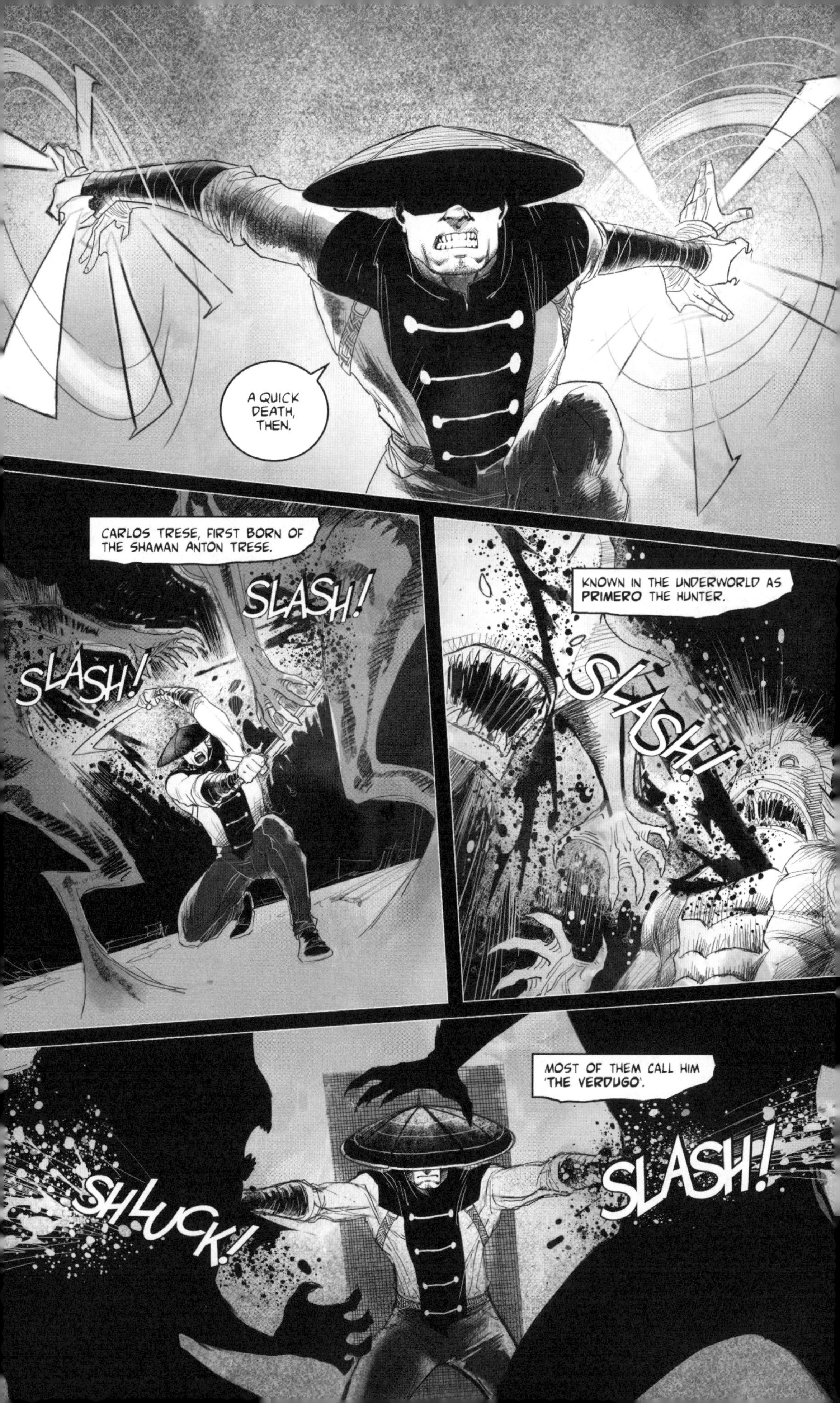
A QUICK DEATH, THEN.
CARLOS TRESE, FIRST BORN OF THE SHAMAN ANTON TRESE.
SLASH!
SLASH!
KNOWN IN THE UNDERWORLD AS PRIMERO THE HUNTER.
SLASH!
MOST OF THEM CALL HIM 'THE VERDUGO'.
SHLUCK!
SLASH!

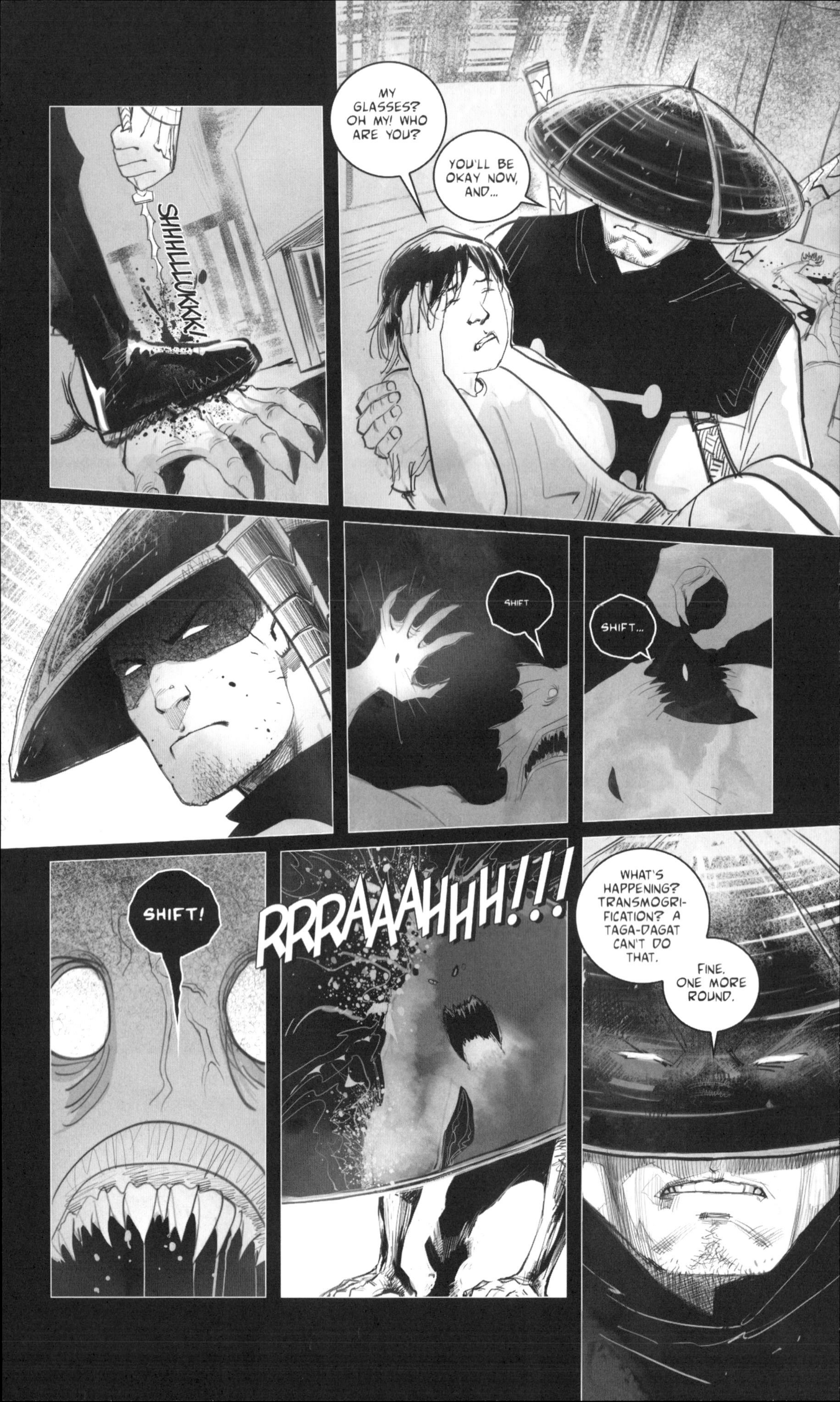
SHHHLLLUKKK!
MY GLASSES? OH MY! WHO ARE YOU?
YOU'LL BE OKAY NOW, AND...
SHIFT
SHIFT...
SHIFT!
RRRAAAHHH!!!
WHAT'S HAPPENING? TRANSMOGRI-FICATION? A TAGA-DAGAT CAN'T DO THAT.
FINE. ONE MORE ROUND.

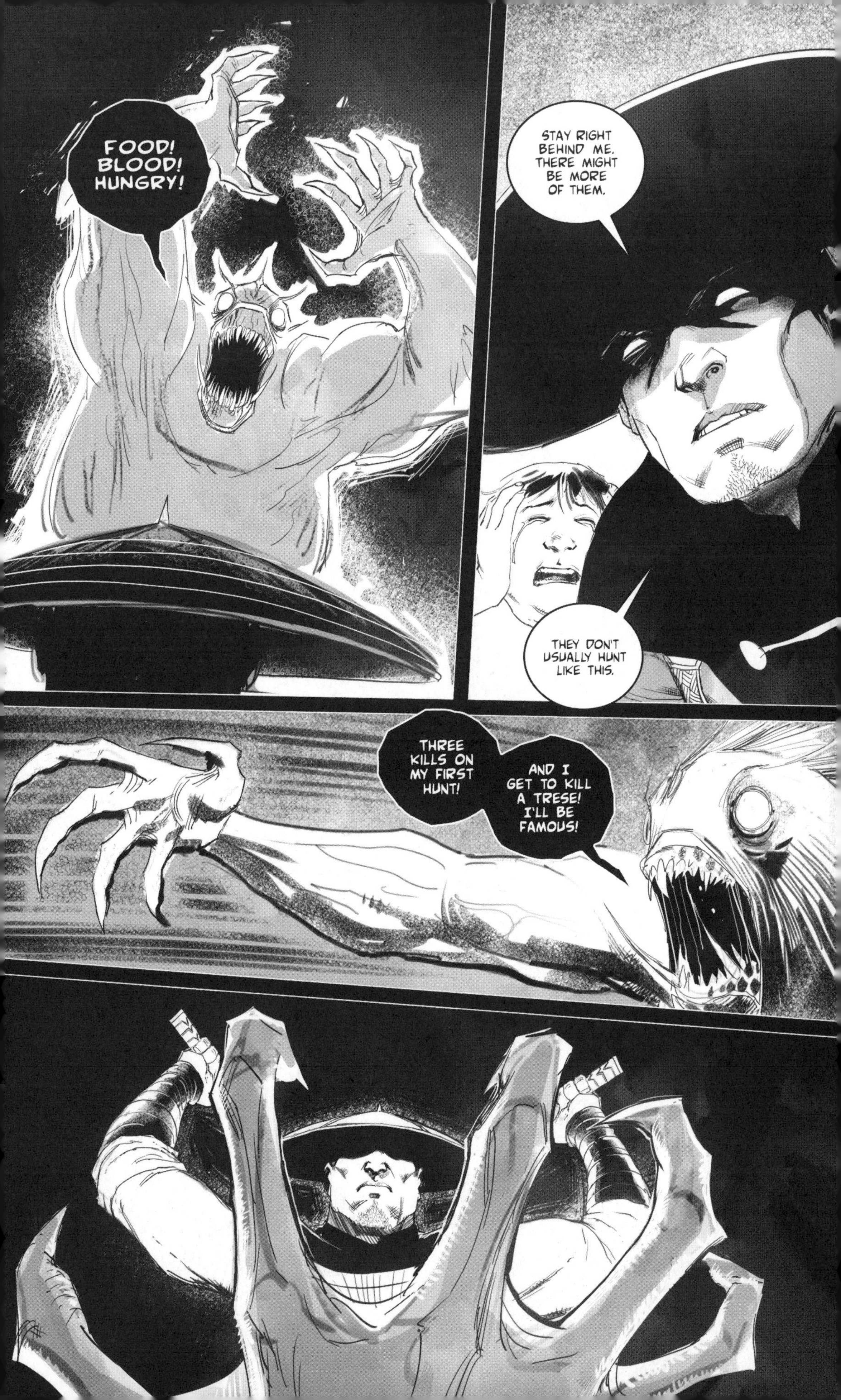
FOOD! BLOOD! HUNGRY!
STAY RIGHT BEHIND ME. THERE MIGHT BE MORE OF THEM.
THEY DON'T USUALLY HUNT LIKE THIS.
THREE KILLS ON MY FIRST HUNT!
AND I GET TO KILL A TRESE! I'LL BE FAMOUS!

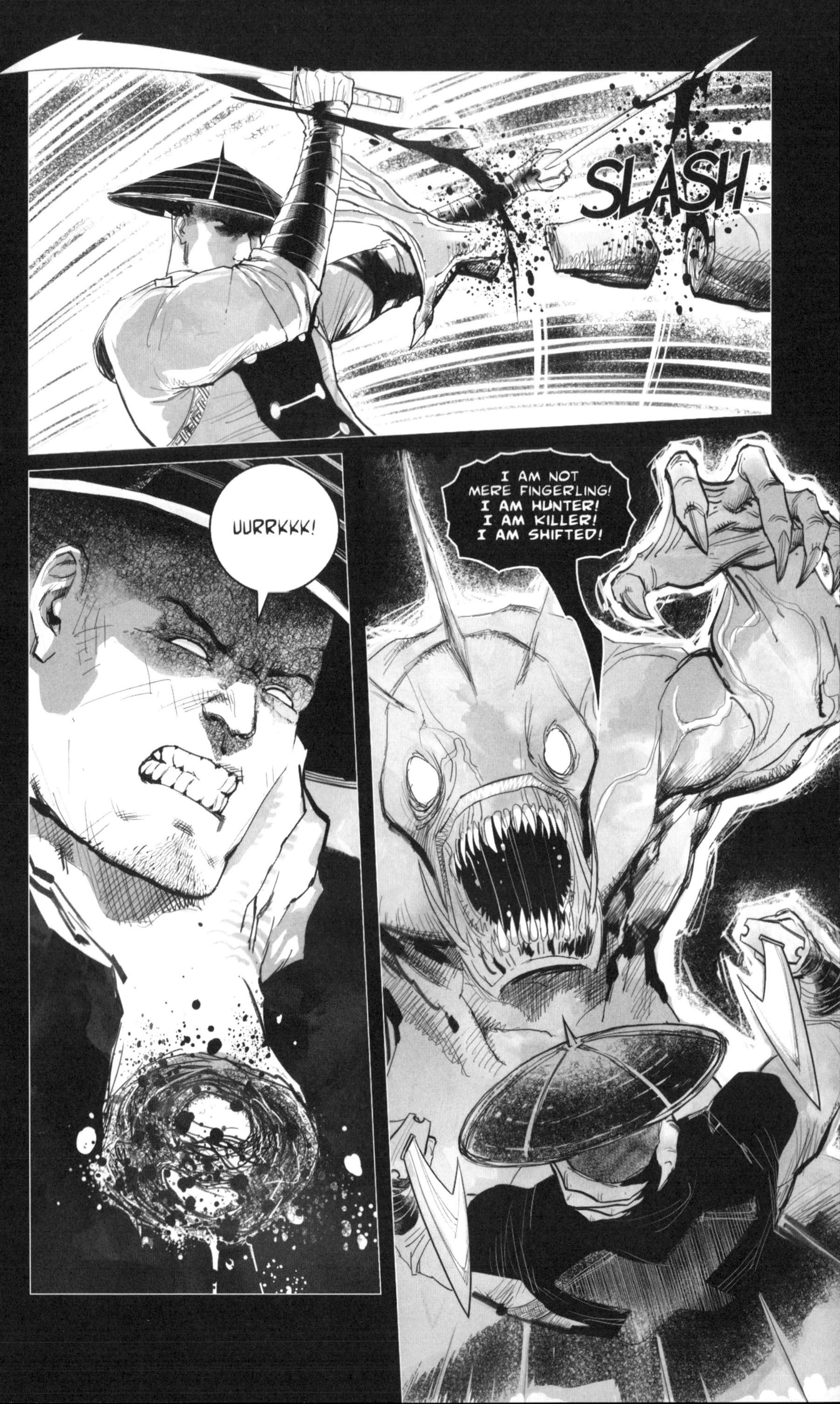
SLASH
UURRKKK!
I AM NOT MERE FINGERLING! I AM HUNTER! I AM KILLER! I AM SHIFTED!

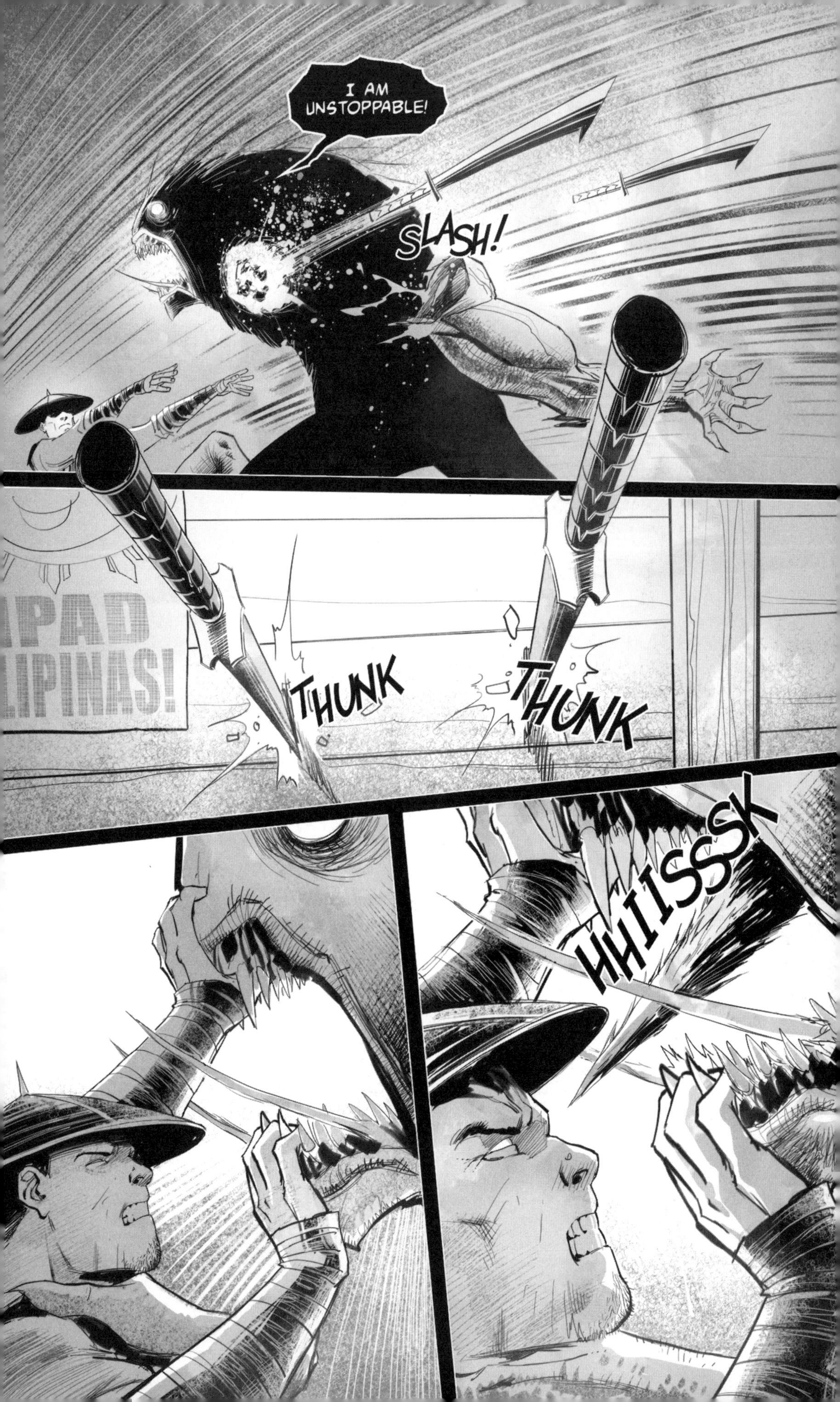
I AM UNSTOPPABLE!
SLASH!
PAD
LIPINAS!
THUNK
THUNK
HHIISSSK

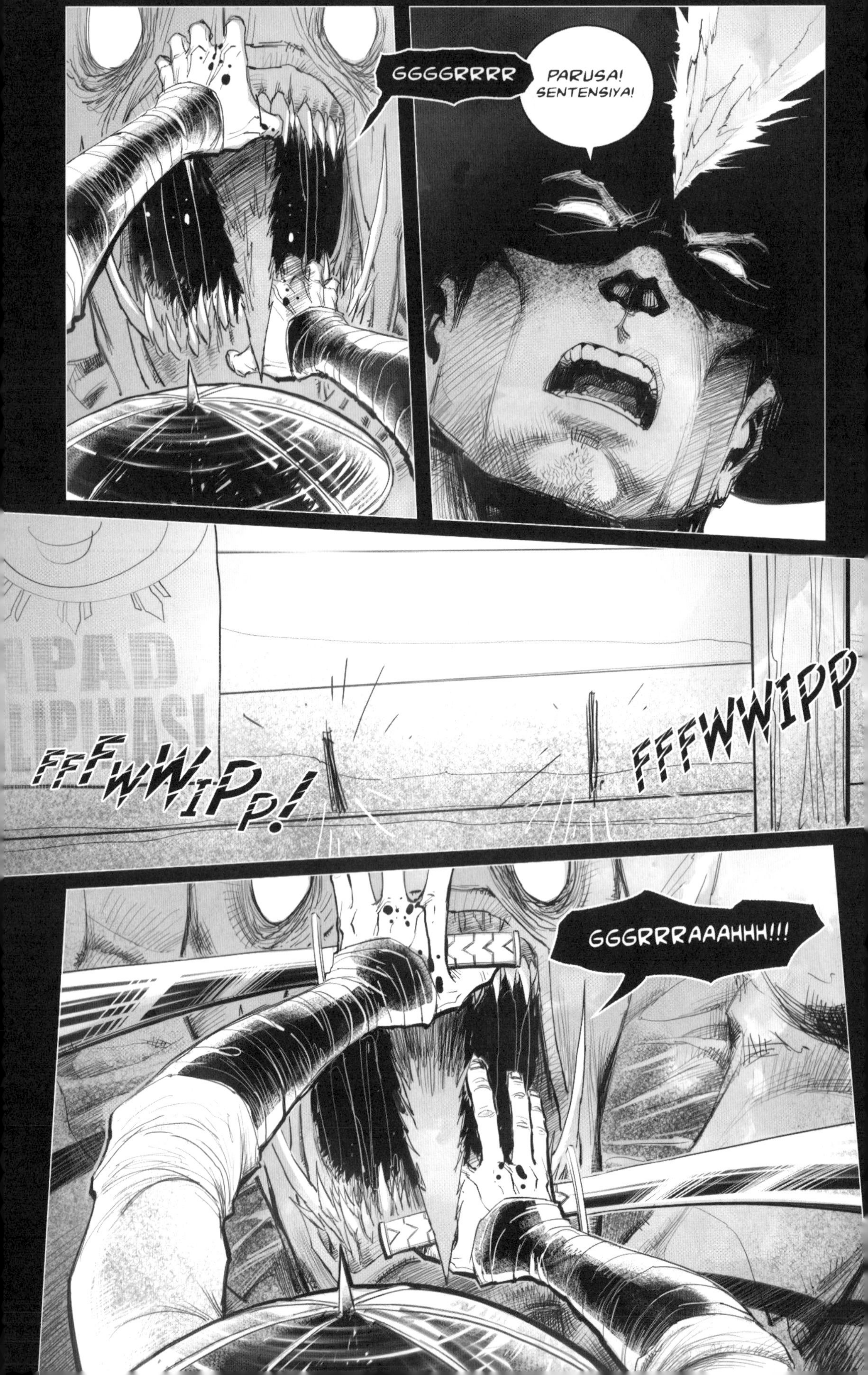
GGGGRRRR
PARUSA! SENTENSIYA!
FFFWWIPP!
FFFWWIPP
GGGRRRAAAHHH!!!

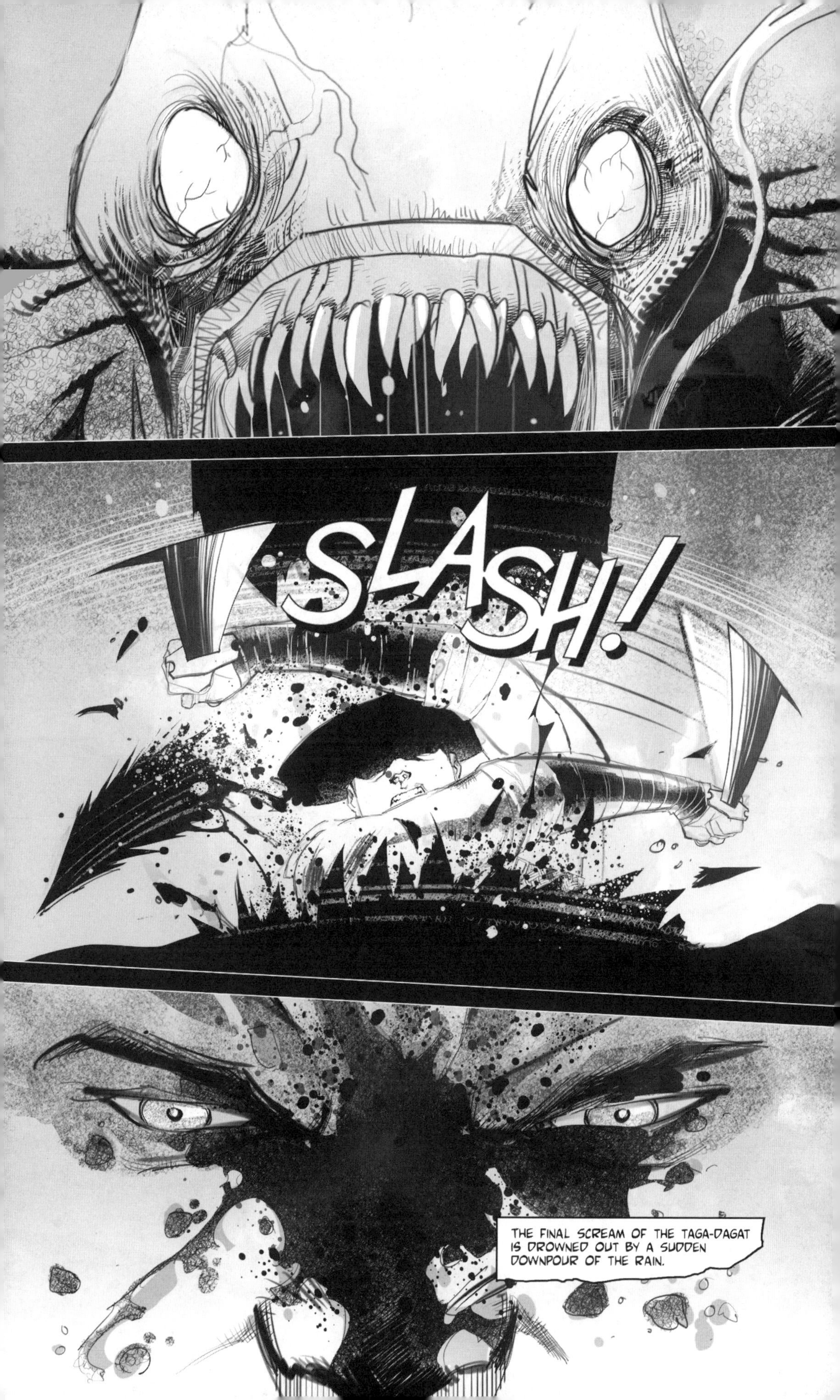
SLASH!
THE FINAL SCREAM OF THE TAGA-DAGAT IS DROWNED OUT BY A SUDDEN DOWNPOUR OF THE RAIN.

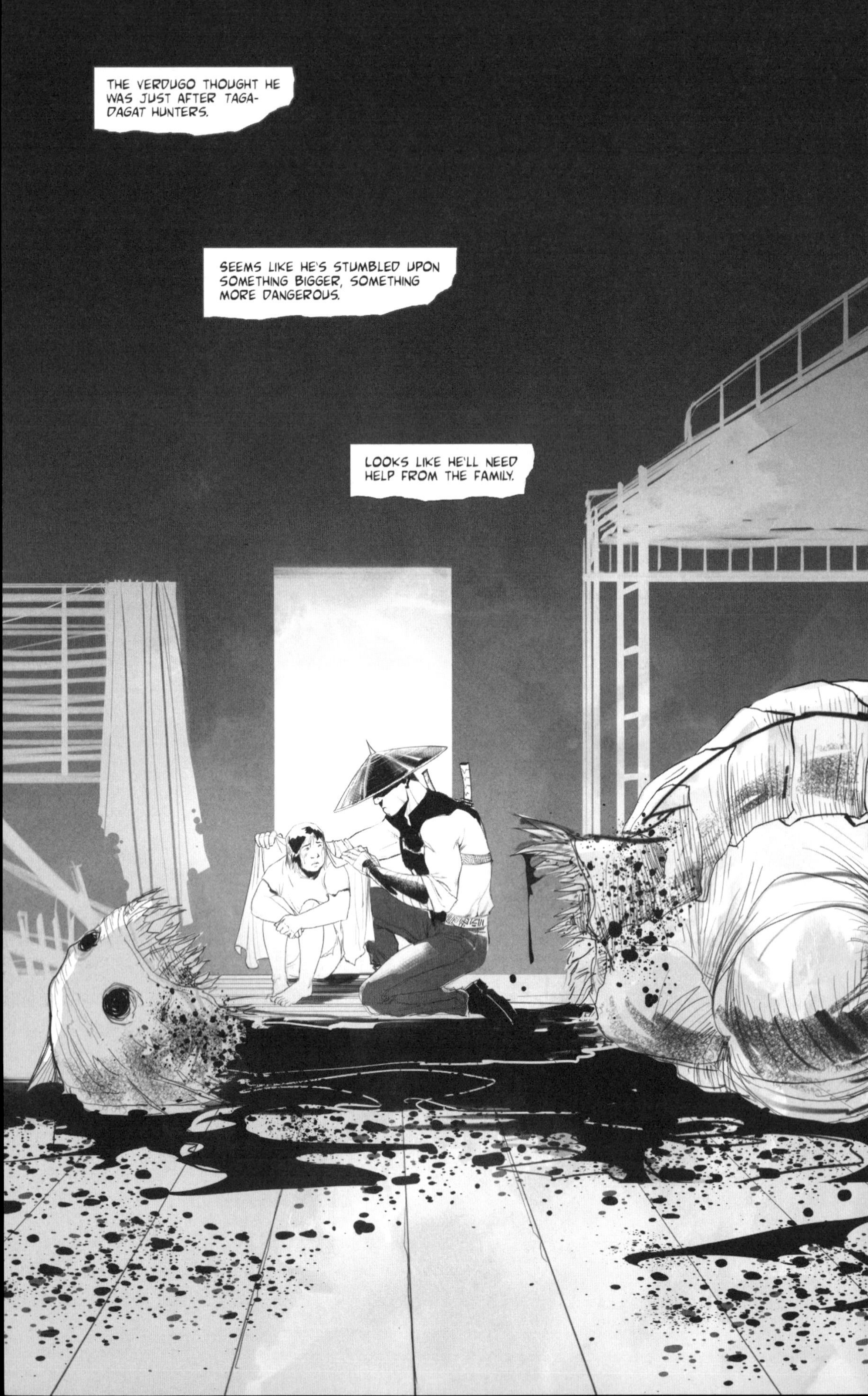
THE VERDUGO THOUGHT HE WAS JUST AFTER TAGA-DAGAT HUNTERS.
SEEMS LIKE HE'S STUMBLED UPON SOMETHING BIGGER, SOMETHING MORE DANGEROUS.
LOOKS LIKE HE'LL NEED HELP FROM THE FAMILY.

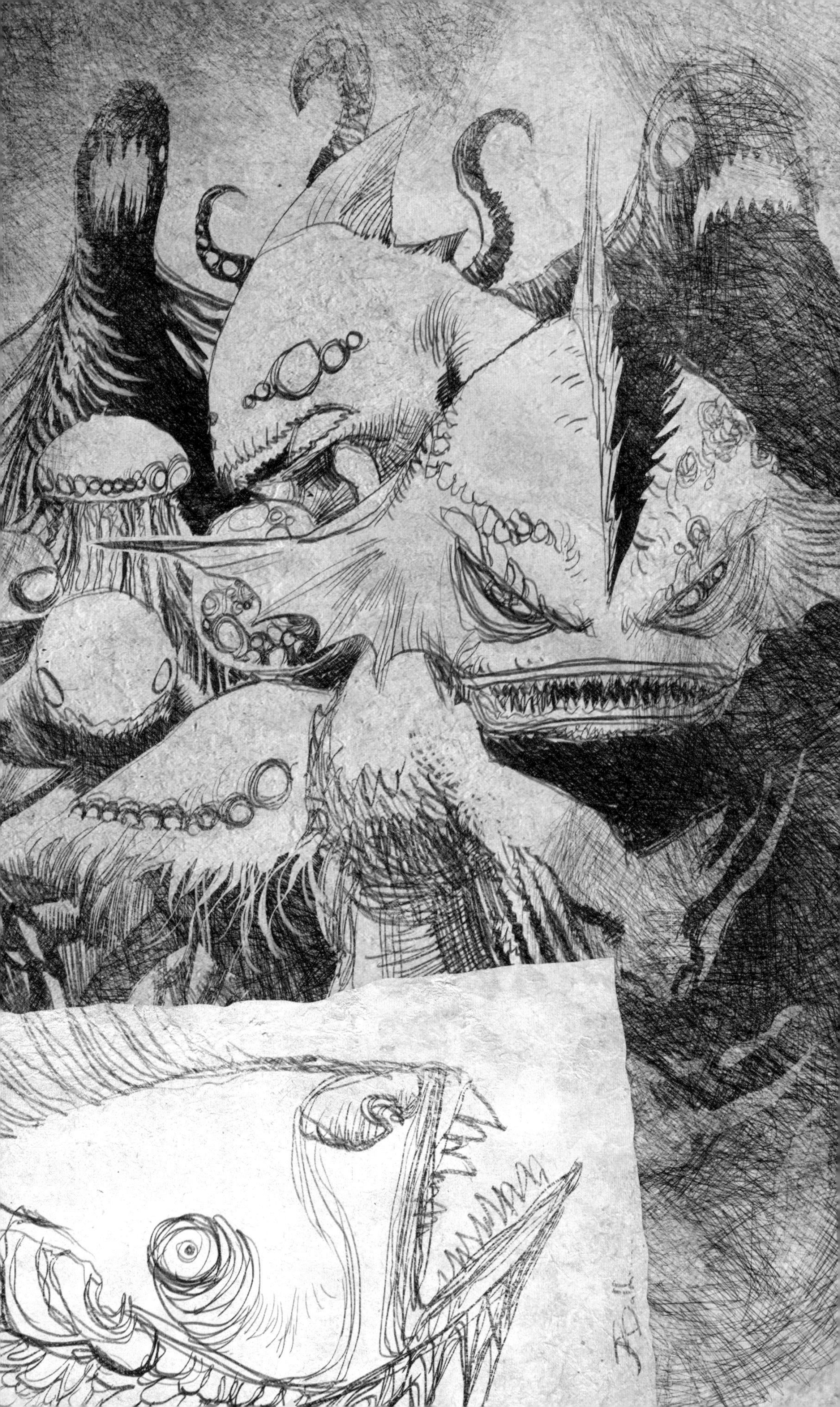

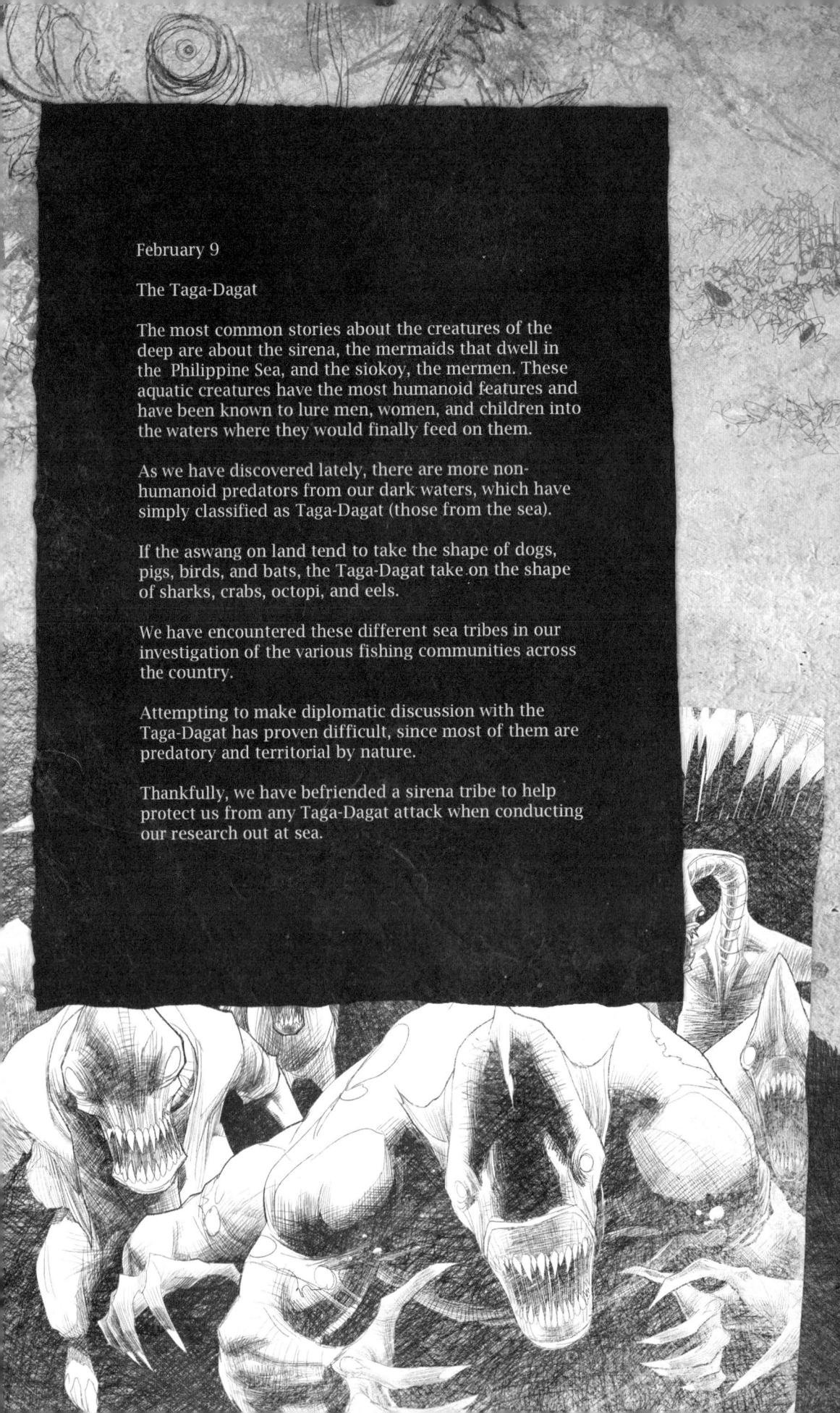

February 9

The Taga-Dagat

The most common stories about the creatures of the deep are about the sirena, the mermaids that dwell in the Philippine Sea, and the siokoy, the mermen. These aquatic creatures have the most humanoid features and have been known to lure men, women, and children into the waters where they would finally feed on them.

As we have discovered lately, there are more non-humanoid predators from our dark waters, which have simply classified as Taga-Dagat (those from the sea).

If the aswang on land tend to take the shape of dogs, pigs, birds, and bats, the Taga-Dagat take on the shape of sharks, crabs, octopi, and eels.

We have encountered these different sea tribes in our investigation of the various fishing communities across the country.

Attempting to make diplomatic discussion with the Taga-Dagat has proven difficult, since most of them are predatory and territorial by nature.

Thankfully, we have befriended a sirena tribe to help protect us from any Taga-Dagat attack when conducting our research out at sea.

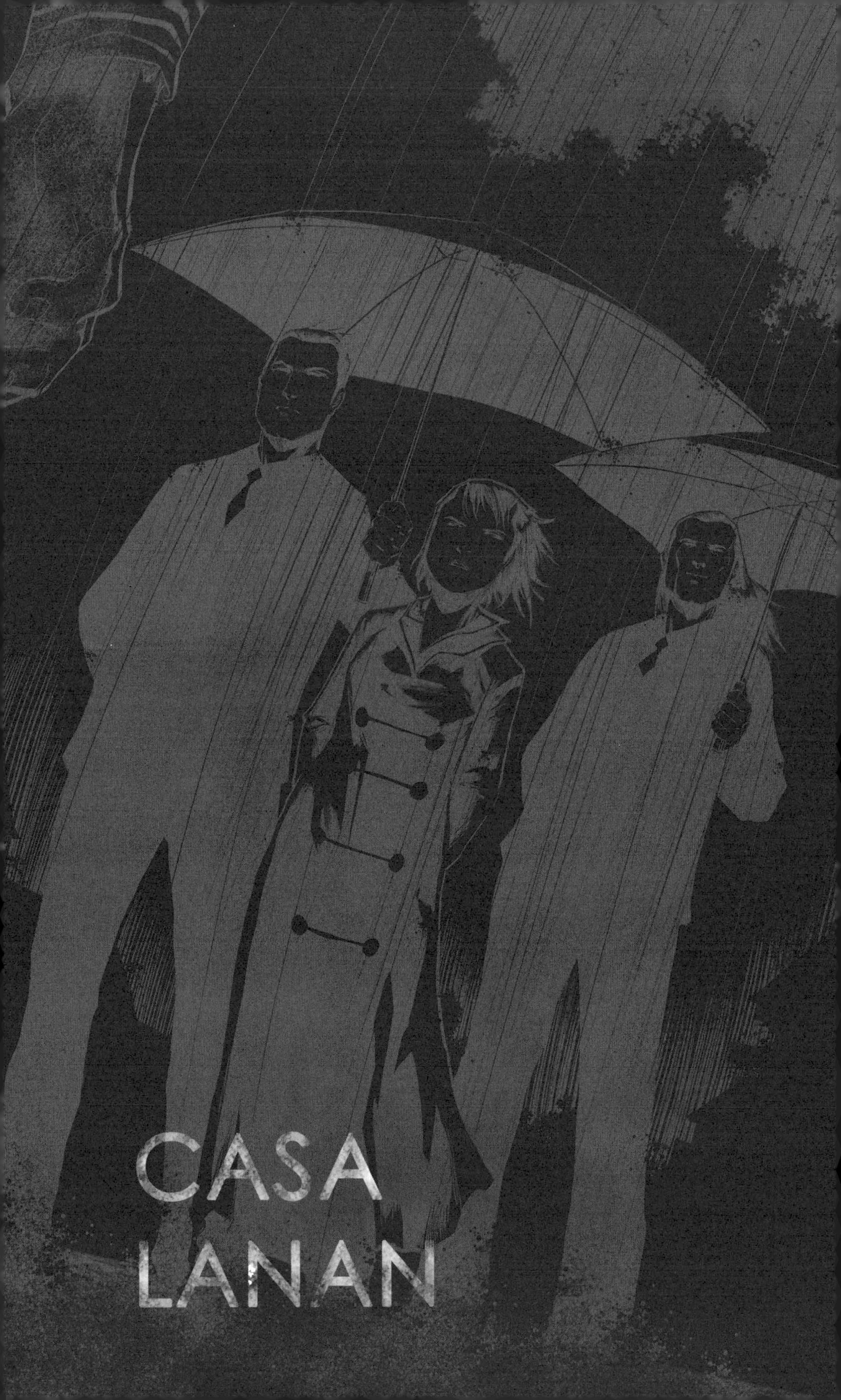
CASA
LANAN

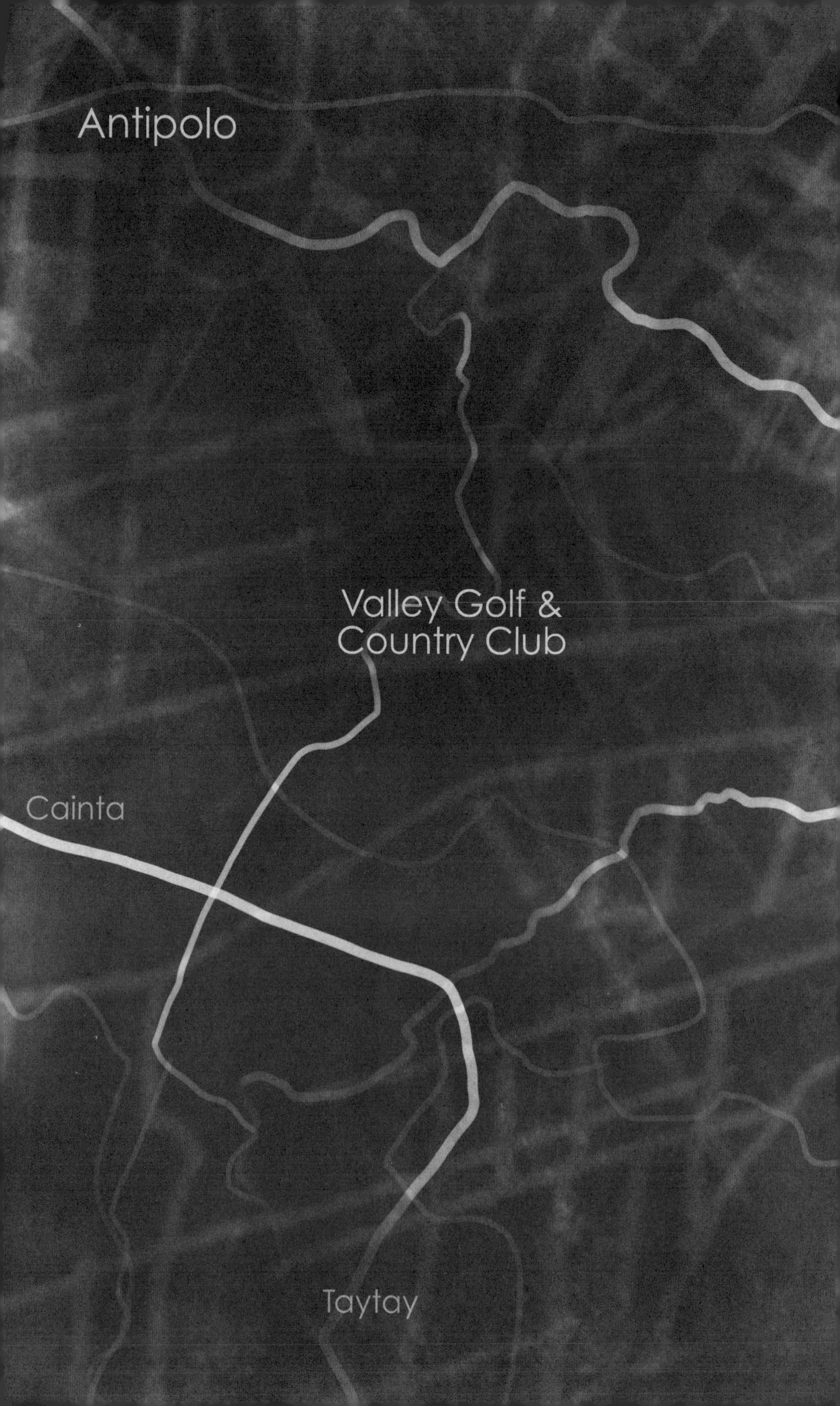
Antipolo
Valley Golf &
Country Club
Cainta
Taytay

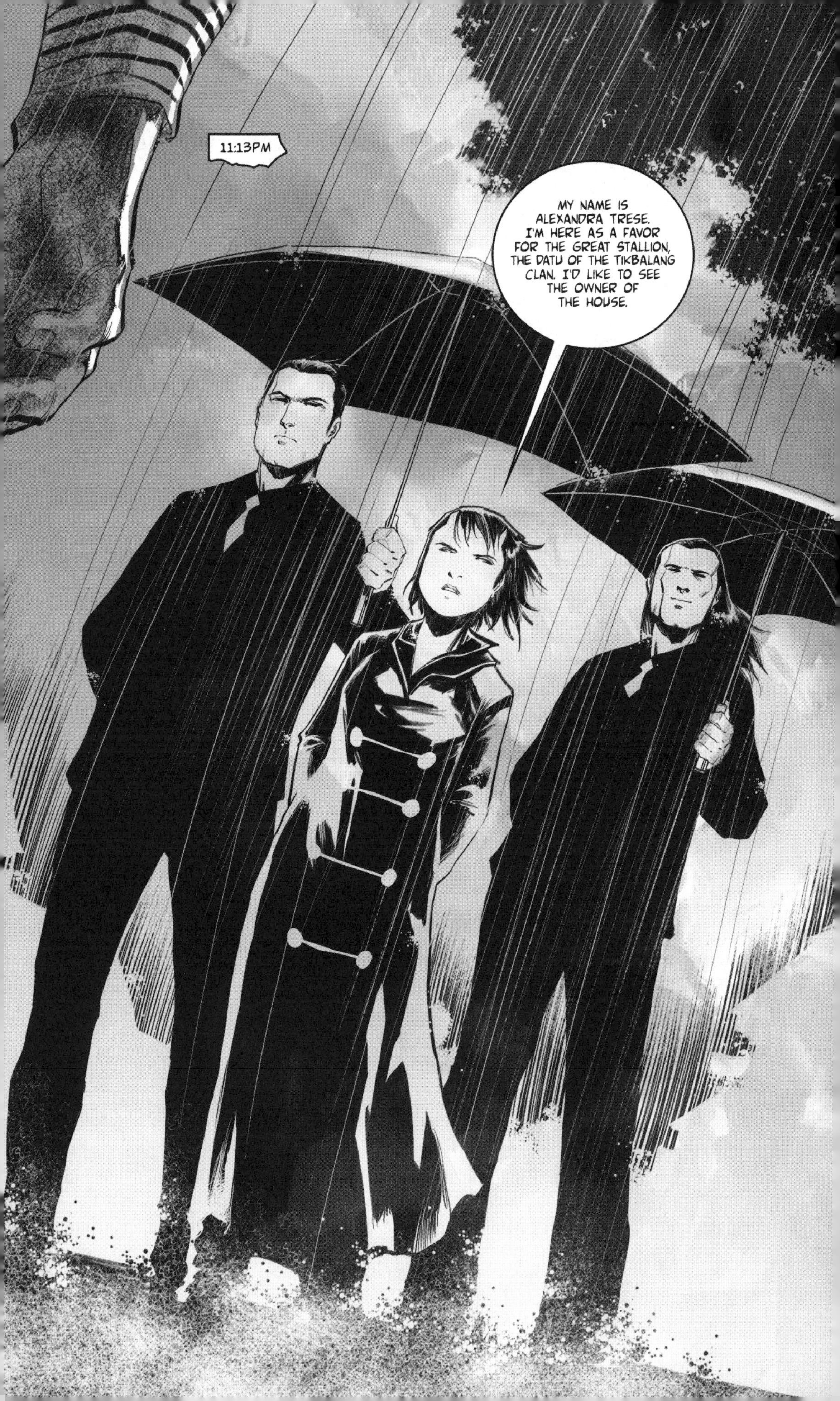
11:13PM
MY NAME IS ALEXANDRA TRESE. I'M HERE AS A FAVOR FOR THE GREAT STALLION, THE DATU OF THE TIKBALANG CLAN. I'D LIKE TO SEE THE OWNER OF THE HOUSE.

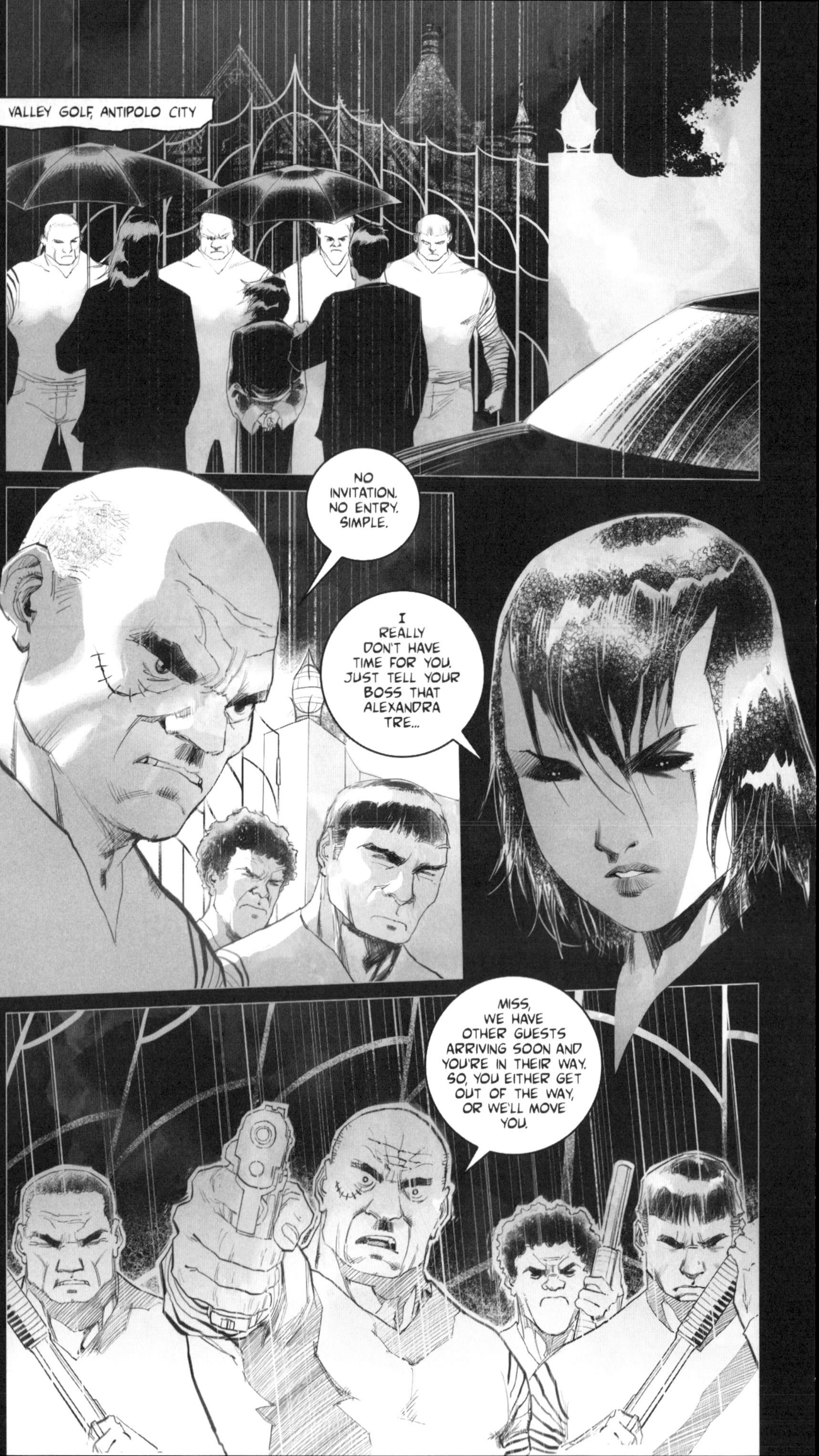
VALLEY GOLF, ANTIPOLO CITY
NO INVITATION. NO ENTRY. SIMPLE.
I REALLY DON'T HAVE TIME FOR YOU. JUST TELL YOUR BOSS THAT ALEXANDRA TRE...
MISS, WE HAVE OTHER GUESTS ARRIVING SOON AND YOU'RE IN THEIR WAY. SO, YOU EITHER GET OUT OF THE WAY, OR WE'LL MOVE YOU.

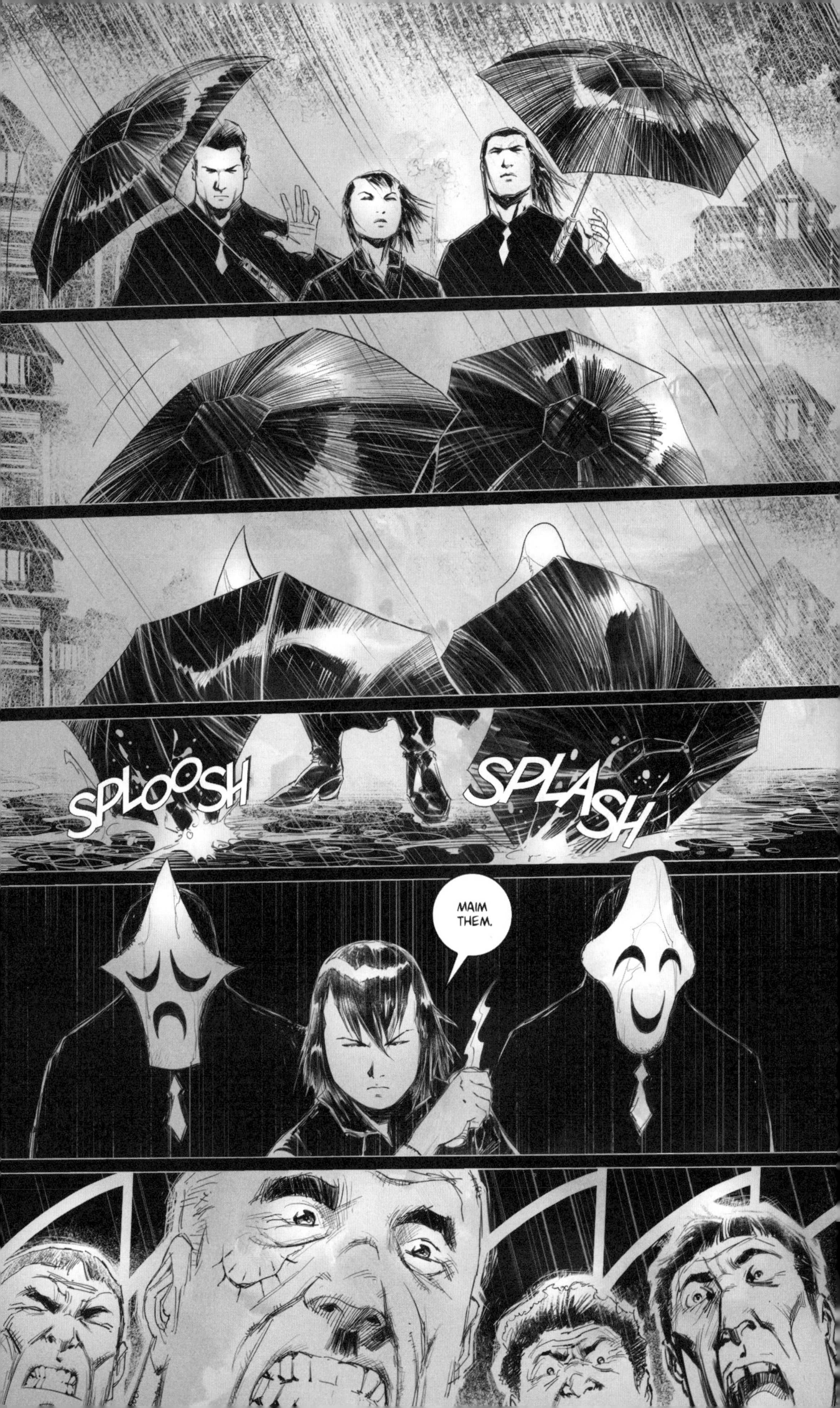
SPLOOSH
SPLASH
MAIM THEM.

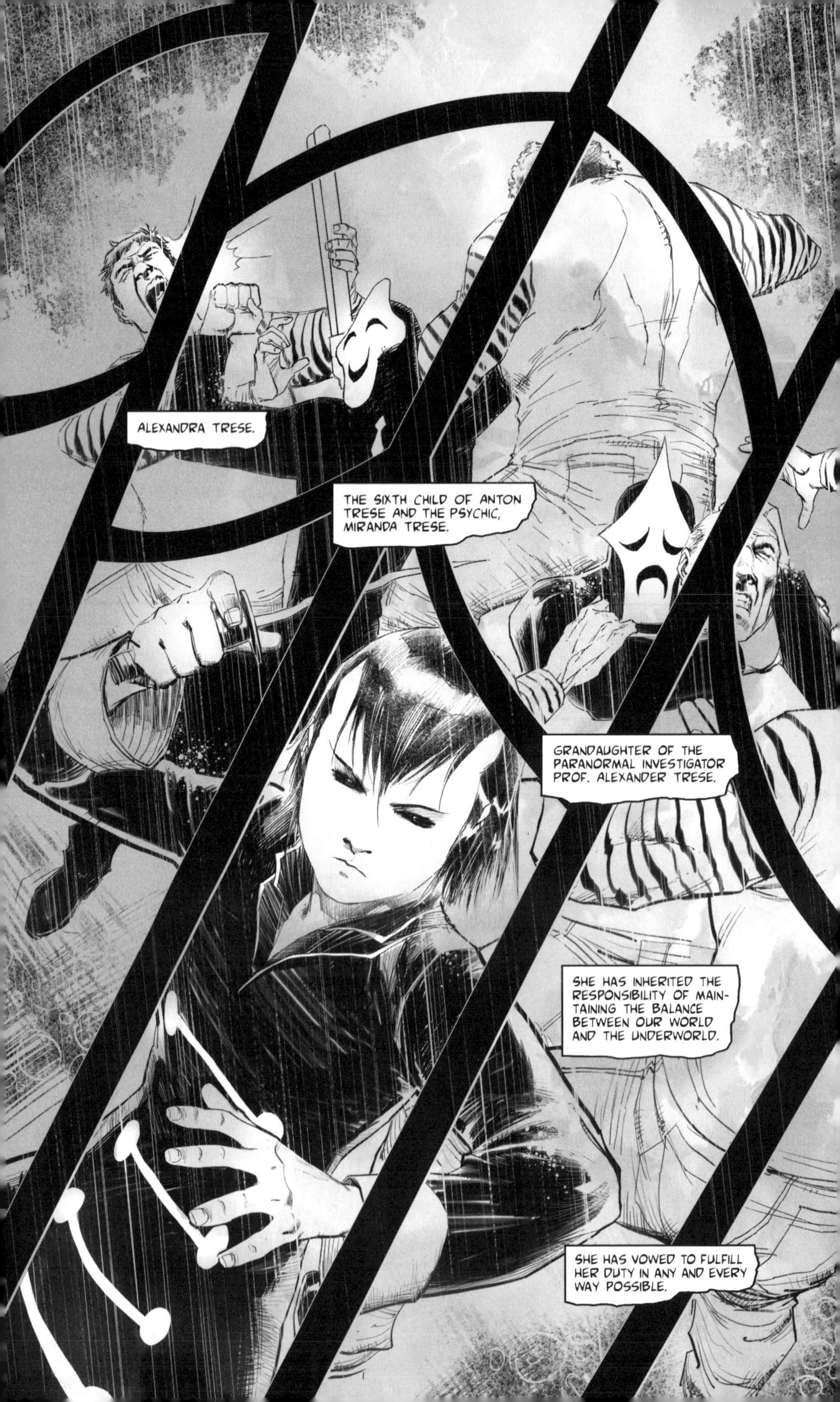
ALEXANDRA TRESE.
THE SIXTH CHILD OF ANTON TRESE AND THE PSYCHIC, MIRANDA TRESE.
GRANDAUGHTER OF THE PARANORMAL INVESTIGATOR PROF. ALEXANDER TRESE.
SHE HAS INHERITED THE RESPONSIBILITY OF MAIN-TAINING THE BALANCE BETWEEN OUR WORLD AND THE UNDERWORLD.
SHE HAS VOWED TO FULFILL HER DUTY IN ANY AND EVERY WAY POSSIBLE.

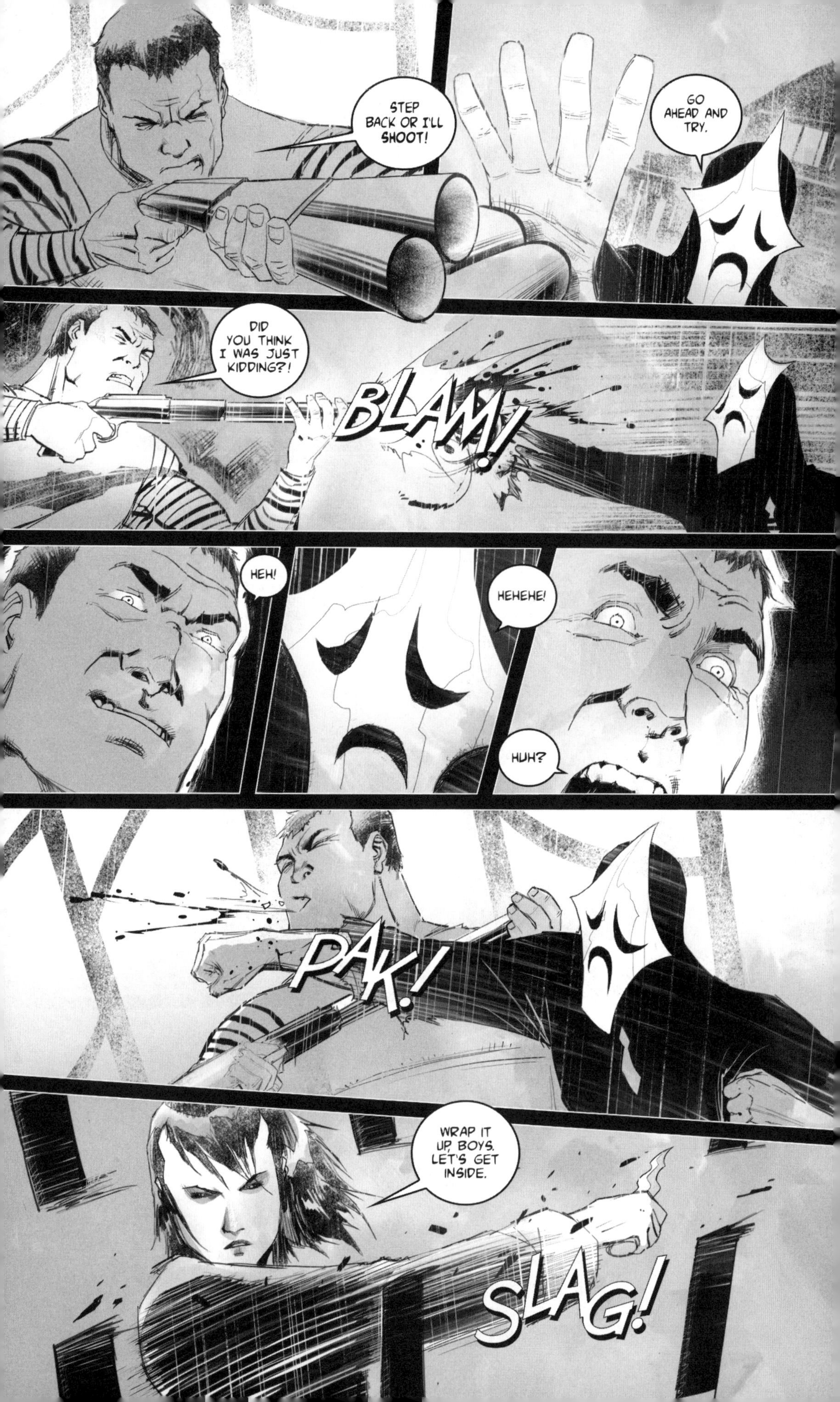
STEP BACK OR I'LL SHOOT!
GO AHEAD AND TRY.
DID YOU THINK I WAS JUST KIDDING?!
BLAM!
HEH!
HEHEHE!
HUH?
PAK!
WRAP IT UP, BOYS. LET'S GET INSIDE.
SLAG!

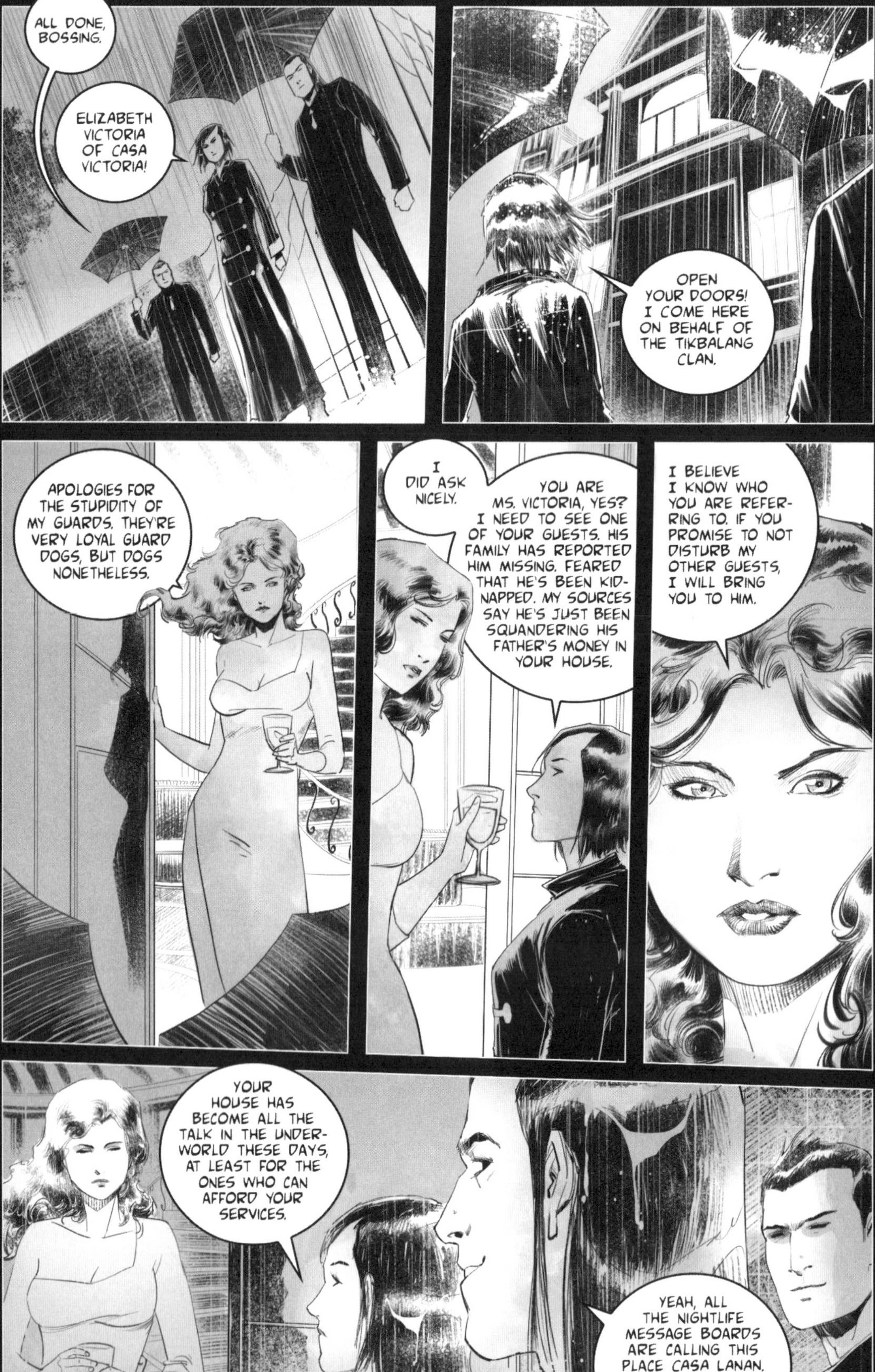
ALL DONE, BOSSING.
ELIZABETH VICTORIA OF CASA VICTORIA!
OPEN YOUR DOORS! I COME HERE ON BEHALF OF THE TIKBALANG CLAN.
APOLOGIES FOR THE STUPIDITY OF MY GUARDS. THEY'RE VERY LOYAL GUARD DOGS, BUT DOGS NONETHELESS.
I DID ASK NICELY.
YOU ARE MS. VICTORIA, YES? I NEED TO SEE ONE OF YOUR GUESTS. HIS FAMILY HAS REPORTED HIM MISSING. FEARED THAT HE'S BEEN KID-NAPPED. MY SOURCES SAY HE'S JUST BEEN SQUANDERING HIS FATHER'S MONEY IN YOUR HOUSE.
I BELIEVE I KNOW WHO YOU ARE REFER-RING TO. IF YOU PROMISE TO NOT DISTURB MY OTHER GUESTS, I WILL BRING YOU TO HIM.
YOUR HOUSE HAS BECOME ALL THE TALK IN THE UNDER-WORLD THESE DAYS, AT LEAST FOR THE ONES WHO CAN AFFORD YOUR SERVICES.
YEAH, ALL THE NIGHTLIFE MESSAGE BOARDS ARE CALLING THIS PLACE CASA LANAN. THEY'RE WONDERING IF IT REALLY EXISTS. HEH!

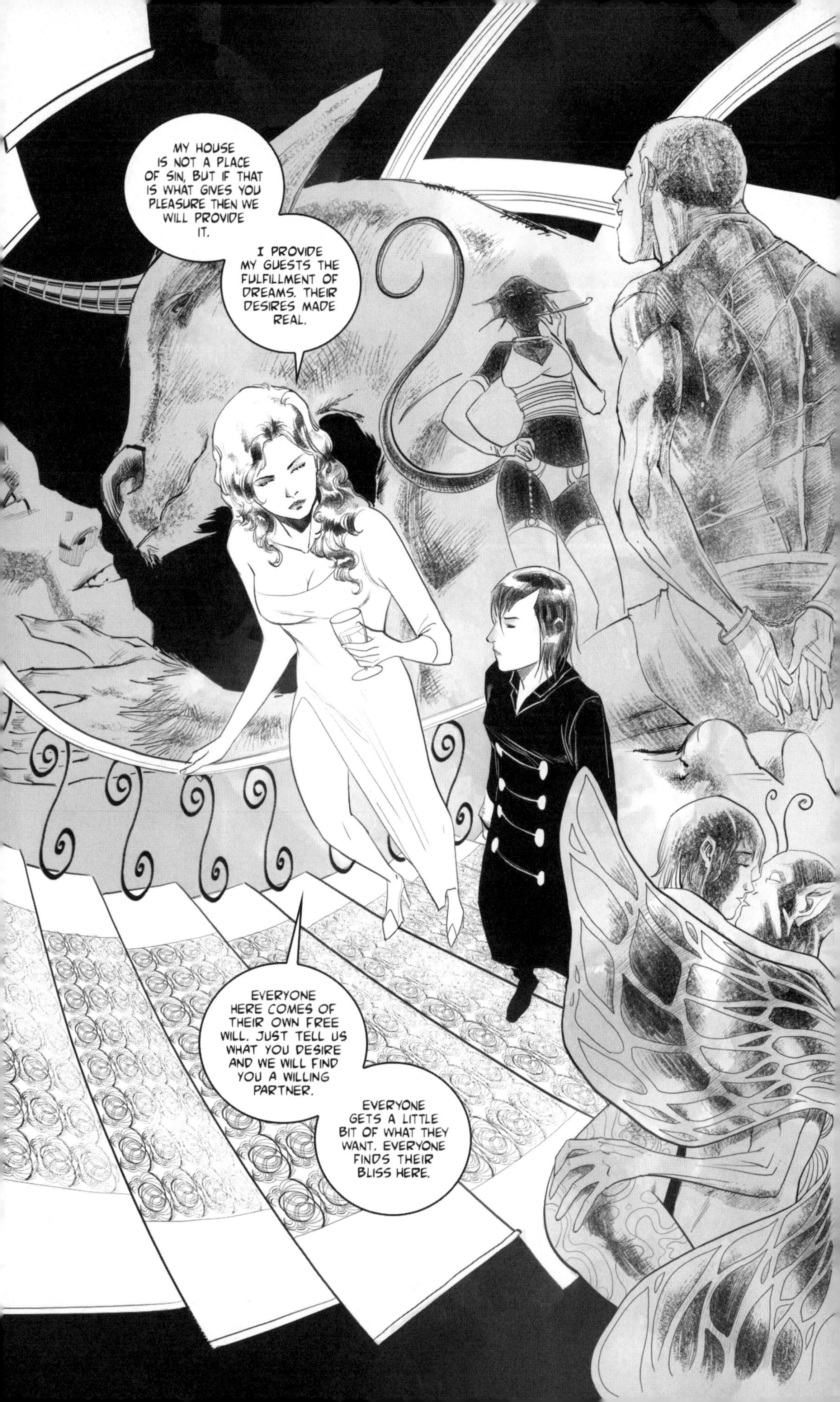
MY HOUSE IS NOT A PLACE OF SIN, BUT IF THAT IS WHAT GIVES YOU PLEASURE THEN WE WILL PROVIDE IT.
I PROVIDE MY GUESTS THE FULFILLMENT OF DREAMS. THEIR DESIRES MADE REAL.
EVERYONE HERE COMES OF THEIR OWN FREE WILL. JUST TELL US WHAT YOU DESIRE AND WE WILL FIND YOU A WILLING PARTNER.
EVERYONE GETS A LITTLE BIT OF WHAT THEY WANT. EVERYONE FINDS THEIR BLISS HERE.

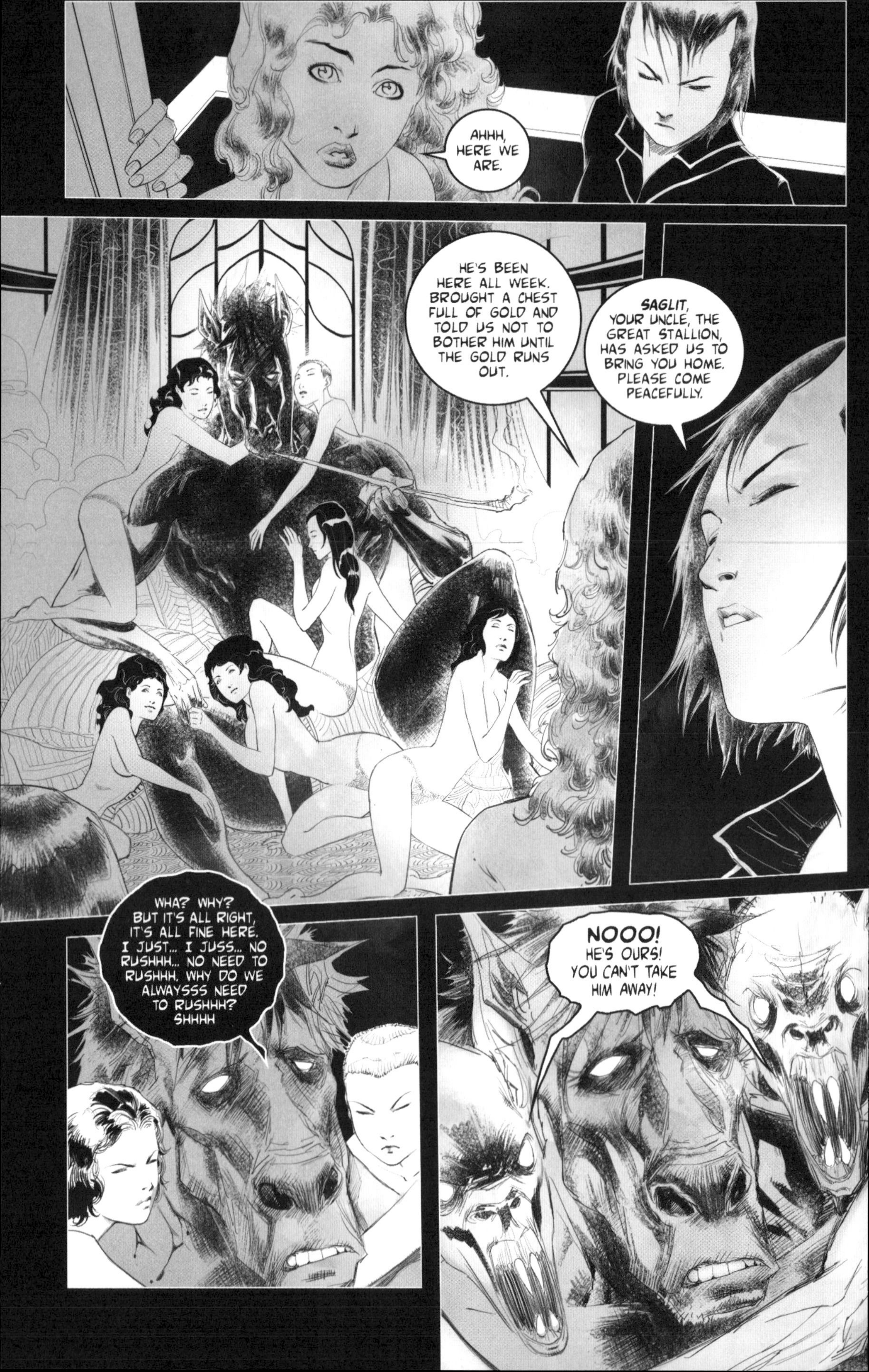

AHHH, HERE WE ARE.
HE'S BEEN HERE ALL WEEK. BROUGHT A CHEST FULL OF GOLD AND TOLD US NOT TO BOTHER HIM UNTIL THE GOLD RUNS OUT.
SAGLIT, YOUR UNCLE, THE GREAT STALLION, HAS ASKED US TO BRING YOU HOME. PLEASE COME PEACEFULLY.
WHA? WHY? BUT IT'S ALL RIGHT, IT'S ALL FINE HERE. I JUST... I JUSS... NO RUSHHH... NO NEED TO RUSHHH. WHY DO WE ALWAYSSS NEED TO RUSHHH? SHHHH
NOOO! HE'S OURS! YOU CAN'T TAKE HIM AWAY!

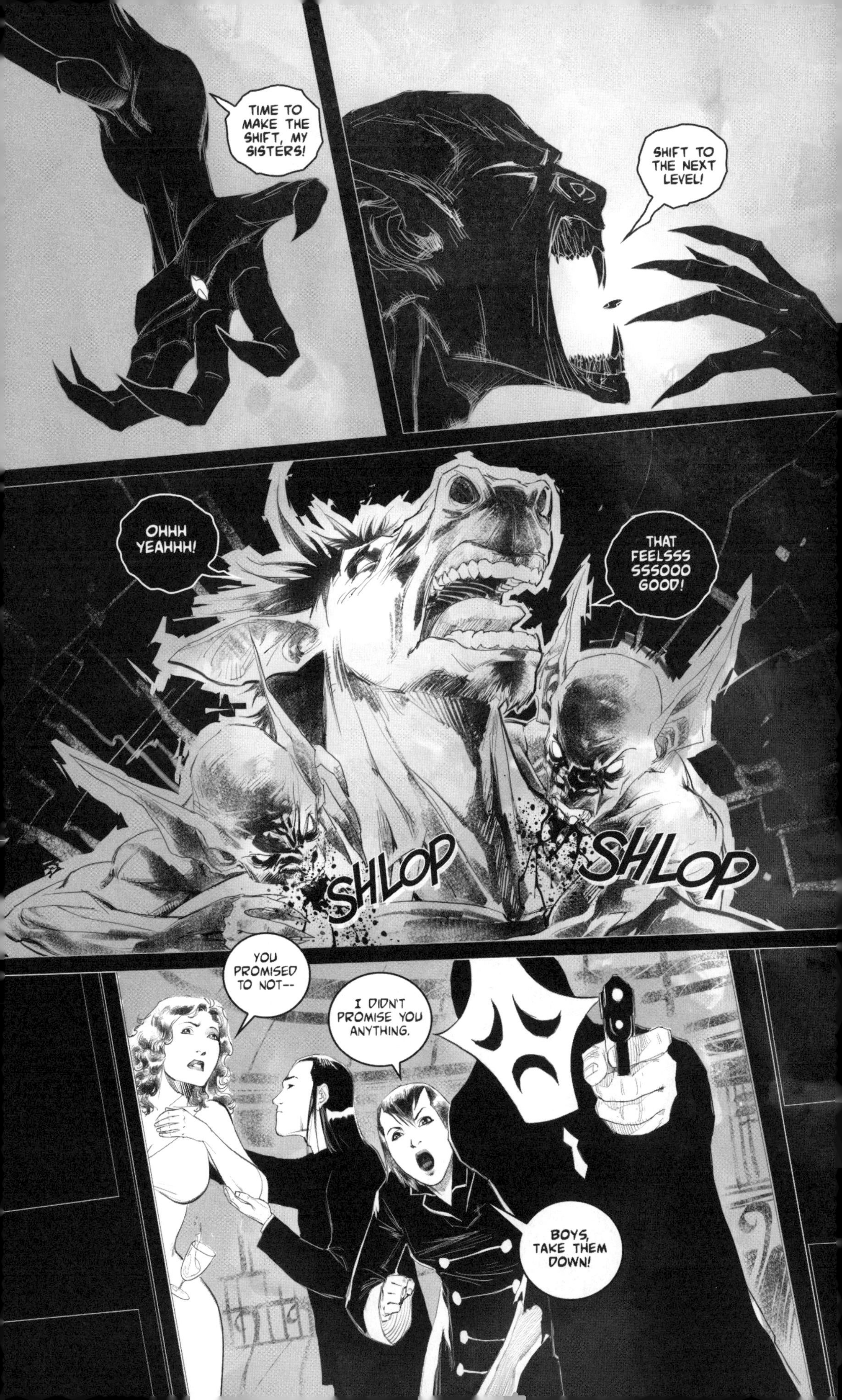
TIME TO MAKE THE SHIFT, MY SISTERS!
SHIFT TO THE NEXT LEVEL!
OHHH YEAHHH!
THAT FEELSSS SSSOOO GOOD!
SHLOP
SHLOP
YOU PROMISED TO NOT--
I DIDN'T PROMISE YOU ANYTHING.
BOYS, TAKE THEM DOWN!

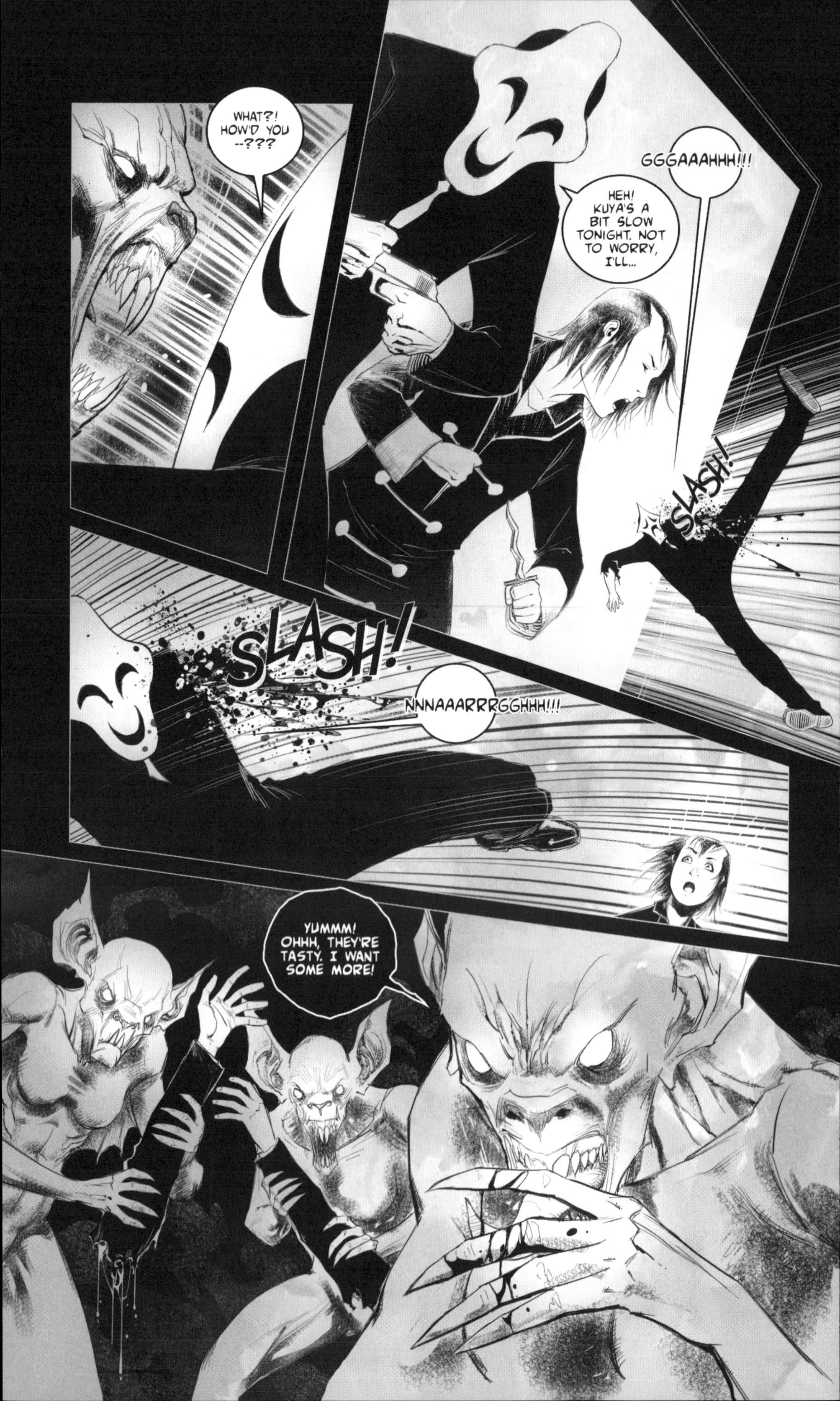
WHAT?! HOW'D YOU --???
HEH! KUYA'S A BIT SLOW TONIGHT. NOT TO WORRY, I'LL...
GGGAAAHHH!!!
SLASH!
SLASH!
NNNAAARRRGGHHH!!!
YUMMM! OHHH, THEY'RE TASTY. I WANT SOME MORE!

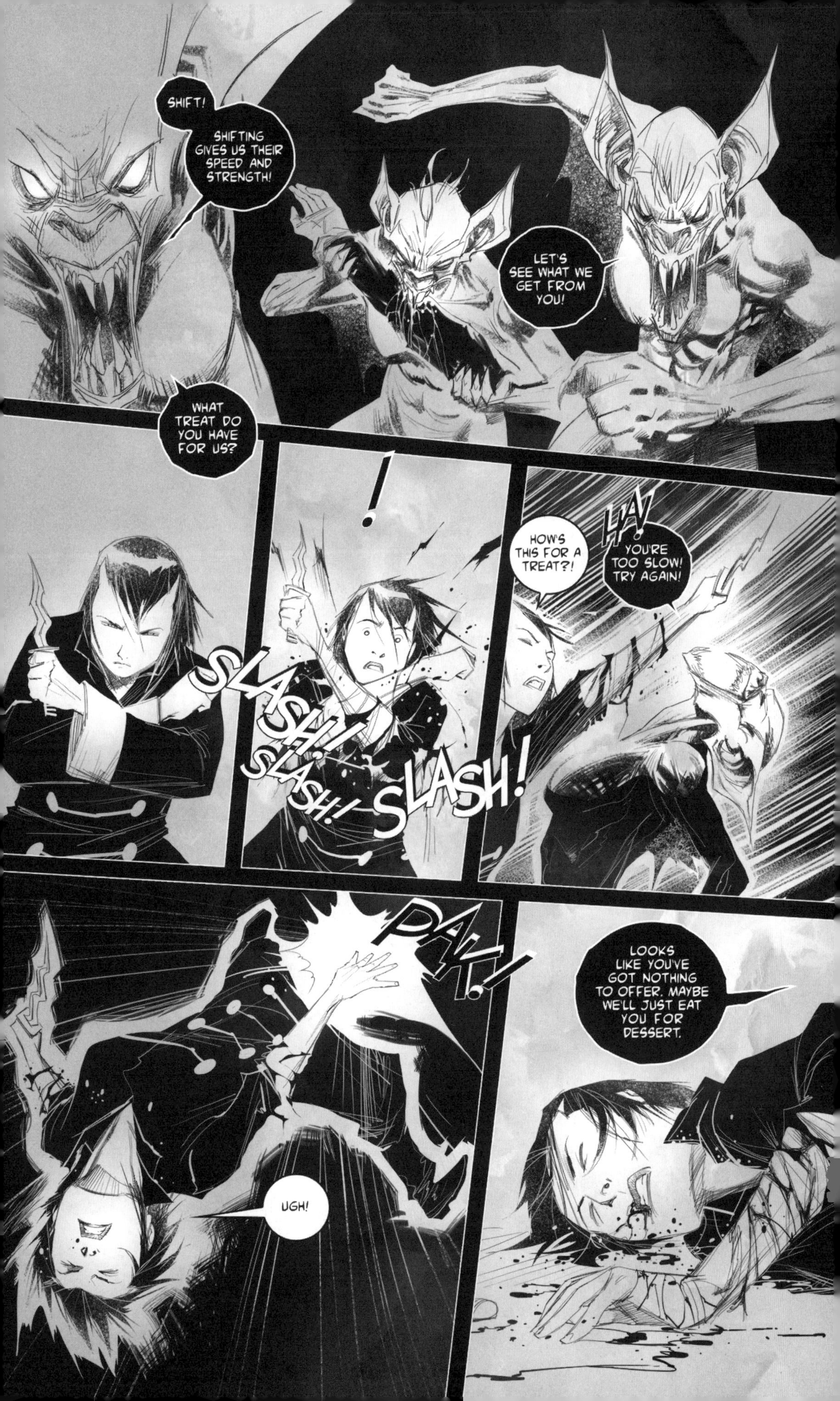
SHIFT!
SHIFTING GIVES US THEIR SPEED AND STRENGTH!
LET'S SEE WHAT WE GET FROM YOU!
WHAT TREAT DO YOU HAVE FOR US?
!
SLASH!
SLASH!
SLASH!
HOW'S THIS FOR A TREAT?!
HA!
YOU'RE TOO SLOW! TRY AGAIN!
PAK!
UGH!
LOOKS LIKE YOU'VE GOT NOTHING TO OFFER. MAYBE WE'LL JUST EAT YOU FOR DESSERT.

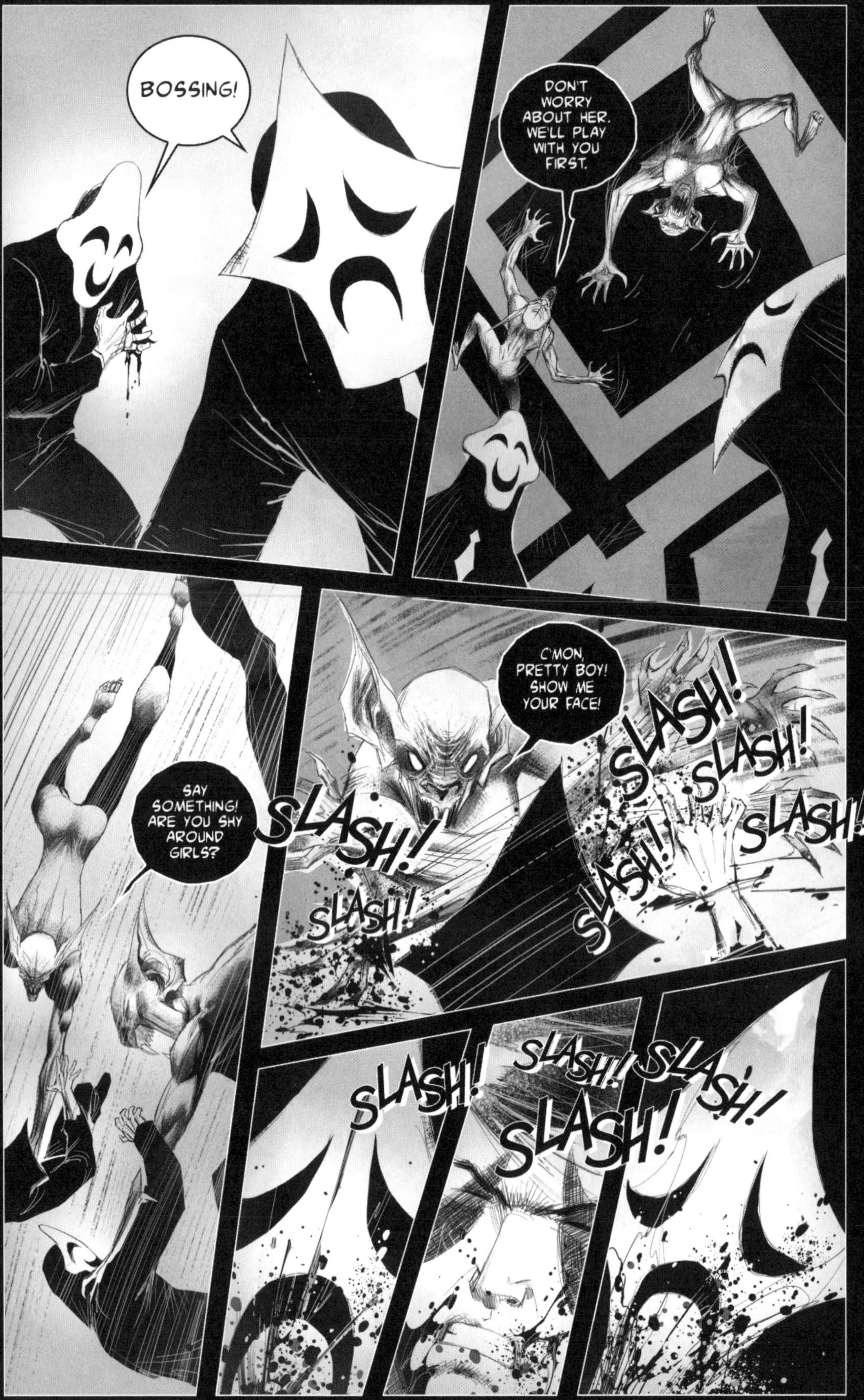

BOSSING!
DON'T WORRY ABOUT HER. WE'LL PLAY WITH YOU FIRST.
SAY SOMETHING! ARE YOU SHY AROUND GIRLS?
C'MON, PRETTY BOY! SHOW ME YOUR FACE!
SLASH!
SLASH!
SLASH!
SLASH!
SLASH!
SLASH!
SLASH!
SLASH!
SLASH!
SLASH!

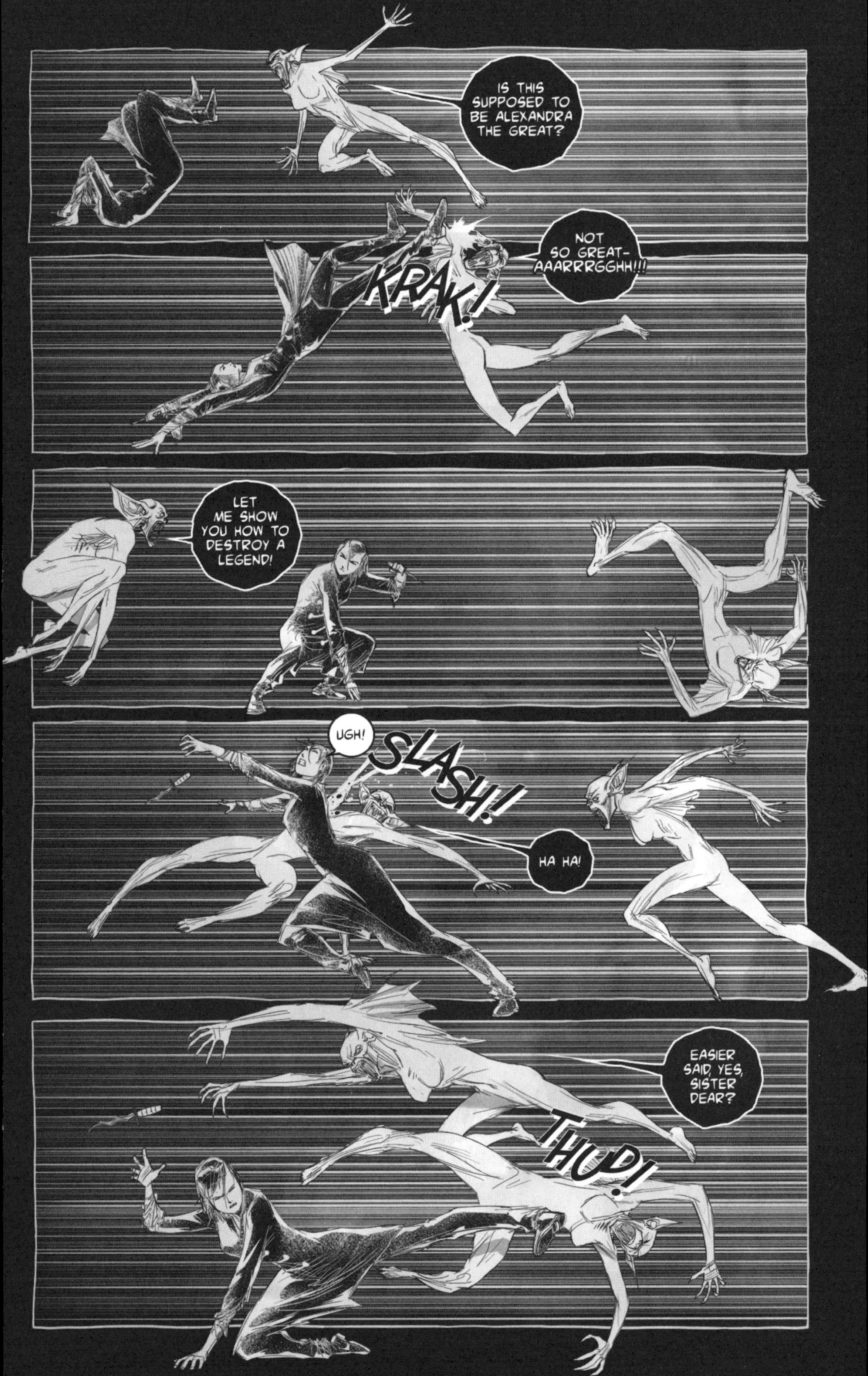
IS THIS SUPPOSED TO BE ALEXANDRA THE GREAT?
NOT SO GREAT-AAARRRGGHH!!!
KRAK!
LET ME SHOW YOU HOW TO DESTROY A LEGEND!
UGH!
SLASH!
HA HA!
EASIER SAID, YES, SISTER DEAR?
THUD!

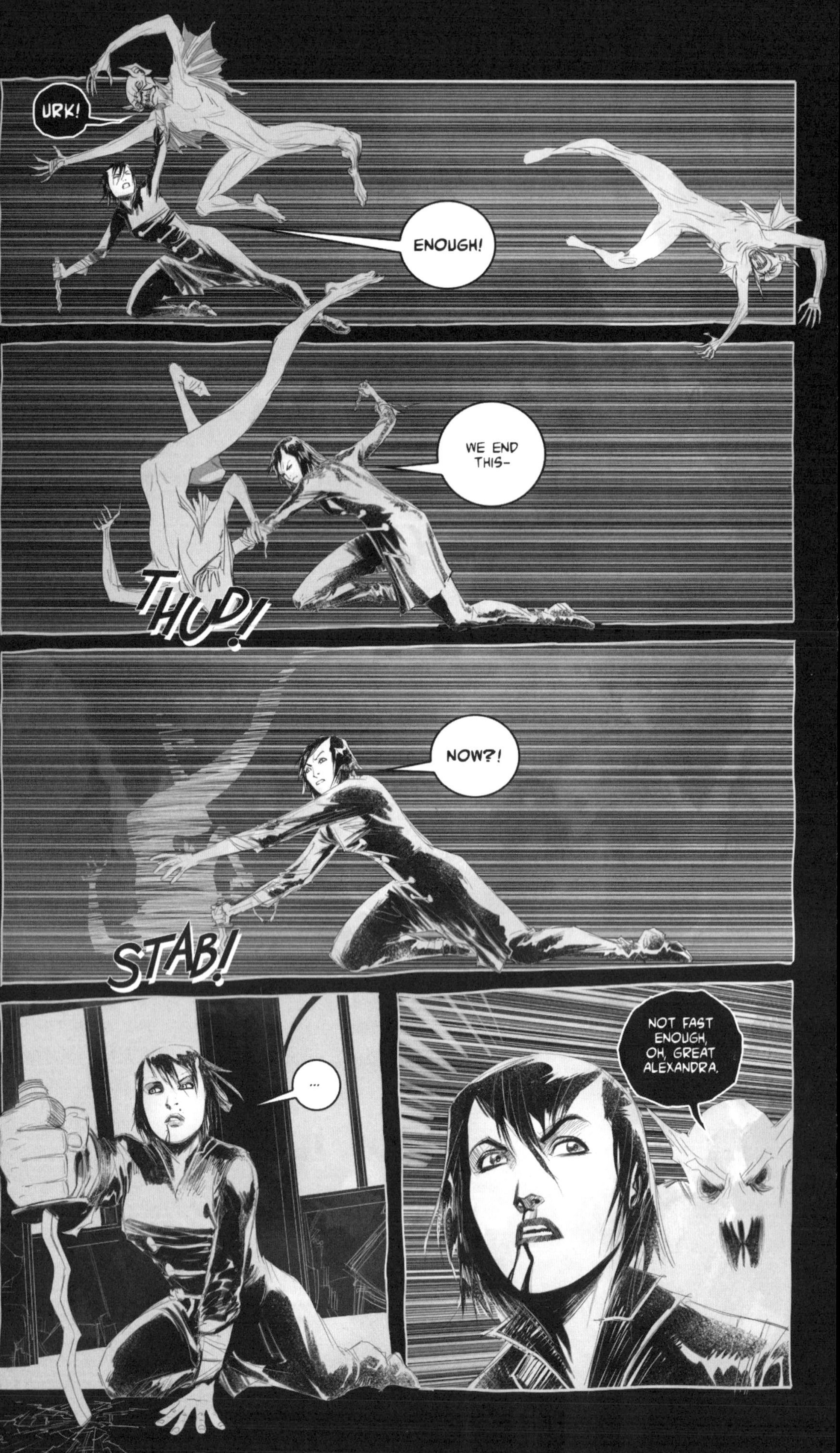
URK!
ENOUGH!
WE END THIS-
THUD!
NOW?!
STAB!
...
NOT FAST ENOUGH, OH, GREAT ALEXANDRA.

THUD! **CRASH!**

klik

THE URBANITE BAR, MAKATI CITY

RINGGG! **RINGGG!** **RINGGG!**

HIHIHI! OH, MAL! YOU'RE SO FUNNY!

HANG ON, LET ME PUT MY PHONE ON SILENT—

HEY HEY! ALEX! FINALLY YOU RETURN MY CALL. WHAT'S UP?

RODEO!

SORRY, GIRLS. HAVE TO GO!

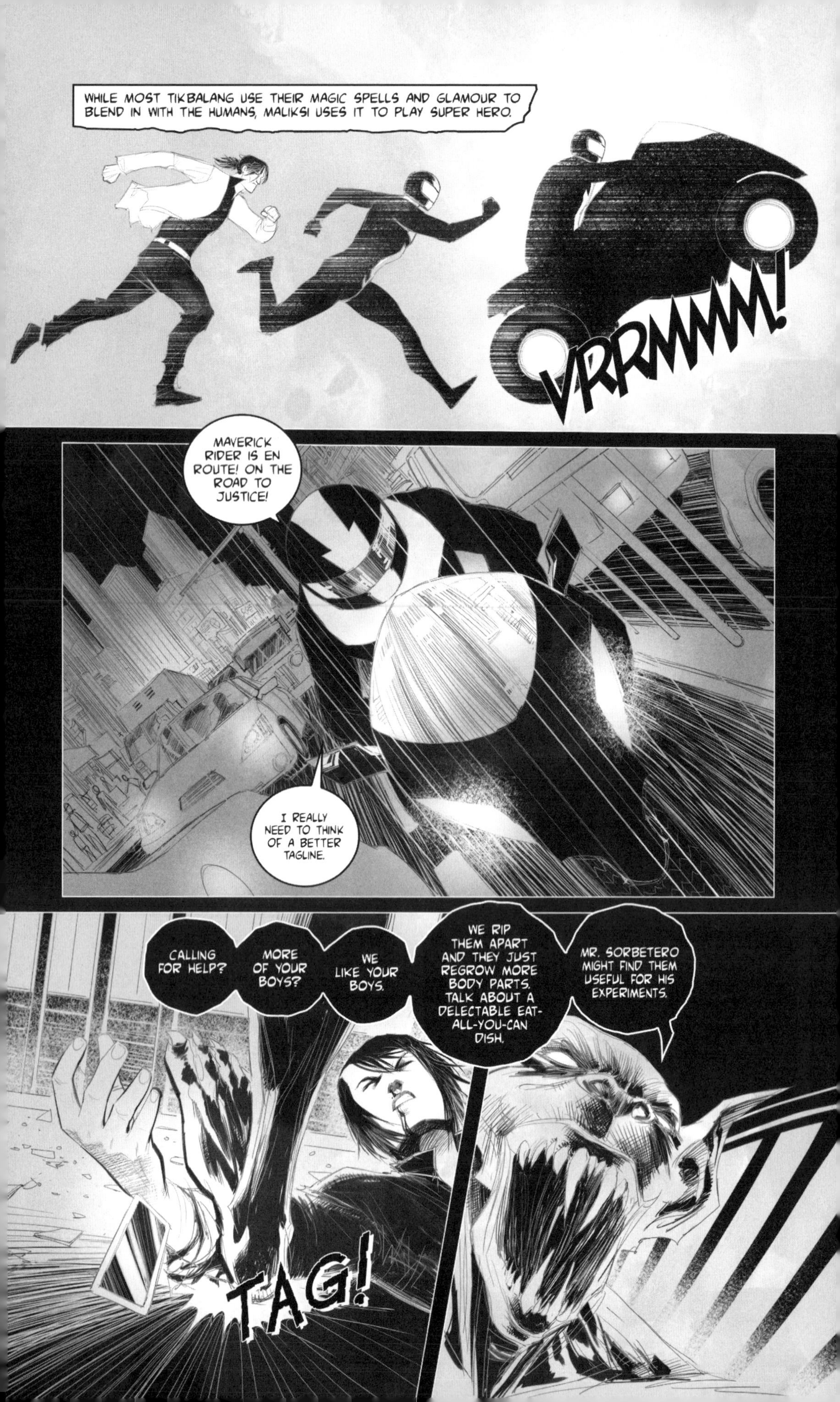

WHILE MOST TIKBALANG USE THEIR MAGIC SPELLS AND GLAMOUR TO BLEND IN WITH THE HUMANS, MALIKSI USES IT TO PLAY SUPER HERO.
VRRMMM!
MAVERICK RIDER IS EN ROUTE! ON THE ROAD TO JUSTICE!
I REALLY NEED TO THINK OF A BETTER TAGLINE.
CALLING FOR HELP?
MORE OF YOUR BOYS?
WE LIKE YOUR BOYS.
WE RIP THEM APART AND THEY JUST REGROW MORE BODY PARTS. TALK ABOUT A DELECTABLE EAT-ALL-YOU-CAN DISH.
MR. SORBETERO MIGHT FIND THEM USEFUL FOR HIS EXPERIMENTS.
TAG!

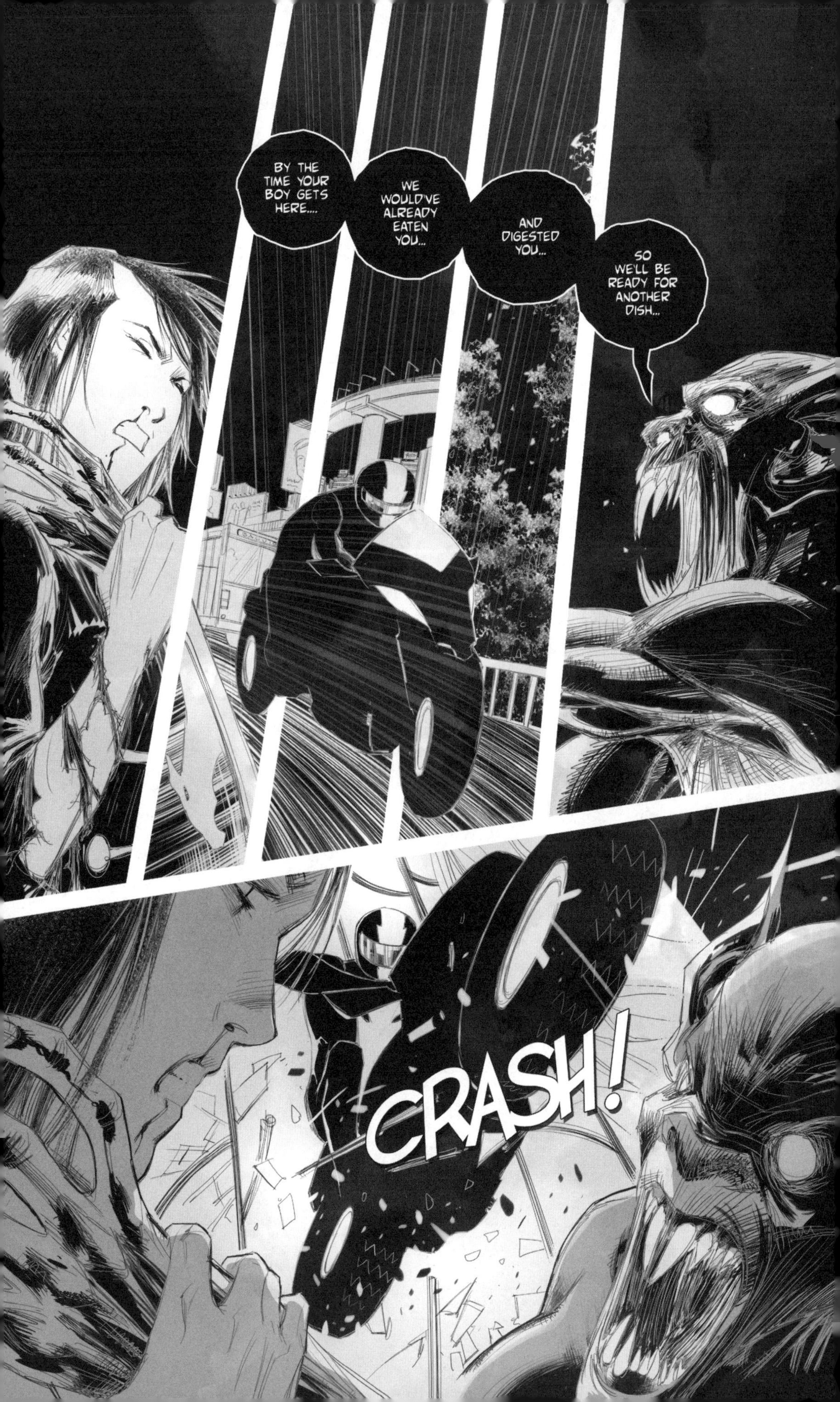
BY THE TIME YOUR BOY GETS HERE....
WE WOULD'VE ALREADY EATEN YOU...
AND DIGESTED YOU...
SO WE'LL BE READY FOR ANOTHER DISH...
CRASH!

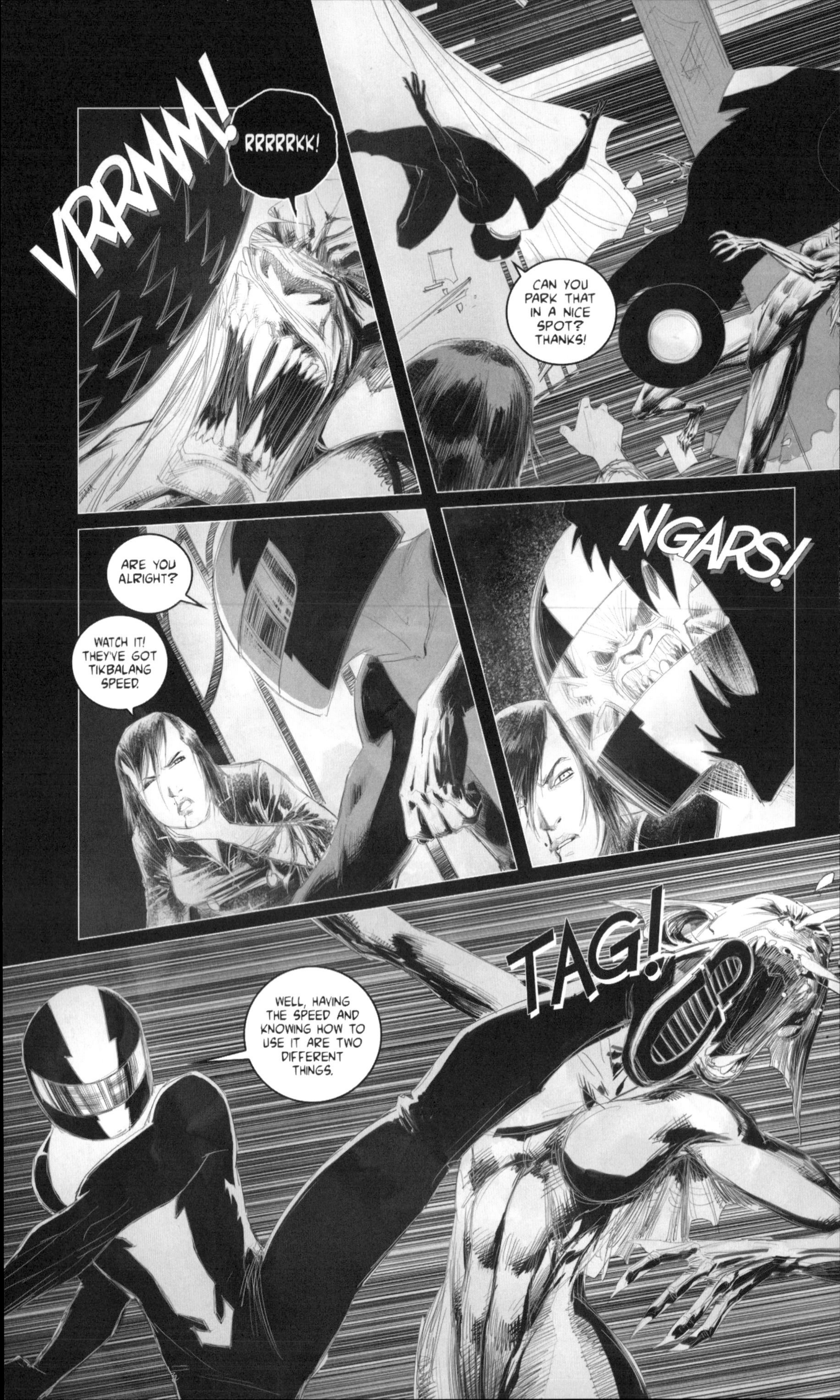
VRRMM!
RRRRRKK!
CAN YOU PARK THAT IN A NICE SPOT? THANKS!
ARE YOU ALRIGHT?
WATCH IT! THEY'VE GOT TIKBALANG SPEED.
NGARS!
TAG!
WELL, HAVING THE SPEED AND KNOWING HOW TO USE IT ARE TWO DIFFERENT THINGS.

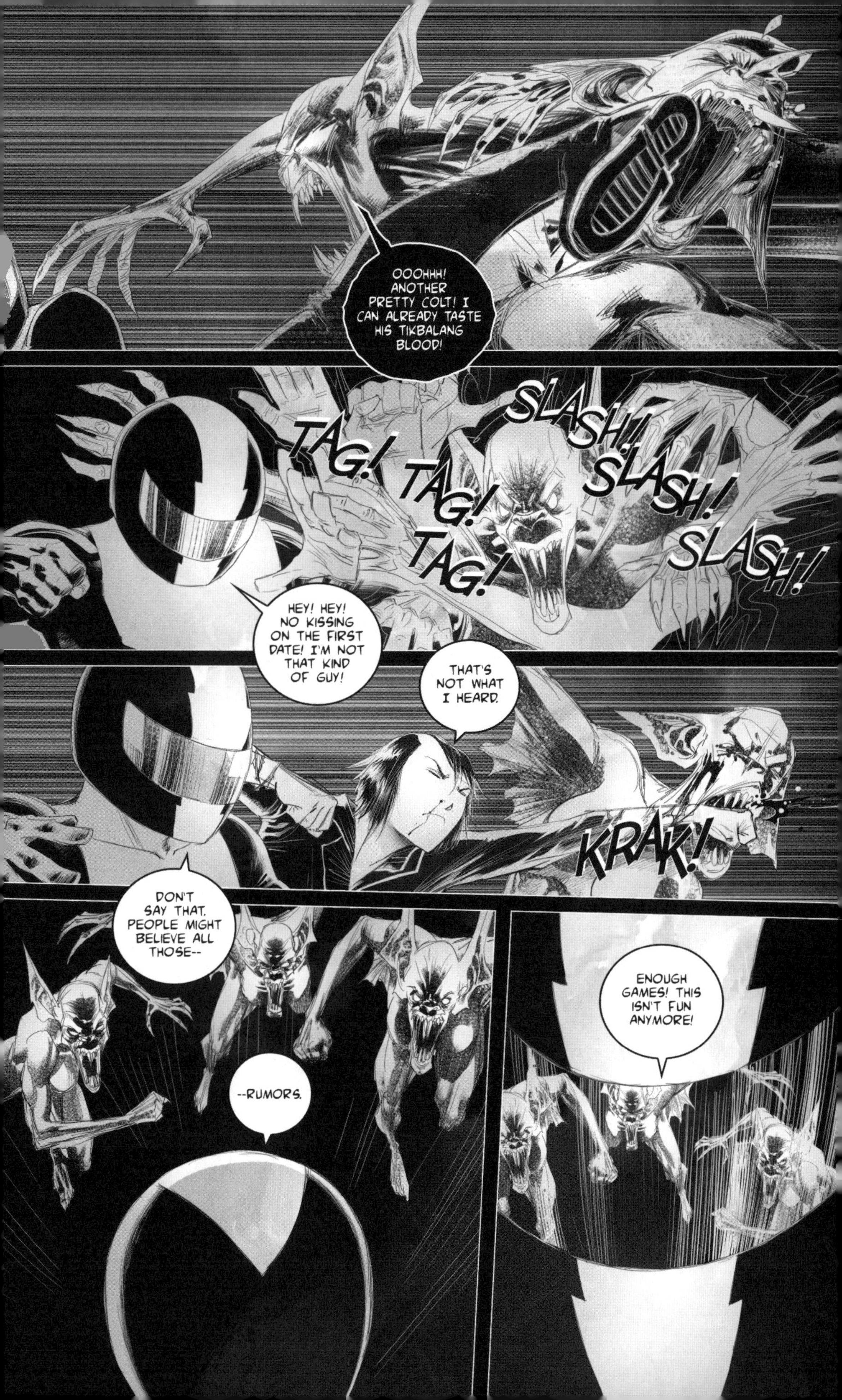
OOOHHH! ANOTHER PRETTY COLT! I CAN ALREADY TASTE HIS TIKBALANG BLOOD!
TAG! TAG! TAG!
SLASH! SLASH! SLASH!
HEY! HEY! NO KISSING ON THE FIRST DATE! I'M NOT THAT KIND OF GUY!
THAT'S NOT WHAT I HEARD.
KRAK!
DON'T SAY THAT. PEOPLE MIGHT BELIEVE ALL THOSE--
--RUMORS.
ENOUGH GAMES! THIS ISN'T FUN ANYMORE!

MALIKSI FINALLY REVEALS HIS TRUE FORM, WHICH MAKES THE ASWANG GASP, PARTLY BECAUSE OF FEAR, BUT MOSTLY BECAUSE OF THEIR CRAVING FOR MORE TIKBALANG BLOOD.

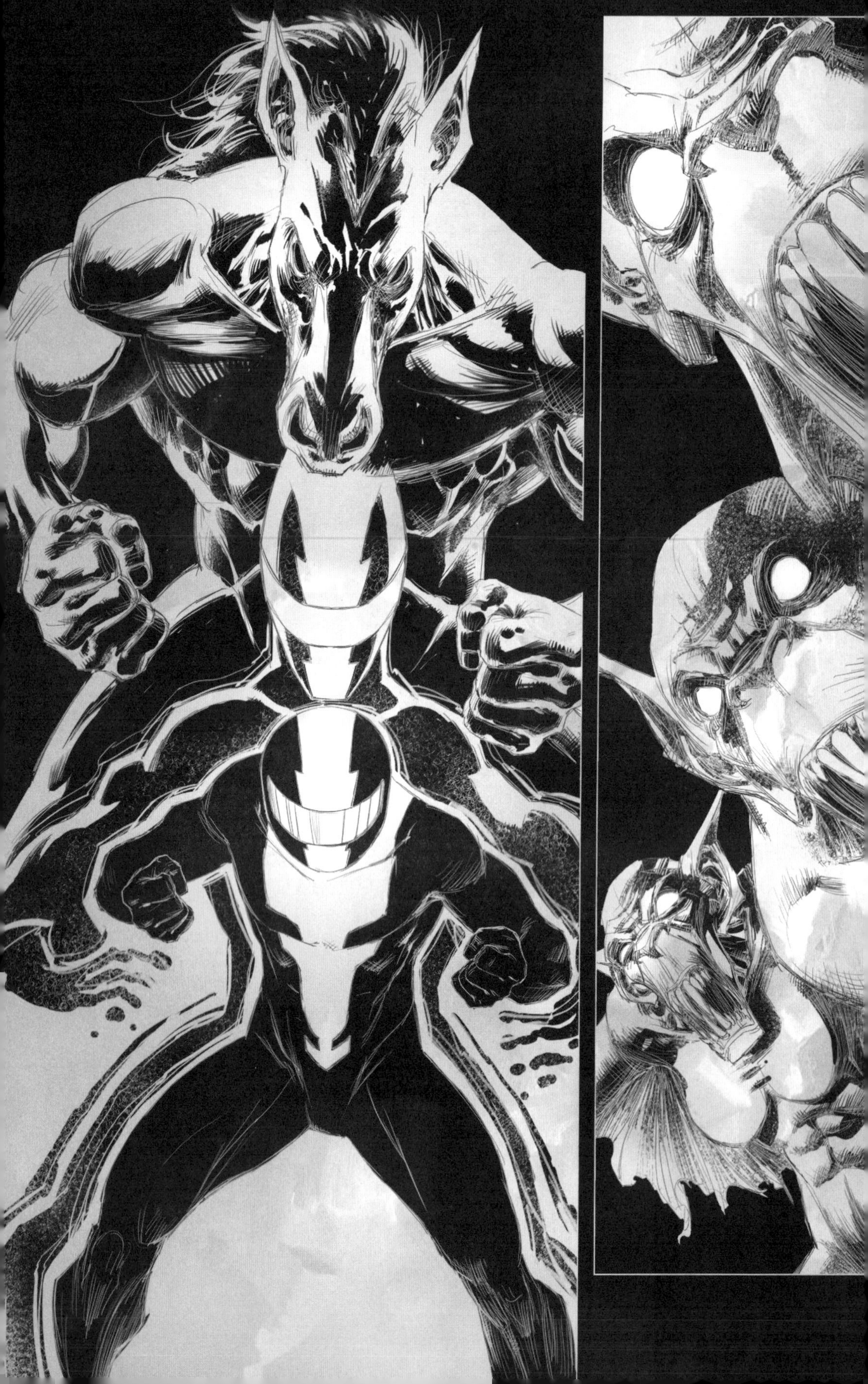

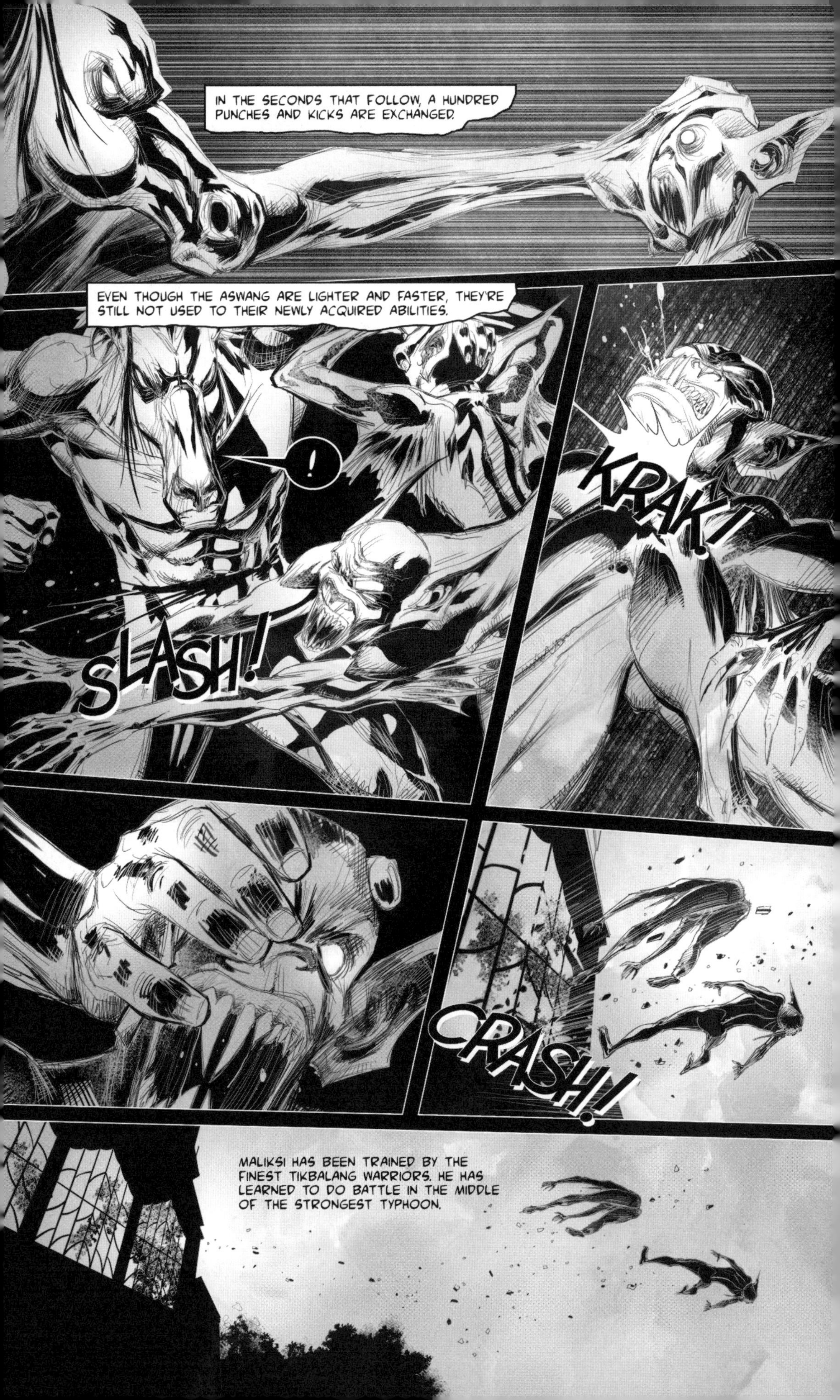
IN THE SECONDS THAT FOLLOW, A HUNDRED PUNCHES AND KICKS ARE EXCHANGED.
EVEN THOUGH THE ASWANG ARE LIGHTER AND FASTER, THEY'RE STILL NOT USED TO THEIR NEWLY ACQUIRED ABILITIES.
!
SLASH!
KRAK!
CRASH!
MALIKSI HAS BEEN TRAINED BY THE FINEST TIKBALANG WARRIORS. HE HAS LEARNED TO DO BATTLE IN THE MIDDLE OF THE STRONGEST TYPHOON.

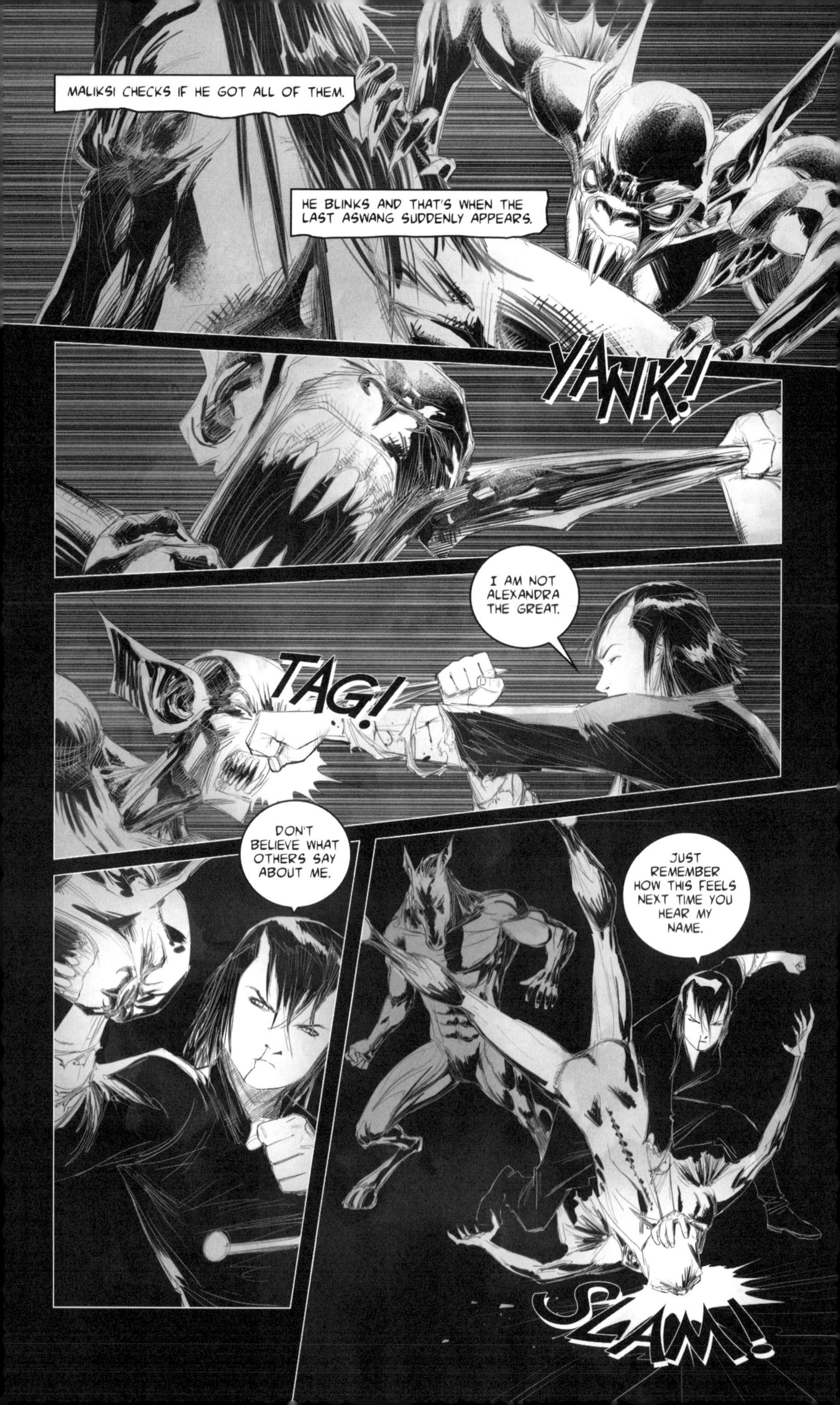
MALIKSI CHECKS IF HE GOT ALL OF THEM.
HE BLINKS AND THAT'S WHEN THE LAST ASWANG SUDDENLY APPEARS.
YANK!
I AM NOT ALEXANDRA THE GREAT.
TAG!
DON'T BELIEVE WHAT OTHERS SAY ABOUT ME.
JUST REMEMBER HOW THIS FEELS NEXT TIME YOU HEAR MY NAME.
SLAM!

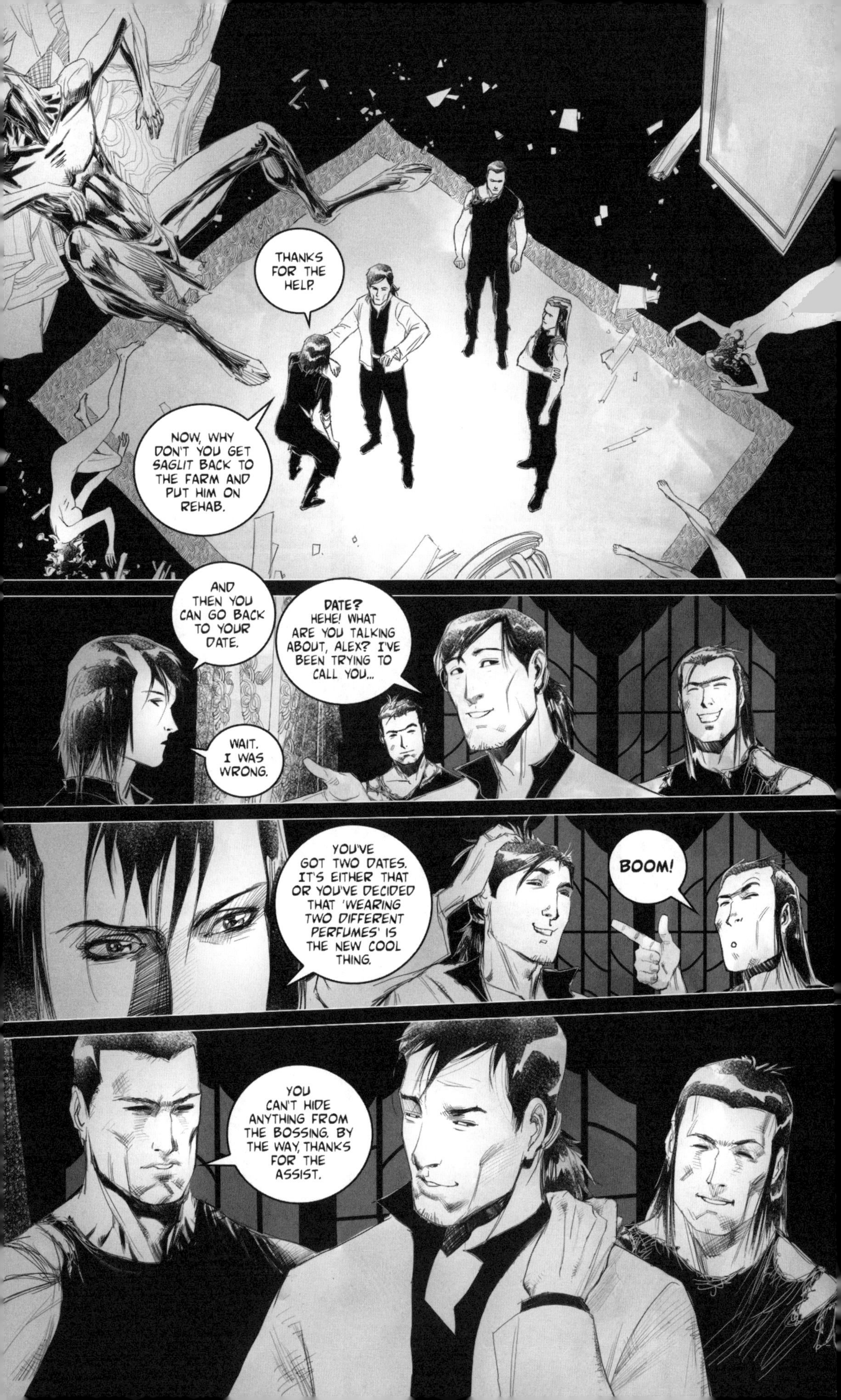
THANKS FOR THE HELP.
NOW, WHY DON'T YOU GET SAGLIT BACK TO THE FARM AND PUT HIM ON REHAB.
AND THEN YOU CAN GO BACK TO YOUR DATE.
DATE? HEHE! WHAT ARE YOU TALKING ABOUT, ALEX? I'VE BEEN TRYING TO CALL YOU...
WAIT. I WAS WRONG.
YOU'VE GOT TWO DATES. IT'S EITHER THAT OR YOU'VE DECIDED THAT 'WEARING TWO DIFFERENT PERFUMES' IS THE NEW COOL THING.
BOOM!
YOU CAN'T HIDE ANYTHING FROM THE BOSSING. BY THE WAY, THANKS FOR THE ASSIST.

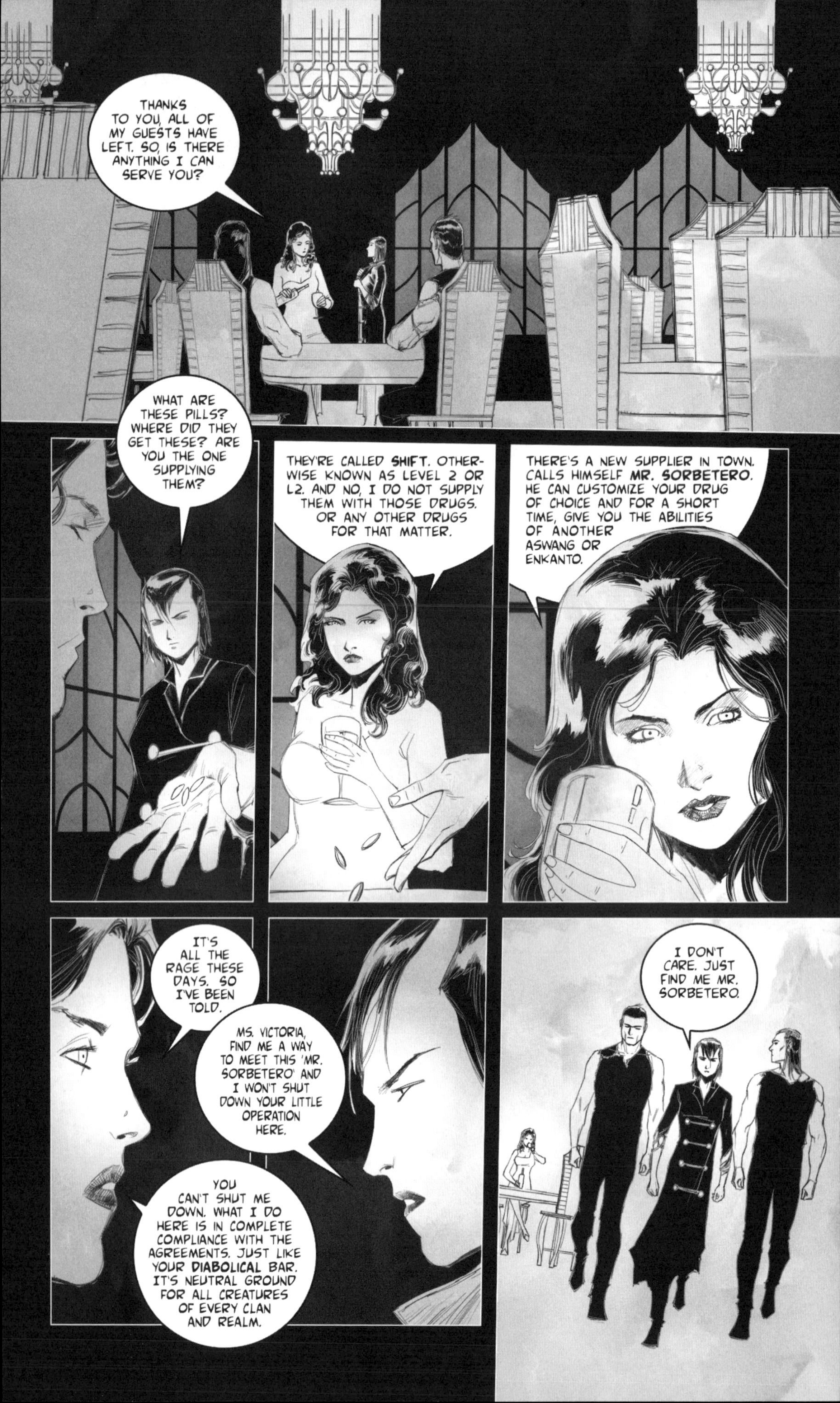
THANKS TO YOU, ALL OF MY GUESTS HAVE LEFT. SO, IS THERE ANYTHING I CAN SERVE YOU?
WHAT ARE THESE PILLS? WHERE DID THEY GET THESE? ARE YOU THE ONE SUPPLYING THEM?
THEY'RE CALLED SHIFT. OTHERWISE KNOWN AS LEVEL 2 OR L2. AND NO, I DO NOT SUPPLY THEM WITH THOSE DRUGS. OR ANY OTHER DRUGS FOR THAT MATTER.
THERE'S A NEW SUPPLIER IN TOWN. CALLS HIMSELF MR. SORBETERO. HE CAN CUSTOMIZE YOUR DRUG OF CHOICE AND FOR A SHORT TIME, GIVE YOU THE ABILITIES OF ANOTHER ASWANG OR ENKANTO.
IT'S ALL THE RAGE THESE DAYS. SO I'VE BEEN TOLD.
MS. VICTORIA, FIND ME A WAY TO MEET THIS 'MR. SORBETERO' AND I WON'T SHUT DOWN YOUR LITTLE OPERATION HERE.
YOU CAN'T SHUT ME DOWN. WHAT I DO HERE IS IN COMPLETE COMPLIANCE WITH THE AGREEMENTS. JUST LIKE YOUR DIABOLICAL BAR. IT'S NEUTRAL GROUND FOR ALL CREATURES OF EVERY CLAN AND REALM.
I DON'T CARE. JUST FIND ME MR. SORBETERO.

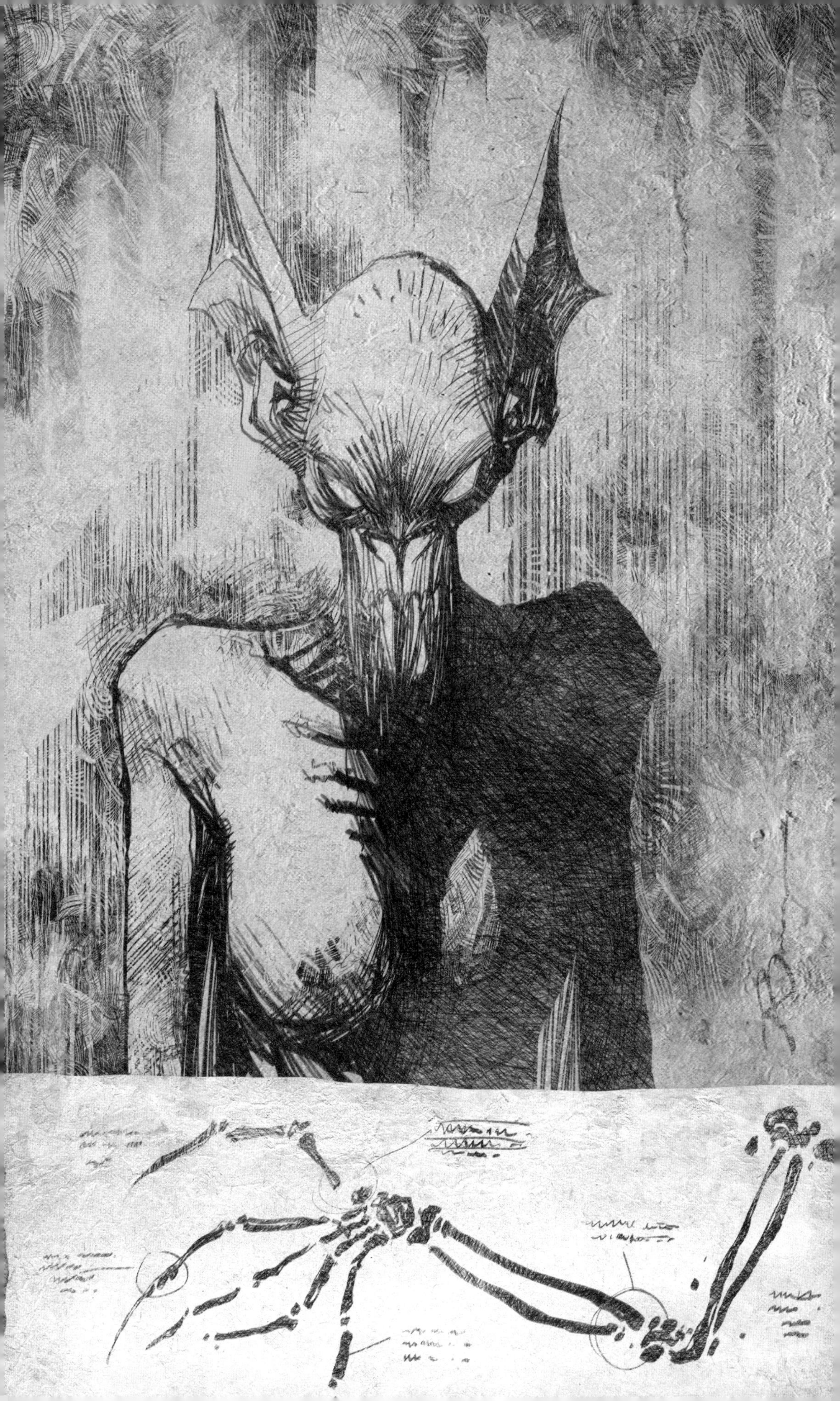

August 14

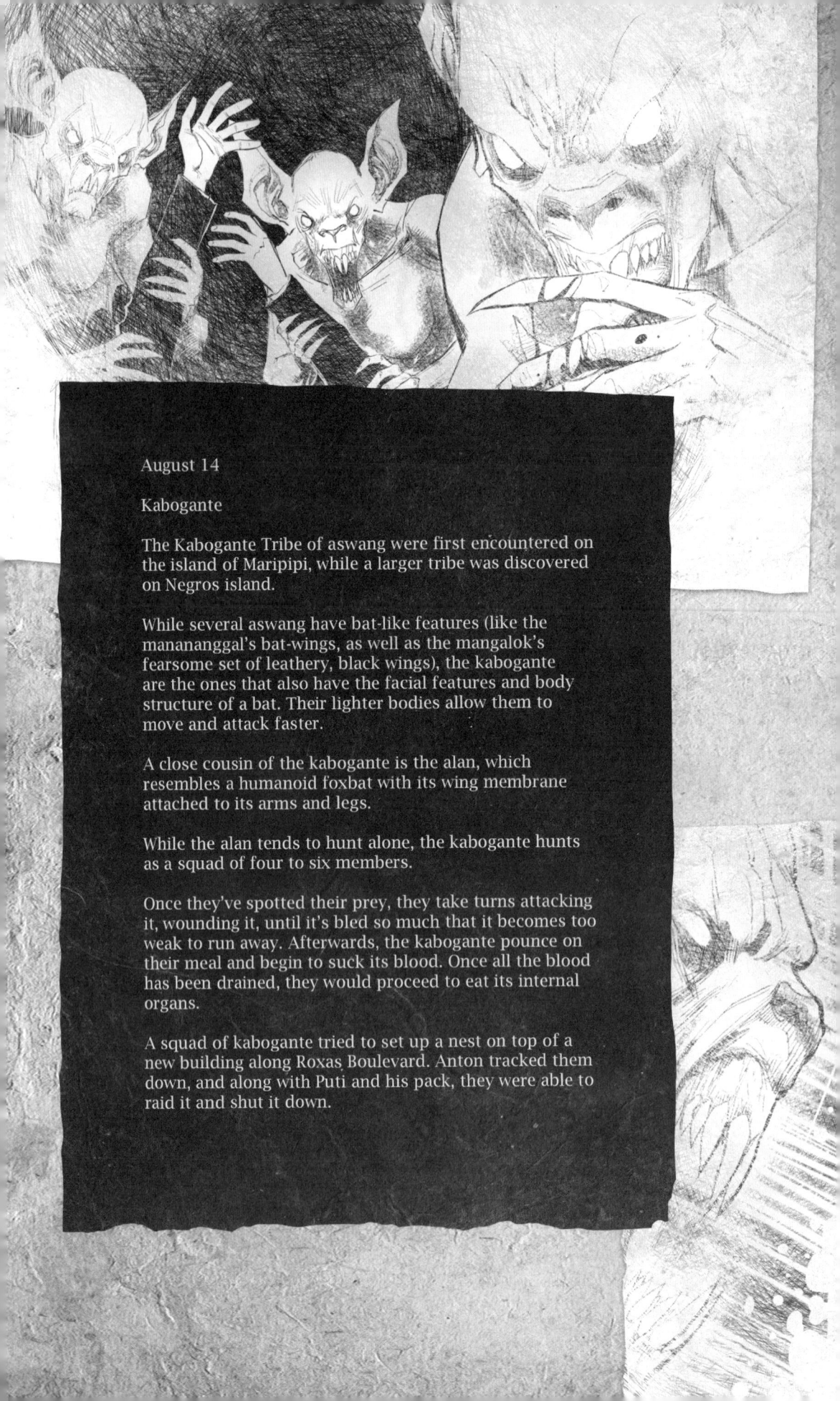

Kabogante

The Kabogante Tribe of aswang were first encountered on the island of Maripipi, while a larger tribe was discovered on Negros island.

While several aswang have bat-like features (like the manananggal's bat-wings, as well as the mangalok's fearsome set of leathery, black wings), the kabogante are the ones that also have the facial features and body structure of a bat. Their lighter bodies allow them to move and attack faster.

A close cousin of the kabogante is the alan, which resembles a humanoid foxbat with its wing membrane attached to its arms and legs.

While the alan tends to hunt alone, the kabogante hunts as a squad of four to six members.

Once they've spotted their prey, they take turns attacking it, wounding it, until it's bled so much that it becomes too weak to run away. Afterwards, the kabogante pounce on their meal and begin to suck its blood. Once all the blood has been drained, they would proceed to eat its internal organs.

A squad of kabogante tried to set up a nest on top of a new building along Roxas Boulevard. Anton tracked them down, and along with Puti and his pack, they were able to raid it and shut it down.

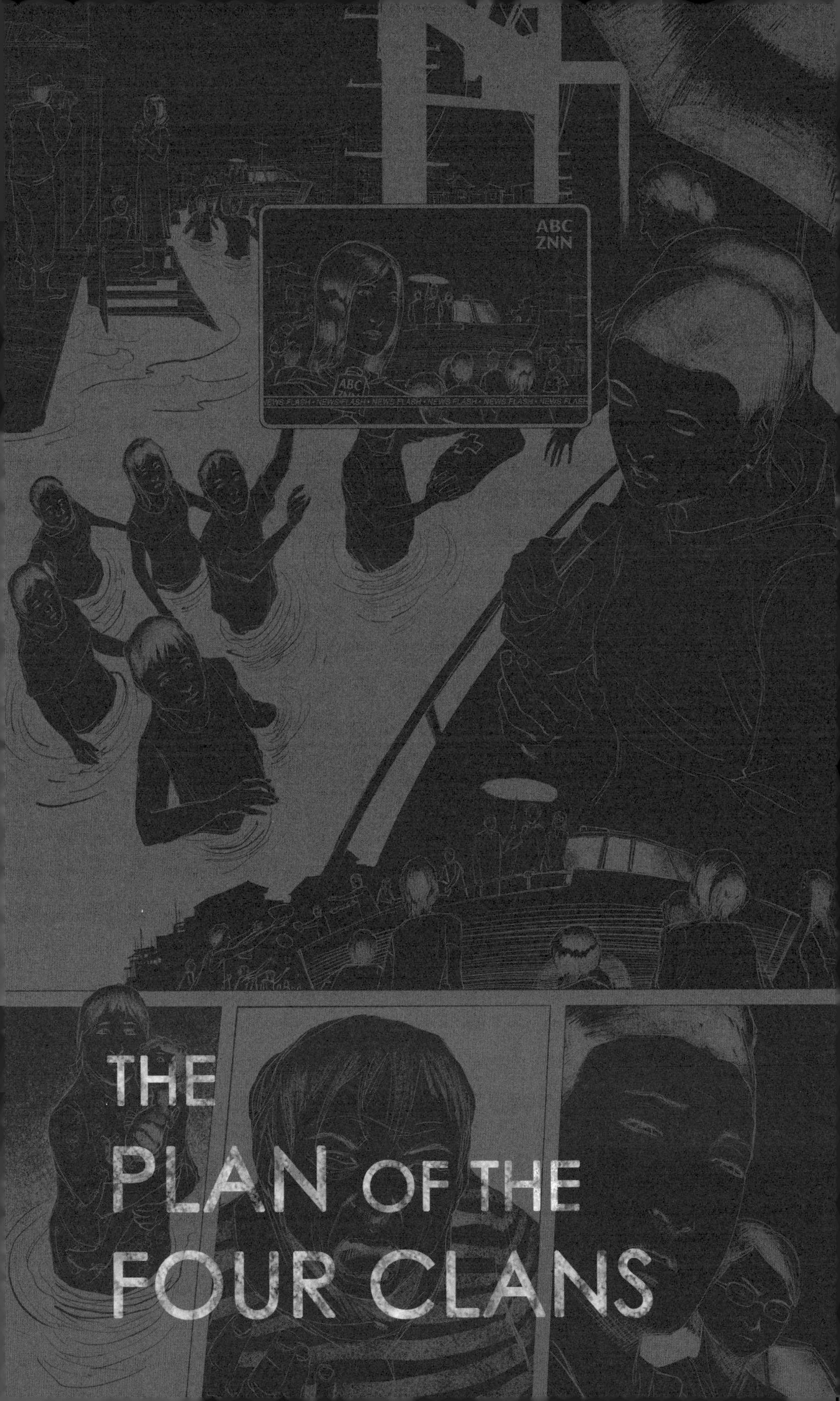
ABC
ZNN
NEWS FLASH • NEWS FLASH • NEWS FLASH • NEWS FLASH • NEWS FLASH • NEWS FLASH
THE
PLAN OF THE
FOUR CLANS

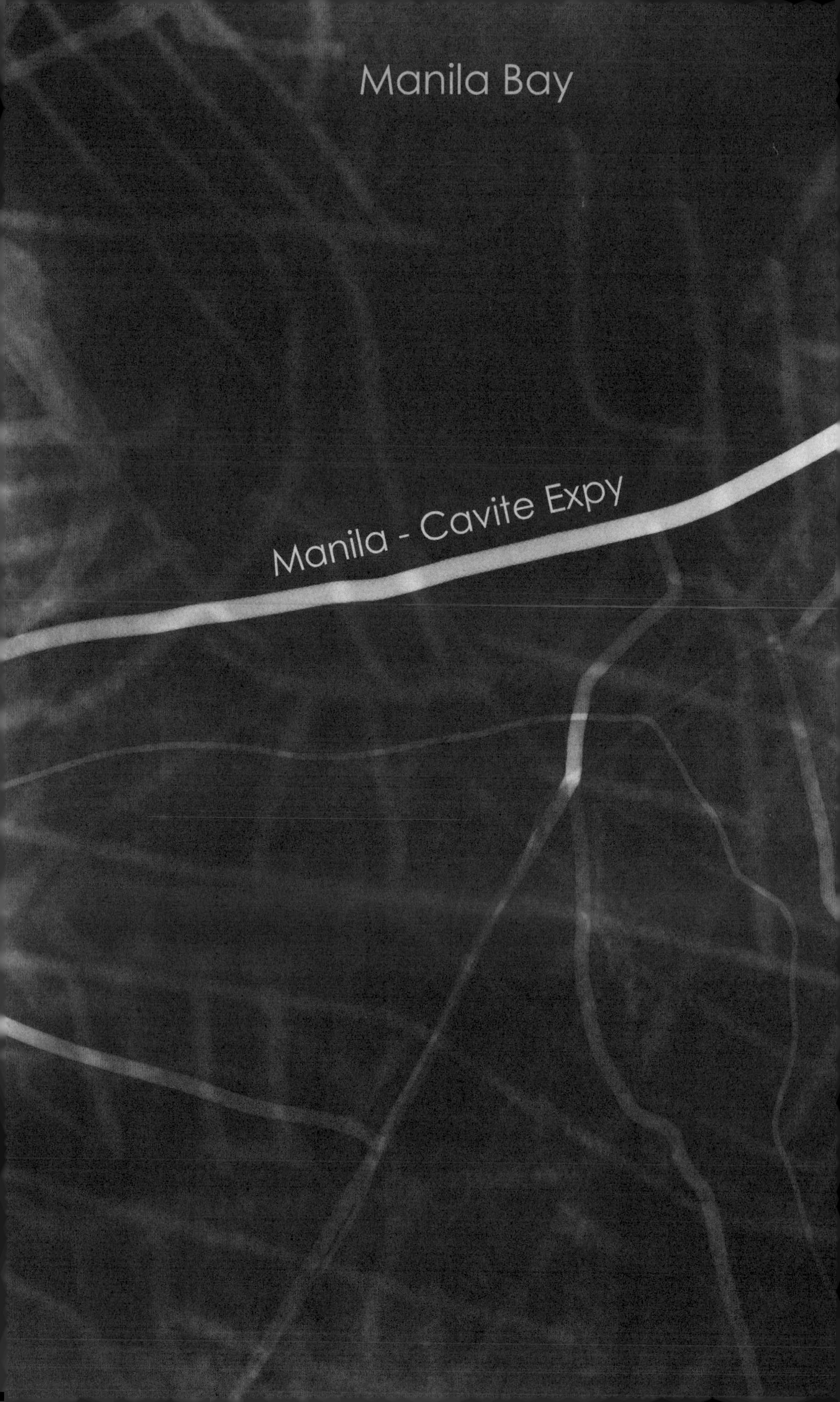
Manila Bay
Manila - Cavite Expy

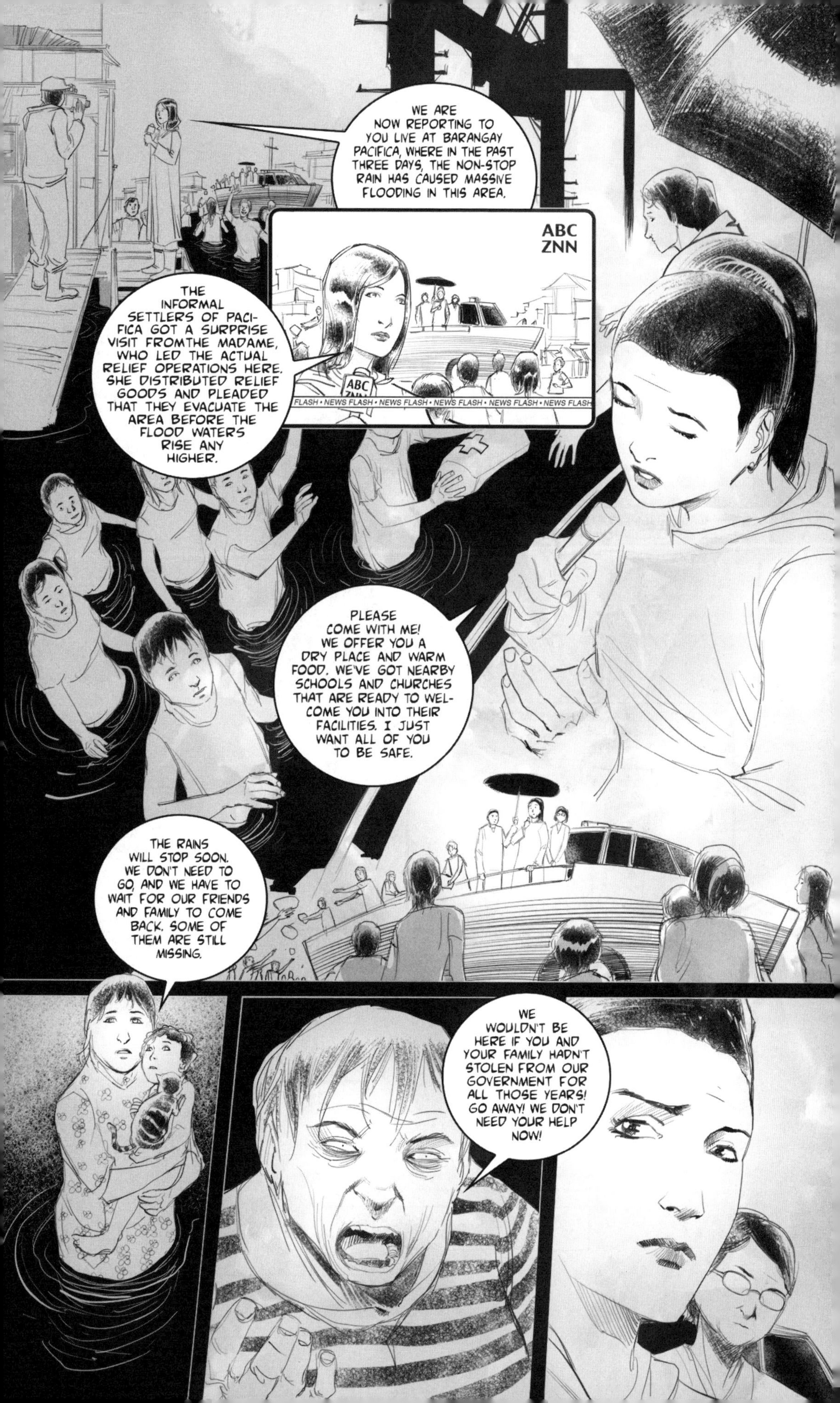
WE ARE NOW REPORTING TO YOU LIVE AT BARANGAY PACIFICA, WHERE IN THE PAST THREE DAYS, THE NON-STOP RAIN HAS CAUSED MASSIVE FLOODING IN THIS AREA.
ABC ZNN
ABC
FLASH • NEWS FLASH • NEWS FLASH • NEWS FLASH • NEWS FLASH • NEWS FLASH
THE INFORMAL SETTLERS OF PACI-FICA GOT A SURPRISE VISIT FROMTHE MADAME, WHO LED THE ACTUAL RELIEF OPERATIONS HERE. SHE DISTRIBUTED RELIEF GOODS AND PLEADED THAT THEY EVACUATE THE AREA BEFORE THE FLOOD WATERS RISE ANY HIGHER.
PLEASE COME WITH ME! WE OFFER YOU A DRY PLACE AND WARM FOOD. WE'VE GOT NEARBY SCHOOLS AND CHURCHES THAT ARE READY TO WEL-COME YOU INTO THEIR FACILITIES. I JUST WANT ALL OF YOU TO BE SAFE.
THE RAINS WILL STOP SOON. WE DON'T NEED TO GO, AND WE HAVE TO WAIT FOR OUR FRIENDS AND FAMILY TO COME BACK. SOME OF THEM ARE STILL MISSING.
WE WOULDN'T BE HERE IF YOU AND YOUR FAMILY HADN'T STOLEN FROM OUR GOVERNMENT FOR ALL THOSE YEARS! GO AWAY! WE DON'T NEED YOUR HELP NOW!

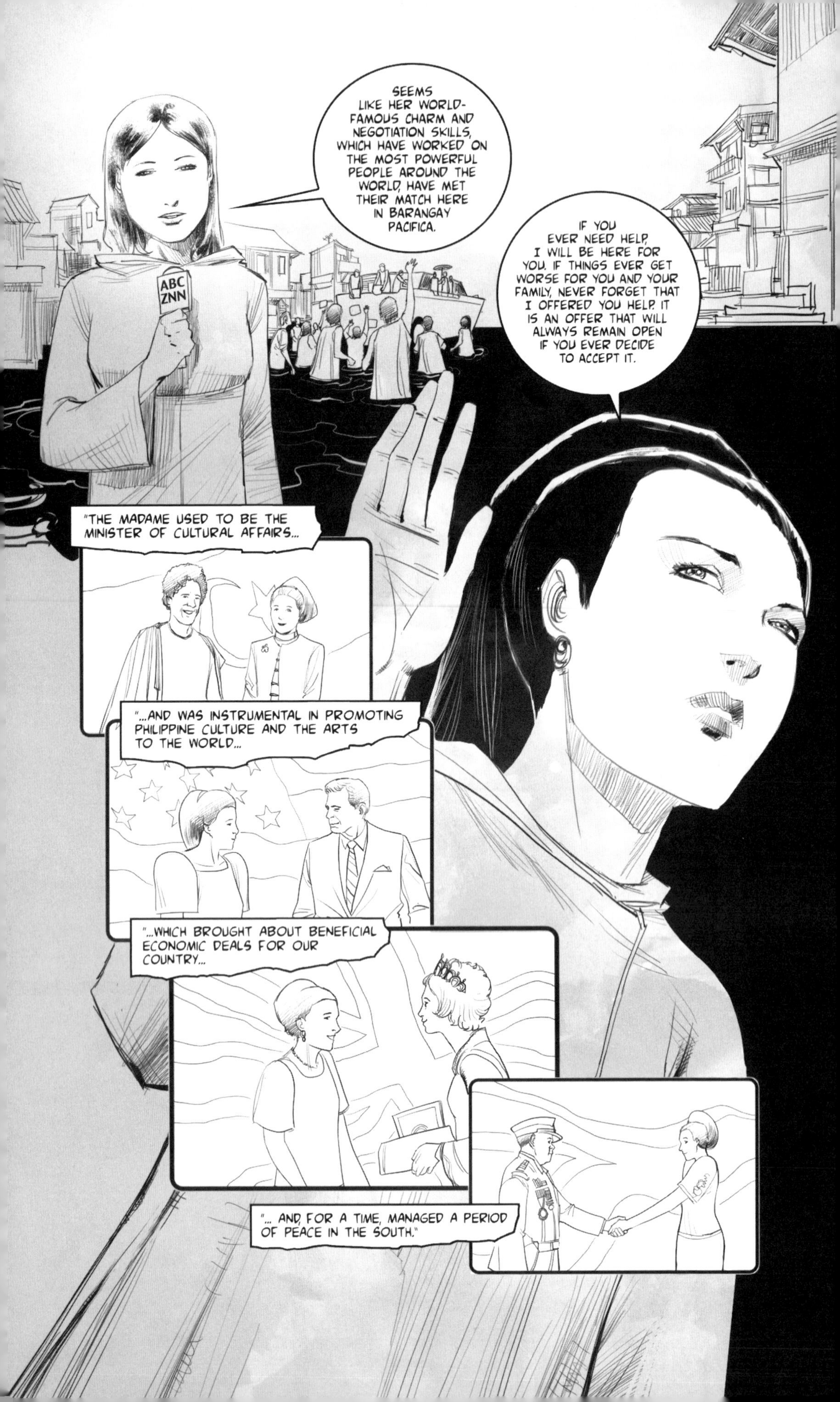
SEEMS LIKE HER WORLD-FAMOUS CHARM AND NEGOTIATION SKILLS, WHICH HAVE WORKED ON THE MOST POWERFUL PEOPLE AROUND THE WORLD, HAVE MET THEIR MATCH HERE IN BARANGAY PACIFICA.
ABC ZNN
IF YOU EVER NEED HELP, I WILL BE HERE FOR YOU. IF THINGS EVER GET WORSE FOR YOU AND YOUR FAMILY, NEVER FORGET THAT I OFFERED YOU HELP. IT IS AN OFFER THAT WILL ALWAYS REMAIN OPEN IF YOU EVER DECIDE TO ACCEPT IT.
"THE MADAME USED TO BE THE MINISTER OF CULTURAL AFFAIRS...
"...AND WAS INSTRUMENTAL IN PROMOTING PHILIPPINE CULTURE AND THE ARTS TO THE WORLD...
"...WHICH BROUGHT ABOUT BENEFICIAL ECONOMIC DEALS FOR OUR COUNTRY...
"... AND, FOR A TIME, MANAGED A PERIOD OF PEACE IN THE SOUTH."

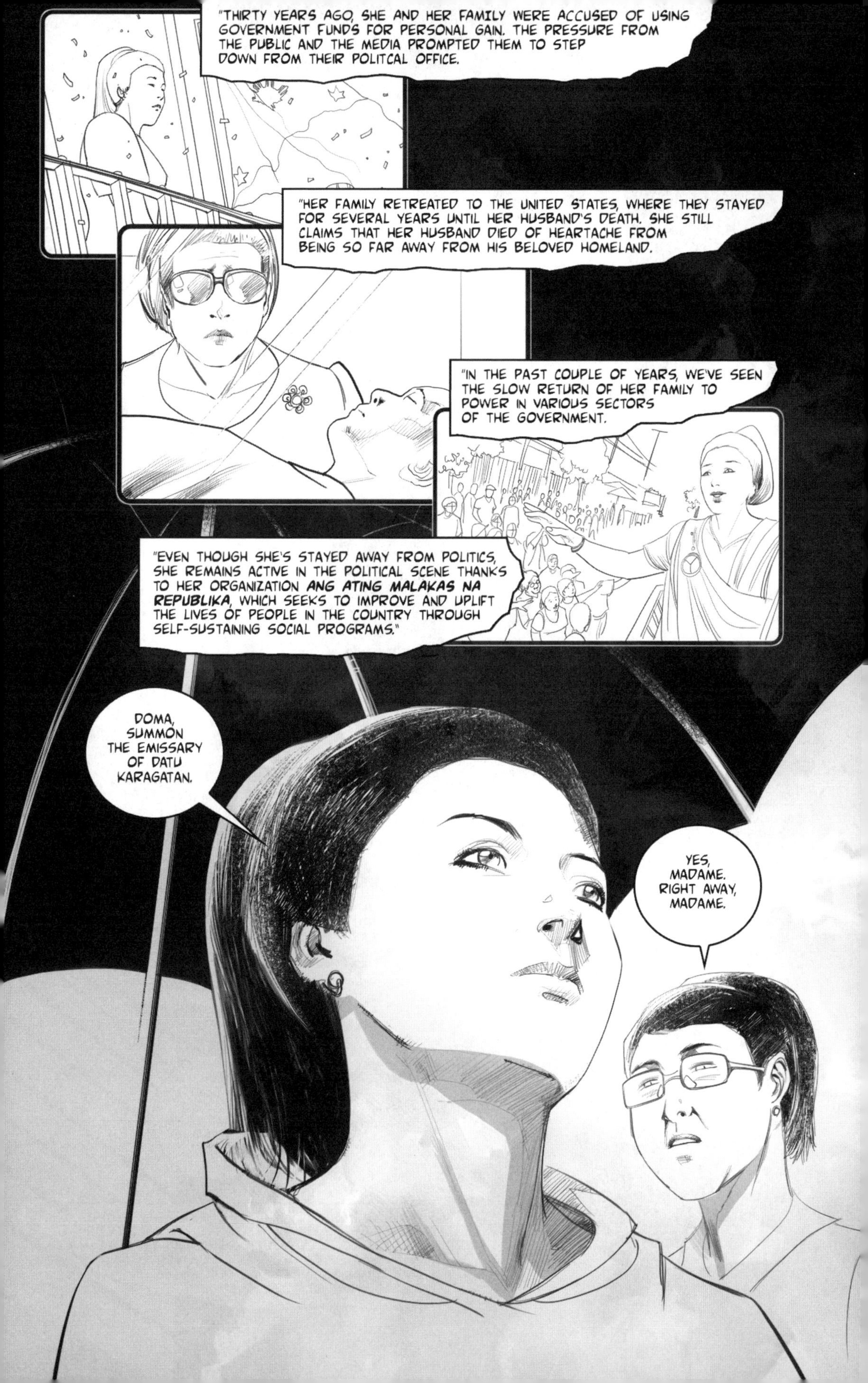
"THIRTY YEARS AGO, SHE AND HER FAMILY WERE ACCUSED OF USING GOVERNMENT FUNDS FOR PERSONAL GAIN. THE PRESSURE FROM THE PUBLIC AND THE MEDIA PROMPTED THEM TO STEP DOWN FROM THEIR POLITCAL OFFICE.
"HER FAMILY RETREATED TO THE UNITED STATES, WHERE THEY STAYED FOR SEVERAL YEARS UNTIL HER HUSBAND'S DEATH. SHE STILL CLAIMS THAT HER HUSBAND DIED OF HEARTACHE FROM BEING SO FAR AWAY FROM HIS BELOVED HOMELAND.
"IN THE PAST COUPLE OF YEARS, WE'VE SEEN THE SLOW RETURN OF HER FAMILY TO POWER IN VARIOUS SECTORS OF THE GOVERNMENT.
"EVEN THOUGH SHE'S STAYED AWAY FROM POLITICS, SHE REMAINS ACTIVE IN THE POLITICAL SCENE THANKS TO HER ORGANIZATION ***ANG ATING MALAKAS NA REPUBLIKA***, WHICH SEEKS TO IMPROVE AND UPLIFT THE LIVES OF PEOPLE IN THE COUNTRY THROUGH SELF-SUSTAINING SOCIAL PROGRAMS."
DOMA, SUMMON THE EMISSARY OF DATU KARAGATAN.
YES, MADAME. RIGHT AWAY, MADAME.

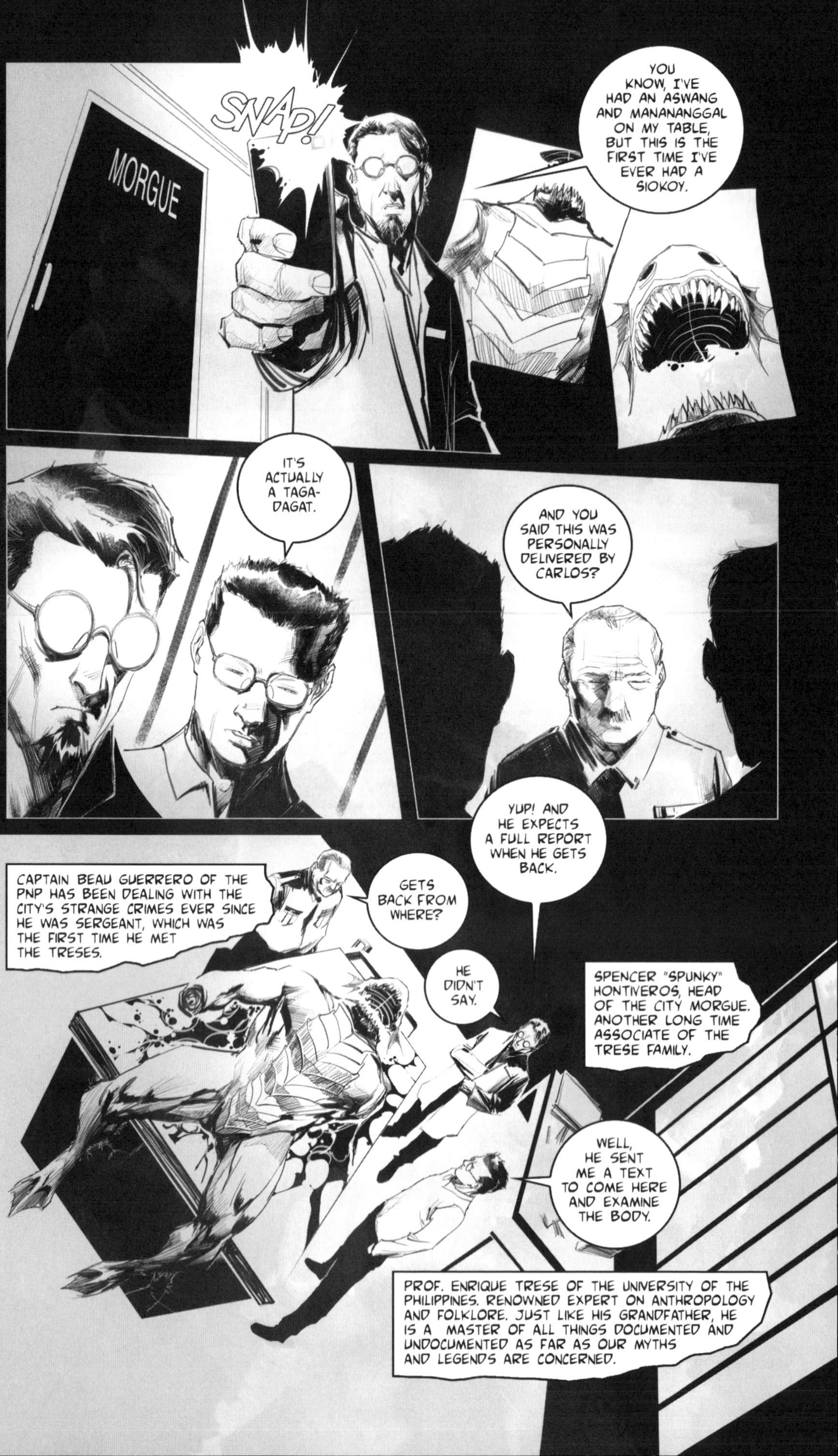

SNAP!
MORGUE
YOU KNOW, I'VE HAD AN ASWANG AND MANANANGGAL ON MY TABLE, BUT THIS IS THE FIRST TIME I'VE EVER HAD A SIOKOY.
IT'S ACTUALLY A TAGA-DAGAT.
AND YOU SAID THIS WAS PERSONALLY DELIVERED BY CARLOS?
YUP! AND HE EXPECTS A FULL REPORT WHEN HE GETS BACK.
CAPTAIN BEAU GUERRERO OF THE PNP HAS BEEN DEALING WITH THE CITY'S STRANGE CRIMES EVER SINCE HE WAS SERGEANT, WHICH WAS THE FIRST TIME HE MET THE TRESES.
GETS BACK FROM WHERE?
HE DIDN'T SAY.
SPENCER "SPUNKY" HONTIVEROS, HEAD OF THE CITY MORGUE. ANOTHER LONG TIME ASSOCIATE OF THE TRESE FAMILY.
WELL, HE SENT ME A TEXT TO COME HERE AND EXAMINE THE BODY.
PROF. ENRIQUE TRESE OF THE UNIVERSITY OF THE PHILIPPINES. RENOWNED EXPERT ON ANTHROPOLOGY AND FOLKLORE. JUST LIKE HIS GRANDFATHER, HE IS A MASTER OF ALL THINGS DOCUMENTED AND UNDOCUMENTED AS FAR AS OUR MYTHS AND LEGENDS ARE CONCERNED.

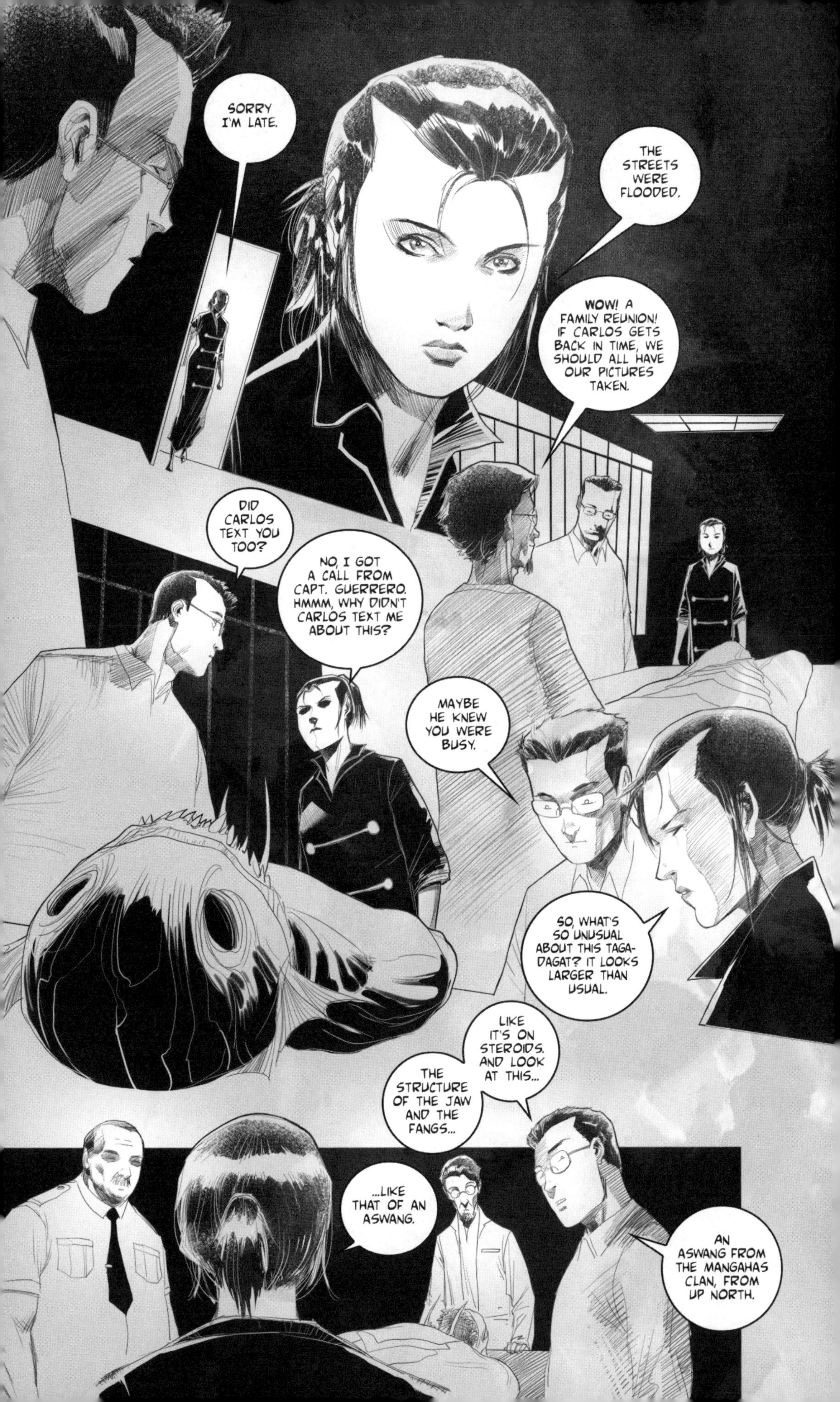
SORRY I'M LATE.
THE STREETS WERE FLOODED.
WOW! A FAMILY REUNION! IF CARLOS GETS BACK IN TIME, WE SHOULD ALL HAVE OUR PICTURES TAKEN.
DID CARLOS TEXT YOU TOO?
NO, I GOT A CALL FROM CAPT. GUERRERO. HMMM, WHY DIDN'T CARLOS TEXT ME ABOUT THIS?
MAYBE HE KNEW YOU WERE BUSY.
SO, WHAT'S SO UNUSUAL ABOUT THIS TAGA-DAGAT? IT LOOKS LARGER THAN USUAL.
LIKE IT'S ON STEROIDS. AND LOOK AT THIS...
THE STRUCTURE OF THE JAW AND THE FANGS...
...LIKE THAT OF AN ASWANG.
AN ASWANG FROM THE MANGAHAS CLAN, FROM UP NORTH.

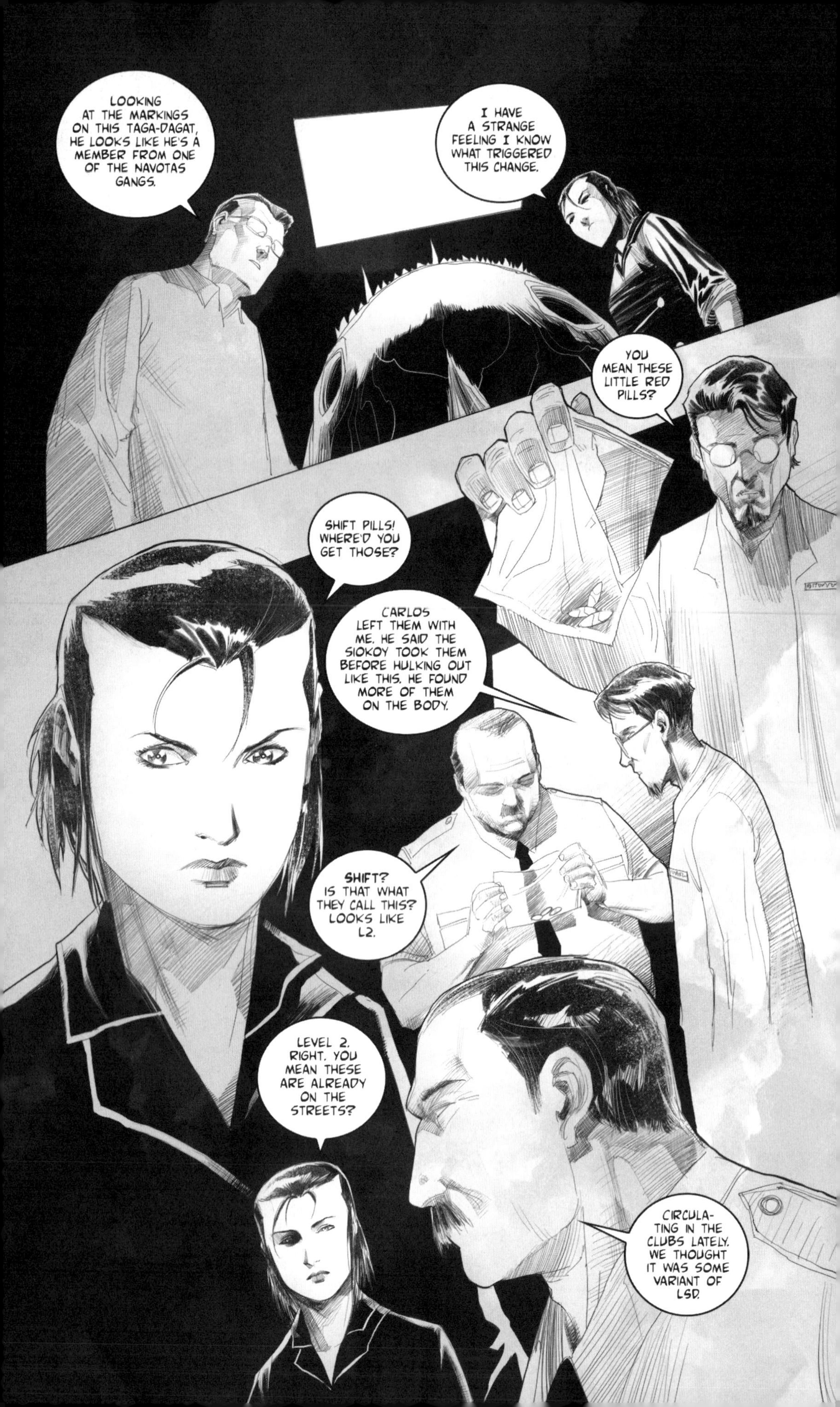
LOOKING AT THE MARKINGS ON THIS TAGA-DAGAT, HE LOOKS LIKE HE'S A MEMBER FROM ONE OF THE NAVOTAS GANGS.
I HAVE A STRANGE FEELING I KNOW WHAT TRIGGERED THIS CHANGE.
YOU MEAN THESE LITTLE RED PILLS?
SHIFT PILLS! WHERE'D YOU GET THOSE?
CARLOS LEFT THEM WITH ME. HE SAID THE SIOKOY TOOK THEM BEFORE HULKING OUT LIKE THIS. HE FOUND MORE OF THEM ON THE BODY.
SHIFT? IS THAT WHAT THEY CALL THIS? LOOKS LIKE L2.
LEVEL 2. RIGHT. YOU MEAN THESE ARE ALREADY ON THE STREETS?
CIRCULATING IN THE CLUBS LATELY. WE THOUGHT IT WAS SOME VARIANT OF LSD.

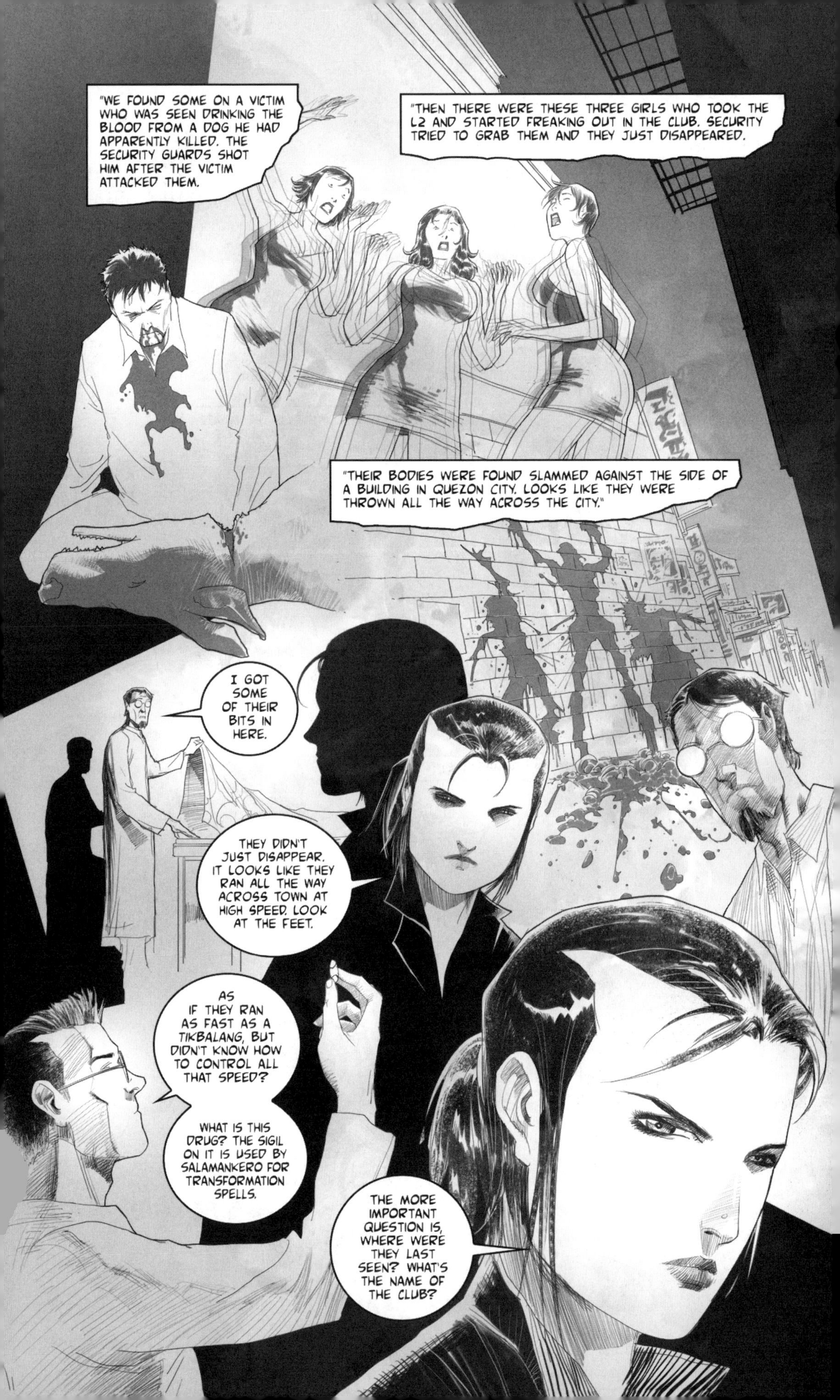
"WE FOUND SOME ON A VICTIM WHO WAS SEEN DRINKING THE BLOOD FROM A DOG HE HAD APPARENTLY KILLED. THE SECURITY GUARDS SHOT HIM AFTER THE VICTIM ATTACKED THEM.
"THEN THERE WERE THESE THREE GIRLS WHO TOOK THE L2 AND STARTED FREAKING OUT IN THE CLUB. SECURITY TRIED TO GRAB THEM AND THEY JUST DISAPPEARED.
"THEIR BODIES WERE FOUND SLAMMED AGAINST THE SIDE OF A BUILDING IN QUEZON CITY. LOOKS LIKE THEY WERE THROWN ALL THE WAY ACROSS THE CITY."
I GOT SOME OF THEIR BITS IN HERE.
THEY DIDN'T JUST DISAPPEAR. IT LOOKS LIKE THEY RAN ALL THE WAY ACROSS TOWN AT HIGH SPEED. LOOK AT THE FEET.
AS IF THEY RAN AS FAST AS A TIKBALANG, BUT DIDN'T KNOW HOW TO CONTROL ALL THAT SPEED?
WHAT IS THIS DRUG? THE SIGIL ON IT IS USED BY SALAMANKERO FOR TRANSFORMATION SPELLS.
THE MORE IMPORTANT QUESTION IS, WHERE WERE THEY LAST SEEN? WHAT'S THE NAME OF THE CLUB?

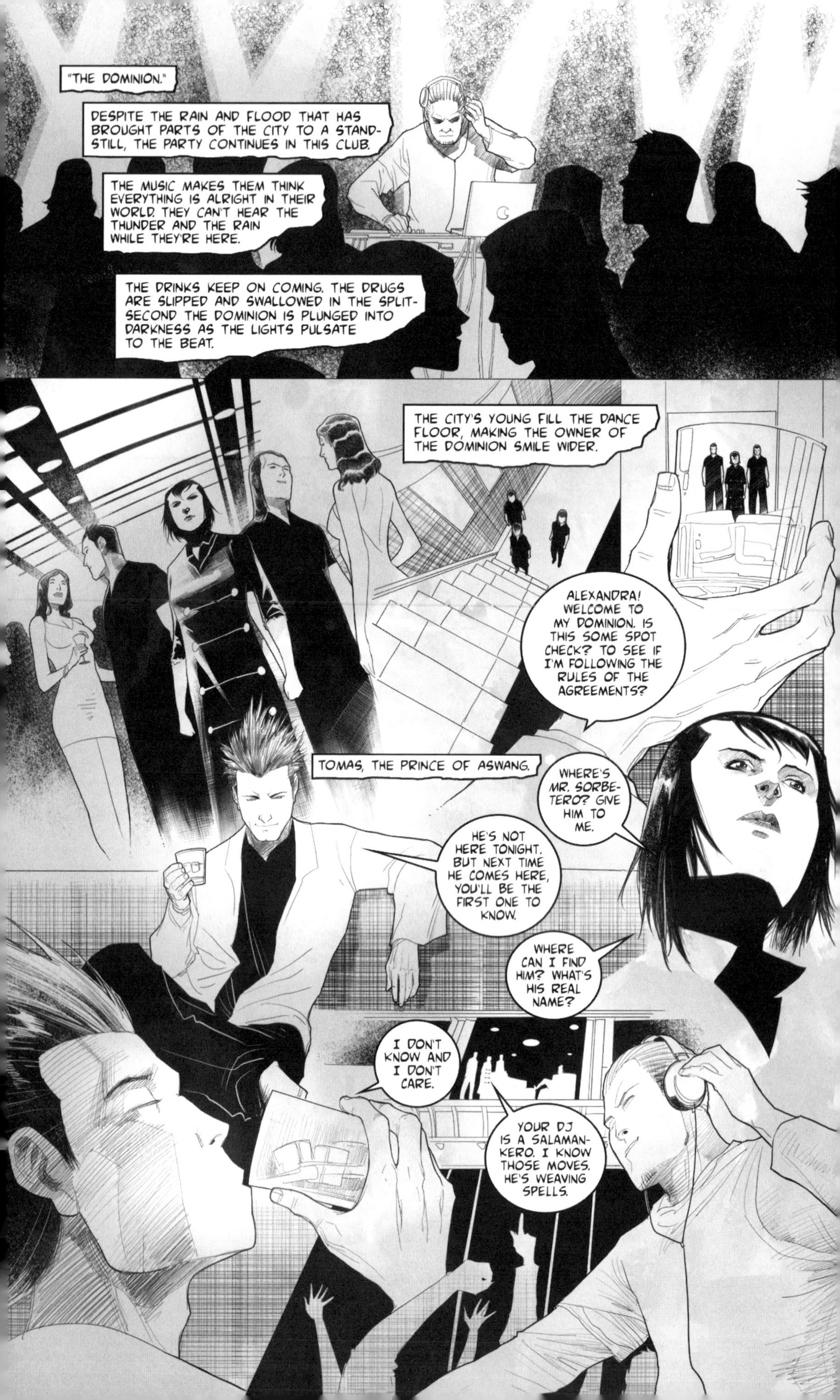

"THE DOMINION."
DESPITE THE RAIN AND FLOOD THAT HAS BROUGHT PARTS OF THE CITY TO A STAND-STILL, THE PARTY CONTINUES IN THIS CLUB.
THE MUSIC MAKES THEM THINK EVERYTHING IS ALRIGHT IN THEIR WORLD. THEY CAN'T HEAR THE THUNDER AND THE RAIN WHILE THEY'RE HERE.
THE DRINKS KEEP ON COMING. THE DRUGS ARE SLIPPED AND SWALLOWED IN THE SPLIT-SECOND THE DOMINION IS PLUNGED INTO DARKNESS AS THE LIGHTS PULSATE TO THE BEAT.
THE CITY'S YOUNG FILL THE DANCE FLOOR, MAKING THE OWNER OF THE DOMINION SMILE WIDER.
ALEXANDRA! WELCOME TO MY DOMINION. IS THIS SOME SPOT CHECK? TO SEE IF I'M FOLLOWING THE RULES OF THE AGREEMENTS?
TOMAS, THE PRINCE OF ASWANG.
WHERE'S MR. SORBETERO? GIVE HIM TO ME.
HE'S NOT HERE TONIGHT. BUT NEXT TIME HE COMES HERE, YOU'LL BE THE FIRST ONE TO KNOW.
WHERE CAN I FIND HIM? WHAT'S HIS REAL NAME?
I DON'T KNOW AND I DON'T CARE.
YOUR DJ IS A SALAMANKERO. I KNOW THOSE MOVES. HE'S WEAVING SPELLS.

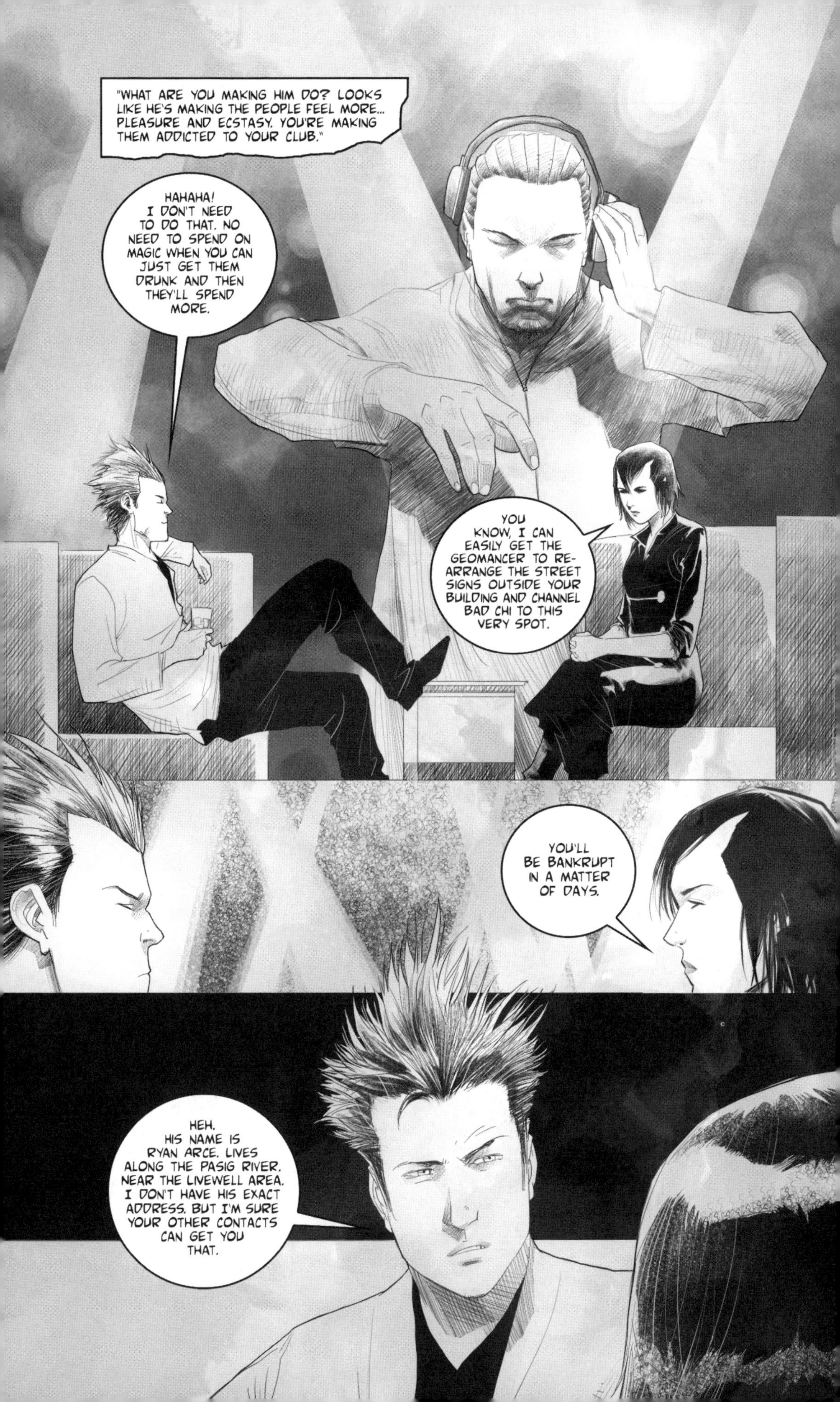
"WHAT ARE YOU MAKING HIM DO? LOOKS LIKE HE'S MAKING THE PEOPLE FEEL MORE... PLEASURE AND ECSTASY. YOU'RE MAKING THEM ADDICTED TO YOUR CLUB."
HAHAHA! I DON'T NEED TO DO THAT. NO NEED TO SPEND ON MAGIC WHEN YOU CAN JUST GET THEM DRUNK AND THEN THEY'LL SPEND MORE.
YOU KNOW, I CAN EASILY GET THE GEOMANCER TO RE-ARRANGE THE STREET SIGNS OUTSIDE YOUR BUILDING AND CHANNEL BAD CHI TO THIS VERY SPOT.
YOU'LL BE BANKRUPT IN A MATTER OF DAYS.
HEH. HIS NAME IS RYAN ARCE. LIVES ALONG THE PASIG RIVER. NEAR THE LIVEWELL AREA. I DON'T HAVE HIS EXACT ADDRESS, BUT I'M SURE YOUR OTHER CONTACTS CAN GET YOU THAT.

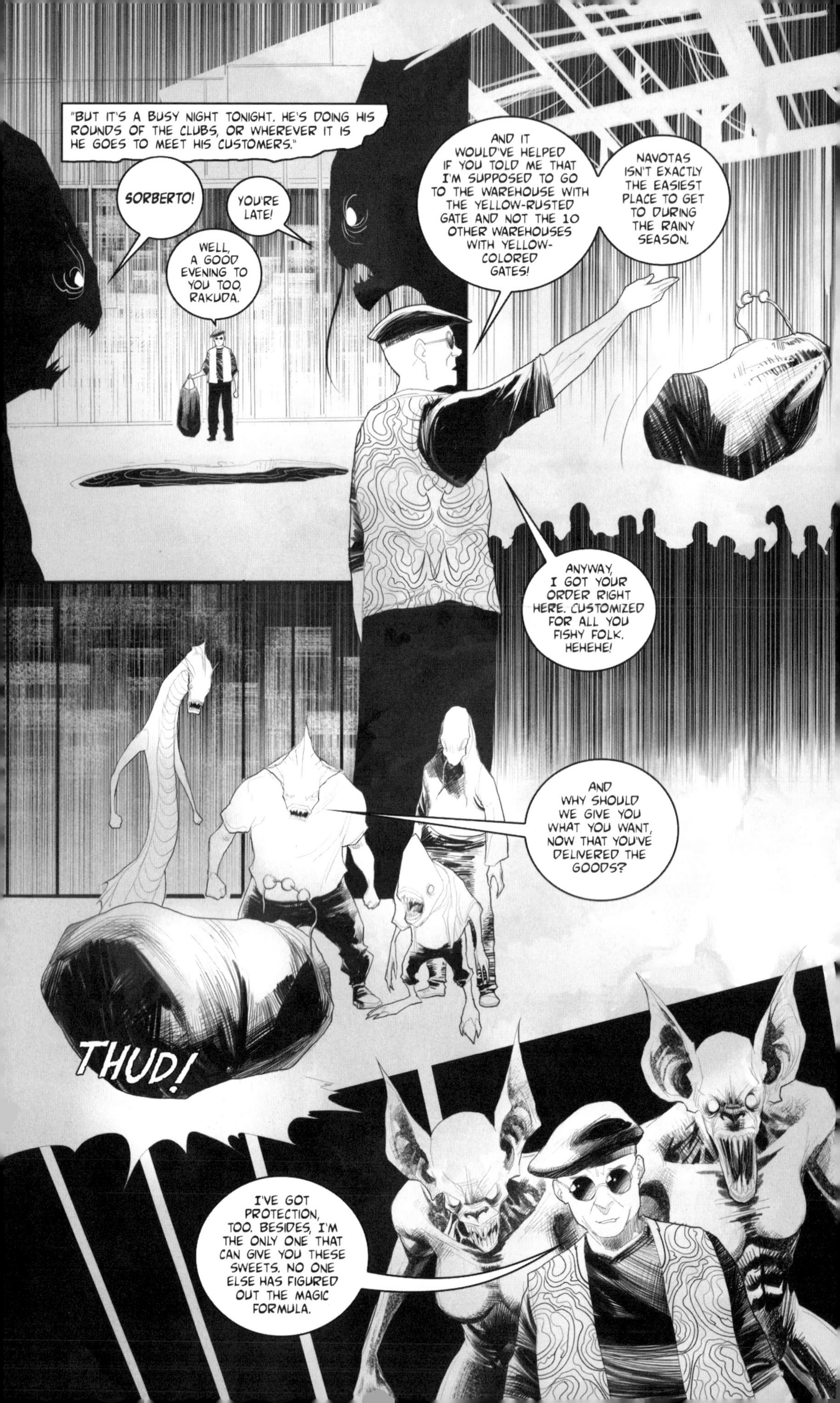
"BUT IT'S A BUSY NIGHT TONIGHT. HE'S DOING HIS ROUNDS OF THE CLUBS, OR WHEREVER IT IS HE GOES TO MEET HIS CUSTOMERS."
SORBERTO!
YOU'RE LATE!
WELL, A GOOD EVENING TO YOU TOO, RAKUDA.
AND IT WOULD'VE HELPED IF YOU TOLD ME THAT I'M SUPPOSED TO GO TO THE WAREHOUSE WITH THE YELLOW-RUSTED GATE AND NOT THE 10 OTHER WAREHOUSES WITH YELLOW-COLORED GATES!
NAVOTAS ISN'T EXACTLY THE EASIEST PLACE TO GET TO DURING THE RAINY SEASON.
ANYWAY, I GOT YOUR ORDER RIGHT HERE. CUSTOMIZED FOR ALL YOU FISHY FOLK. HEHEHE!
AND WHY SHOULD WE GIVE YOU WHAT YOU WANT, NOW THAT YOU'VE DELIVERED THE GOODS?
THUD!
I'VE GOT PROTECTION, TOO. BESIDES, I'M THE ONLY ONE THAT CAN GIVE YOU THESE SWEETS. NO ONE ELSE HAS FIGURED OUT THE MAGIC FORMULA.

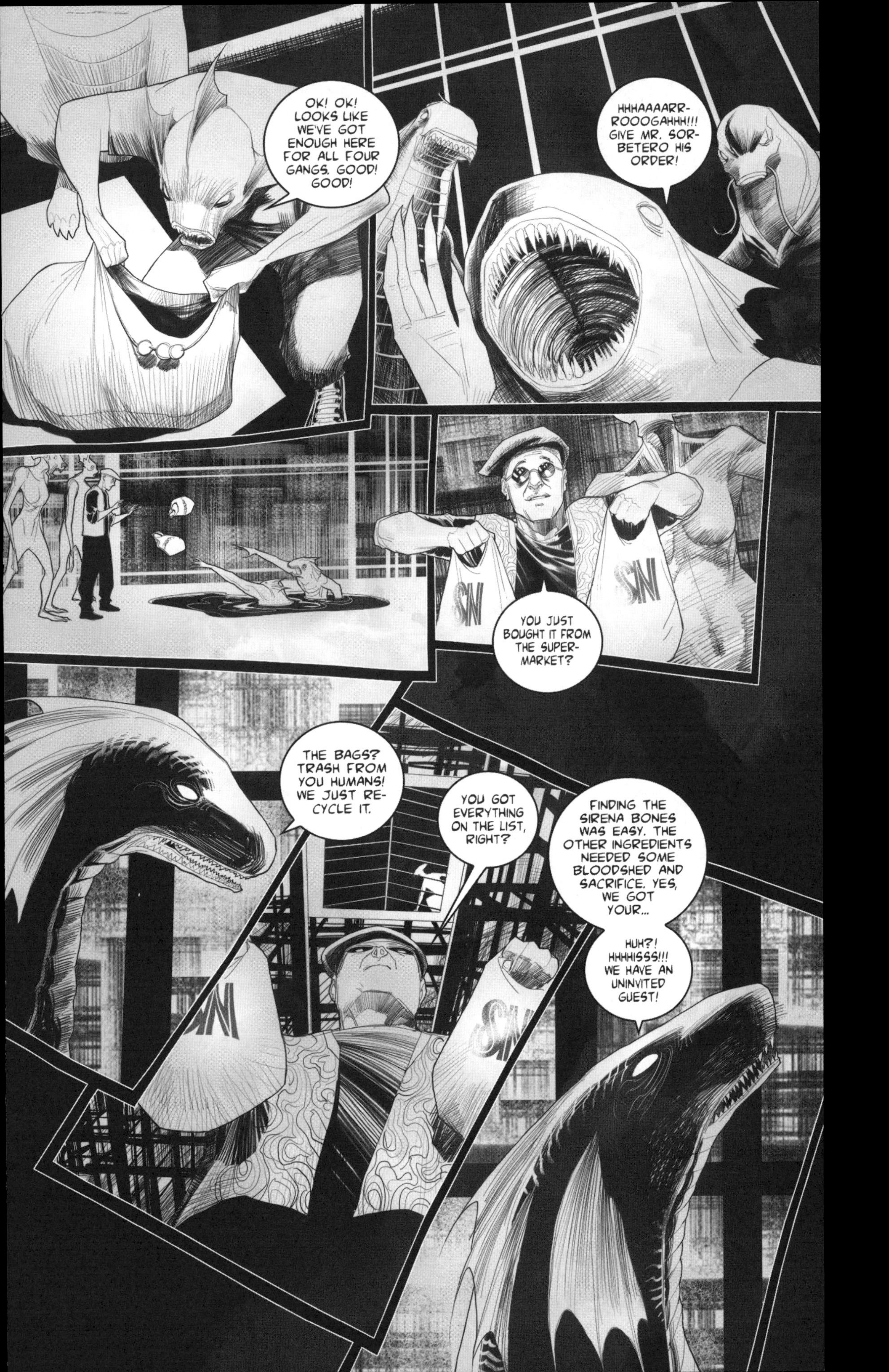
OK! OK! LOOKS LIKE WE'VE GOT ENOUGH HERE FOR ALL FOUR GANGS. GOOD! GOOD!
HHHAAAARR-ROOOGAHHH!!! GIVE MR. SOR-BETERO HIS ORDER!
YOU JUST BOUGHT IT FROM THE SUPER-MARKET?
THE BAGS? TRASH FROM YOU HUMANS! WE JUST RE-CYCLE IT.
YOU GOT EVERYTHING ON THE LIST, RIGHT?
FINDING THE SIRENA BONES WAS EASY. THE OTHER INGREDIENTS NEEDED SOME BLOODSHED AND SACRIFICE. YES, WE GOT YOUR...
HUH?! HHHHISSS!!! WE HAVE AN UNINVITED GUEST!

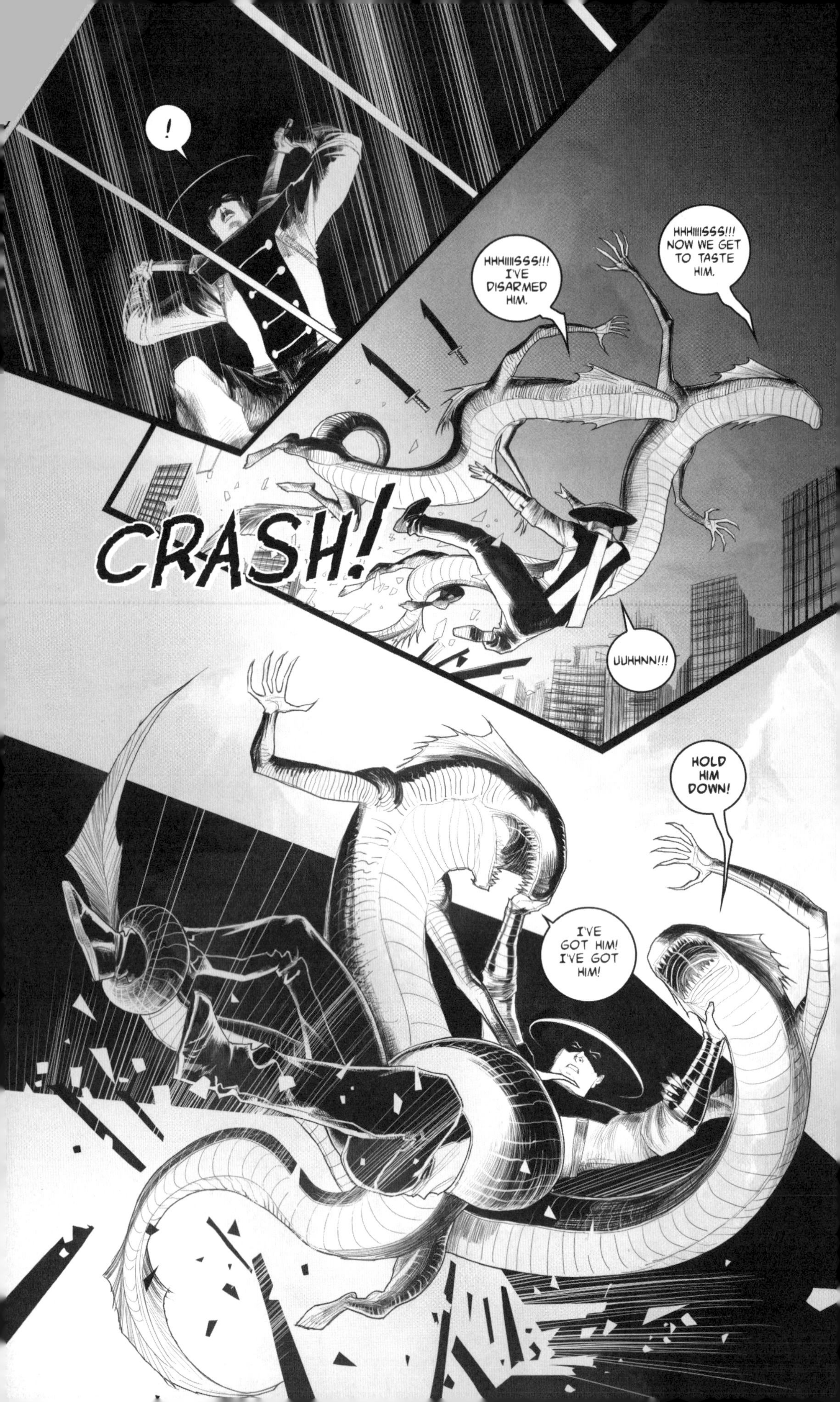
!
HHHIIIISSS!!! I'VE DISARMED HIM.
HHHIIIISSS!!! NOW WE GET TO TASTE HIM.
CRASH!
UUHHNN!!!
HOLD HIM DOWN!
I'VE GOT HIM! I'VE GOT HIM!

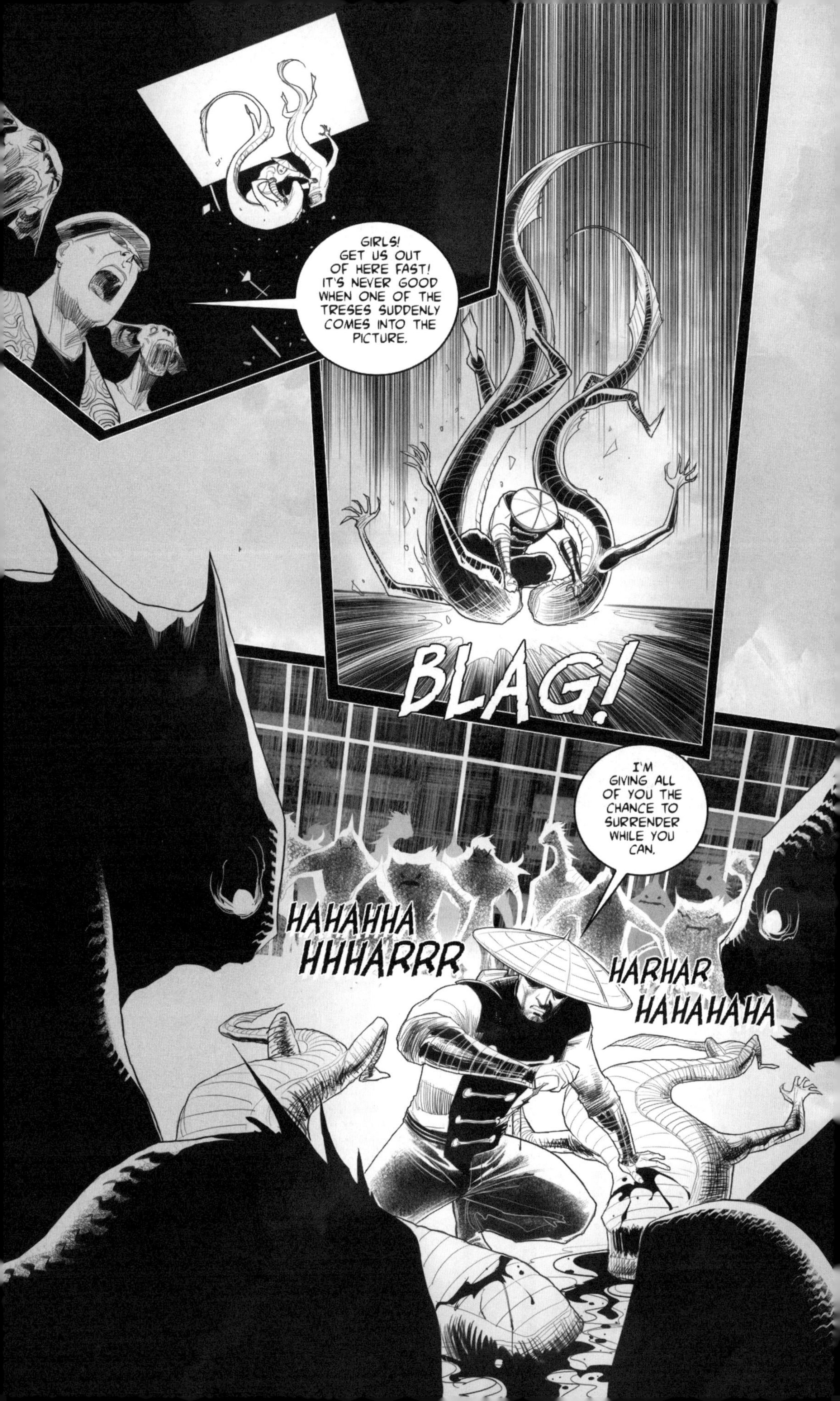
GIRLS! GET US OUT OF HERE FAST! IT'S NEVER GOOD WHEN ONE OF THE TRESES SUDDENLY COMES INTO THE PICTURE.
BLAG!
I'M GIVING ALL OF YOU THE CHANCE TO SURRENDER WHILE YOU CAN.
HAHAHHA HHHARRR
HARHAR HAHAHAHA

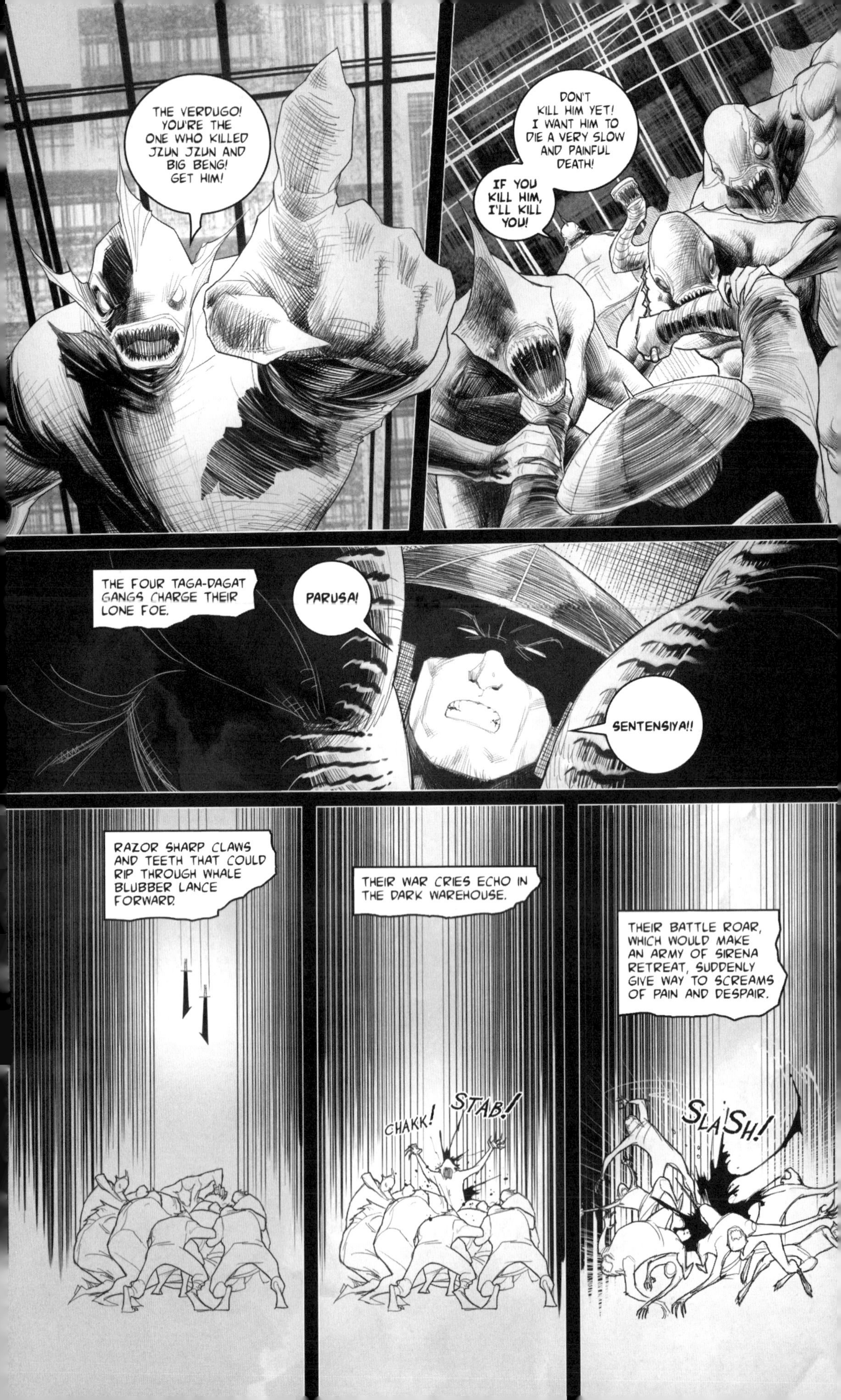
THE VERDUGO! YOU'RE THE ONE WHO KILLED JZUN JZUN AND BIG BENG! GET HIM!
DON'T KILL HIM YET! I WANT HIM TO DIE A VERY SLOW AND PAINFUL DEATH!
IF YOU KILL HIM, I'LL KILL YOU!
THE FOUR TAGA-DAGAT GANGS CHARGE THEIR LONE FOE.
PARUSA!
SENTENSIYA!!
RAZOR SHARP CLAWS AND TEETH THAT COULD RIP THROUGH WHALE BLUBBER LANCE FORWARD.
THEIR WAR CRIES ECHO IN THE DARK WAREHOUSE.
CHAKK!
STAB!
THEIR BATTLE ROAR, WHICH WOULD MAKE AN ARMY OF SIRENA RETREAT, SUDDENLY GIVE WAY TO SCREAMS OF PAIN AND DESPAIR.
SLASH!

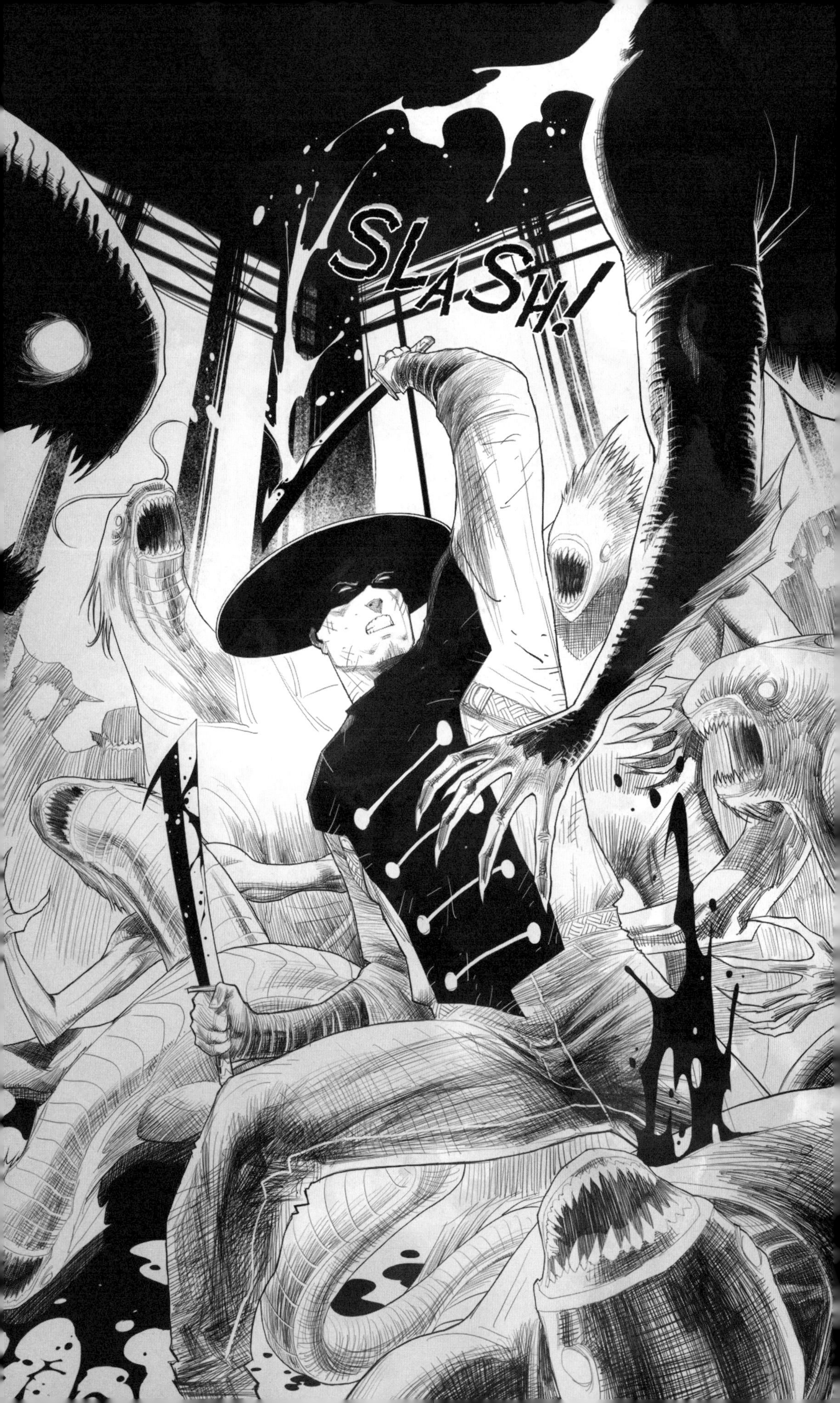
SLASH!

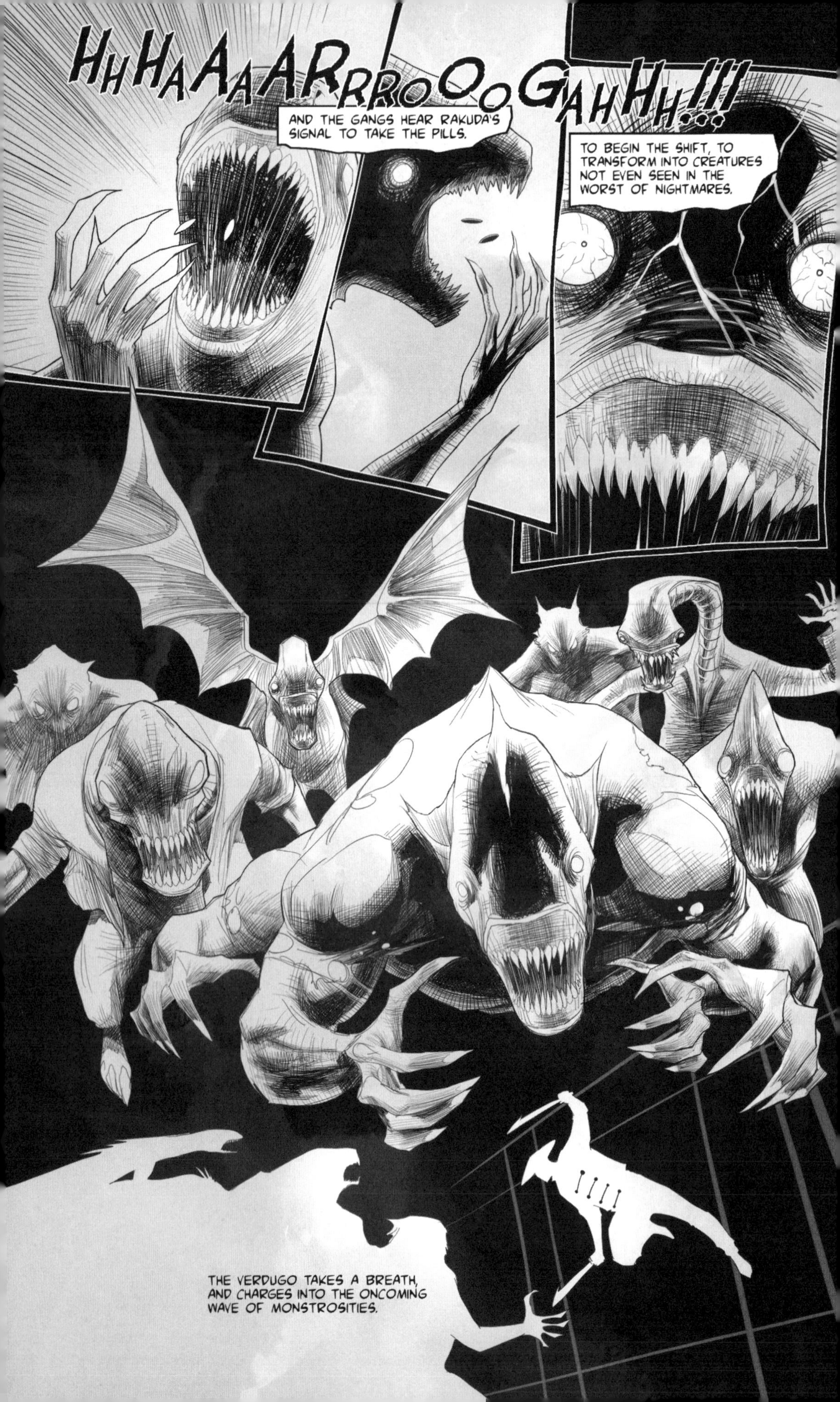
HHHAAAAARRROOOOGAHHH!!!
AND THE GANGS HEAR RAKUDA'S SIGNAL TO TAKE THE PILLS.
TO BEGIN THE SHIFT, TO TRANSFORM INTO CREATURES NOT EVEN SEEN IN THE WORST OF NIGHTMARES.
THE VERDUGO TAKES A BREATH, AND CHARGES INTO THE ONCOMING WAVE OF MONSTROSITIES.

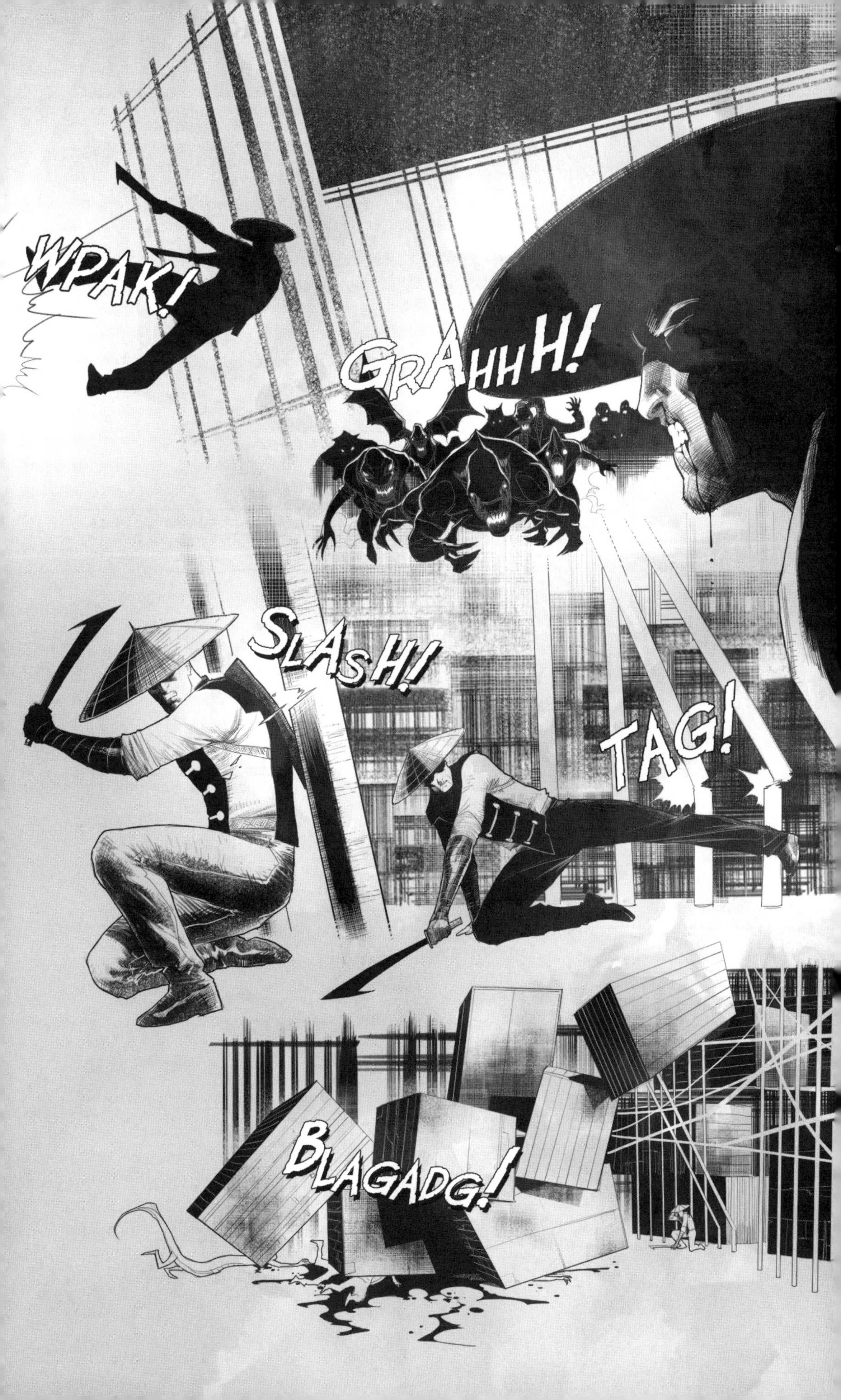

WPAK!
GRAHHH!
SLASH!
TAG!
BLAGADG!

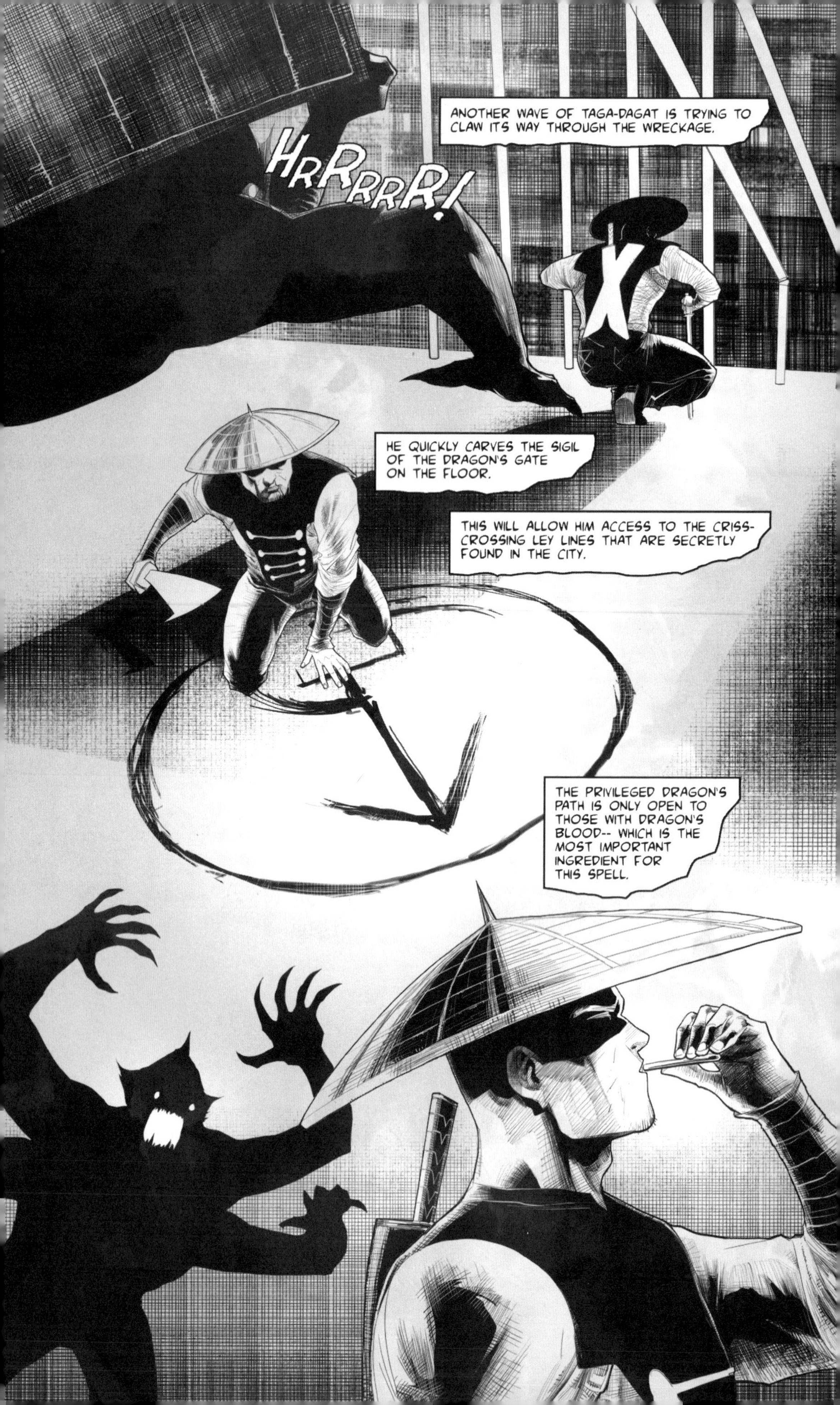
ANOTHER WAVE OF TAGA-DAGAT IS TRYING TO CLAW ITS WAY THROUGH THE WRECKAGE.
HRRRRRR!
HE QUICKLY CARVES THE SIGIL OF THE DRAGON'S GATE ON THE FLOOR.
THIS WILL ALLOW HIM ACCESS TO THE CRISS-CROSSING LEY LINES THAT ARE SECRETLY FOUND IN THE CITY.
THE PRIVILEGED DRAGON'S PATH IS ONLY OPEN TO THOSE WITH DRAGON'S BLOOD-- WHICH IS THE MOST IMPORTANT INGREDIENT FOR THIS SPELL.

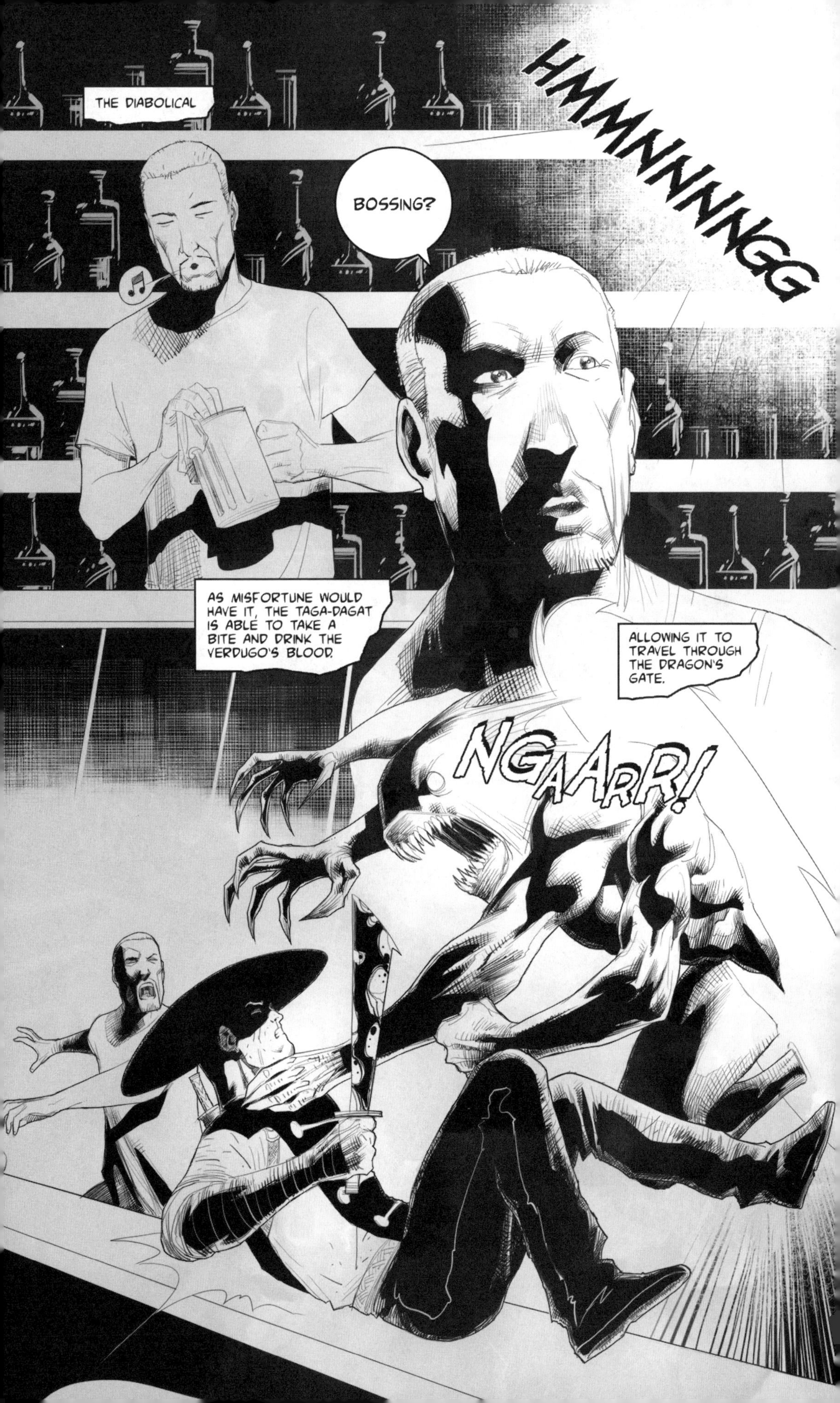
THE DIABOLICAL
HMMNNNNGG
BOSSING?
AS MISFORTUNE WOULD HAVE IT, THE TAGA-DAGAT IS ABLE TO TAKE A BITE AND DRINK THE VERDUGO'S BLOOD.
ALLOWING IT TO TRAVEL THROUGH THE DRAGON'S GATE.
NGAARR!

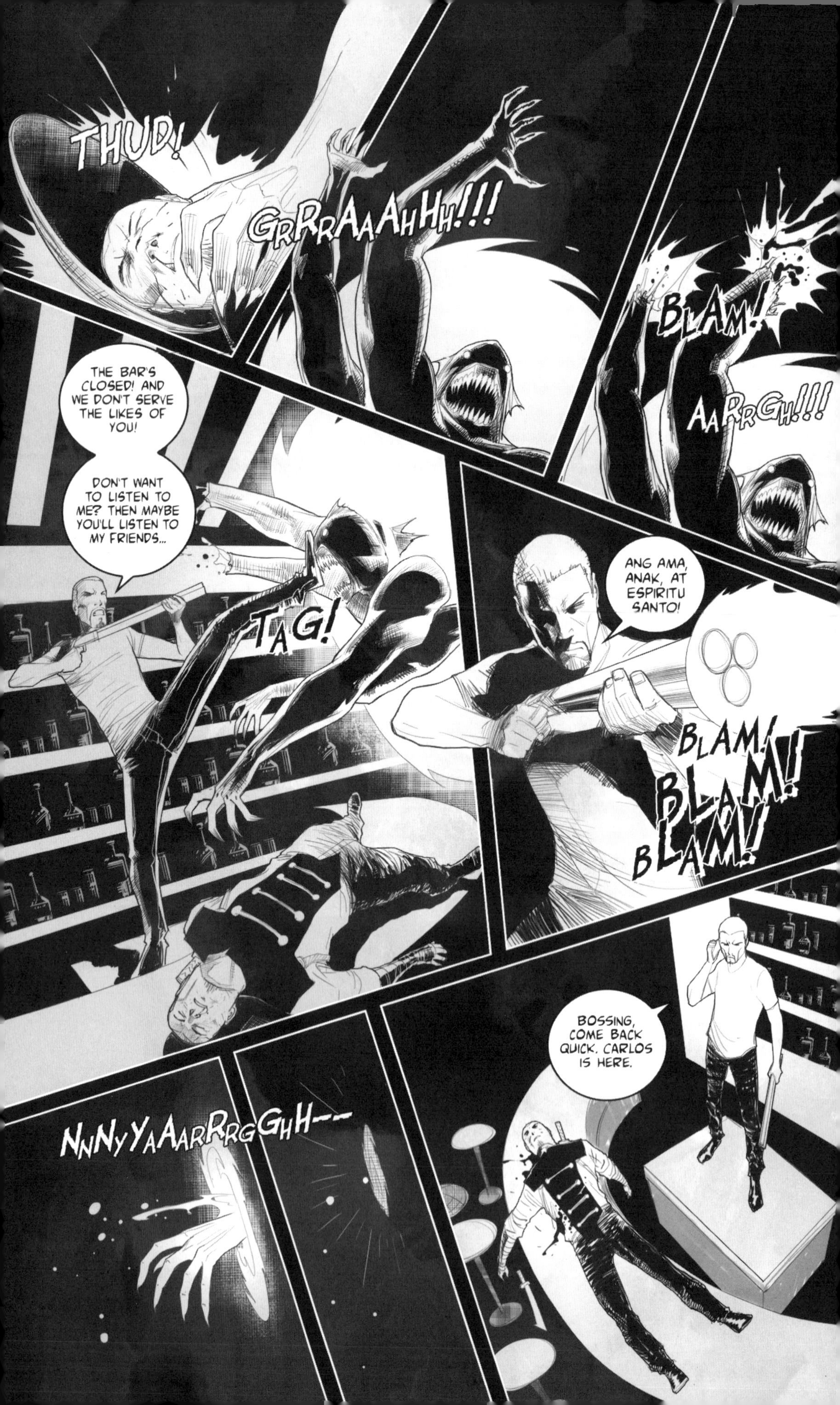
THUD!
GRRRAAAHHH!!!
BLAM!
AARRGH!!!
THE BAR'S CLOSED! AND WE DON'T SERVE THE LIKES OF YOU!
DON'T WANT TO LISTEN TO ME? THEN MAYBE YOU'LL LISTEN TO MY FRIENDS...
TAG!
ANG AMA, ANAK, AT ESPIRITU SANTO!
BLAM! BLAM! BLAM!
NNNYYAAARRRGGHH---
BOSSING, COME BACK QUICK. CARLOS IS HERE.

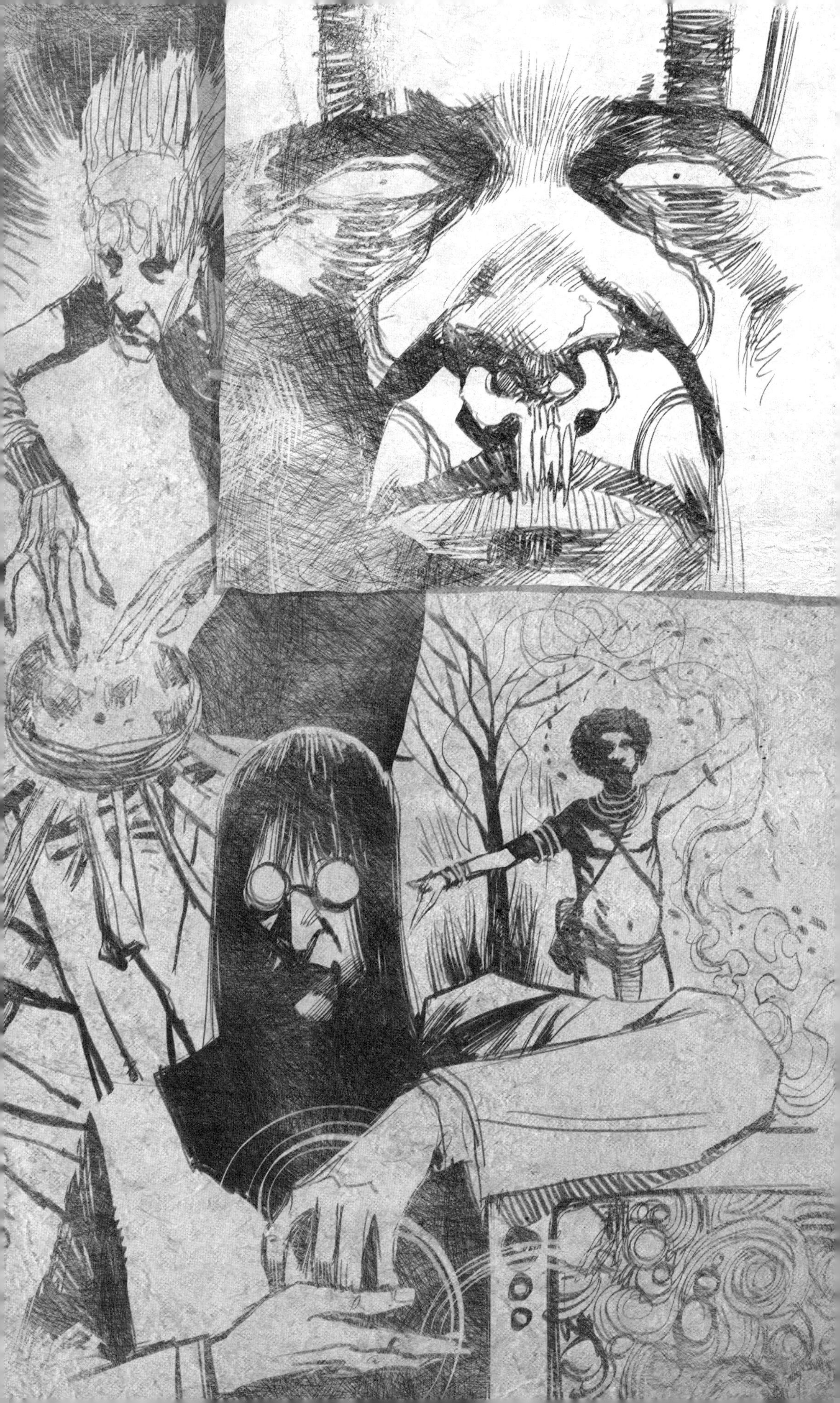

July 22

Salamangkero

Magician. Sorcerer. Wizard. Witch Doctor. The salamangkero is all of these and more.

A salamangkero may start off as an albularyo, a healer that uses the local plants and herbs to help the community. In the course of learning which plants can be used to heal, they also learn about which flora and fauna can be used to harm, maim, and even kill.

As they learn and improve their knowledge, the salamangkero learn to cast spells on a victim through food or a drink, by touching the target with concocted oils on specific body parts.

Eventually, they are able to transmit these spells over vast distances.

As technology has progressed, the salamangkero has also figured out ways to cast spells using radio waves, broadcasting them through TV sets, weaving spells using musical instruments and by spinning turntables, and of course, by tapping the right words on a mobile phone and pressing "send".

It is possible to create and cast a counter-spell, but it would, more often than not, require knowing the origins of the spell and finding out the name and location of the salamangkero.

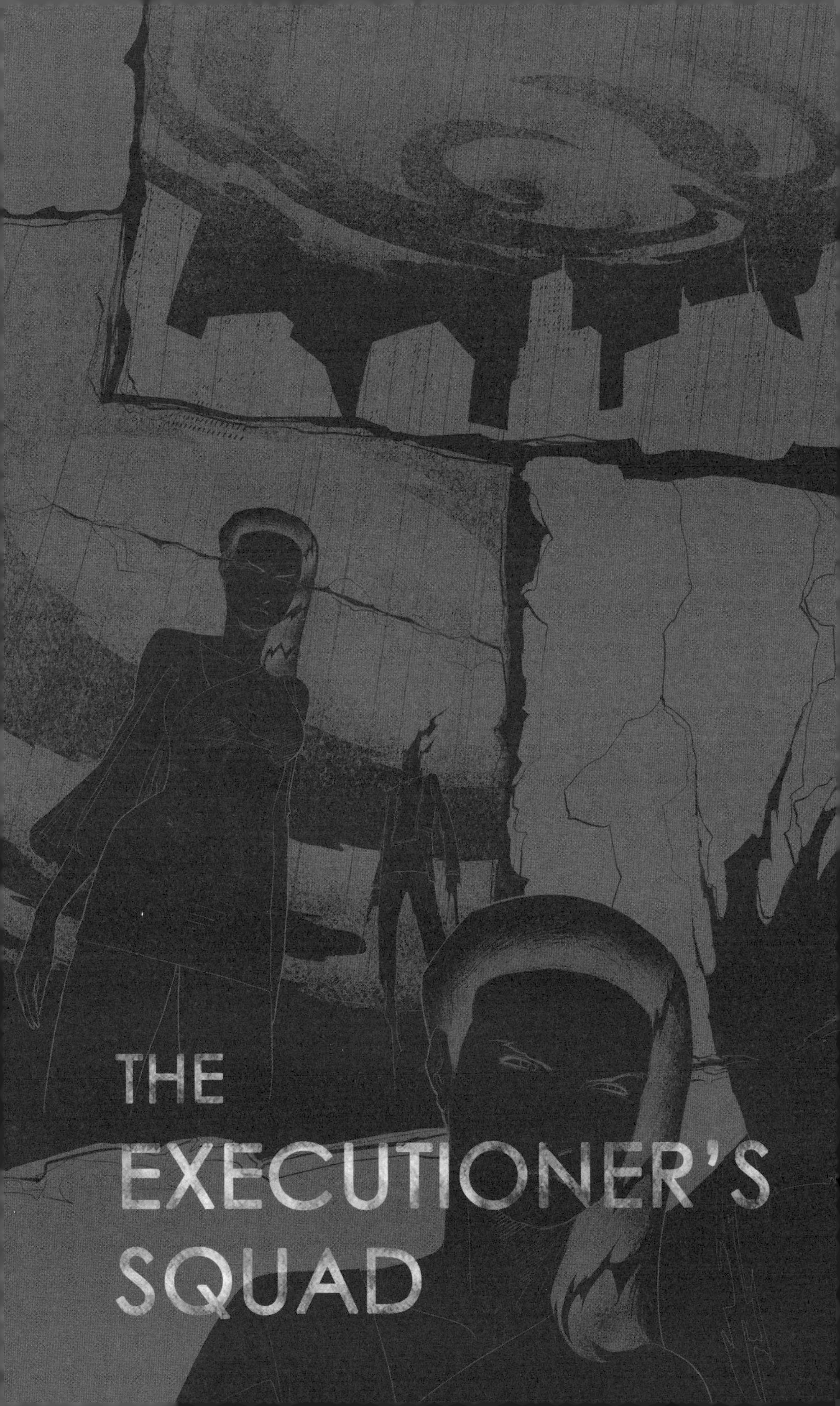
THE
EXECUTIONER'S
SQUAD

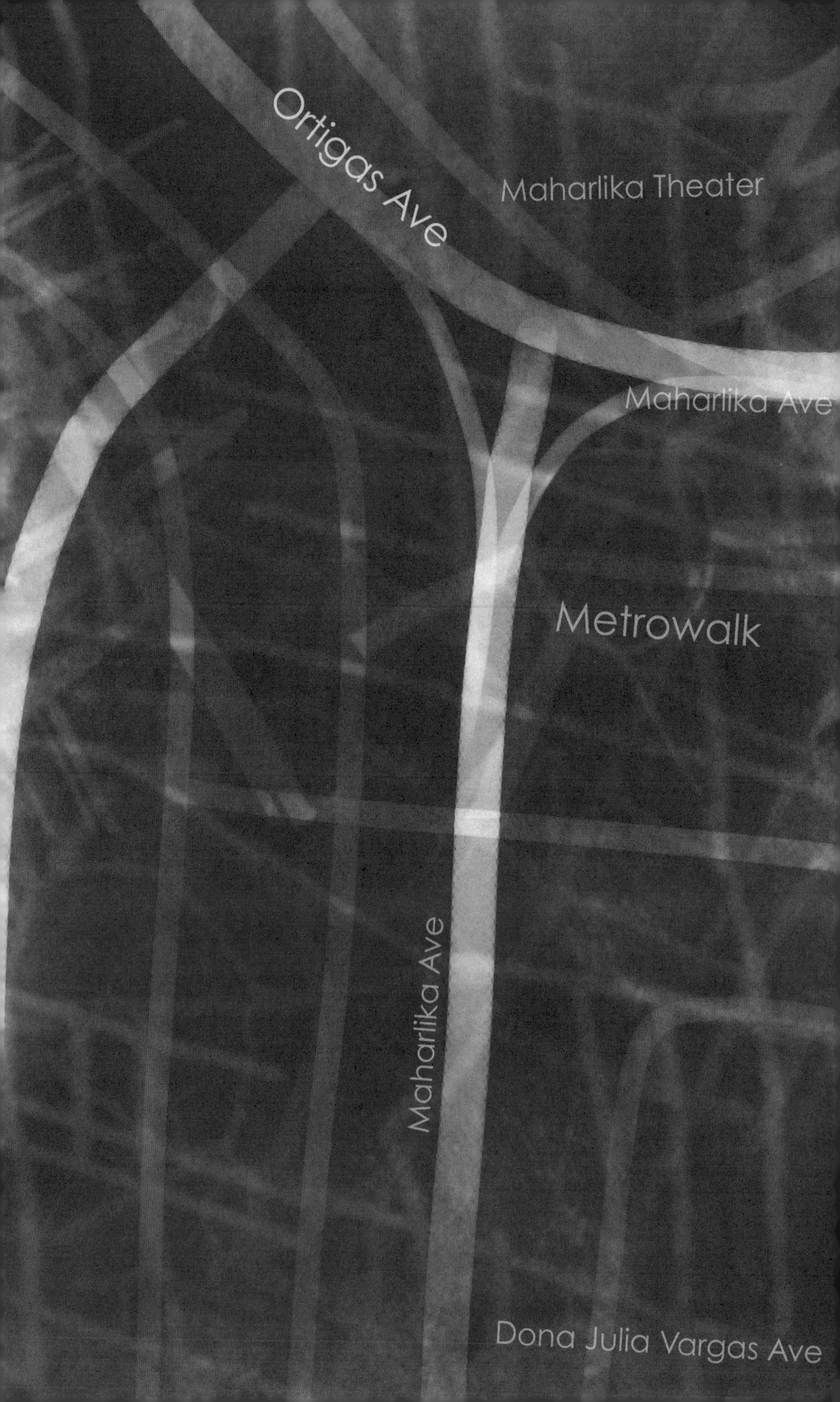
Ortigas Ave
Maharlika Theater
Maharlika Ave
Metrowalk
Maharlika Ave
Dona Julia Vargas Ave

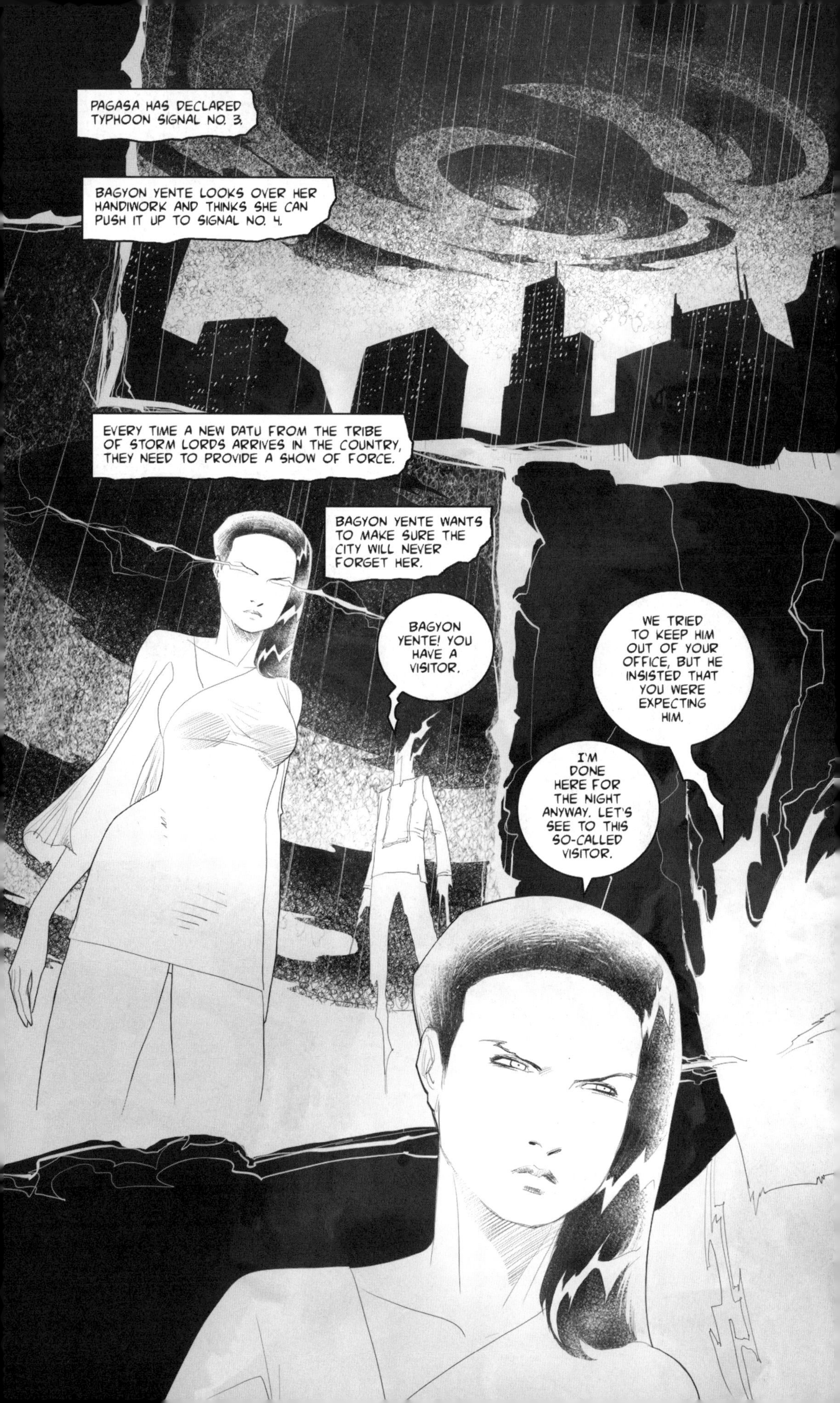
PAGASA HAS DECLARED TYPHOON SIGNAL NO. 3.
BAGYON YENTE LOOKS OVER HER HANDIWORK AND THINKS SHE CAN PUSH IT UP TO SIGNAL NO. 4.
EVERY TIME A NEW DATU FROM THE TRIBE OF STORM LORDS ARRIVES IN THE COUNTRY, THEY NEED TO PROVIDE A SHOW OF FORCE.
BAGYON YENTE WANTS TO MAKE SURE THE CITY WILL NEVER FORGET HER.
BAGYON YENTE! YOU HAVE A VISITOR.
WE TRIED TO KEEP HIM OUT OF YOUR OFFICE, BUT HE INSISTED THAT YOU WERE EXPECTING HIM.
I'M DONE HERE FOR THE NIGHT ANYWAY. LET'S SEE TO THIS SO-CALLED VISITOR.

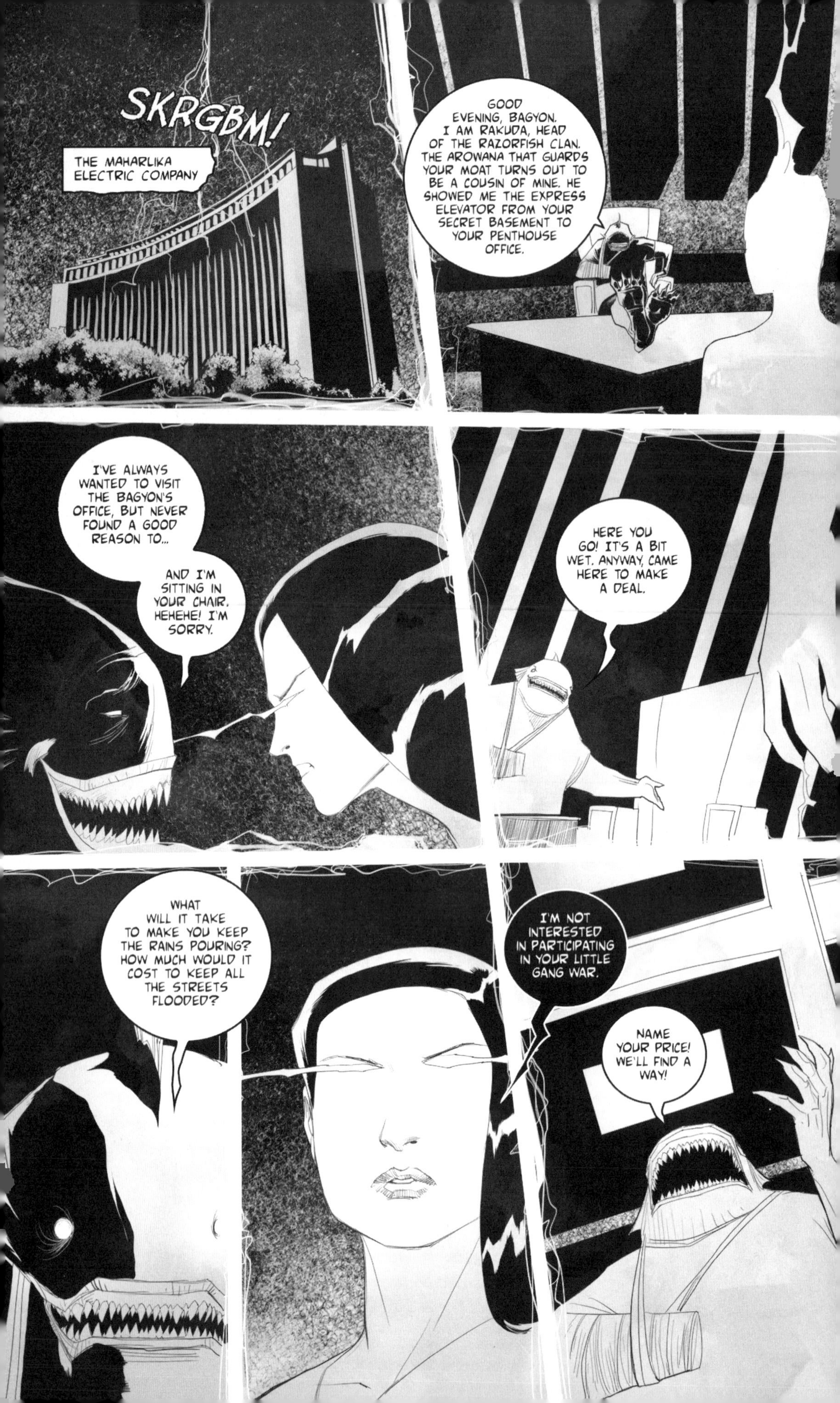
SKRGBM!
THE MAHARLIKA ELECTRIC COMPANY
GOOD EVENING, BAGYON. I AM RAKUDA, HEAD OF THE RAZORFISH CLAN. THE AROWANA THAT GUARDS YOUR MOAT TURNS OUT TO BE A COUSIN OF MINE. HE SHOWED ME THE EXPRESS ELEVATOR FROM YOUR SECRET BASEMENT TO YOUR PENTHOUSE OFFICE.
I'VE ALWAYS WANTED TO VISIT THE BAGYON'S OFFICE, BUT NEVER FOUND A GOOD REASON TO...
AND I'M SITTING IN YOUR CHAIR. HEHEHE! I'M SORRY.
HERE YOU GO! IT'S A BIT WET. ANYWAY, CAME HERE TO MAKE A DEAL.
WHAT WILL IT TAKE TO MAKE YOU KEEP THE RAINS POURING? HOW MUCH WOULD IT COST TO KEEP ALL THE STREETS FLOODED?
I'M NOT INTERESTED IN PARTICIPATING IN YOUR LITTLE GANG WAR.
NAME YOUR PRICE! WE'LL FIND A WAY!

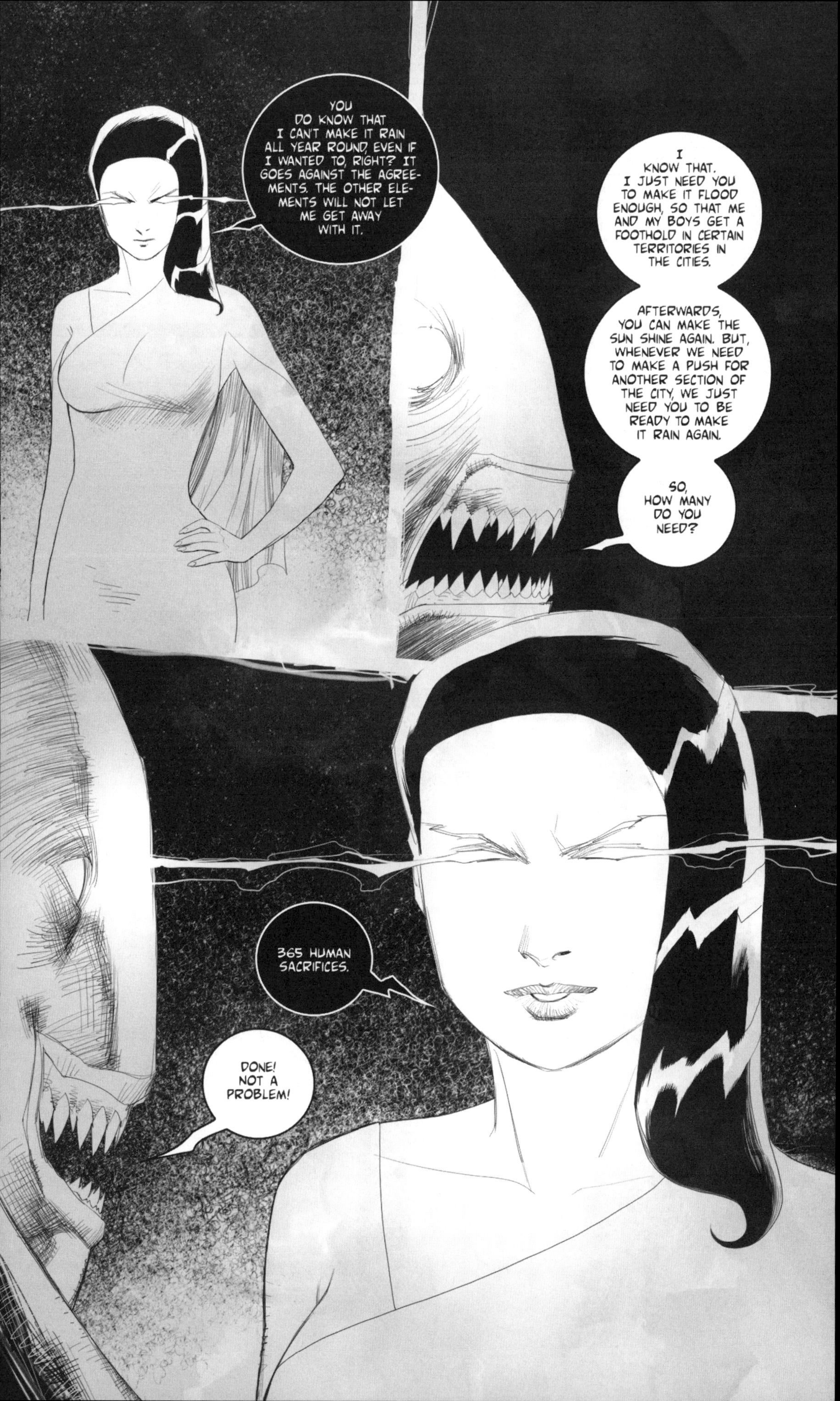
YOU DO KNOW THAT I CAN'T MAKE IT RAIN ALL YEAR ROUND, EVEN IF I WANTED TO, RIGHT? IT GOES AGAINST THE AGREE-MENTS. THE OTHER ELE-MENTS WILL NOT LET ME GET AWAY WITH IT.
I KNOW THAT. I JUST NEED YOU TO MAKE IT FLOOD ENOUGH, SO THAT ME AND MY BOYS GET A FOOTHOLD IN CERTAIN TERRITORIES IN THE CITIES.
AFTERWARDS, YOU CAN MAKE THE SUN SHINE AGAIN. BUT, WHENEVER WE NEED TO MAKE A PUSH FOR ANOTHER SECTION OF THE CITY, WE JUST NEED YOU TO BE READY TO MAKE IT RAIN AGAIN.
SO, HOW MANY DO YOU NEED?
365 HUMAN SACRIFICES.
DONE! NOT A PROBLEM!

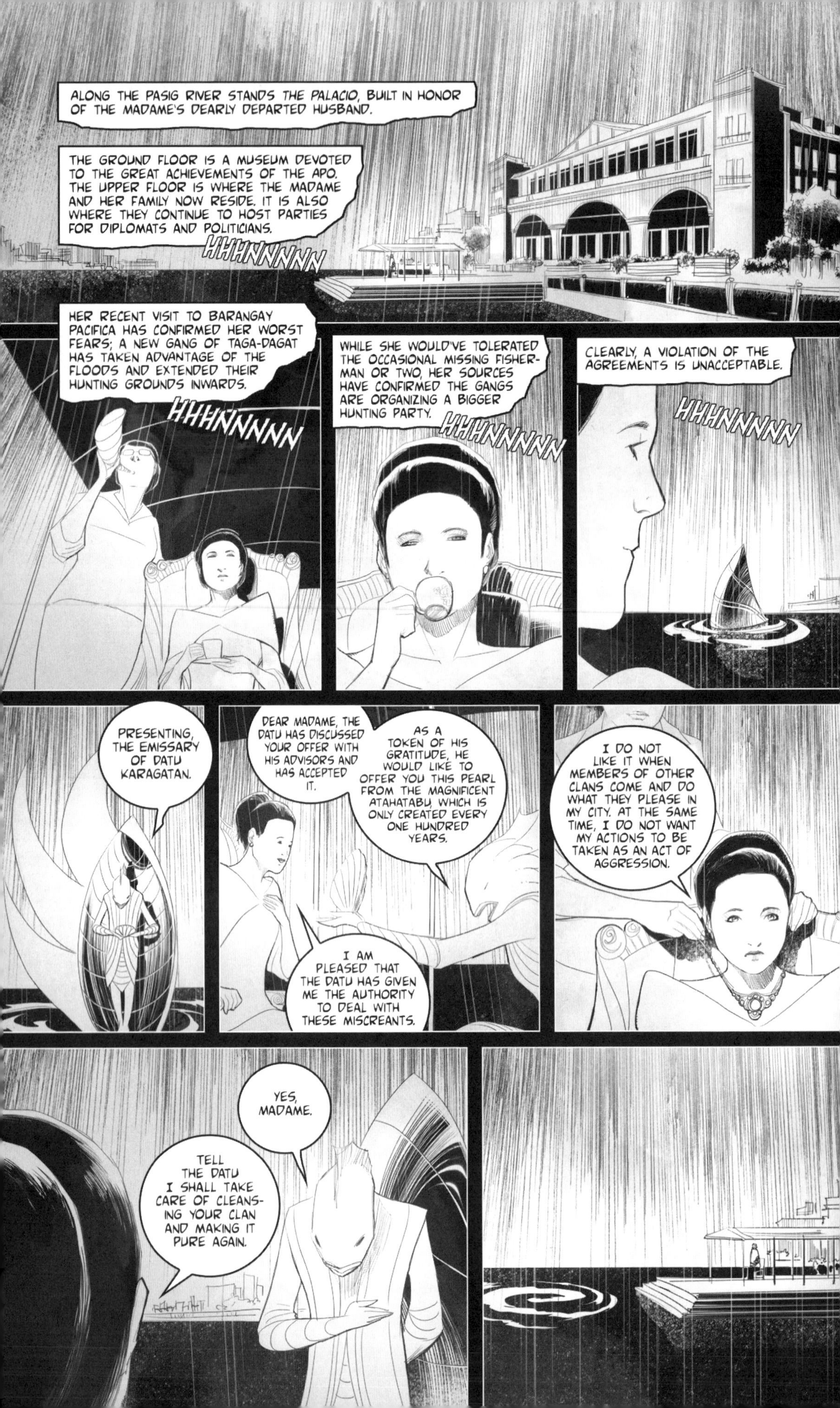
ALONG THE PASIG RIVER STANDS THE PALACIO, BUILT IN HONOR OF THE MADAME'S DEARLY DEPARTED HUSBAND.
THE GROUND FLOOR IS A MUSEUM DEVOTED TO THE GREAT ACHIEVEMENTS OF THE APO. THE UPPER FLOOR IS WHERE THE MADAME AND HER FAMILY NOW RESIDE. IT IS ALSO WHERE THEY CONTINUE TO HOST PARTIES FOR DIPLOMATS AND POLITICIANS.
HHHNNNNN
HER RECENT VISIT TO BARANGAY PACIFICA HAS CONFIRMED HER WORST FEARS; A NEW GANG OF TAGA-DAGAT HAS TAKEN ADVANTAGE OF THE FLOODS AND EXTENDED THEIR HUNTING GROUNDS INWARDS.
HHHNNNNN
WHILE SHE WOULD'VE TOLERATED THE OCCASIONAL MISSING FISHERMAN OR TWO, HER SOURCES HAVE CONFIRMED THE GANGS ARE ORGANIZING A BIGGER HUNTING PARTY.
HHHNNNNN
CLEARLY, A VIOLATION OF THE AGREEMENTS IS UNACCEPTABLE.
HHHNNNNN
PRESENTING, THE EMISSARY OF DATU KARAGATAN.
DEAR MADAME, THE DATU HAS DISCUSSED YOUR OFFER WITH HIS ADVISORS AND HAS ACCEPTED IT.
AS A TOKEN OF HIS GRATITUDE, HE WOULD LIKE TO OFFER YOU THIS PEARL FROM THE MAGNIFICENT ATAHATABU, WHICH IS ONLY CREATED EVERY ONE HUNDRED YEARS.
I AM PLEASED THAT THE DATU HAS GIVEN ME THE AUTHORITY TO DEAL WITH THESE MISCREANTS.
I DO NOT LIKE IT WHEN MEMBERS OF OTHER CLANS COME AND DO WHAT THEY PLEASE IN MY CITY. AT THE SAME TIME, I DO NOT WANT MY ACTIONS TO BE TAKEN AS AN ACT OF AGGRESSION.
TELL THE DATU I SHALL TAKE CARE OF CLEANSING YOUR CLAN AND MAKING IT PURE AGAIN.
YES, MADAME.

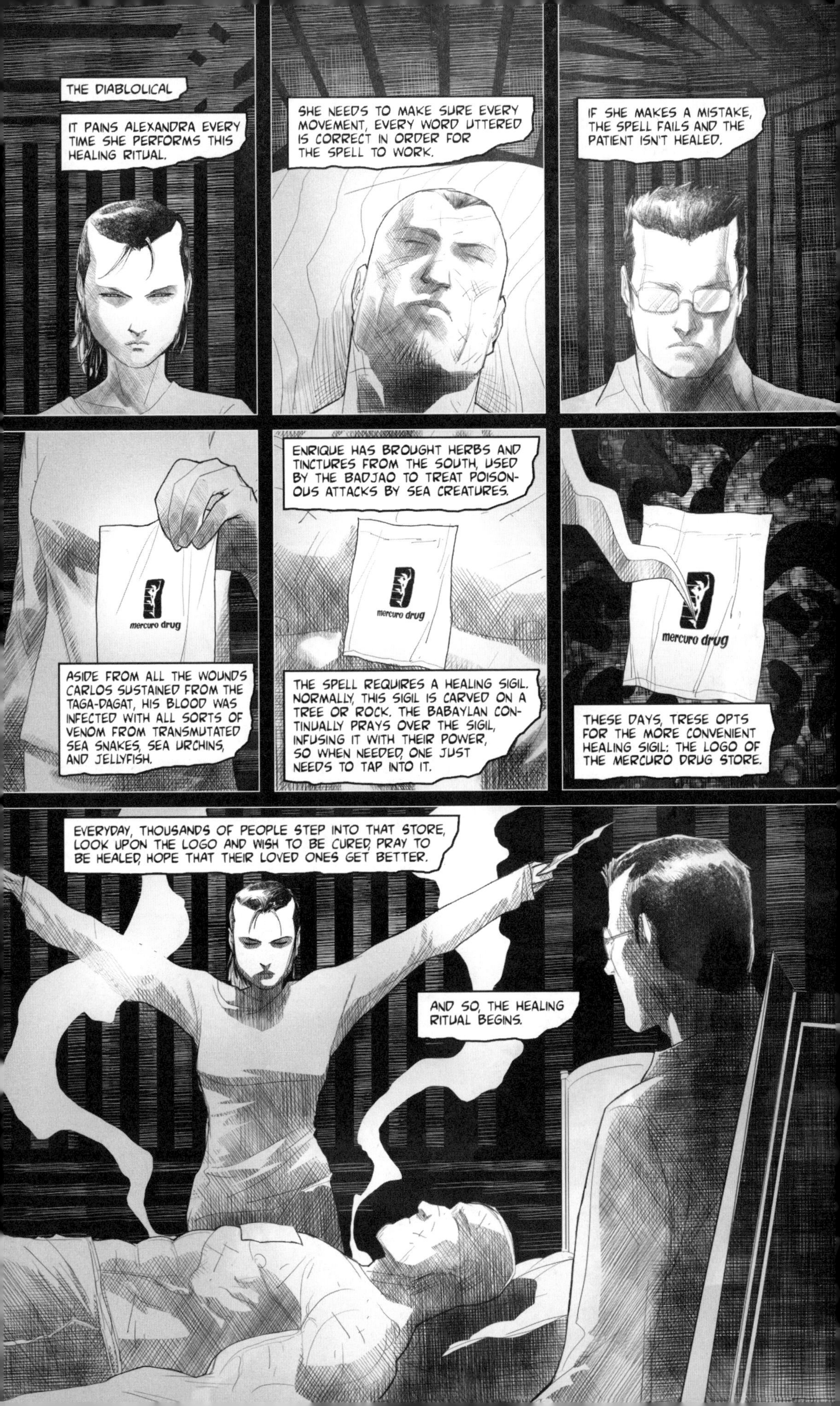
THE DIABLOLICAL
IT PAINS ALEXANDRA EVERY TIME SHE PERFORMS THIS HEALING RITUAL.
SHE NEEDS TO MAKE SURE EVERY MOVEMENT, EVERY WORD UTTERED IS CORRECT IN ORDER FOR THE SPELL TO WORK.
IF SHE MAKES A MISTAKE, THE SPELL FAILS AND THE PATIENT ISN'T HEALED.
mercuro drug
ASIDE FROM ALL THE WOUNDS CARLOS SUSTAINED FROM THE TAGA-DAGAT, HIS BLOOD WAS INFECTED WITH ALL SORTS OF VENOM FROM TRANSMUTATED SEA SNAKES, SEA URCHINS, AND JELLYFISH.
ENRIQUE HAS BROUGHT HERBS AND TINCTURES FROM THE SOUTH, USED BY THE BADJAO TO TREAT POISONOUS ATTACKS BY SEA CREATURES.
mercuro drug
THE SPELL REQUIRES A HEALING SIGIL. NORMALLY, THIS SIGIL IS CARVED ON A TREE OR ROCK. THE BABAYLAN CONTINUALLY PRAYS OVER THE SIGIL, INFUSING IT WITH THEIR POWER, SO WHEN NEEDED, ONE JUST NEEDS TO TAP INTO IT.
mercuro drug
THESE DAYS, TRESE OPTS FOR THE MORE CONVENIENT HEALING SIGIL: THE LOGO OF THE MERCURO DRUG STORE.
EVERYDAY, THOUSANDS OF PEOPLE STEP INTO THAT STORE, LOOK UPON THE LOGO AND WISH TO BE CURED, PRAY TO BE HEALED, HOPE THAT THEIR LOVED ONES GET BETTER.
AND SO, THE HEALING RITUAL BEGINS.

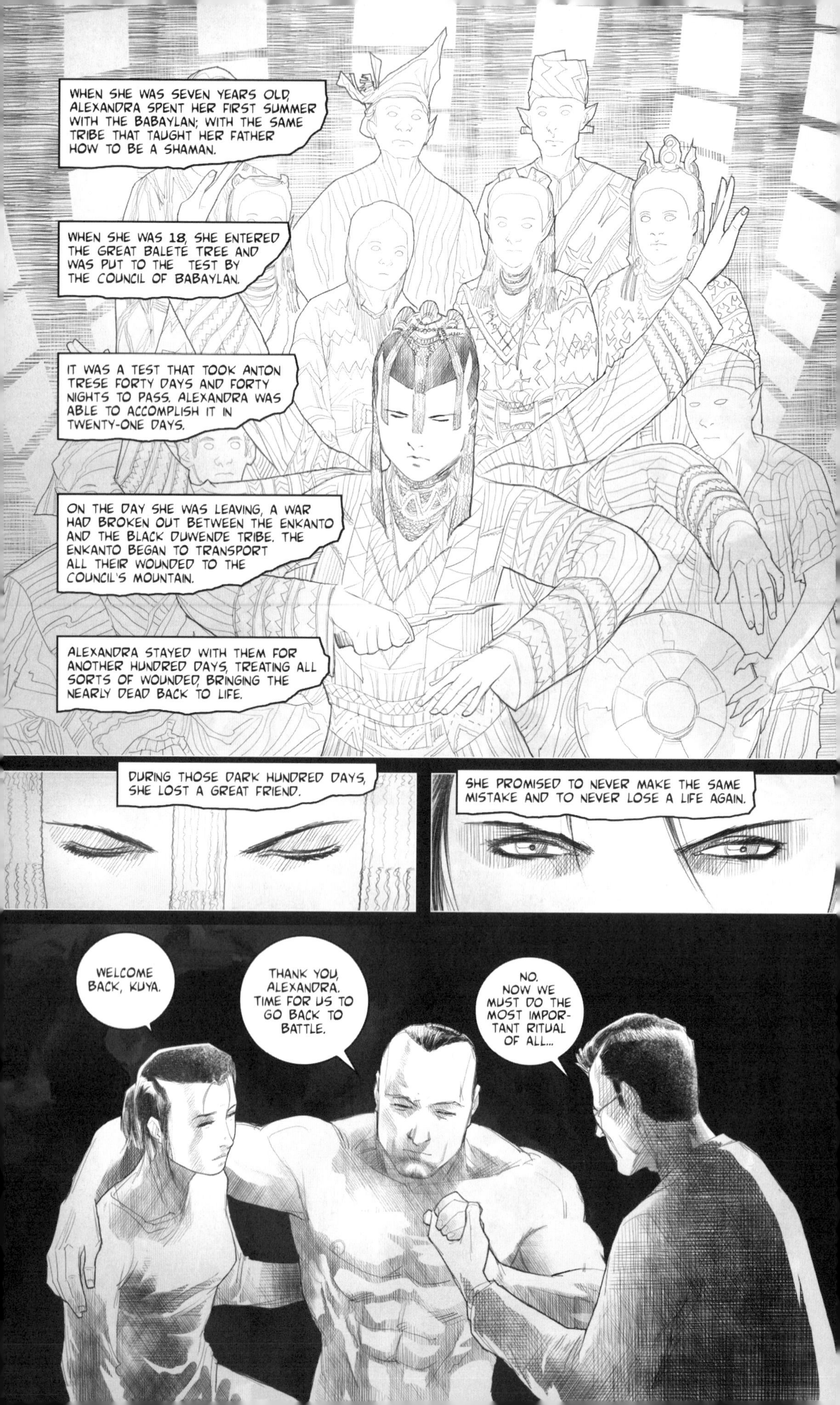
WHEN SHE WAS SEVEN YEARS OLD, ALEXANDRA SPENT HER FIRST SUMMER WITH THE BABAYLAN; WITH THE SAME TRIBE THAT TAUGHT HER FATHER HOW TO BE A SHAMAN.
WHEN SHE WAS 18, SHE ENTERED THE GREAT BALETE TREE AND WAS PUT TO THE TEST BY THE COUNCIL OF BABAYLAN.
IT WAS A TEST THAT TOOK ANTON TRESE FORTY DAYS AND FORTY NIGHTS TO PASS. ALEXANDRA WAS ABLE TO ACCOMPLISH IT IN TWENTY-ONE DAYS.
ON THE DAY SHE WAS LEAVING, A WAR HAD BROKEN OUT BETWEEN THE ENKANTO AND THE BLACK DUWENDE TRIBE. THE ENKANTO BEGAN TO TRANSPORT ALL THEIR WOUNDED TO THE COUNCIL'S MOUNTAIN.
ALEXANDRA STAYED WITH THEM FOR ANOTHER HUNDRED DAYS, TREATING ALL SORTS OF WOUNDED, BRINGING THE NEARLY DEAD BACK TO LIFE.
DURING THOSE DARK HUNDRED DAYS, SHE LOST A GREAT FRIEND.
SHE PROMISED TO NEVER MAKE THE SAME MISTAKE AND TO NEVER LOSE A LIFE AGAIN.
WELCOME BACK, KUYA.
THANK YOU, ALEXANDRA. TIME FOR US TO GO BACK TO BATTLE.
NO. NOW WE MUST DO THE MOST IMPORTANT RITUAL OF ALL...

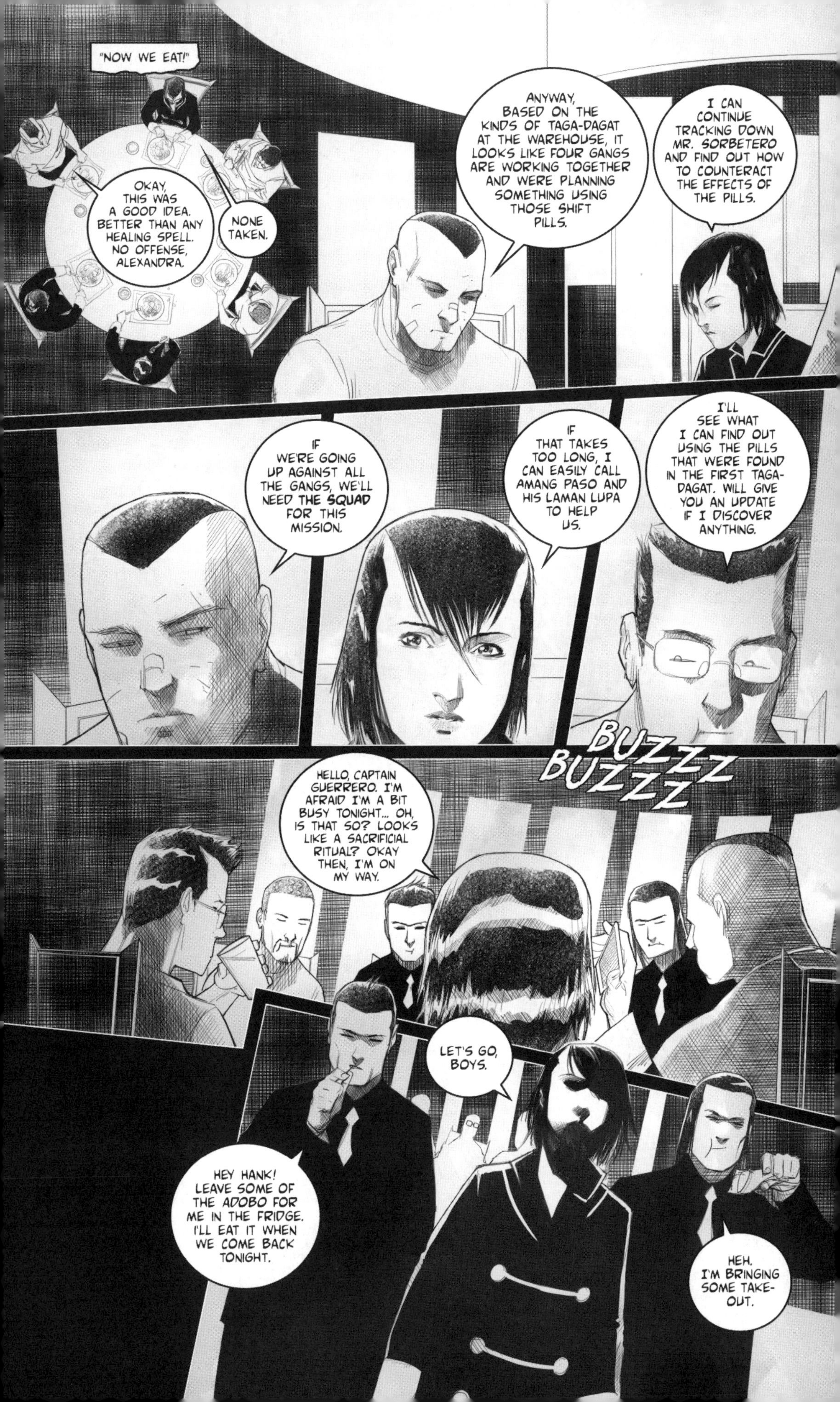

"NOW WE EAT!"
OKAY, THIS WAS A GOOD IDEA. BETTER THAN ANY HEALING SPELL. NO OFFENSE, ALEXANDRA.
NONE TAKEN.
ANYWAY, BASED ON THE KINDS OF TAGA-DAGAT AT THE WAREHOUSE, IT LOOKS LIKE FOUR GANGS ARE WORKING TOGETHER AND WERE PLANNING SOMETHING USING THOSE SHIFT PILLS.
I CAN CONTINUE TRACKING DOWN MR. SORBETERO AND FIND OUT HOW TO COUNTERACT THE EFFECTS OF THE PILLS.
IF WE'RE GOING UP AGAINST ALL THE GANGS, WE'LL NEED THE SQUAD FOR THIS MISSION.
IF THAT TAKES TOO LONG, I CAN EASILY CALL AMANG PASO AND HIS LAMAN LUPA TO HELP US.
I'LL SEE WHAT I CAN FIND OUT USING THE PILLS THAT WERE FOUND IN THE FIRST TAGA-DAGAT. WILL GIVE YOU AN UPDATE IF I DISCOVER ANYTHING.
BUZZZ BUZZZZ
HELLO, CAPTAIN GUERRERO. I'M AFRAID I'M A BIT BUSY TONIGHT... OH, IS THAT SO? LOOKS LIKE A SACRIFICIAL RITUAL? OKAY THEN, I'M ON MY WAY.
LET'S GO, BOYS.
HEY HANK! LEAVE SOME OF THE ADOBO FOR ME IN THE FRIDGE. I'LL EAT IT WHEN WE COME BACK TONIGHT.
HEH. I'M BRINGING SOME TAKE-OUT.

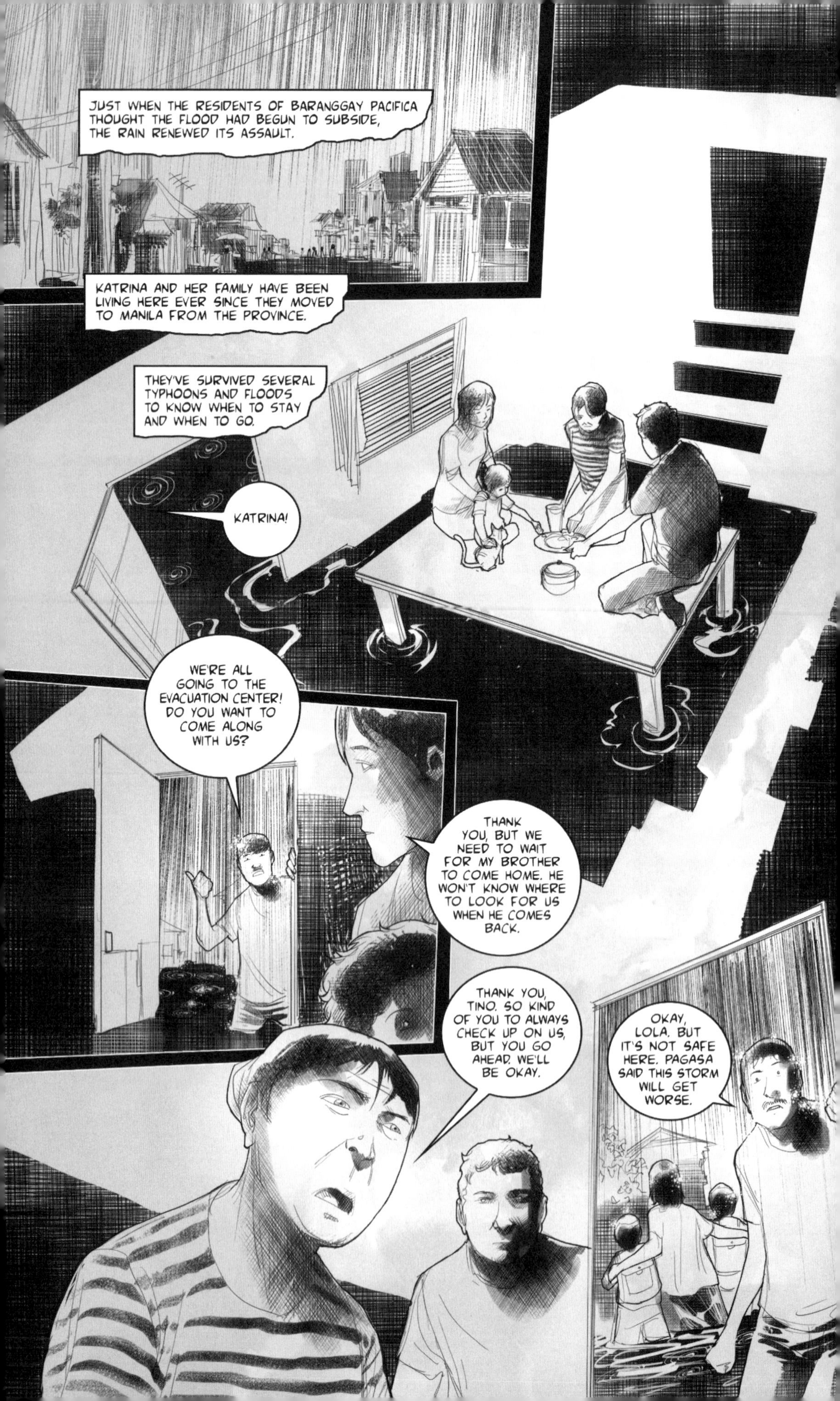
JUST WHEN THE RESIDENTS OF BARANGGAY PACIFICA THOUGHT THE FLOOD HAD BEGUN TO SUBSIDE, THE RAIN RENEWED ITS ASSAULT.
KATRINA AND HER FAMILY HAVE BEEN LIVING HERE EVER SINCE THEY MOVED TO MANILA FROM THE PROVINCE.
THEY'VE SURVIVED SEVERAL TYPHOONS AND FLOODS TO KNOW WHEN TO STAY AND WHEN TO GO.
KATRINA!
WE'RE ALL GOING TO THE EVACUATION CENTER! DO YOU WANT TO COME ALONG WITH US?
THANK YOU, BUT WE NEED TO WAIT FOR MY BROTHER TO COME HOME. HE WON'T KNOW WHERE TO LOOK FOR US WHEN HE COMES BACK.
THANK YOU, TINO. SO KIND OF YOU TO ALWAYS CHECK UP ON US, BUT YOU GO AHEAD. WE'LL BE OKAY.
OKAY, LOLA. BUT IT'S NOT SAFE HERE. PAGASA SAID THIS STORM WILL GET WORSE.

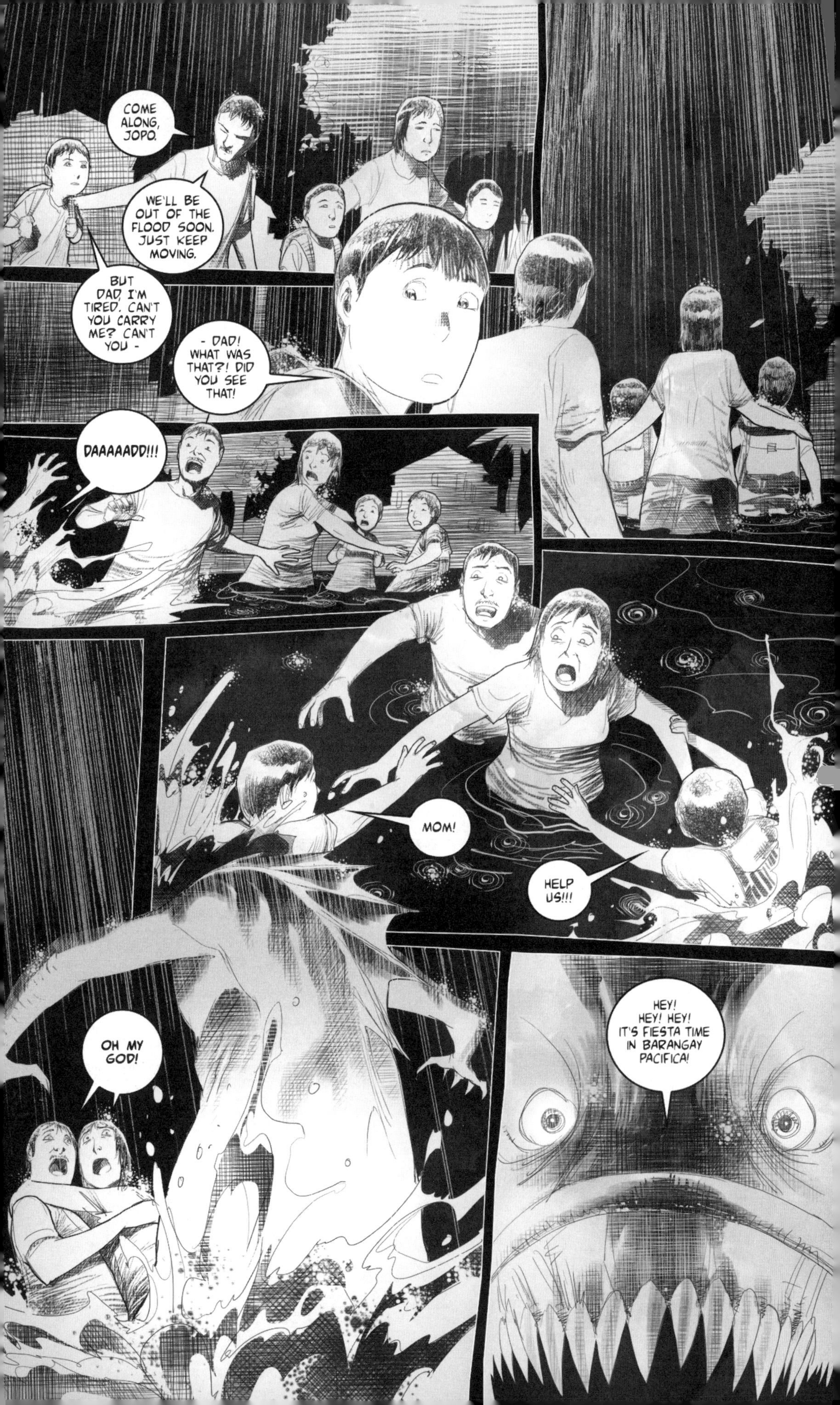
COME ALONG, JOPO.
WE'LL BE OUT OF THE FLOOD SOON. JUST KEEP MOVING.
BUT DAD, I'M TIRED. CAN'T YOU CARRY ME? CAN'T YOU -
- DAD! WHAT WAS THAT?! DID YOU SEE THAT!
DAAAAADD!!!
MOM!
HELP US!!!
OH MY GOD!
HEY! HEY! HEY! IT'S FIESTA TIME IN BARANGAY PACIFICA!

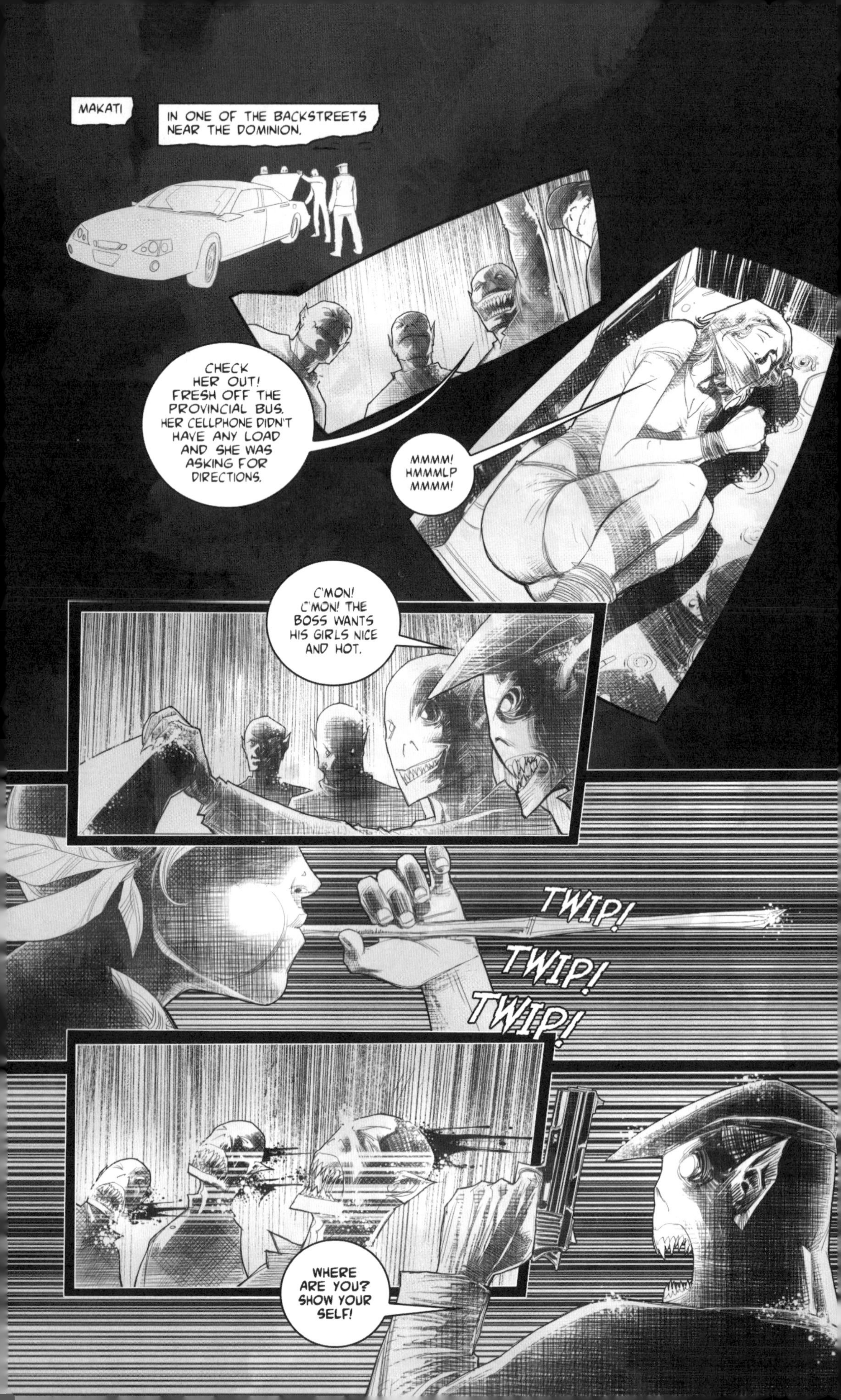

MAKATI
IN ONE OF THE BACKSTREETS NEAR THE DOMINION.
CHECK HER OUT! FRESH OFF THE PROVINCIAL BUS. HER CELLPHONE DIDN'T HAVE ANY LOAD AND SHE WAS ASKING FOR DIRECTIONS.
MMMM! HMMMLP MMMM!
C'MON! C'MON! THE BOSS WANTS HIS GIRLS NICE AND HOT.
TWIP!
TWIP!
TWIP!
WHERE ARE YOU? SHOW YOUR SELF!

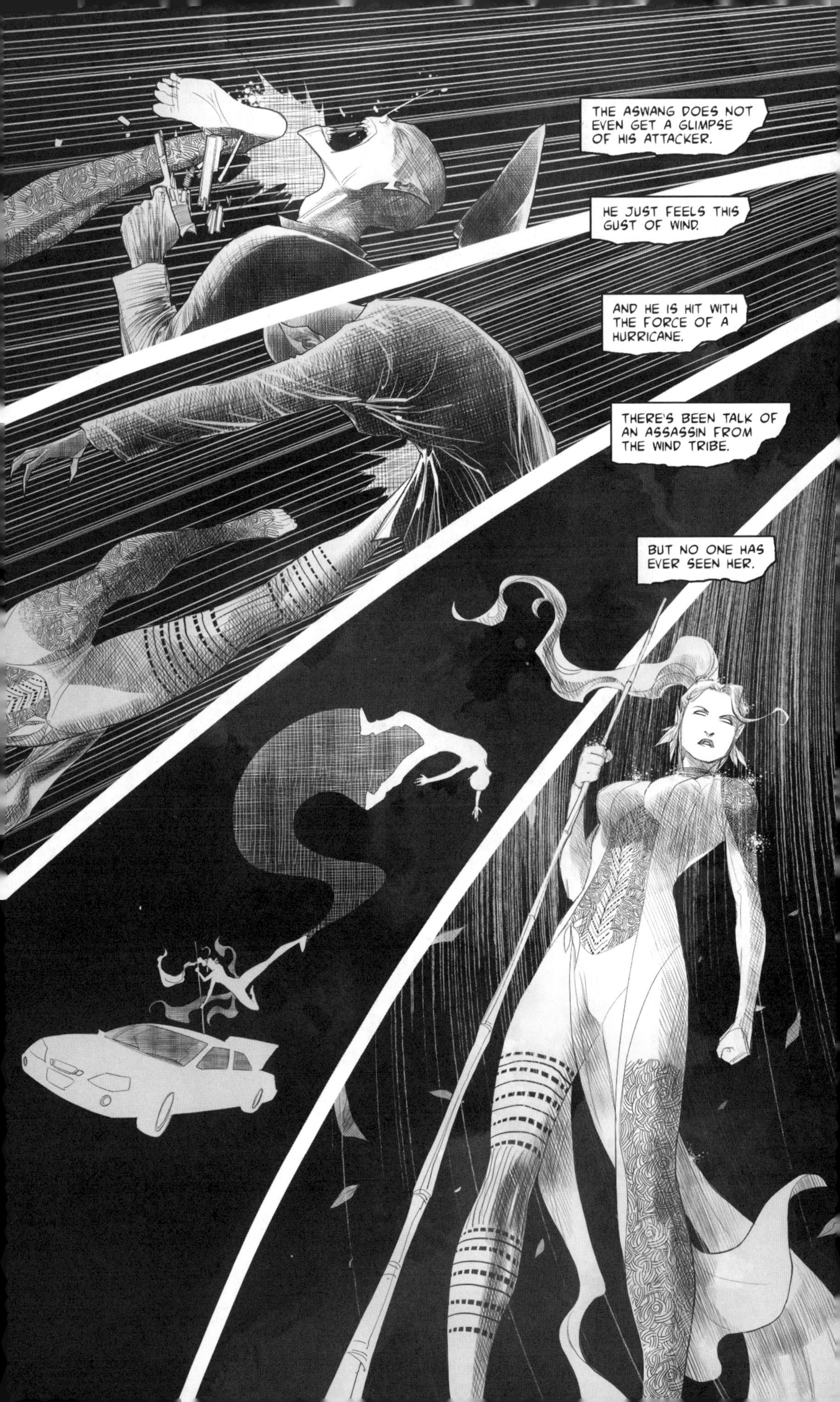
THE ASWANG DOES NOT EVEN GET A GLIMPSE OF HIS ATTACKER.
HE JUST FEELS THIS GUST OF WIND.
AND HE IS HIT WITH THE FORCE OF A HURRICANE.
THERE'S BEEN TALK OF AN ASSASSIN FROM THE WIND TRIBE.
BUT NO ONE HAS EVER SEEN HER.

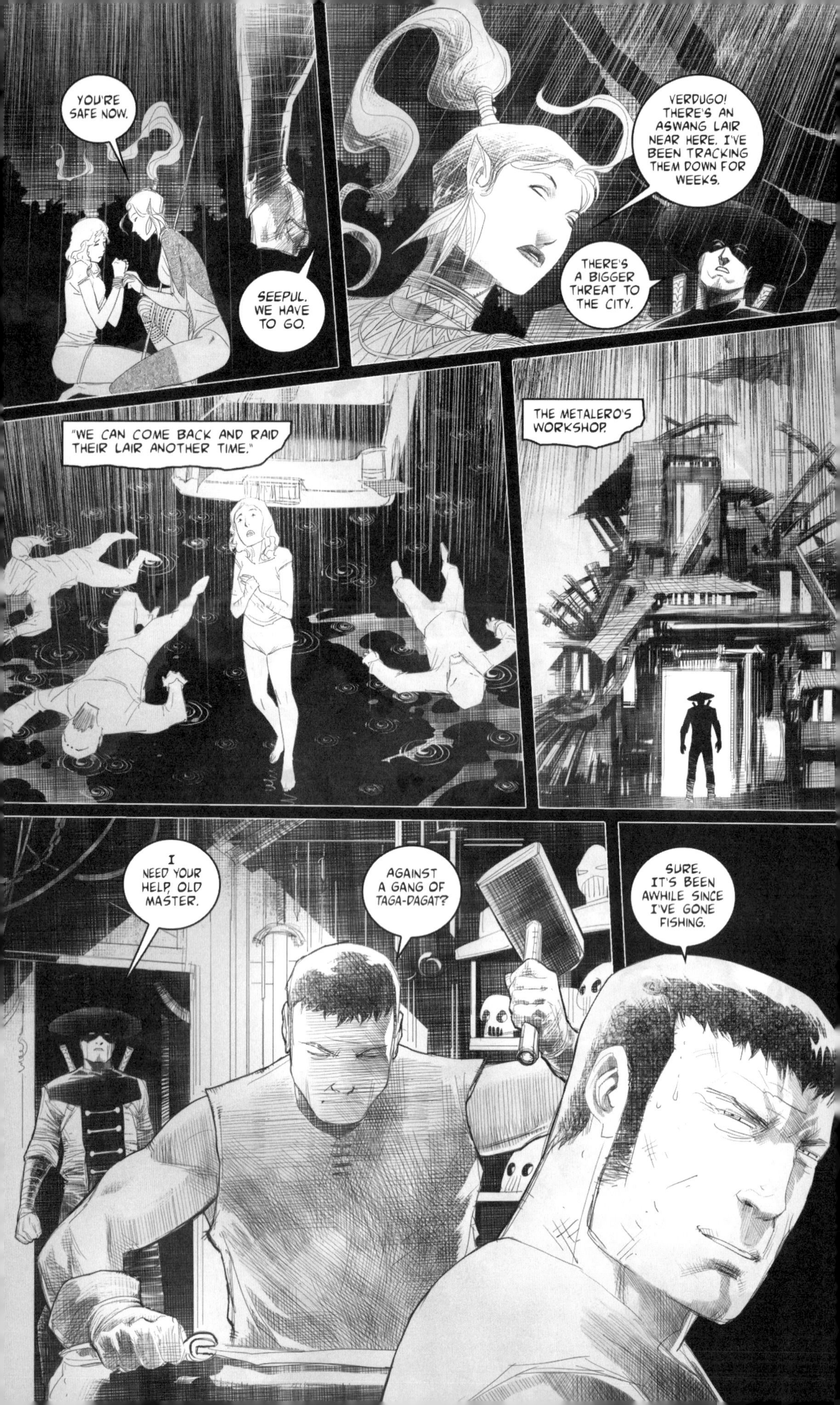
YOU'RE SAFE NOW.
SEEPUL. WE HAVE TO GO.
VERDUGO! THERE'S AN ASWANG LAIR NEAR HERE. I'VE BEEN TRACKING THEM DOWN FOR WEEKS.
THERE'S A BIGGER THREAT TO THE CITY.
"WE CAN COME BACK AND RAID THEIR LAIR ANOTHER TIME."
THE METALERO'S WORKSHOP.
I NEED YOUR HELP, OLD MASTER.
AGAINST A GANG OF TAGA-DAGAT?
SURE. IT'S BEEN AWHILE SINCE I'VE GONE FISHING.

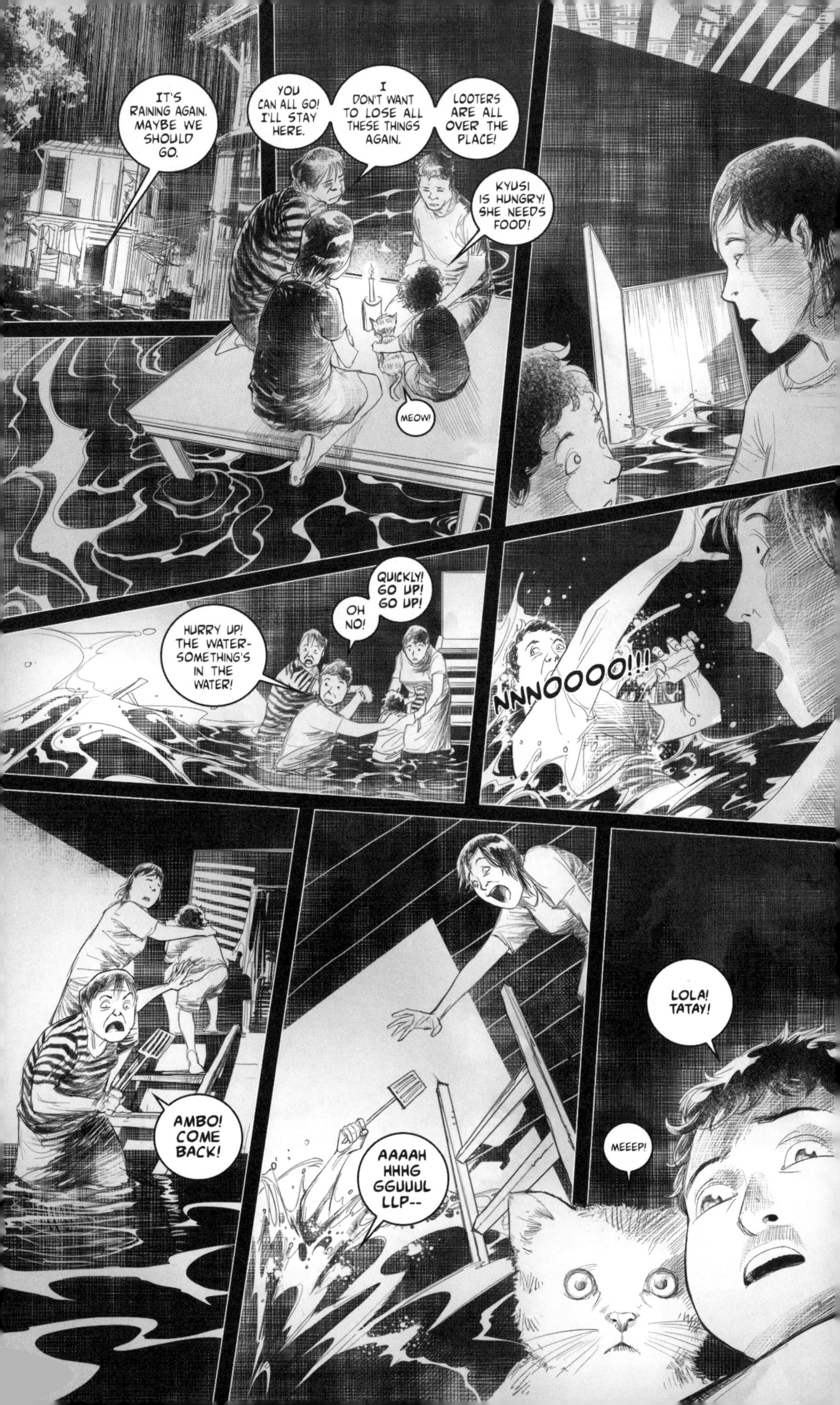
IT'S RAINING AGAIN. MAYBE WE SHOULD GO.
YOU CAN ALL GO! I'LL STAY HERE.
I DON'T WANT TO LOSE ALL THESE THINGS AGAIN.
LOOTERS ARE ALL OVER THE PLACE!
KYUSI IS HUNGRY! SHE NEEDS FOOD!
MEOW!
QUICKLY! GO UP! GO UP!
OH NO!
HURRY UP! THE WATER- SOMETHING'S IN THE WATER!
NNNOOOOO!!!
AMBO! COME BACK!
AAAAH HHHG GGUUUL LLP--
LOLA! TATAY!
MEEEP!

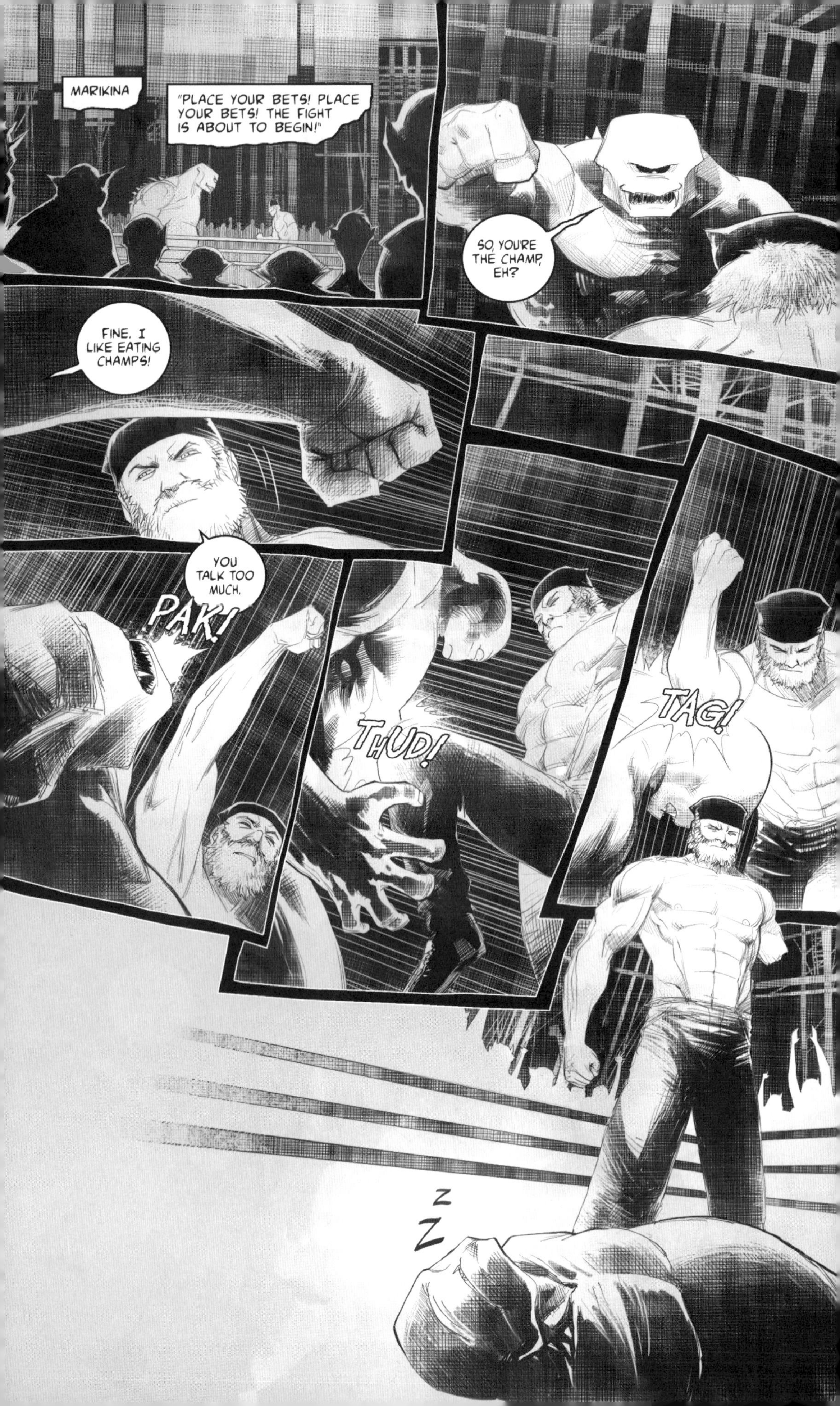
MARIKINA
"PLACE YOUR BETS! PLACE YOUR BETS! THE FIGHT IS ABOUT TO BEGIN!"
SO, YOU'RE THE CHAMP, EH?
FINE. I LIKE EATING CHAMPS!
YOU TALK TOO MUCH.
PAK!
THUD!
TAG!
Z
Z

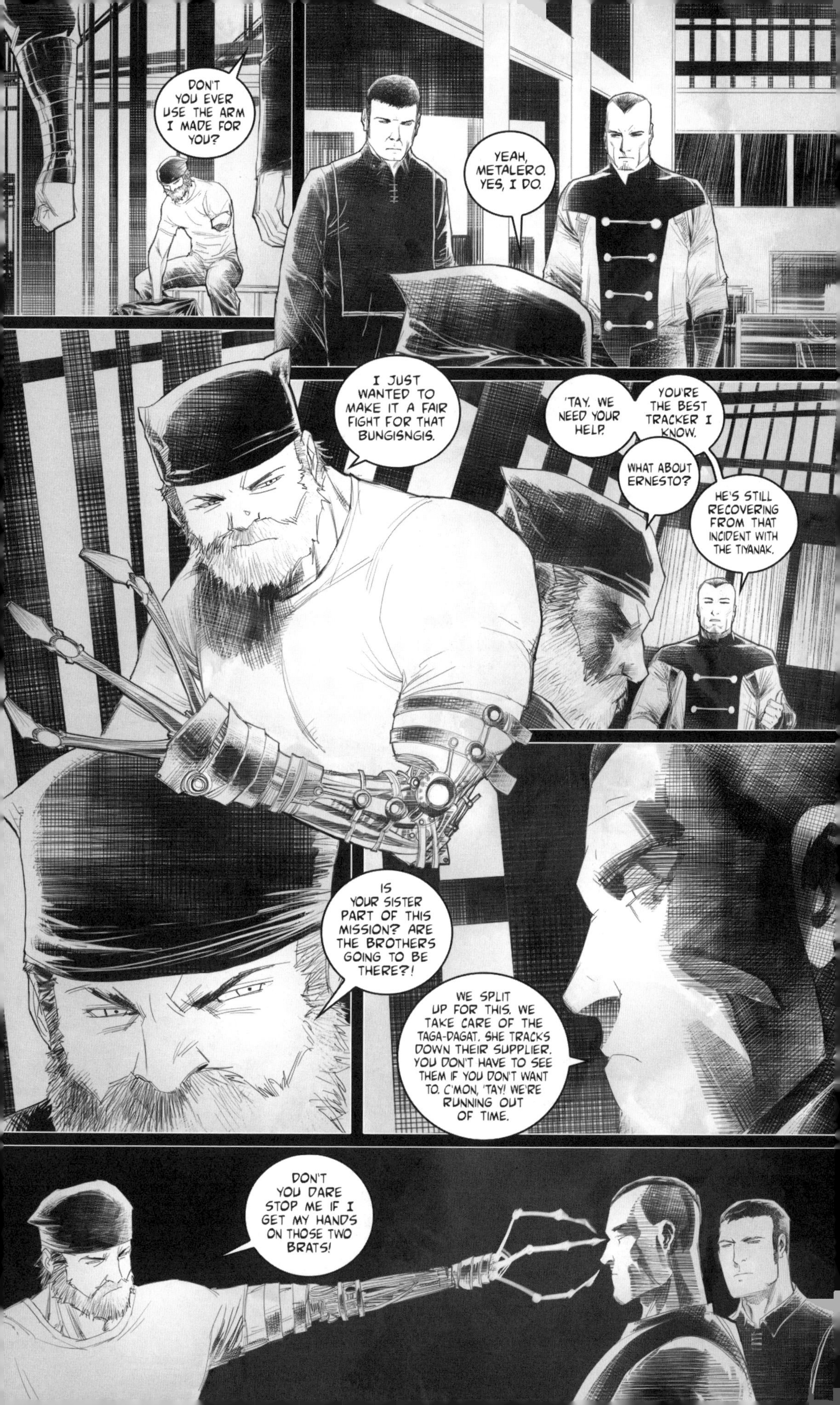
DON'T YOU EVER USE THE ARM I MADE FOR YOU?
YEAH, METALERO. YES, I DO.
I JUST WANTED TO MAKE IT A FAIR FIGHT FOR THAT BUNGISNGIS.
'TAY. WE NEED YOUR HELP.
YOU'RE THE BEST TRACKER I KNOW.
WHAT ABOUT ERNESTO?
HE'S STILL RECOVERING FROM THAT INCIDENT WITH THE TIYANAK.
IS YOUR SISTER PART OF THIS MISSION? ARE THE BROTHERS GOING TO BE THERE?!
WE SPLIT UP FOR THIS. WE TAKE CARE OF THE TAGA-DAGAT. SHE TRACKS DOWN THEIR SUPPLIER. YOU DON'T HAVE TO SEE THEM IF YOU DON'T WANT TO. C'MON, 'TAY! WE'RE RUNNING OUT OF TIME.
DON'T YOU DARE STOP ME IF I GET MY HANDS ON THOSE TWO BRATS!

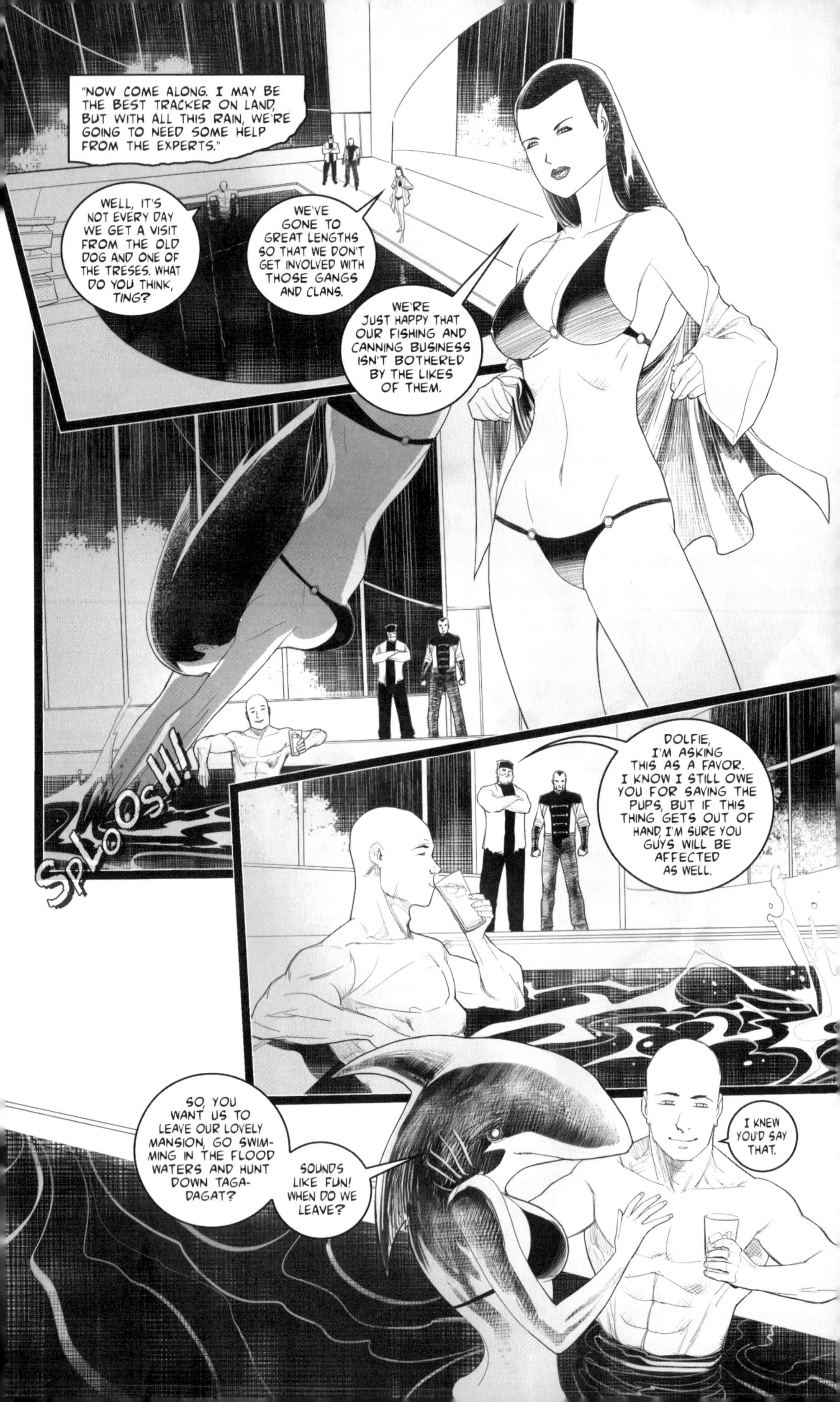
"NOW COME ALONG. I MAY BE THE BEST TRACKER ON LAND, BUT WITH ALL THIS RAIN, WE'RE GOING TO NEED SOME HELP FROM THE EXPERTS."
WELL, IT'S NOT EVERY DAY WE GET A VISIT FROM THE OLD DOG AND ONE OF THE TRESES. WHAT DO YOU THINK, TING?
WE'VE GONE TO GREAT LENGTHS SO THAT WE DON'T GET INVOLVED WITH THOSE GANGS AND CLANS.
WE'RE JUST HAPPY THAT OUR FISHING AND CANNING BUSINESS ISN'T BOTHERED BY THE LIKES OF THEM.
SPLOOSH!!
DOLFIE, I'M ASKING THIS AS A FAVOR. I KNOW I STILL OWE YOU FOR SAVING THE PUPS, BUT IF THIS THING GETS OUT OF HAND, I'M SURE YOU GUYS WILL BE AFFECTED AS WELL.
SO, YOU WANT US TO LEAVE OUR LOVELY MANSION, GO SWIMMING IN THE FLOOD WATERS AND HUNT DOWN TAGA-DAGAT?
SOUNDS LIKE FUN! WHEN DO WE LEAVE?
I KNEW YOU'D SAY THAT.

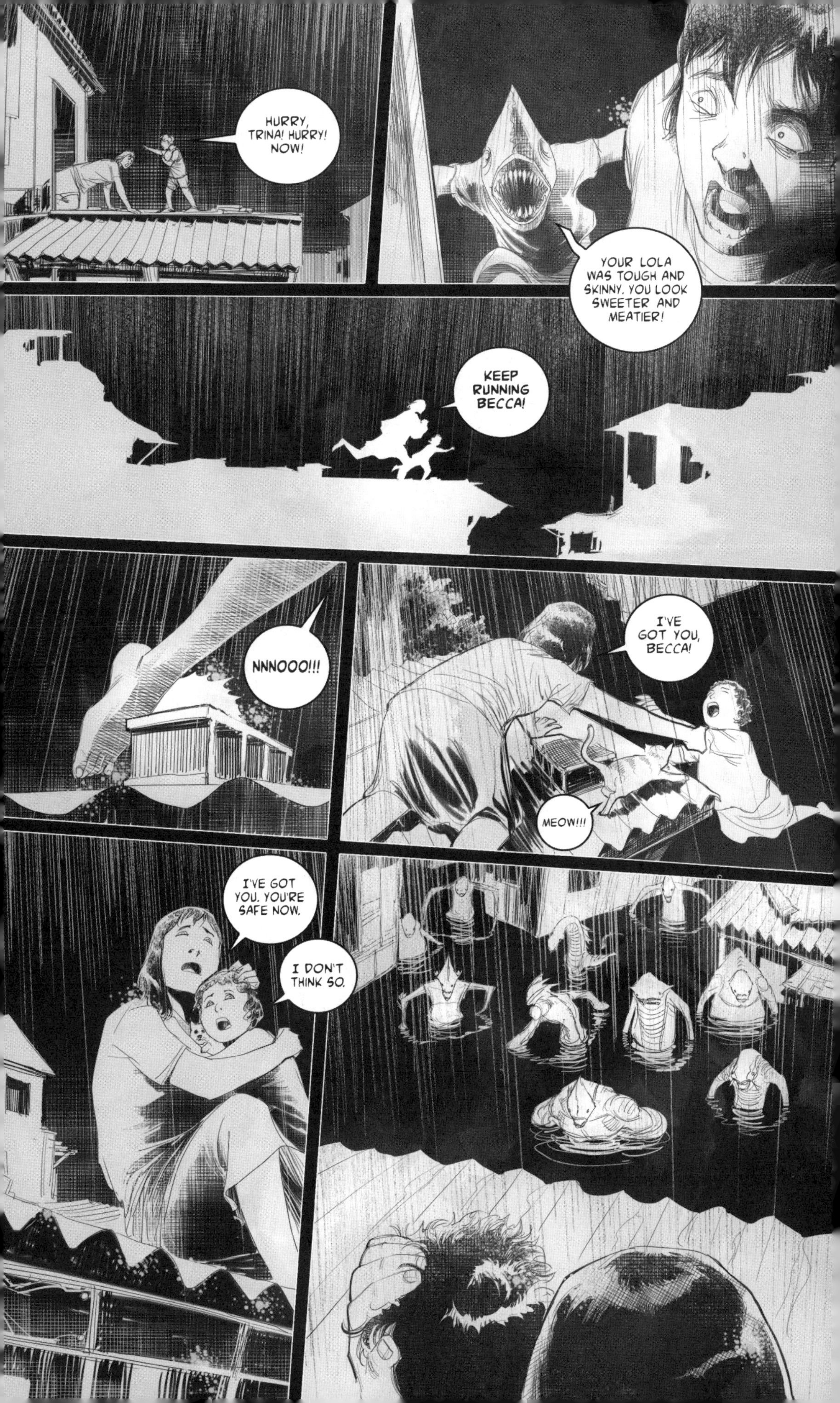
HURRY, TRINA! HURRY! NOW!
YOUR LOLA WAS TOUGH AND SKINNY. YOU LOOK SWEETER AND MEATIER!
KEEP RUNNING BECCA!
NNNOOO!!!
I'VE GOT YOU, BECCA!
MEOW!!!
I'VE GOT YOU. YOU'RE SAFE NOW.
I DON'T THINK SO.

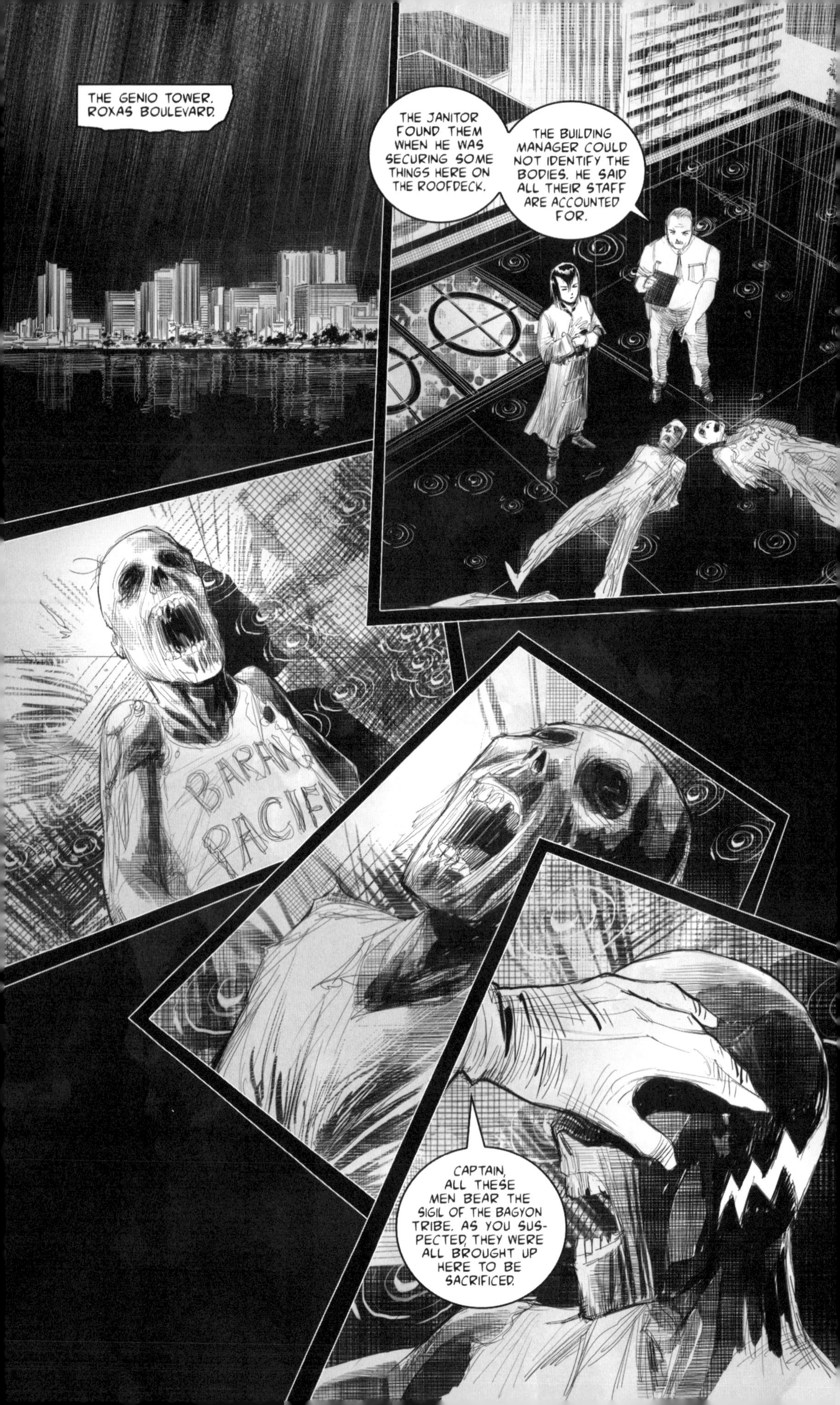
THE GENIO TOWER. ROXAS BOULEVARD.
THE JANITOR FOUND THEM WHEN HE WAS SECURING SOME THINGS HERE ON THE ROOFDECK.
THE BUILDING MANAGER COULD NOT IDENTIFY THE BODIES. HE SAID ALL THEIR STAFF ARE ACCOUNTED FOR.
CAPTAIN, ALL THESE MEN BEAR THE SIGIL OF THE BAGYON TRIBE. AS YOU SUSPECTED, THEY WERE ALL BROUGHT UP HERE TO BE SACRIFICED.

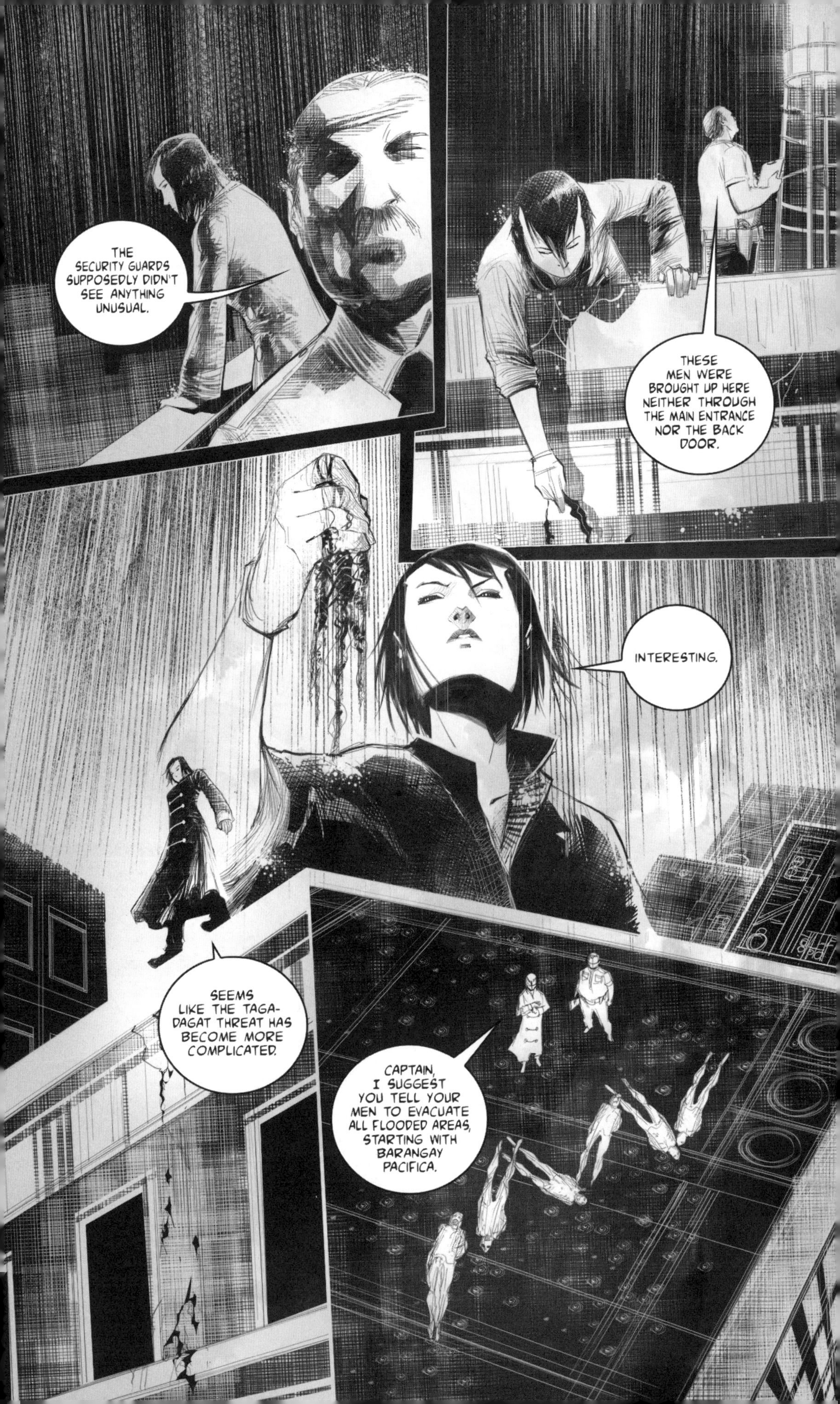
THE SECURITY GUARDS SUPPOSEDLY DIDN'T SEE ANYTHING UNUSUAL.
THESE MEN WERE BROUGHT UP HERE NEITHER THROUGH THE MAIN ENTRANCE NOR THE BACK DOOR.
INTERESTING.
SEEMS LIKE THE TAGA-DAGAT THREAT HAS BECOME MORE COMPLICATED.
CAPTAIN, I SUGGEST YOU TELL YOUR MEN TO EVACUATE ALL FLOODED AREAS, STARTING WITH BARANGAY PACIFICA.

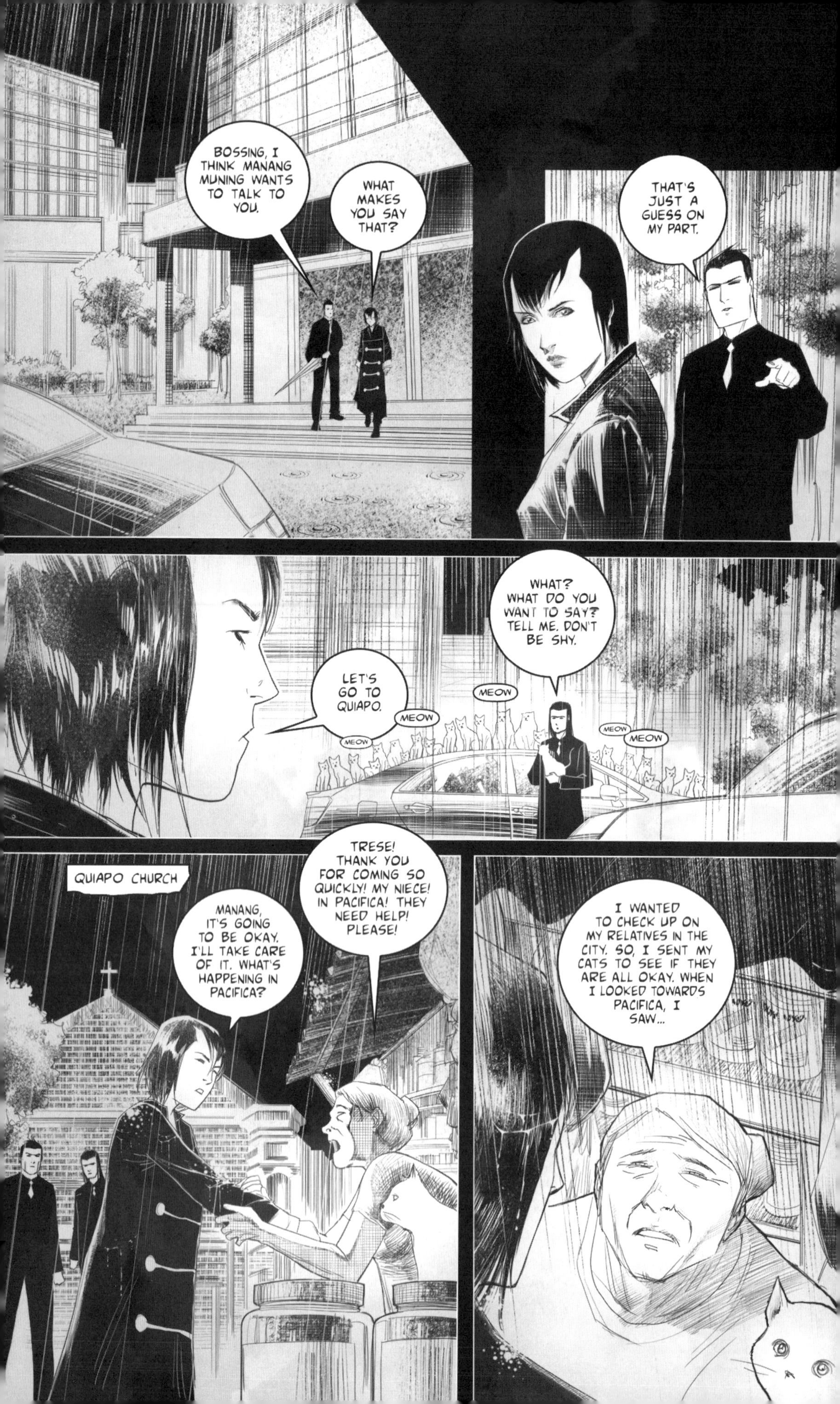

BOSSING, I THINK MANANG MUNING WANTS TO TALK TO YOU.
WHAT MAKES YOU SAY THAT?
THAT'S JUST A GUESS ON MY PART.
WHAT? WHAT DO YOU WANT TO SAY? TELL ME. DON'T BE SHY.
MEOW
LET'S GO TO QUIAPO.
MEOW
MEOW
MEOW
MEOW
QUIAPO CHURCH
TRESE! THANK YOU FOR COMING SO QUICKLY! MY NIECE! IN PACIFICA! THEY NEED HELP! PLEASE!
MANANG, IT'S GOING TO BE OKAY. I'LL TAKE CARE OF IT. WHAT'S HAPPENING IN PACIFICA?
I WANTED TO CHECK UP ON MY RELATIVES IN THE CITY. SO, I SENT MY CATS TO SEE IF THEY ARE ALL OKAY. WHEN I LOOKED TOWARDS PACIFICA, I SAW...

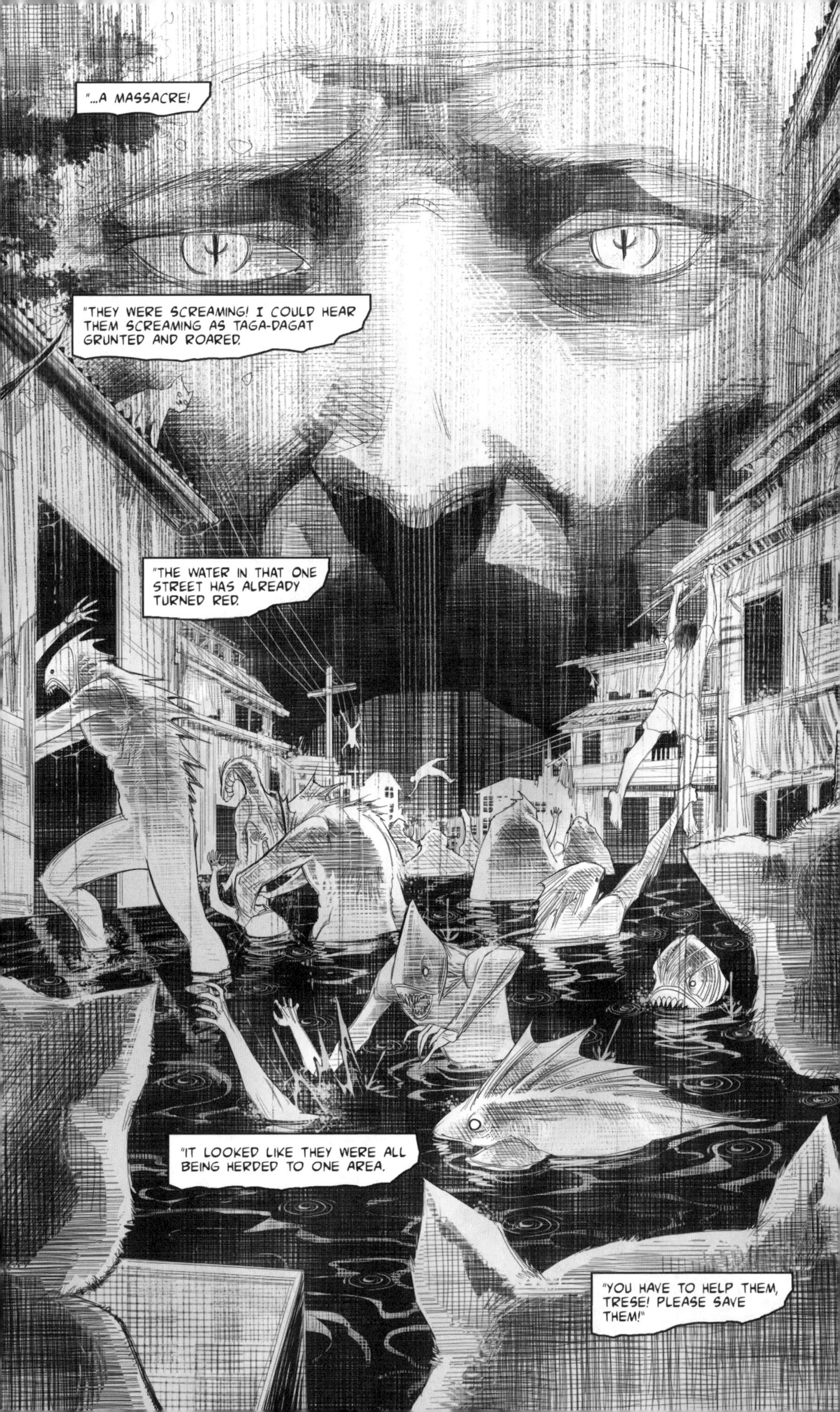
"...A MASSACRE!
"THEY WERE SCREAMING! I COULD HEAR THEM SCREAMING AS TAGA-DAGAT GRUNTED AND ROARED.
"THE WATER IN THAT ONE STREET HAS ALREADY TURNED RED.
"IT LOOKED LIKE THEY WERE ALL BEING HERDED TO ONE AREA.
"YOU HAVE TO HELP THEM, TRESE! PLEASE SAVE THEM!"

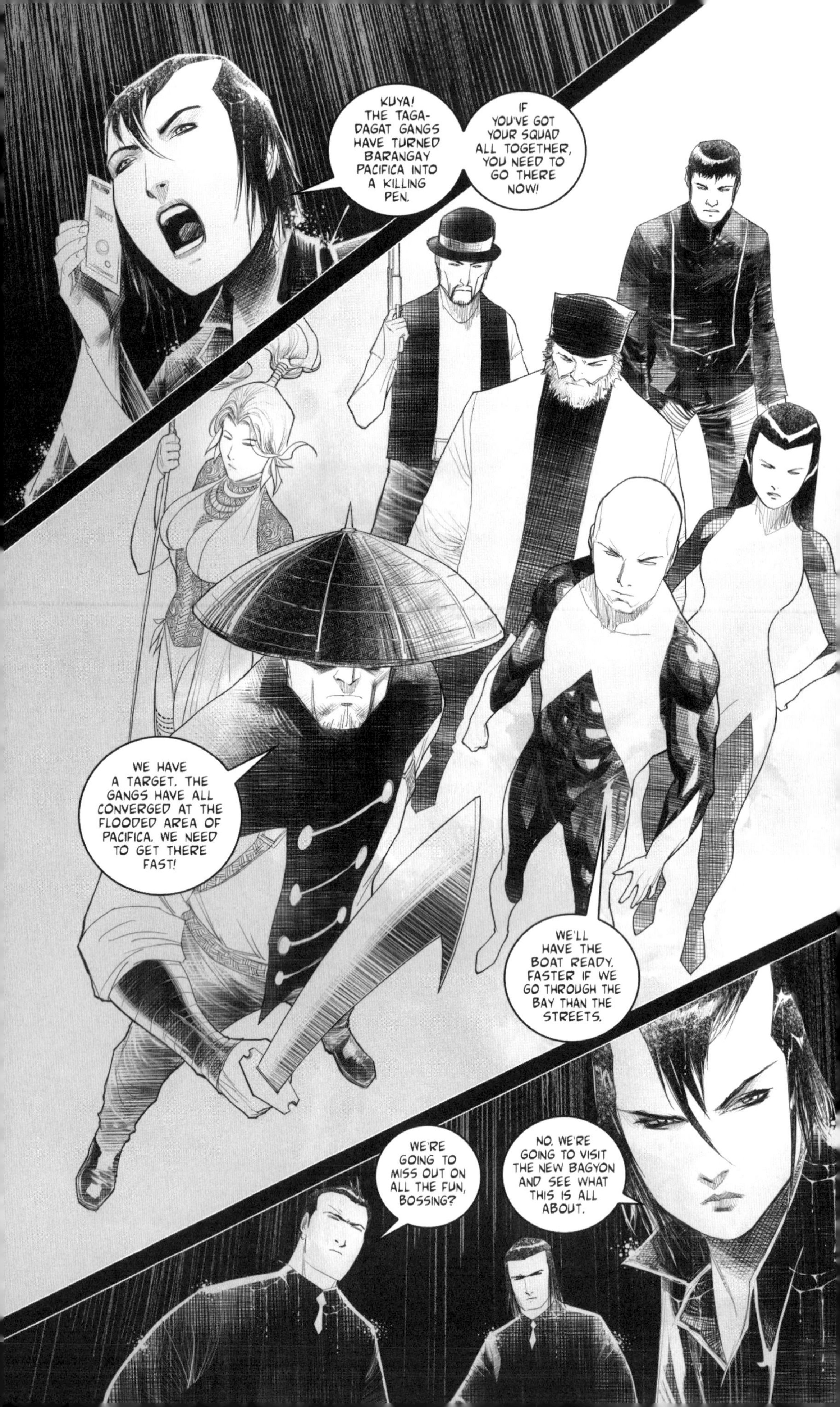

KUYA! THE TAGA-DAGAT GANGS HAVE TURNED BARANGAY PACIFICA INTO A KILLING PEN.
IF YOU'VE GOT YOUR SQUAD ALL TOGETHER, YOU NEED TO GO THERE NOW!
WE HAVE A TARGET. THE GANGS HAVE ALL CONVERGED AT THE FLOODED AREA OF PACIFICA. WE NEED TO GET THERE FAST!
WE'LL HAVE THE BOAT READY. FASTER IF WE GO THROUGH THE BAY THAN THE STREETS.
WE'RE GOING TO MISS OUT ON ALL THE FUN, BOSSING?
NO. WE'RE GOING TO VISIT THE NEW BAGYON AND SEE WHAT THIS IS ALL ABOUT.

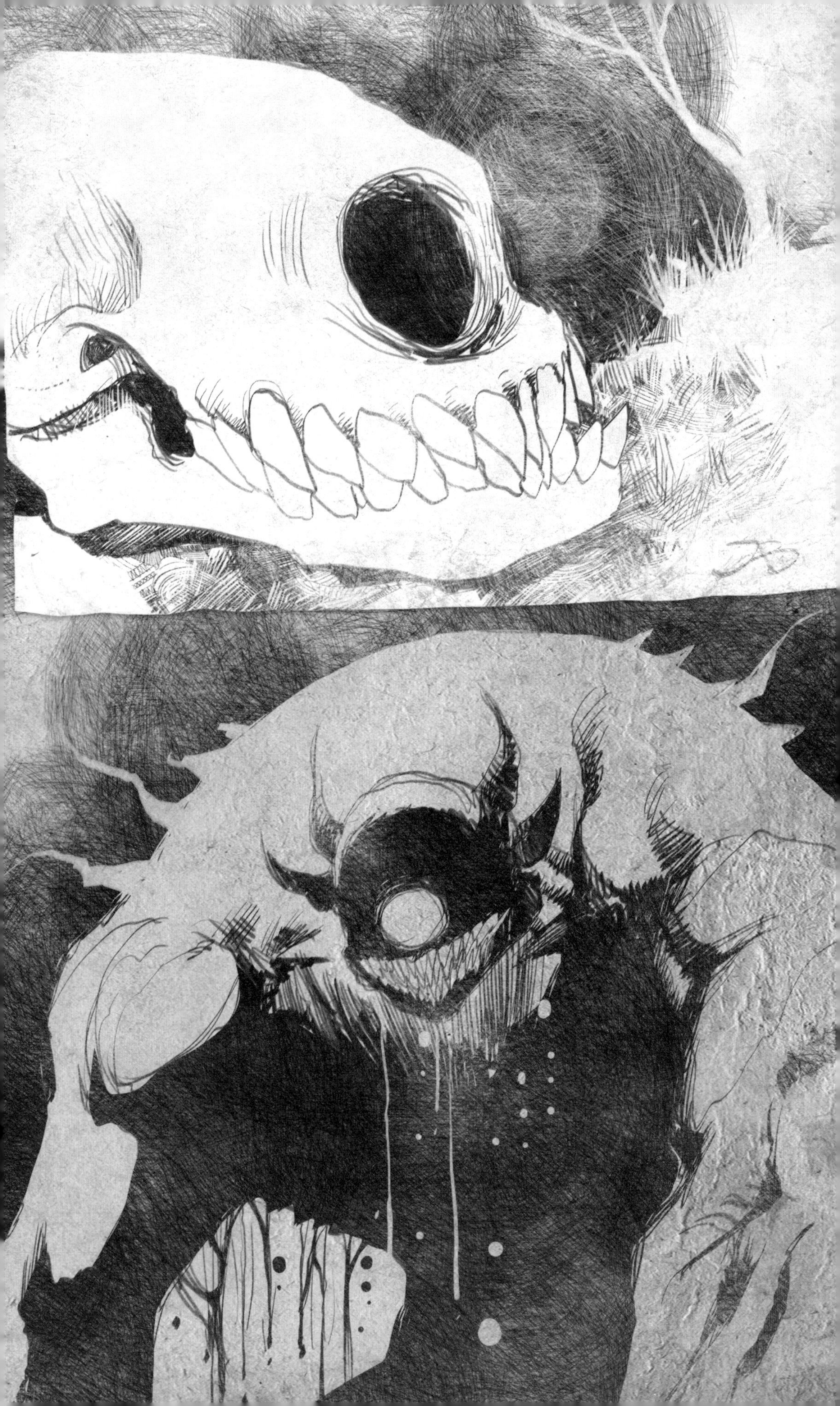

October 1

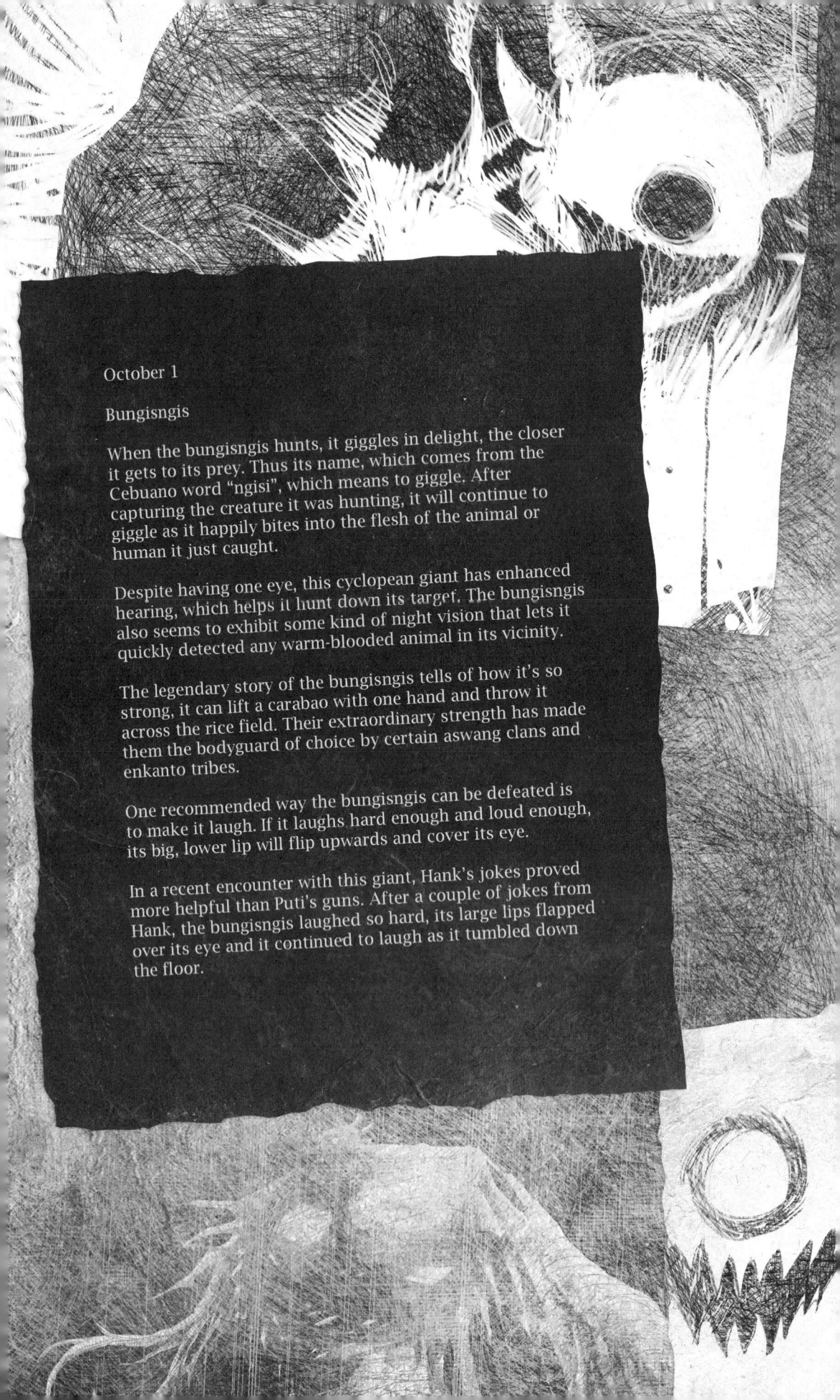

Bungisngis

When the bungisngis hunts, it giggles in delight, the closer it gets to its prey. Thus its name, which comes from the Cebuano word "ngisi", which means to giggle. After capturing the creature it was hunting, it will continue to giggle as it happily bites into the flesh of the animal or human it just caught.

Despite having one eye, this cyclopean giant has enhanced hearing, which helps it hunt down its target. The bungisngis also seems to exhibit some kind of night vision that lets it quickly detected any warm-blooded animal in its vicinity.

The legendary story of the bungisngis tells of how it's so strong, it can lift a carabao with one hand and throw it across the rice field. Their extraordinary strength has made them the bodyguard of choice by certain aswang clans and enkanto tribes.

One recommended way the bungisngis can be defeated is to make it laugh. If it laughs hard enough and loud enough, its big, lower lip will flip upwards and cover its eye.

In a recent encounter with this giant, Hank's jokes proved more helpful than Puti's guns. After a couple of jokes from Hank, the bungisngis laughed so hard, its large lips flapped over its eye and it continued to laugh as it tumbled down the floor.

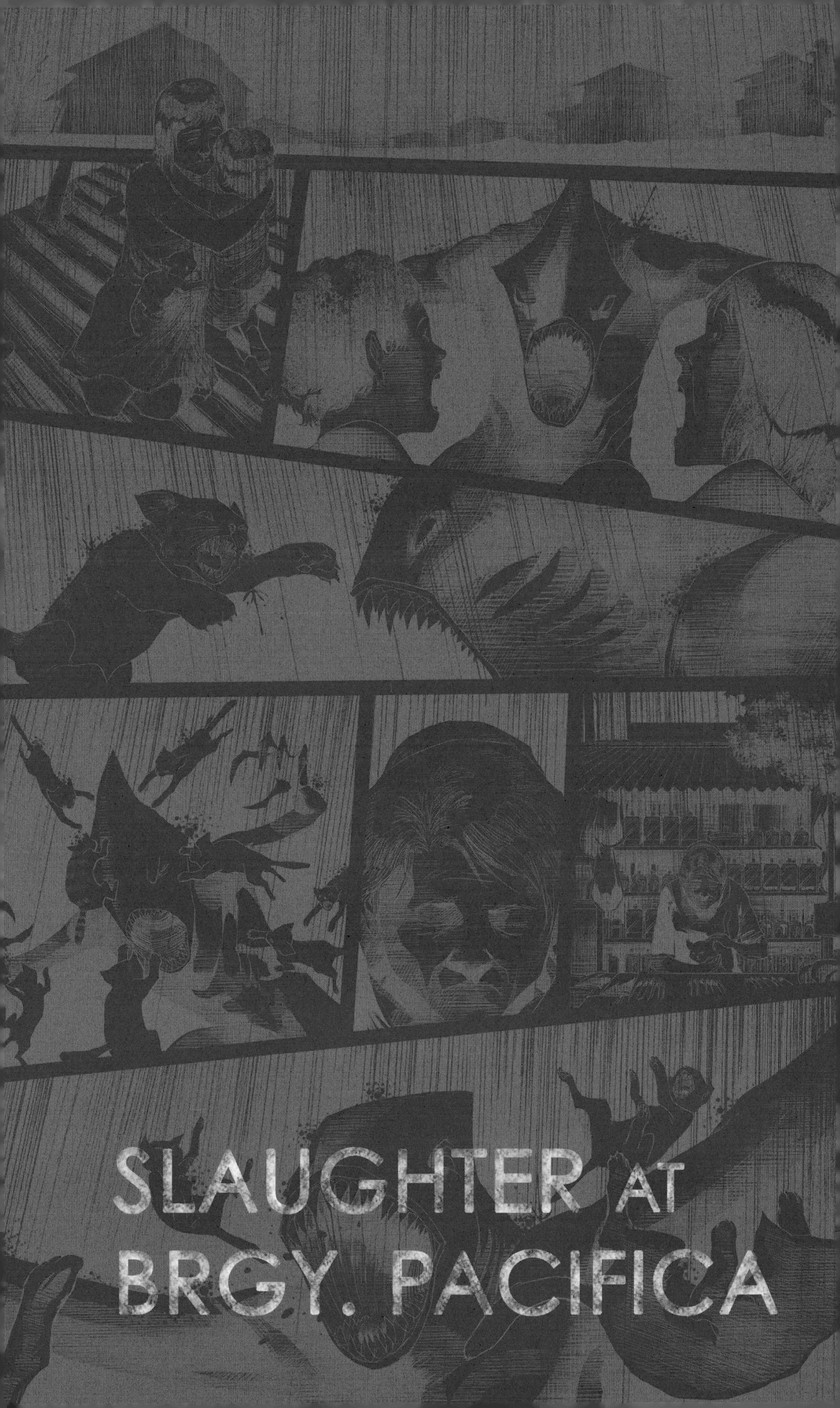
SLAUGHTER AT
BRGY. PACIFICA

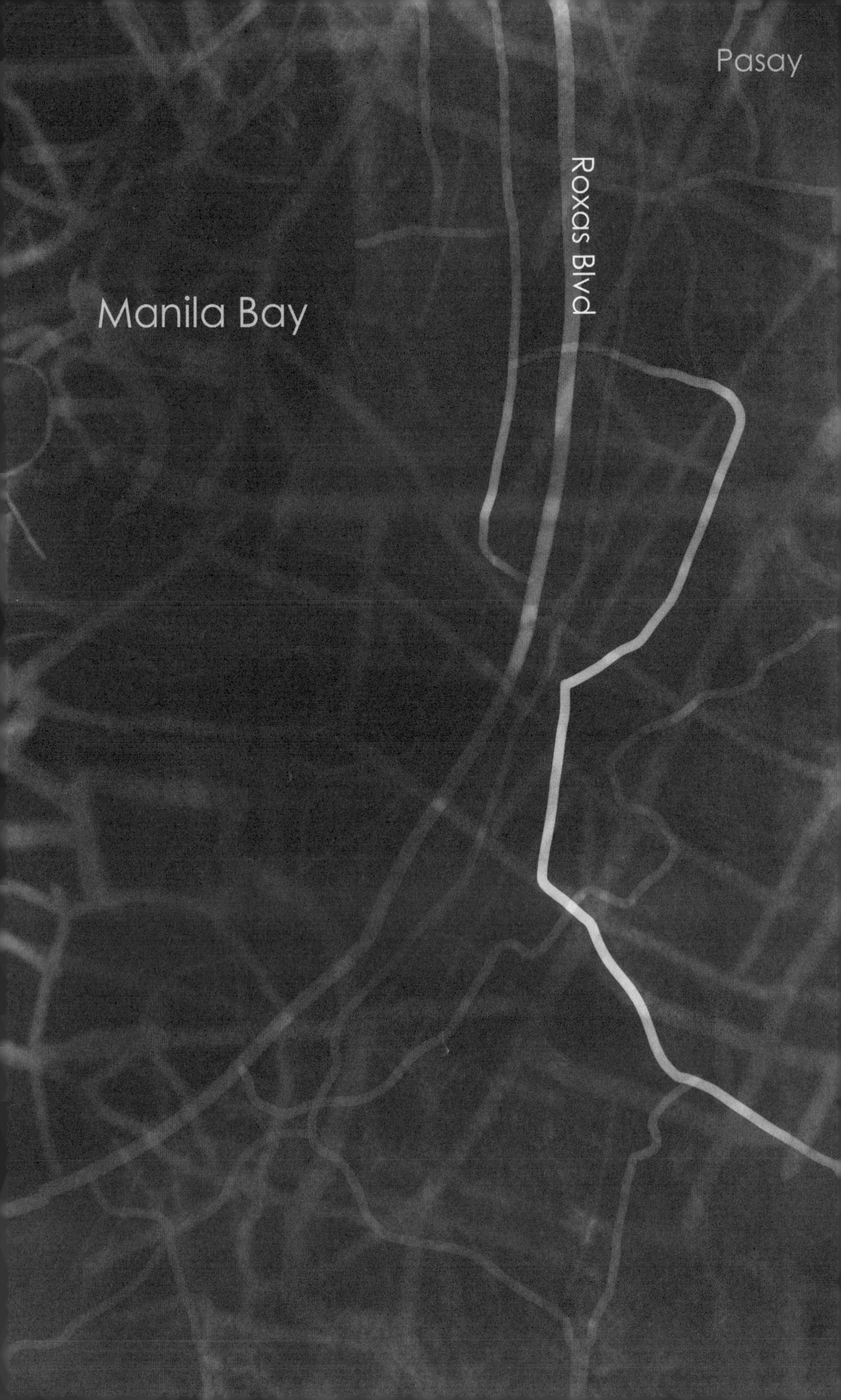
Pasay
Roxas Blvd
Manila Bay

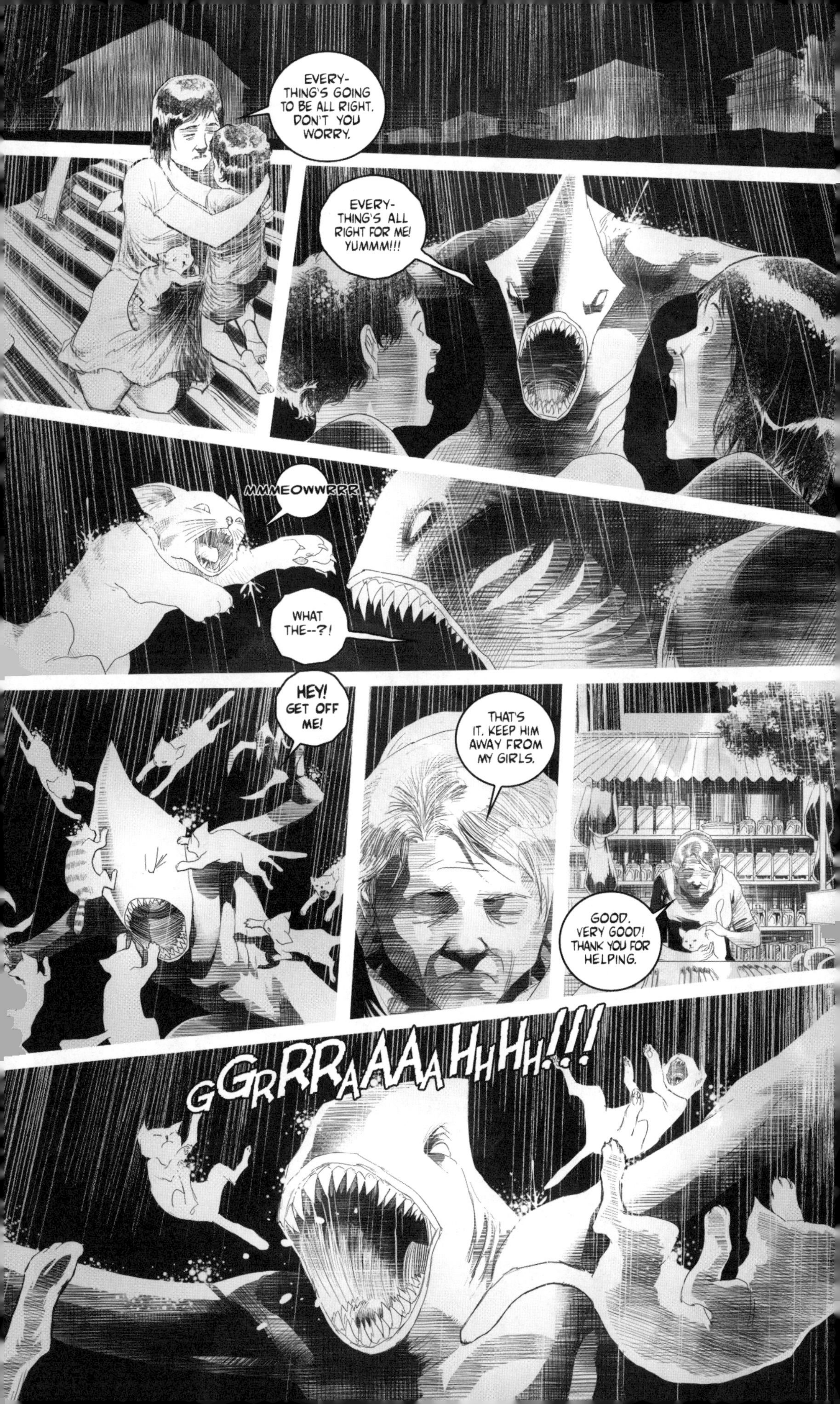
EVERY-THING'S GOING TO BE ALL RIGHT. DON'T YOU WORRY.
EVERY-THING'S ALL RIGHT FOR ME! YUMMM!!!
MMMEOWWRRR
WHAT THE--?!
HEY! GET OFF ME!
THAT'S IT. KEEP HIM AWAY FROM MY GIRLS.
GOOD. VERY GOOD! THANK YOU FOR HELPING.
GGRRRAAAAHHHH!!!

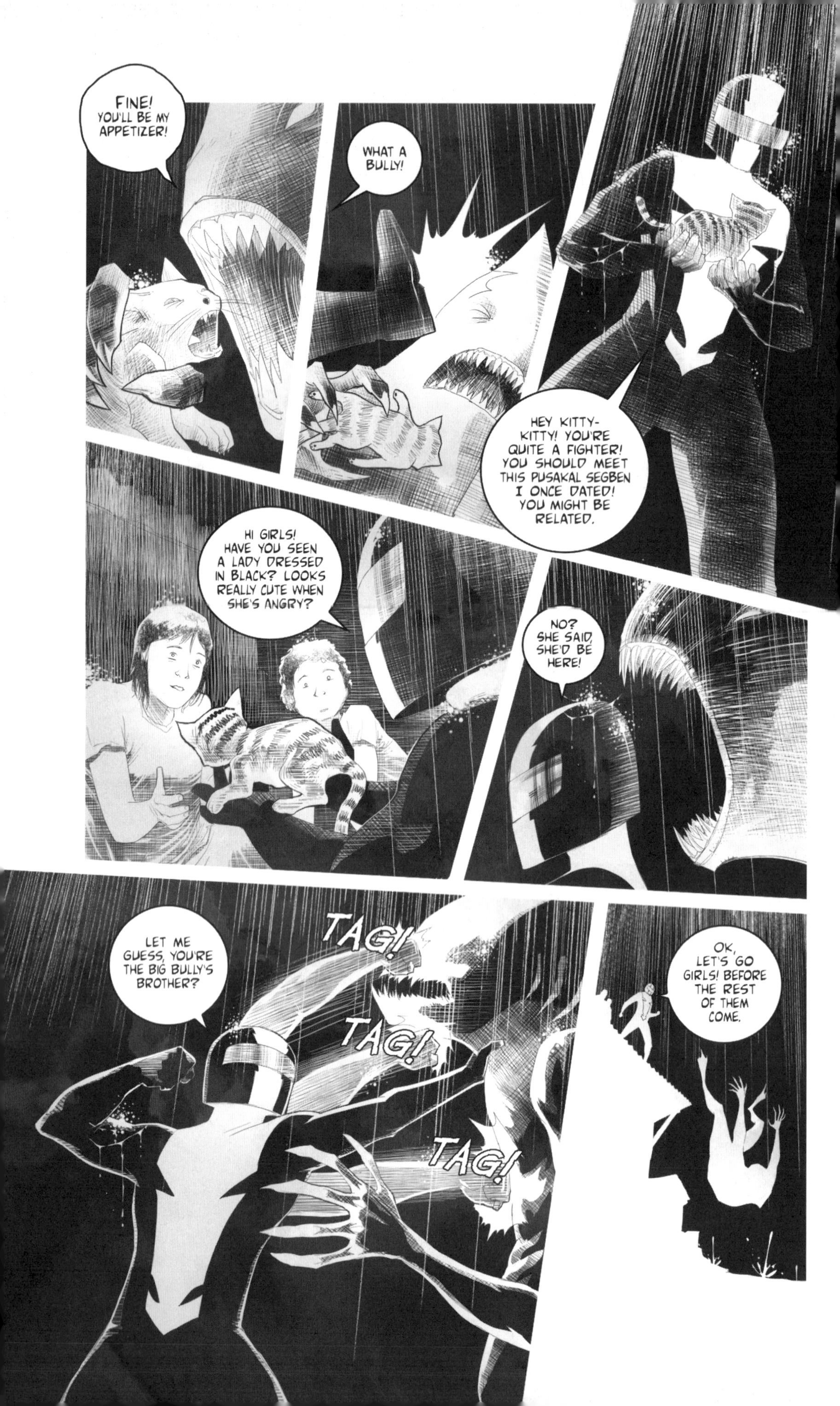
FINE! YOU'LL BE MY APPETIZER!
WHAT A BULLY!
HEY KITTY-KITTY! YOU'RE QUITE A FIGHTER! YOU SHOULD MEET THIS PUSAKAL SEGBEN I ONCE DATED! YOU MIGHT BE RELATED.
HI GIRLS! HAVE YOU SEEN A LADY DRESSED IN BLACK? LOOKS REALLY CUTE WHEN SHE'S ANGRY?
NO? SHE SAID, SHE'D BE HERE!
LET ME GUESS, YOU'RE THE BIG BULLY'S BROTHER?
TAG!
TAG!
TAG!
OK, LET'S GO GIRLS! BEFORE THE REST OF THEM COME.

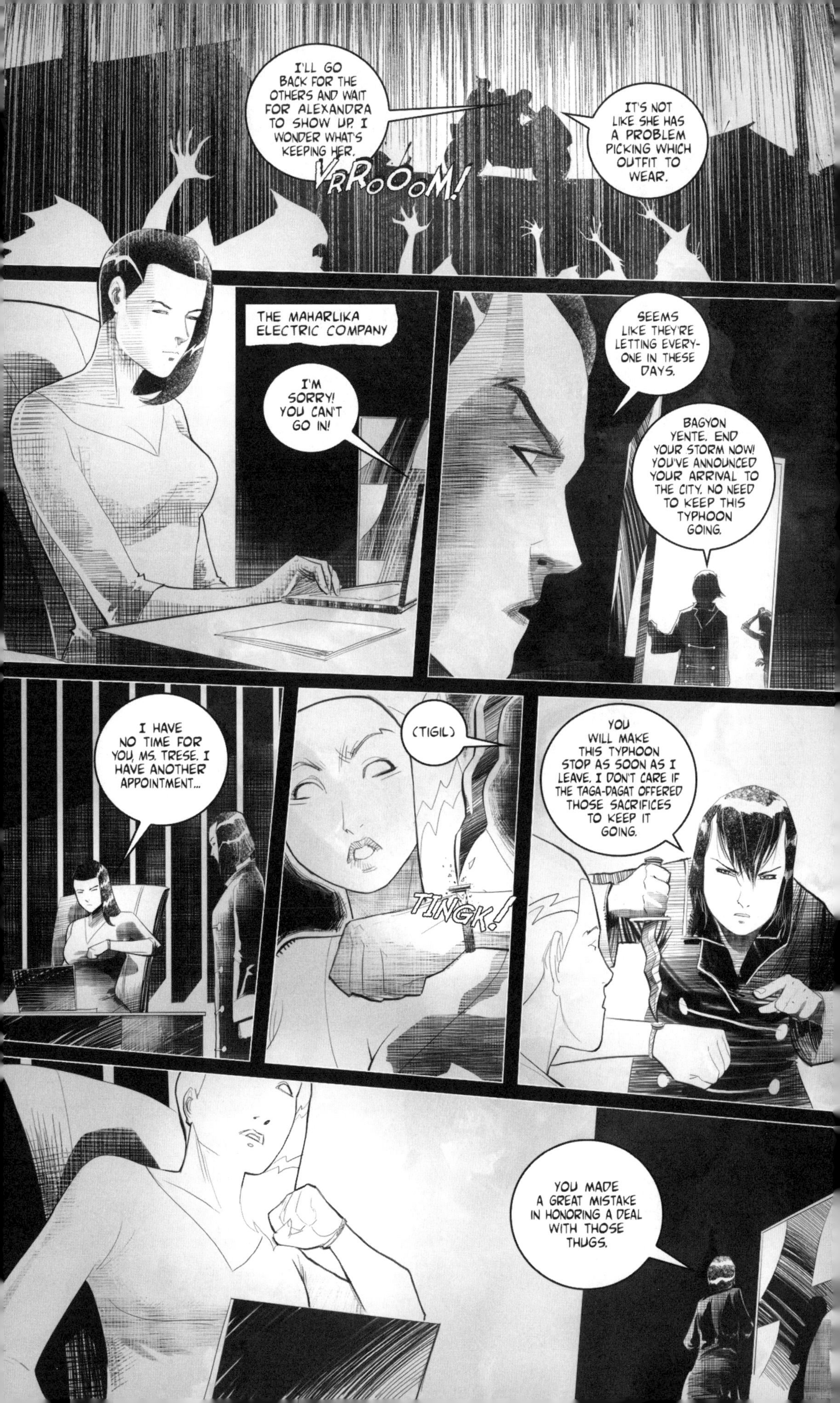
I'LL GO BACK FOR THE OTHERS AND WAIT FOR ALEXANDRA TO SHOW UP. I WONDER WHAT'S KEEPING HER.
IT'S NOT LIKE SHE HAS A PROBLEM PICKING WHICH OUTFIT TO WEAR.
VRROOOOM!
THE MAHARLIKA ELECTRIC COMPANY
I'M SORRY! YOU CAN'T GO IN!
SEEMS LIKE THEY'RE LETTING EVERY-ONE IN THESE DAYS.
BAGYON YENTE. END YOUR STORM NOW! YOU'VE ANNOUNCED YOUR ARRIVAL TO THE CITY. NO NEED TO KEEP THIS TYPHOON GOING.
I HAVE NO TIME FOR YOU, MS. TRESE. I HAVE ANOTHER APPOINTMENT...
(TIGIL)
TINGK!
YOU WILL MAKE THIS TYPHOON STOP AS SOON AS I LEAVE. I DON'T CARE IF THE TAGA-DAGAT OFFERED THOSE SACRIFICES TO KEEP IT GOING.
YOU MADE A GREAT MISTAKE IN HONORING A DEAL WITH THOSE THUGS.

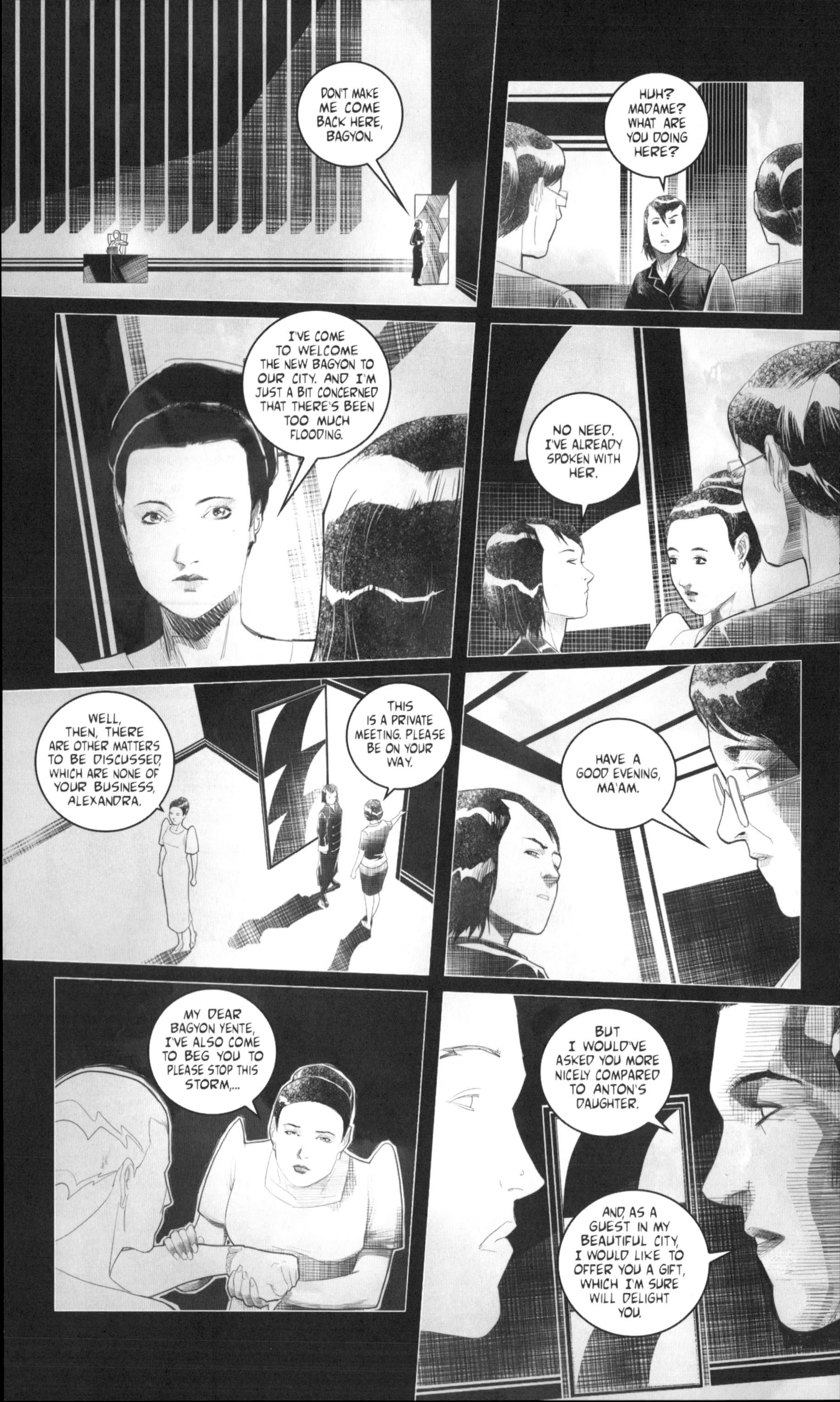
DON'T MAKE ME COME BACK HERE, BAGYON.
HUH? MADAME? WHAT ARE YOU DOING HERE?
I'VE COME TO WELCOME THE NEW BAGYON TO OUR CITY. AND I'M JUST A BIT CONCERNED THAT THERE'S BEEN TOO MUCH FLOODING.
NO NEED. I'VE ALREADY SPOKEN WITH HER.
WELL, THEN, THERE ARE OTHER MATTERS TO BE DISCUSSED, WHICH ARE NONE OF YOUR BUSINESS, ALEXANDRA.
THIS IS A PRIVATE MEETING. PLEASE BE ON YOUR WAY.
HAVE A GOOD EVENING, MA'AM.
MY DEAR BAGYON YENTE, I'VE ALSO COME TO BEG YOU TO PLEASE STOP THIS STORM,...
BUT I WOULD'VE ASKED YOU MORE NICELY COMPARED TO ANTON'S DAUGHTER.
AND, AS A GUEST IN MY BEAUTIFUL CITY, I WOULD LIKE TO OFFER YOU A GIFT, WHICH I'M SURE WILL DELIGHT YOU.

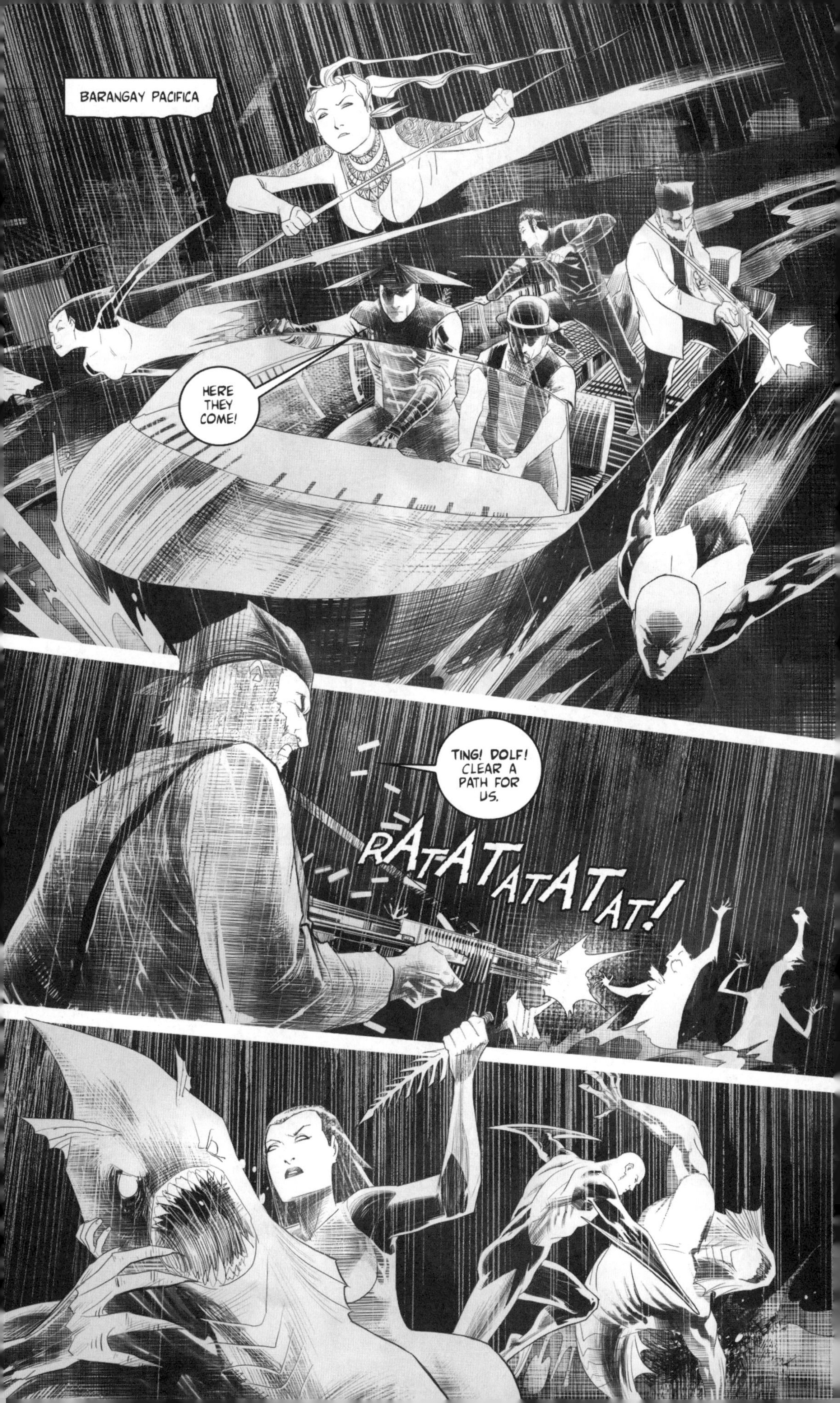
BARANGAY PACIFICA
HERE THEY COME!
TING! DOLF! CLEAR A PATH FOR US.
RATATATATATAT!

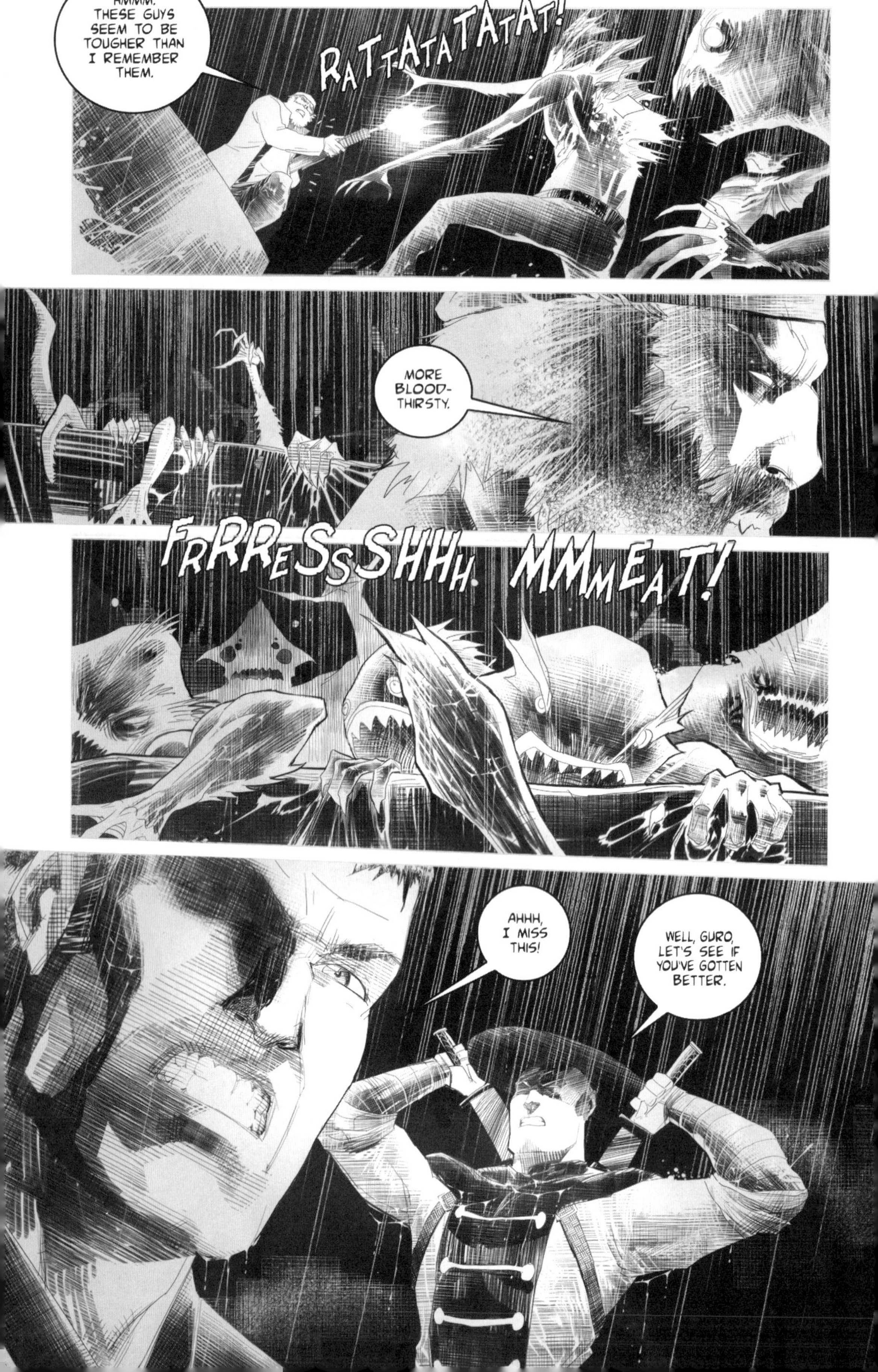

HMMM. THESE GUYS SEEM TO BE TOUGHER THAN I REMEMBER THEM.
RATTATATATAT!
MORE BLOOD-THIRSTY.
FRRRESSSHHH
MMMEAT!
AHHH, I MISS THIS!
WELL, GURO, LET'S SEE IF YOU'VE GOTTEN BETTER.

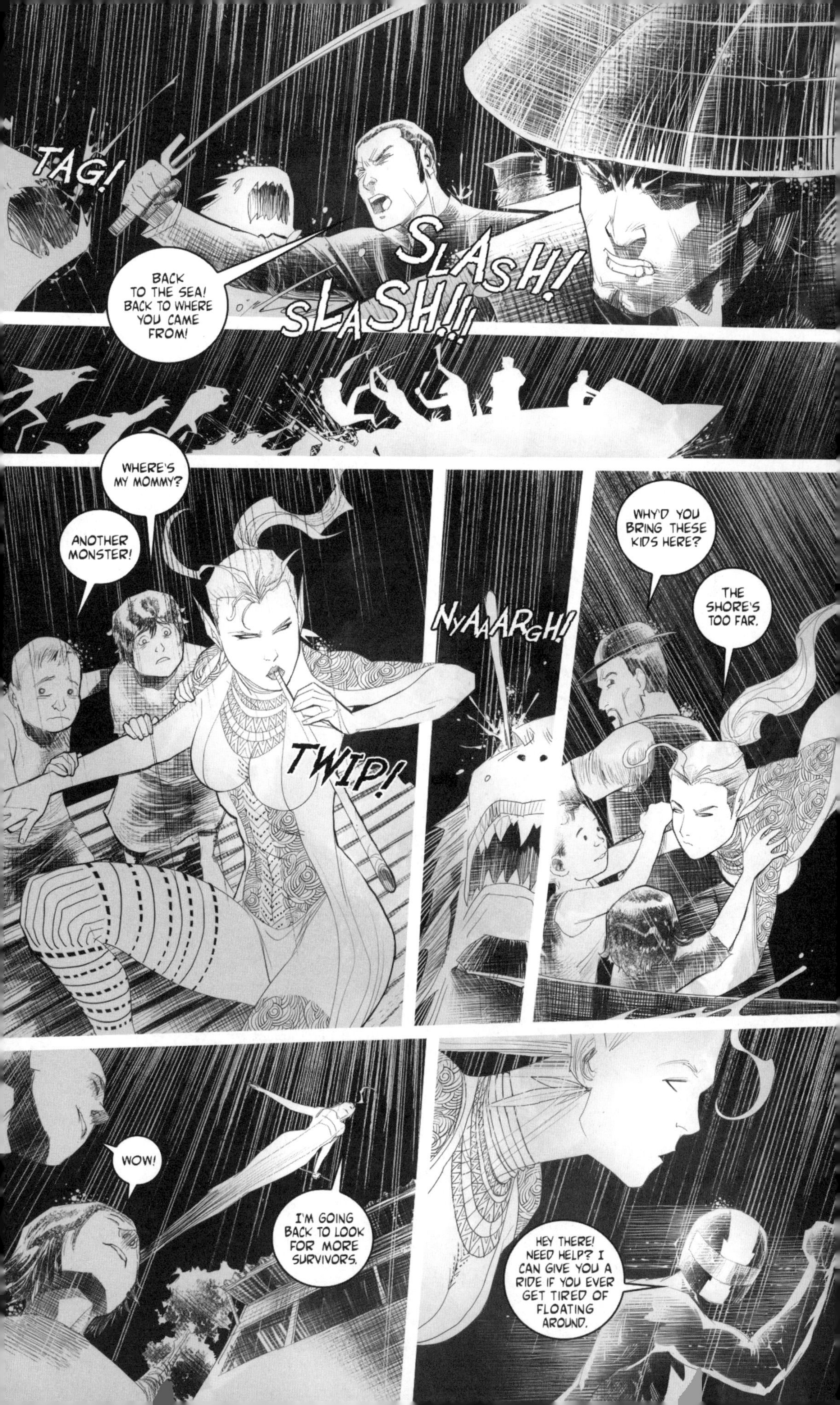
TAG!
BACK TO THE SEA! BACK TO WHERE YOU CAME FROM!
SLASH!
SLASH!!!
WHERE'S MY MOMMY?
ANOTHER MONSTER!
TWIP!
NYAAARGH!
WHY'D YOU BRING THESE KIDS HERE?
THE SHORE'S TOO FAR.
WOW!
I'M GOING BACK TO LOOK FOR MORE SURVIVORS.
HEY THERE! NEED HELP? I CAN GIVE YOU A RIDE IF YOU EVER GET TIRED OF FLOATING AROUND.

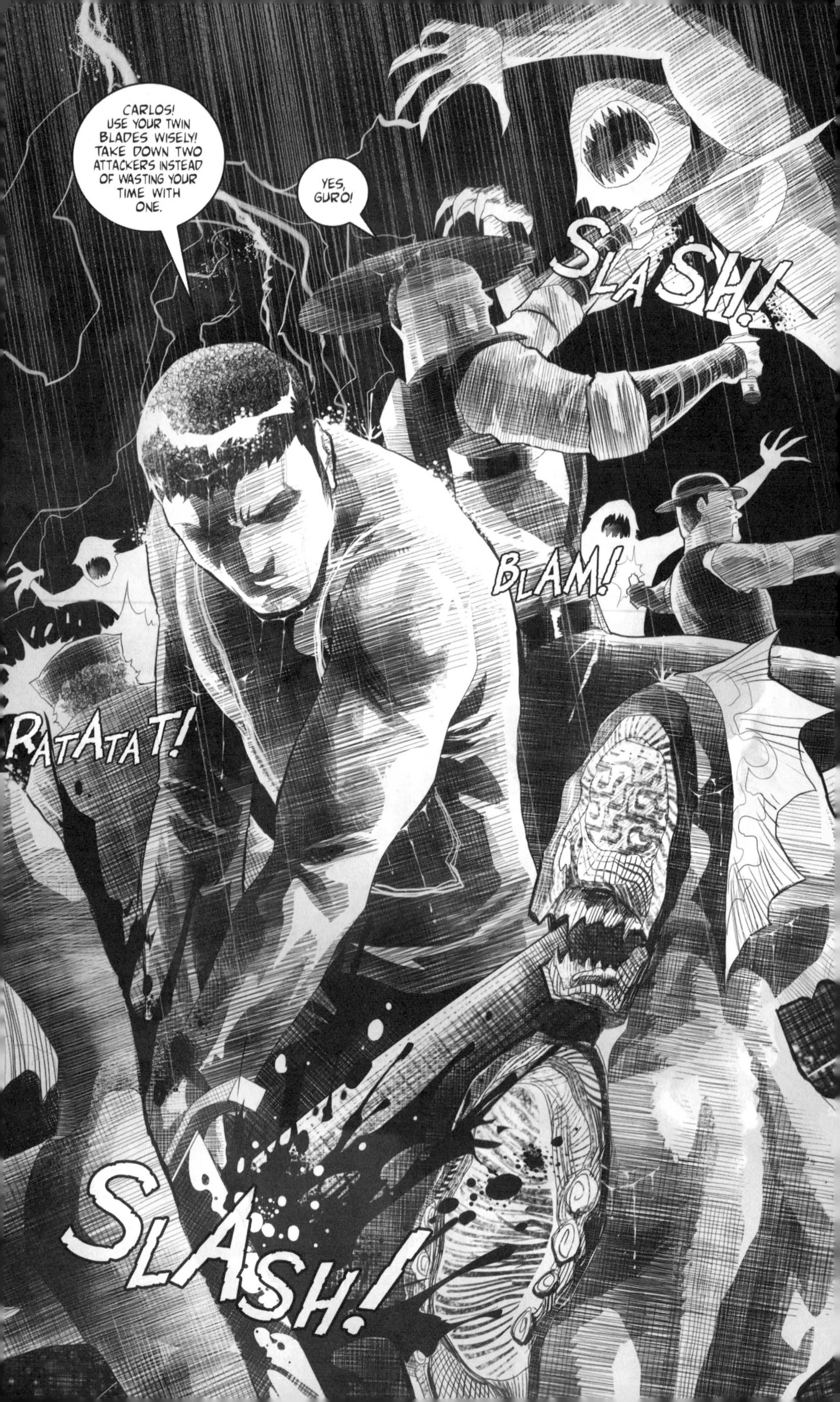

CARLOS! USE YOUR TWIN BLADES WISELY! TAKE DOWN TWO ATTACKERS INSTEAD OF WASTING YOUR TIME WITH ONE.
YES, GURO!
SLASH!
BLAM!
RATATAT!
SLASH!

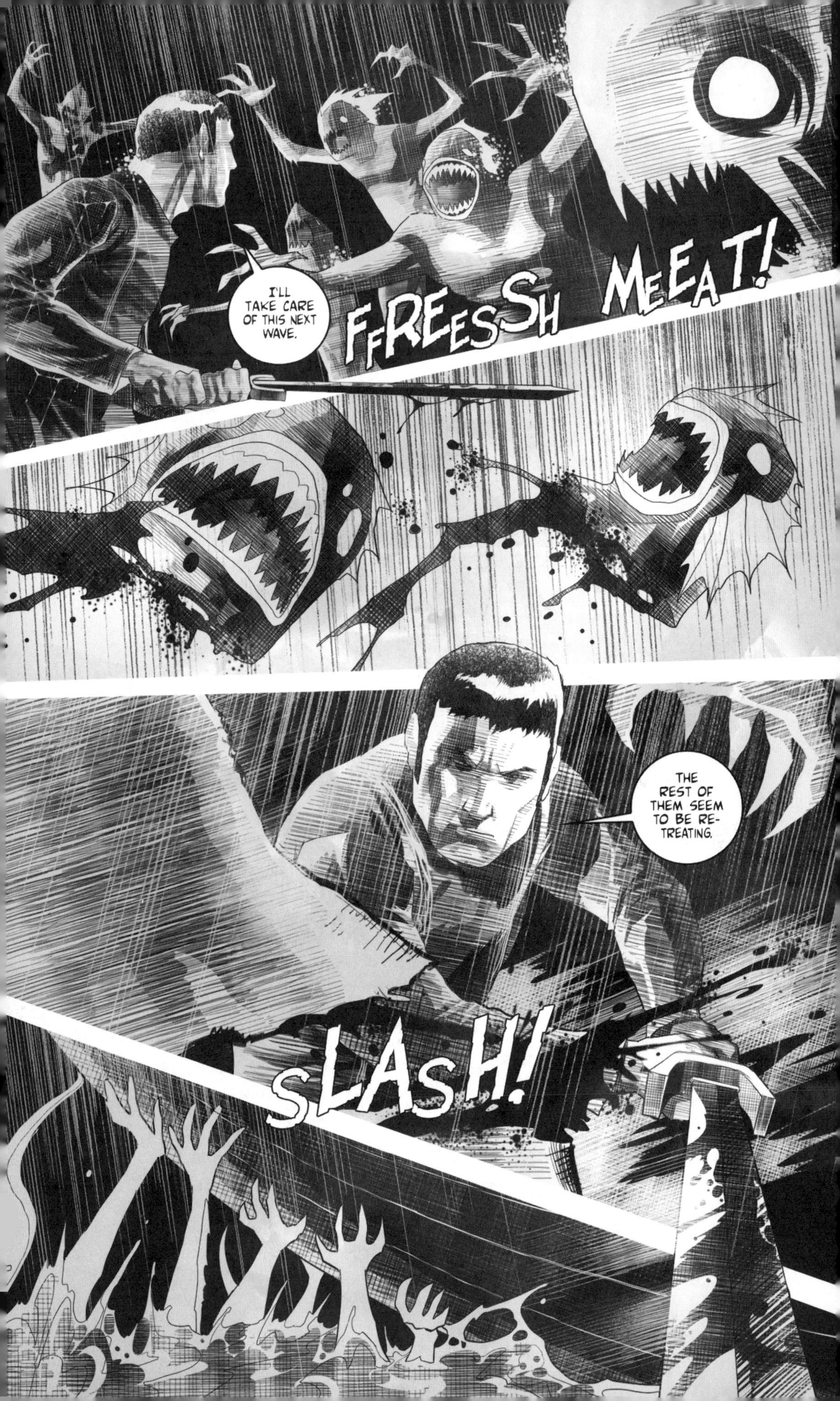
I'LL TAKE CARE OF THIS NEXT WAVE.
FFREESSH MEEAT!
THE REST OF THEM SEEM TO BE RE-TREATING.
SLASH!

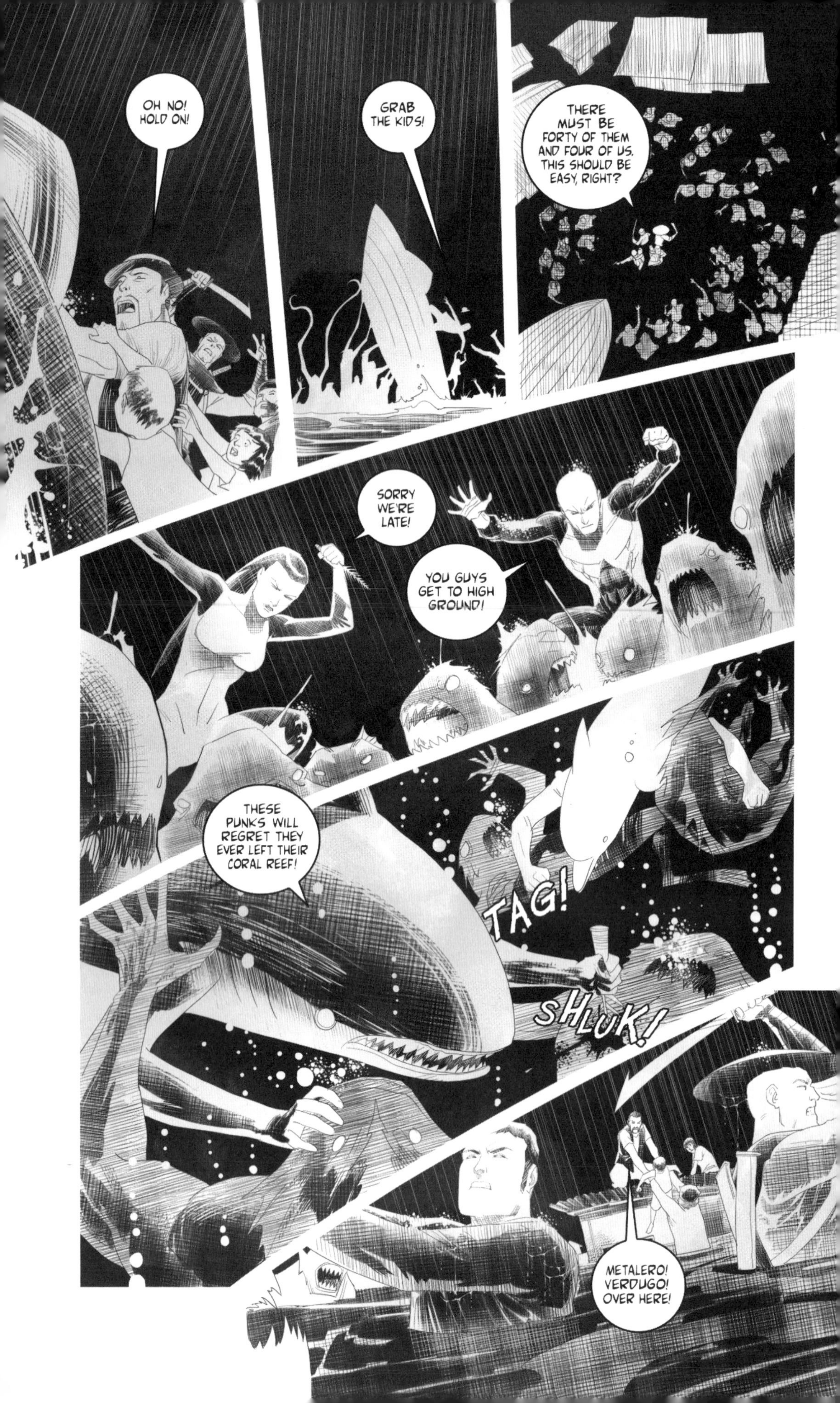
OH NO! HOLD ON!
GRAB THE KIDS!
THERE MUST BE FORTY OF THEM AND FOUR OF US. THIS SHOULD BE EASY, RIGHT?
SORRY WE'RE LATE!
YOU GUYS GET TO HIGH GROUND!
THESE PUNKS WILL REGRET THEY EVER LEFT THEIR CORAL REEF!
TAG!
SHLUK!
METALERO! VERDUGO! OVER HERE!

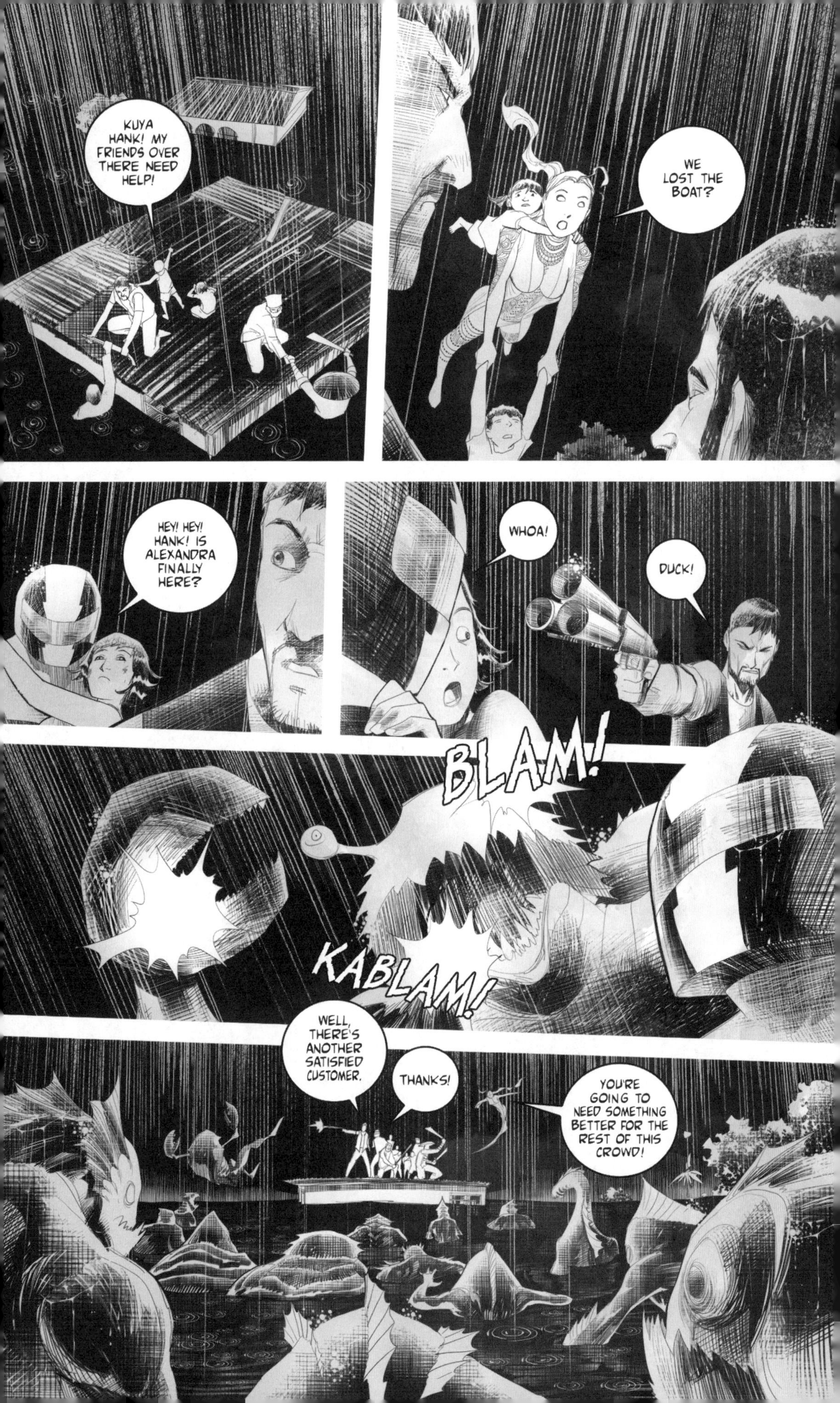
KUYA HANK! MY FRIENDS OVER THERE NEED HELP!
WE LOST THE BOAT?
HEY! HEY! HANK! IS ALEXANDRA FINALLY HERE?
WHOA!
DUCK!
BLAM!
KABLAM!
WELL, THERE'S ANOTHER SATISFIED CUSTOMER.
THANKS!
YOU'RE GOING TO NEED SOMETHING BETTER FOR THE REST OF THIS CROWD!

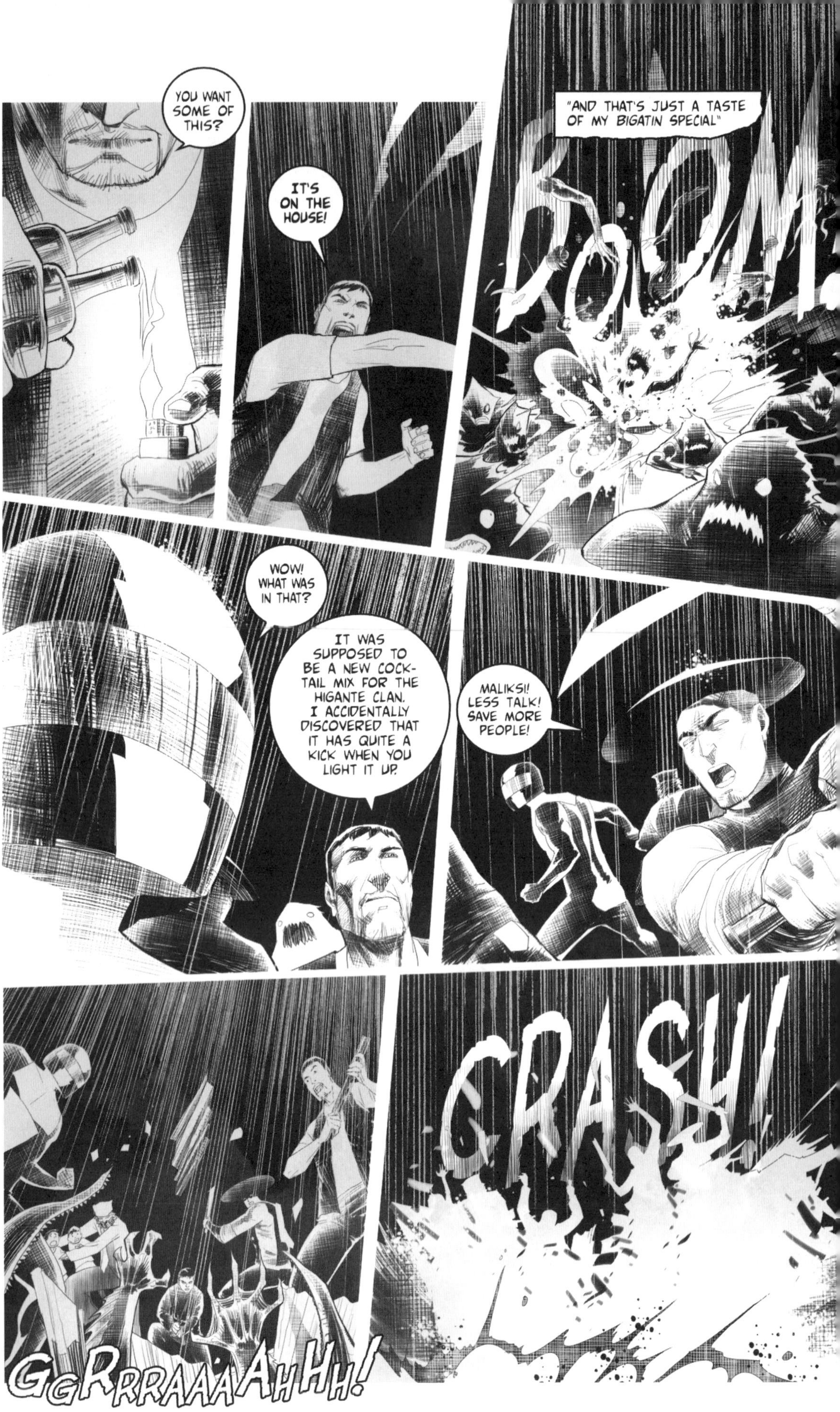
YOU WANT SOME OF THIS?
IT'S ON THE HOUSE!
"AND THAT'S JUST A TASTE OF MY BIGATIN SPECIAL"
BOOM!
WOW! WHAT WAS IN THAT?
IT WAS SUPPOSED TO BE A NEW COCK-TAIL MIX FOR THE HIGANTE CLAN. I ACCIDENTALLY DISCOVERED THAT IT HAS QUITE A KICK WHEN YOU LIGHT IT UP.
MALIKSI! LESS TALK! SAVE MORE PEOPLE!
GGRRRRAAAAHHHH!
CRASH!

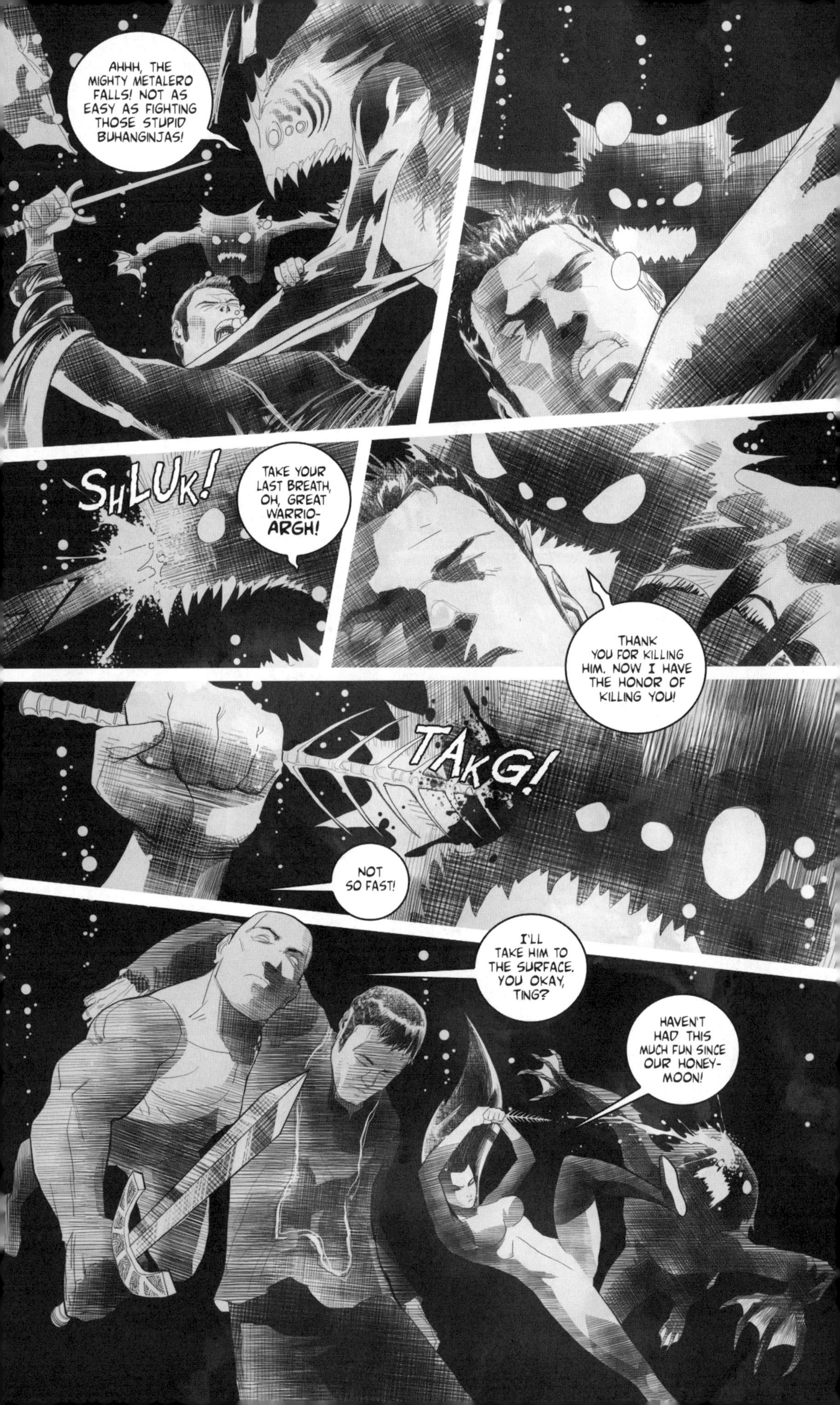

AHHH, THE MIGHTY METALERO FALLS! NOT AS EASY AS FIGHTING THOSE STUPID BUHANGINJAS!
SHLUK!
TAKE YOUR LAST BREATH, OH, GREAT WARRIO-ARGH!
THANK YOU FOR KILLING HIM. NOW I HAVE THE HONOR OF KILLING YOU!
TAKG!
NOT SO FAST!
I'LL TAKE HIM TO THE SURFACE. YOU OKAY, TING?
HAVEN'T HAD THIS MUCH FUN SINCE OUR HONEY-MOON!

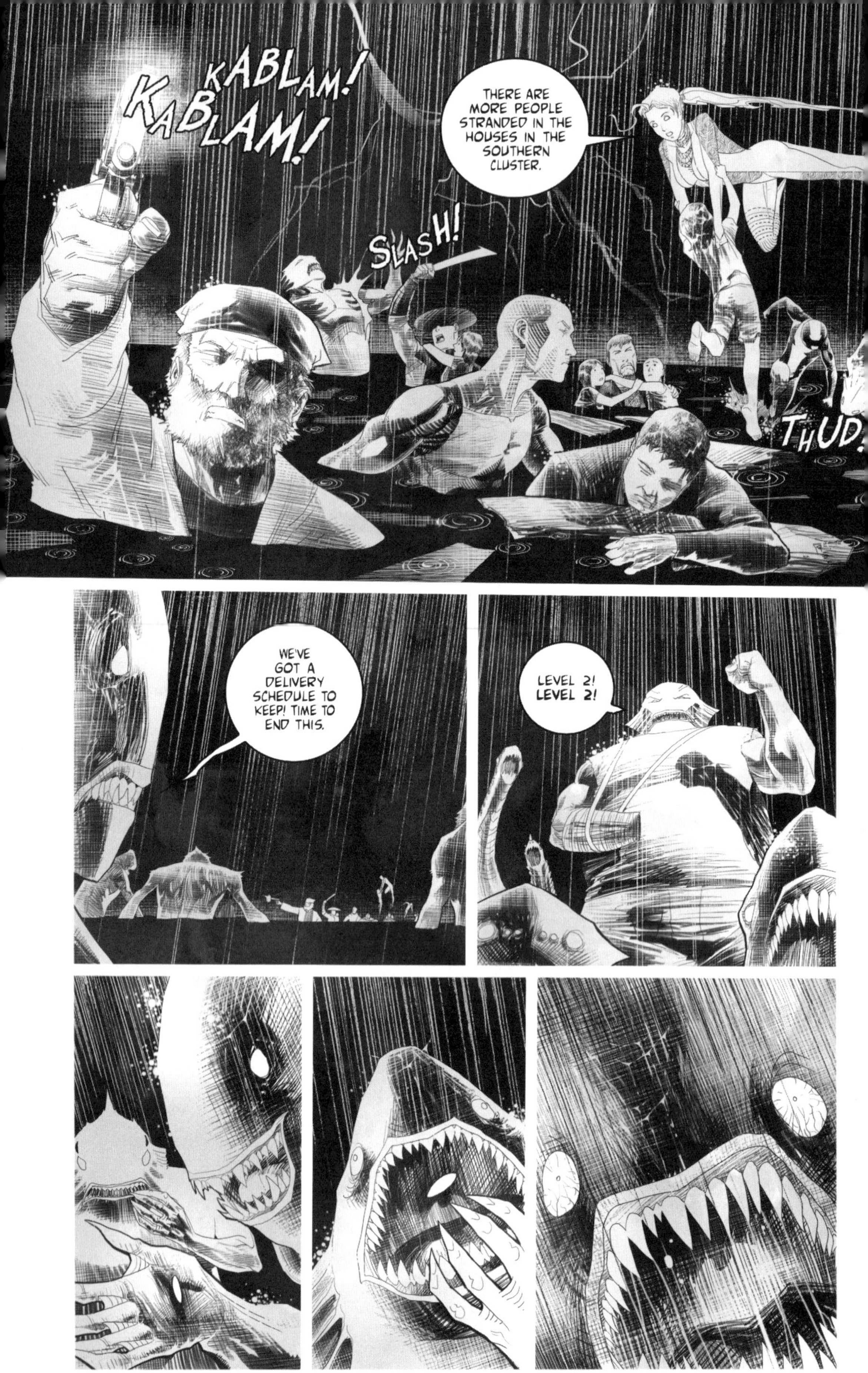
KABLAM!
KABLAM!
THERE ARE MORE PEOPLE STRANDED IN THE HOUSES IN THE SOUTHERN CLUSTER.
SLASH!
THUD.
WE'VE GOT A DELIVERY SCHEDULE TO KEEP! TIME TO END THIS.
LEVEL 2! LEVEL 2!

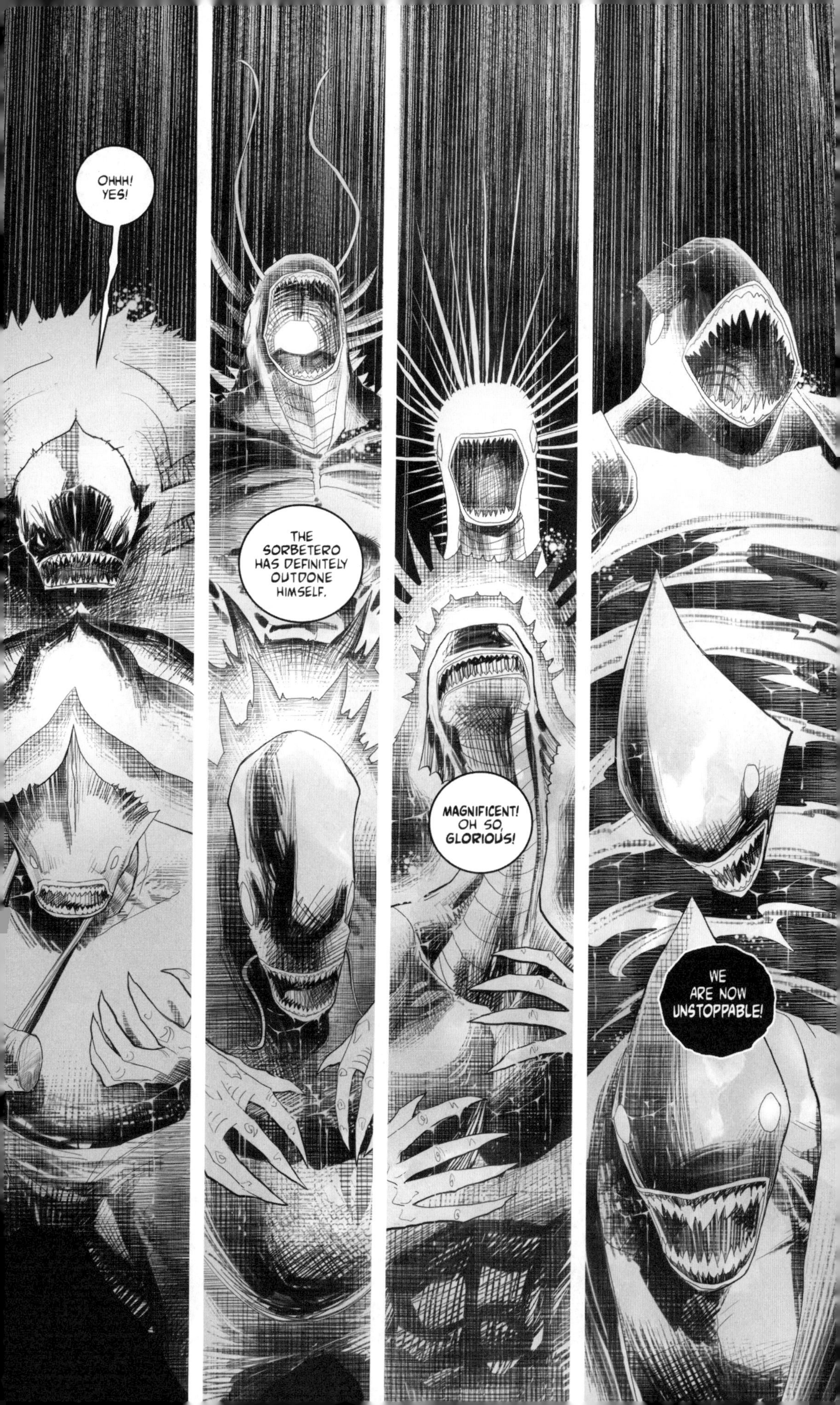
OHHH! YES!
THE SORBETERO HAS DEFINITELY OUTDONE HIMSELF.
MAGNIFICENT! OH SO, GLORIOUS!
WE ARE NOW UNSTOPPABLE!

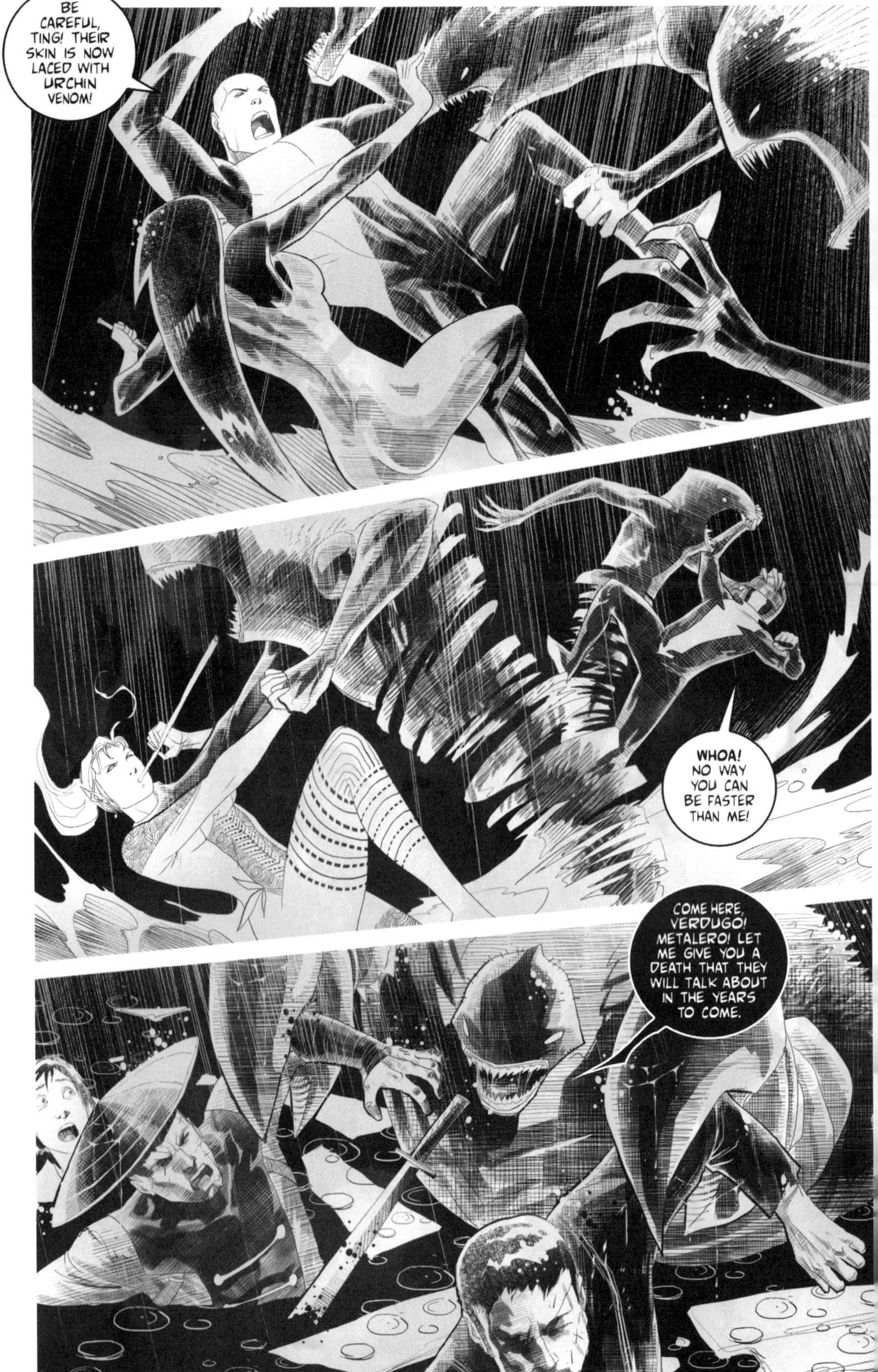
BE CAREFUL, TING! THEIR SKIN IS NOW LACED WITH URCHIN VENOM!
WHOA! NO WAY YOU CAN BE FASTER THAN ME!
COME HERE, VERDUGO! METALERO! LET ME GIVE YOU A DEATH THAT THEY WILL TALK ABOUT IN THE YEARS TO COME.

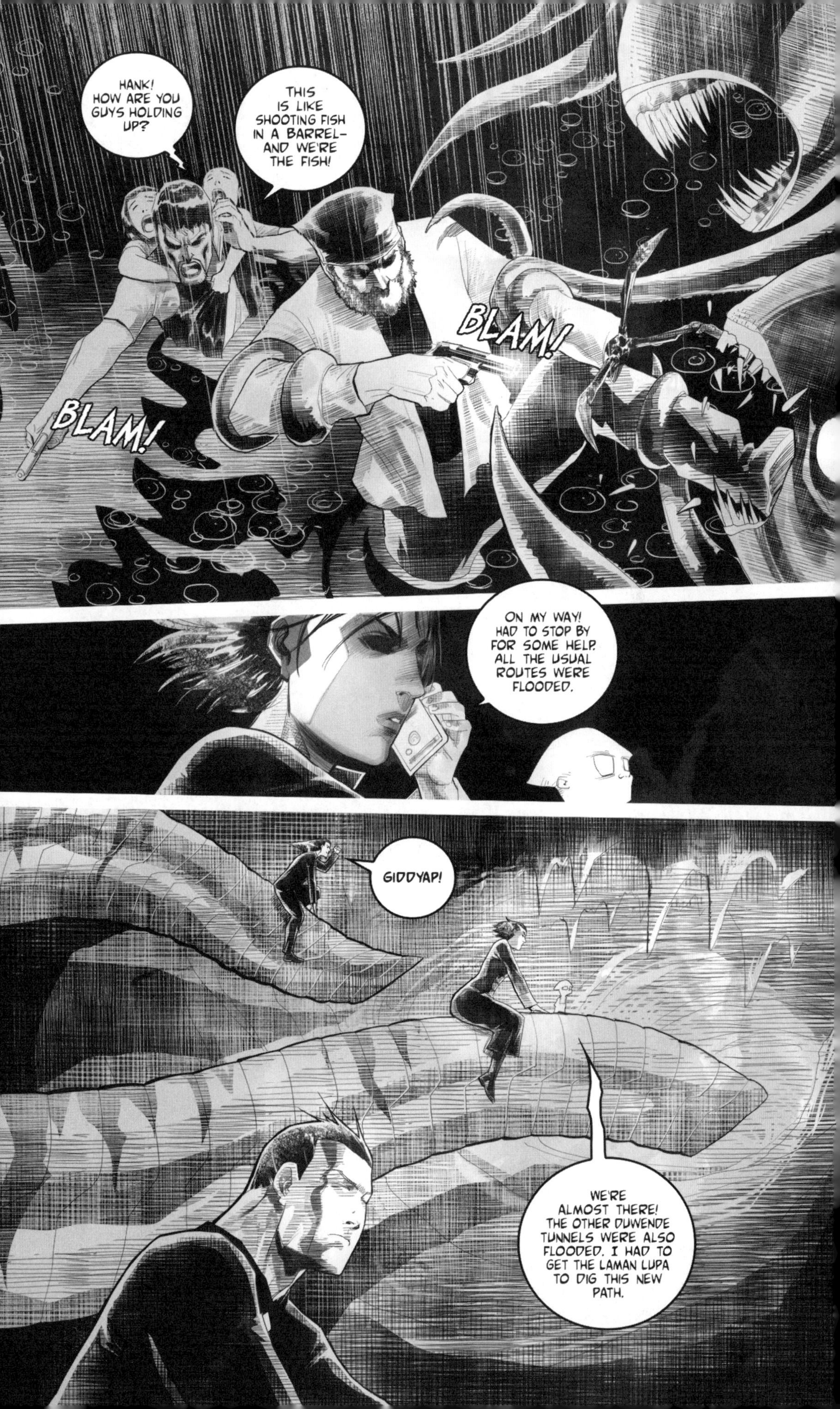
HANK! HOW ARE YOU GUYS HOLDING UP?
THIS IS LIKE SHOOTING FISH IN A BARREL-AND WE'RE THE FISH!
BLAM!
BLAM!
ON MY WAY! HAD TO STOP BY FOR SOME HELP. ALL THE USUAL ROUTES WERE FLOODED.
GIDDYAP!
WE'RE ALMOST THERE! THE OTHER DUWENDE TUNNELS WERE ALSO FLOODED. I HAD TO GET THE LAMAN LUPA TO DIG THIS NEW PATH.

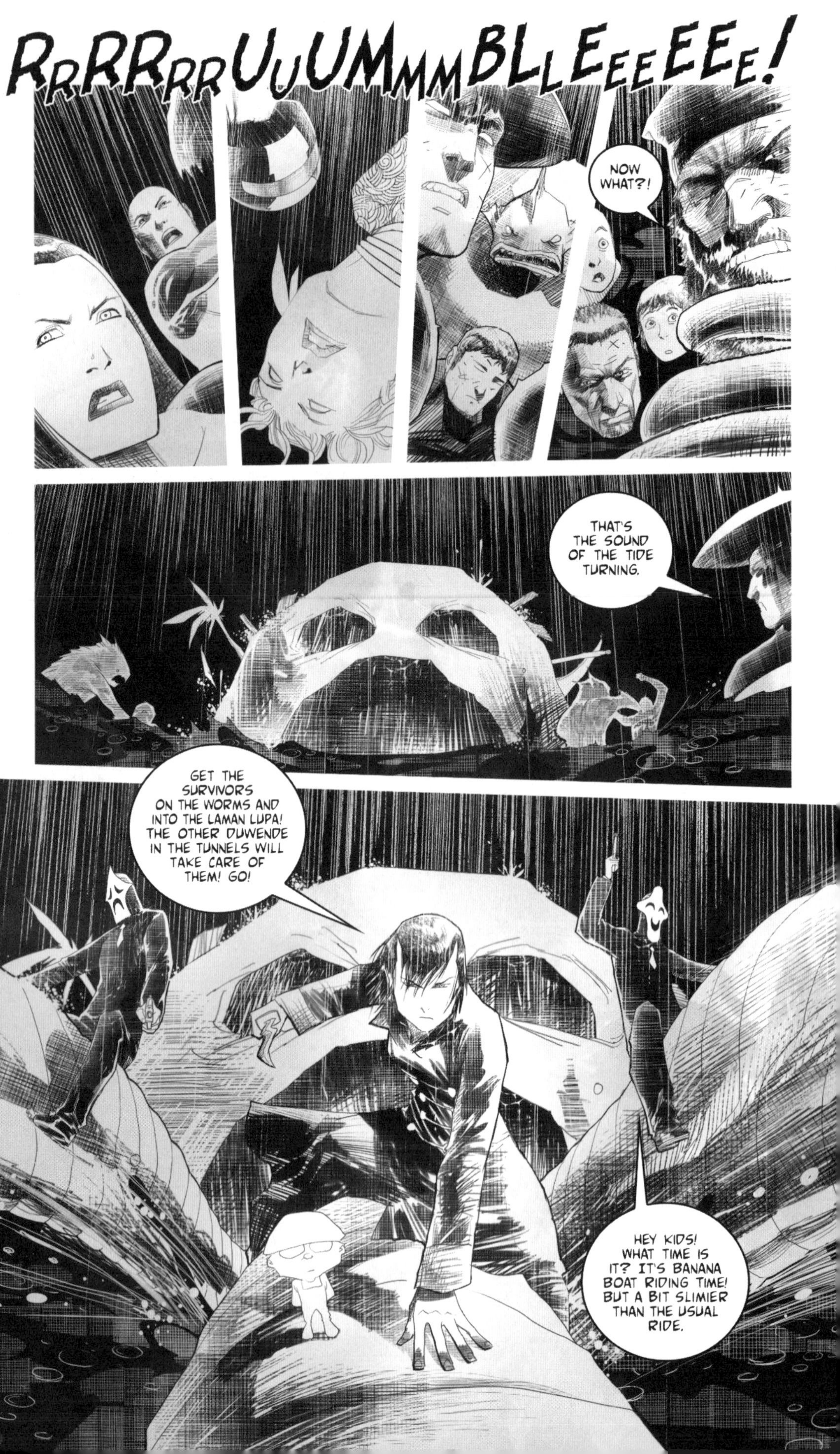
RRRRRRUUUMMMBLLEEEEEE!
NOW WHAT?!
THAT'S THE SOUND OF THE TIDE TURNING.
GET THE SURVIVORS ON THE WORMS AND INTO THE LAMAN LUPA! THE OTHER DUWENDE IN THE TUNNELS WILL TAKE CARE OF THEM! GO!
HEY KIDS! WHAT TIME IS IT? IT'S BANANA BOAT RIDING TIME! BUT A BIT SLIMIER THAN THE USUAL RIDE.

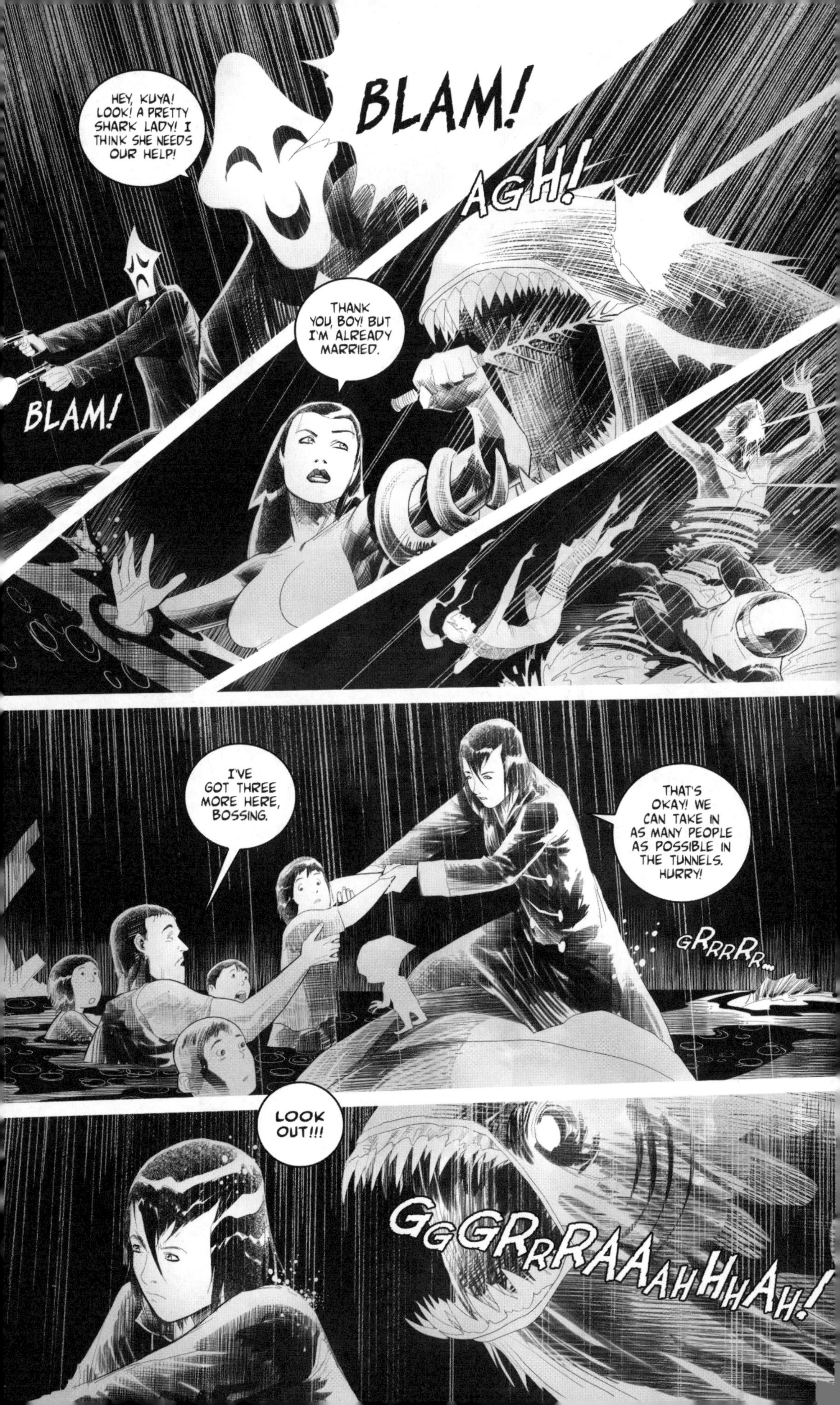
HEY, KUYA! LOOK! A PRETTY SHARK LADY! I THINK SHE NEEDS OUR HELP!
BLAM!
BLAM!
AGH!
THANK YOU, BOY! BUT I'M ALREADY MARRIED.
I'VE GOT THREE MORE HERE, BOSSING.
THAT'S OKAY! WE CAN TAKE IN AS MANY PEOPLE AS POSSIBLE IN THE TUNNELS. HURRY!
GRRRRR...
LOOK OUT!!!
GGGRRRRAAAAHHHAH!

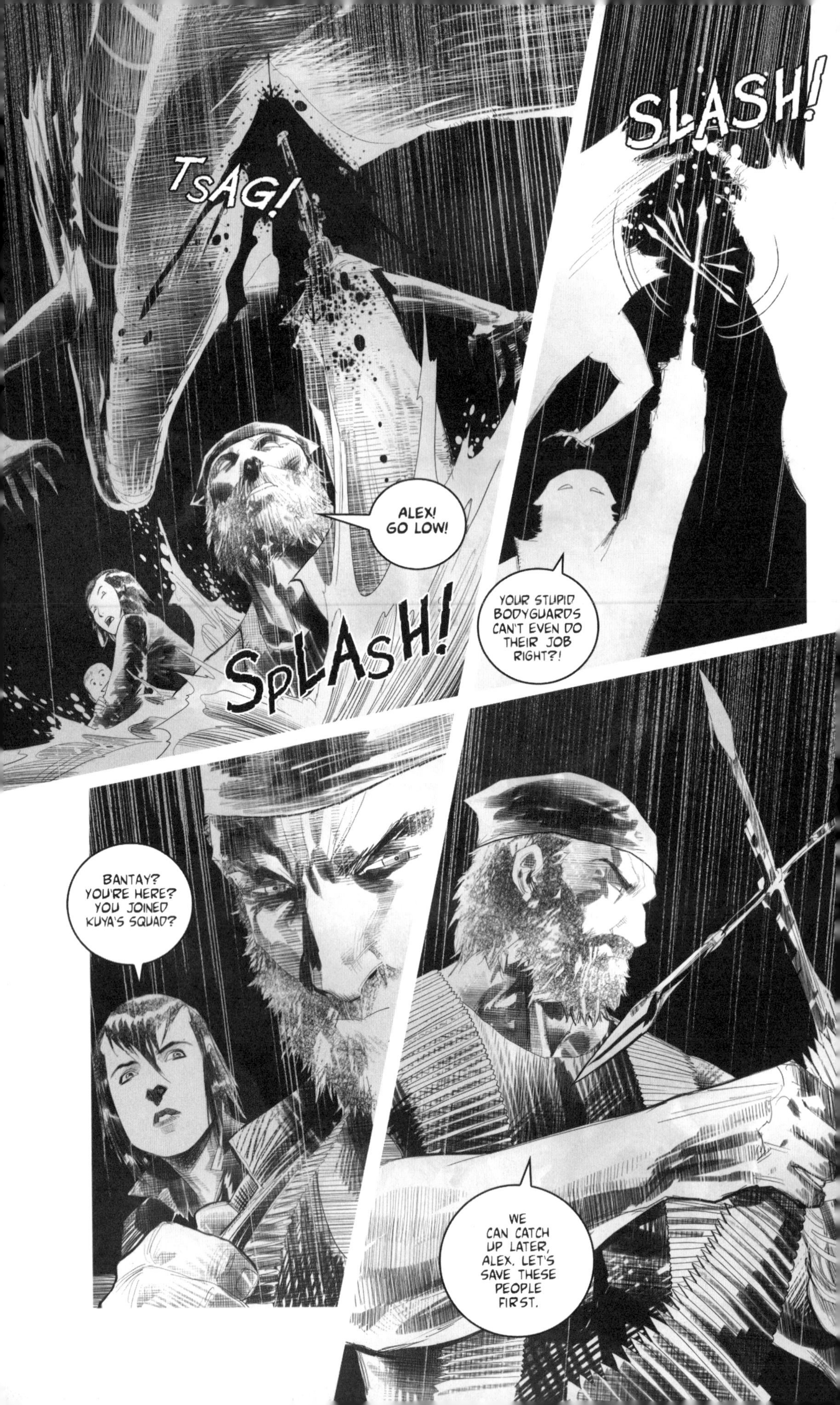
TSAG!
SLASH!
ALEX! GO LOW!
SPLASH!
YOUR STUPID BODYGUARDS CAN'T EVEN DO THEIR JOB RIGHT?!
BANTAY? YOU'RE HERE? YOU JOINED KUYA'S SQUAD?
WE CAN CATCH UP LATER, ALEX. LET'S SAVE THESE PEOPLE FIRST.

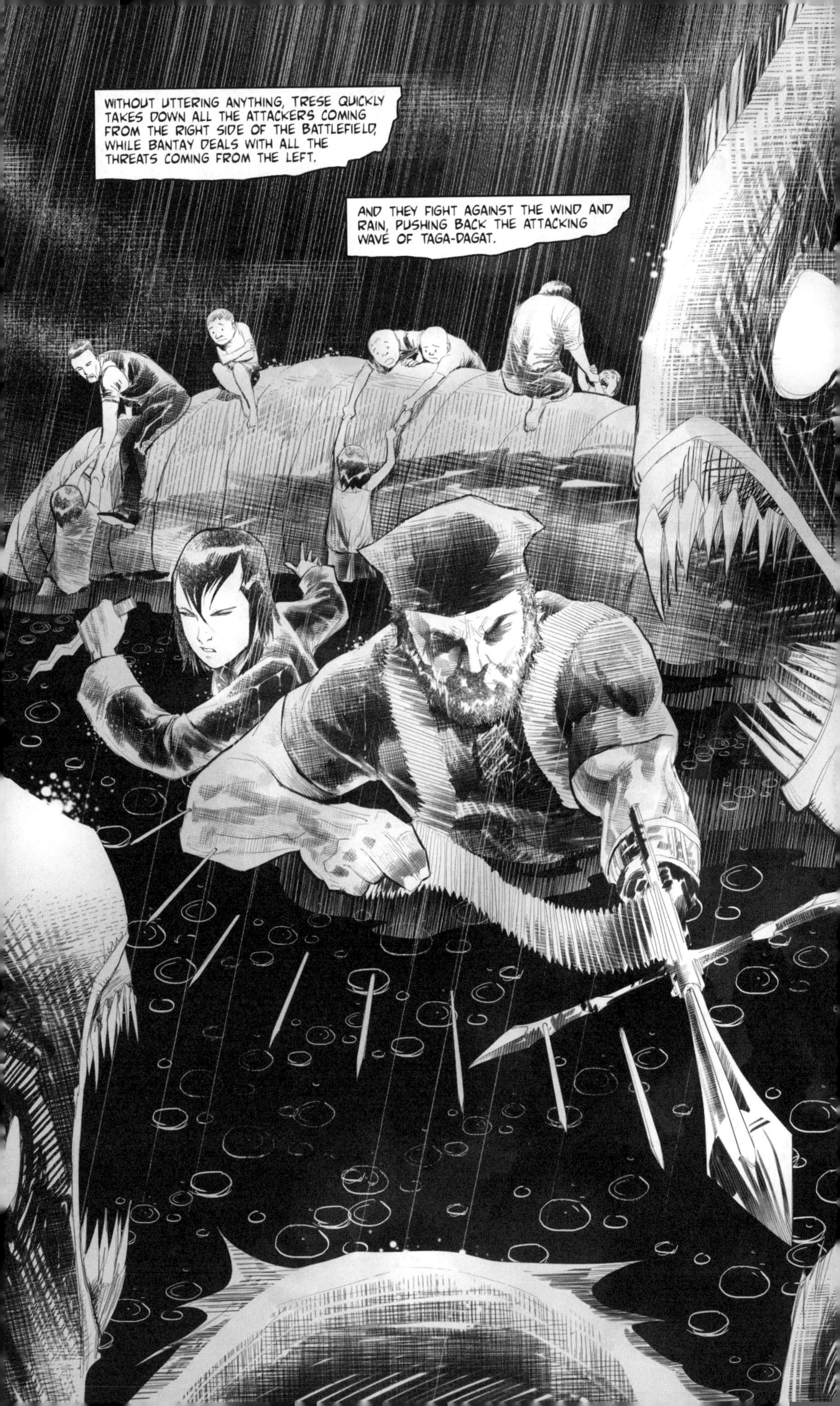
WITHOUT UTTERING ANYTHING, TRESE QUICKLY TAKES DOWN ALL THE ATTACKERS COMING FROM THE RIGHT SIDE OF THE BATTLEFIELD, WHILE BANTAY DEALS WITH ALL THE THREATS COMING FROM THE LEFT.
AND THEY FIGHT AGAINST THE WIND AND RAIN, PUSHING BACK THE ATTACKING WAVE OF TAGA-DAGAT.

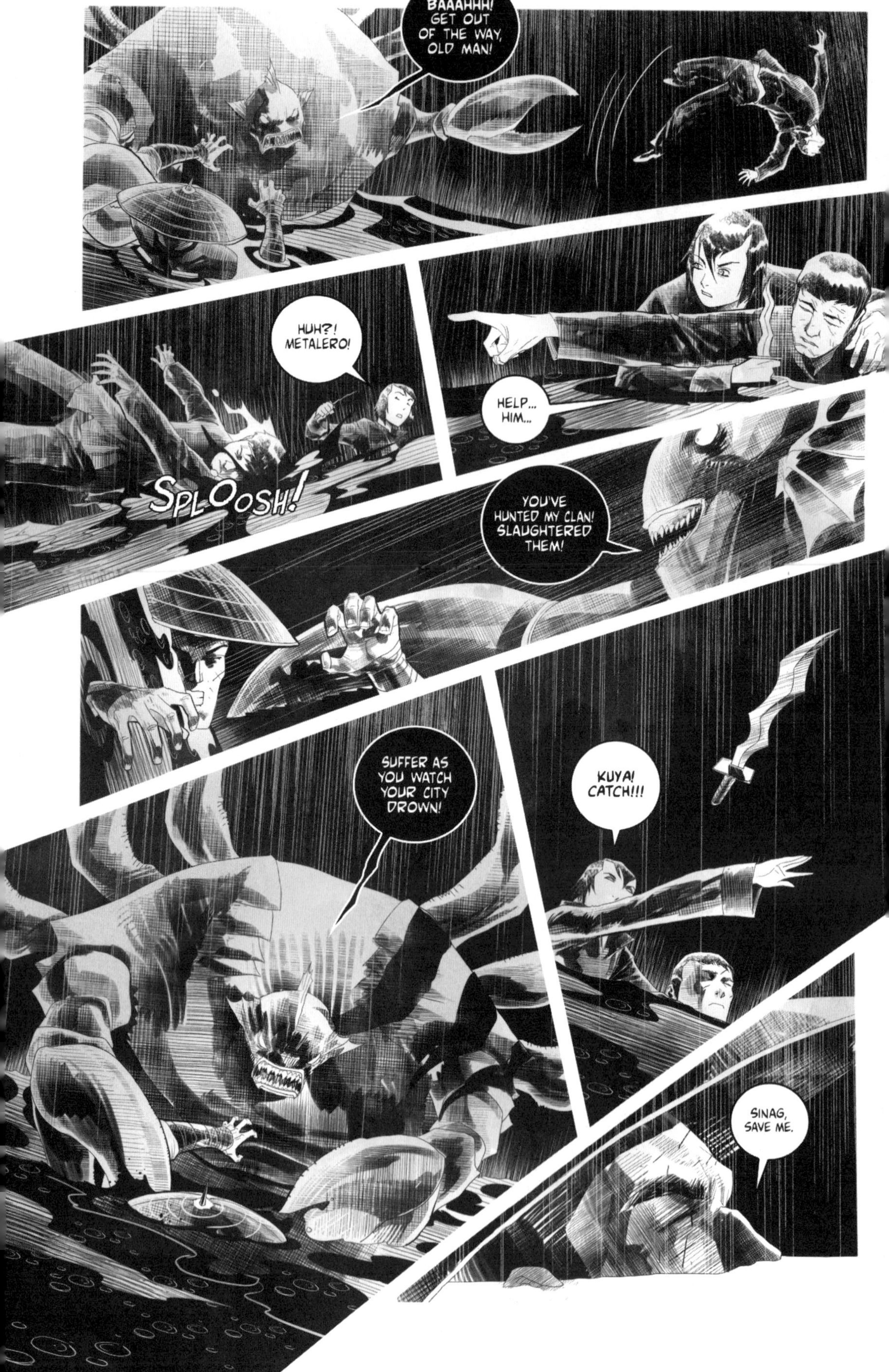
BAAAHHH! GET OUT OF THE WAY, OLD MAN!
HUH?! METALERO!
SPLOOSH!
HELP... HIM...
YOU'VE HUNTED MY CLAN! SLAUGHTERED THEM!
SUFFER AS YOU WATCH YOUR CITY DROWN!
KUYA! CATCH!!!
SINAG, SAVE ME.

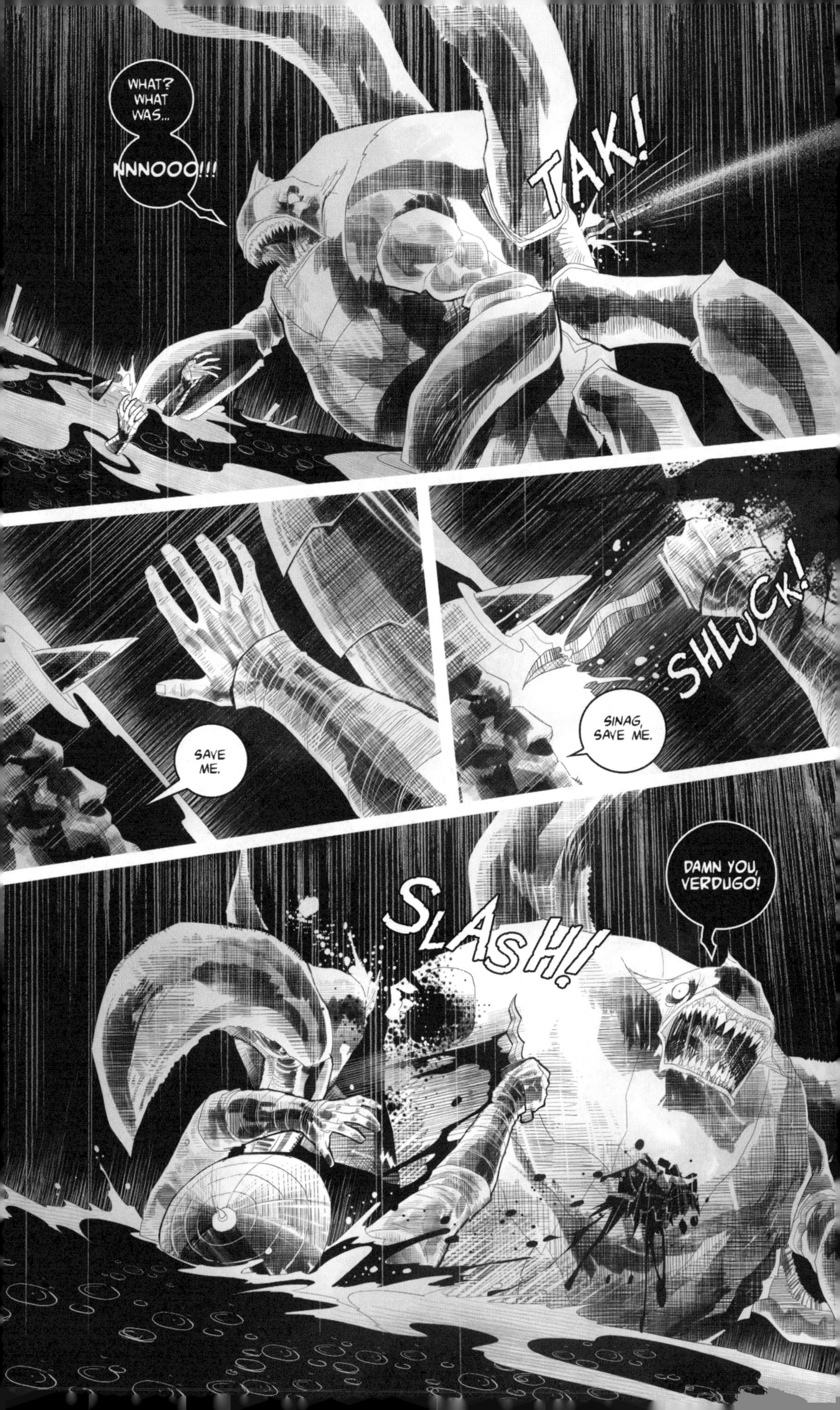
WHAT? WHAT WAS...
NNNOOO!!!
TAK!
SAVE ME.
SHLUCK!
SINAG, SAVE ME.
SLASH!
DAMN YOU, VERDUGO!

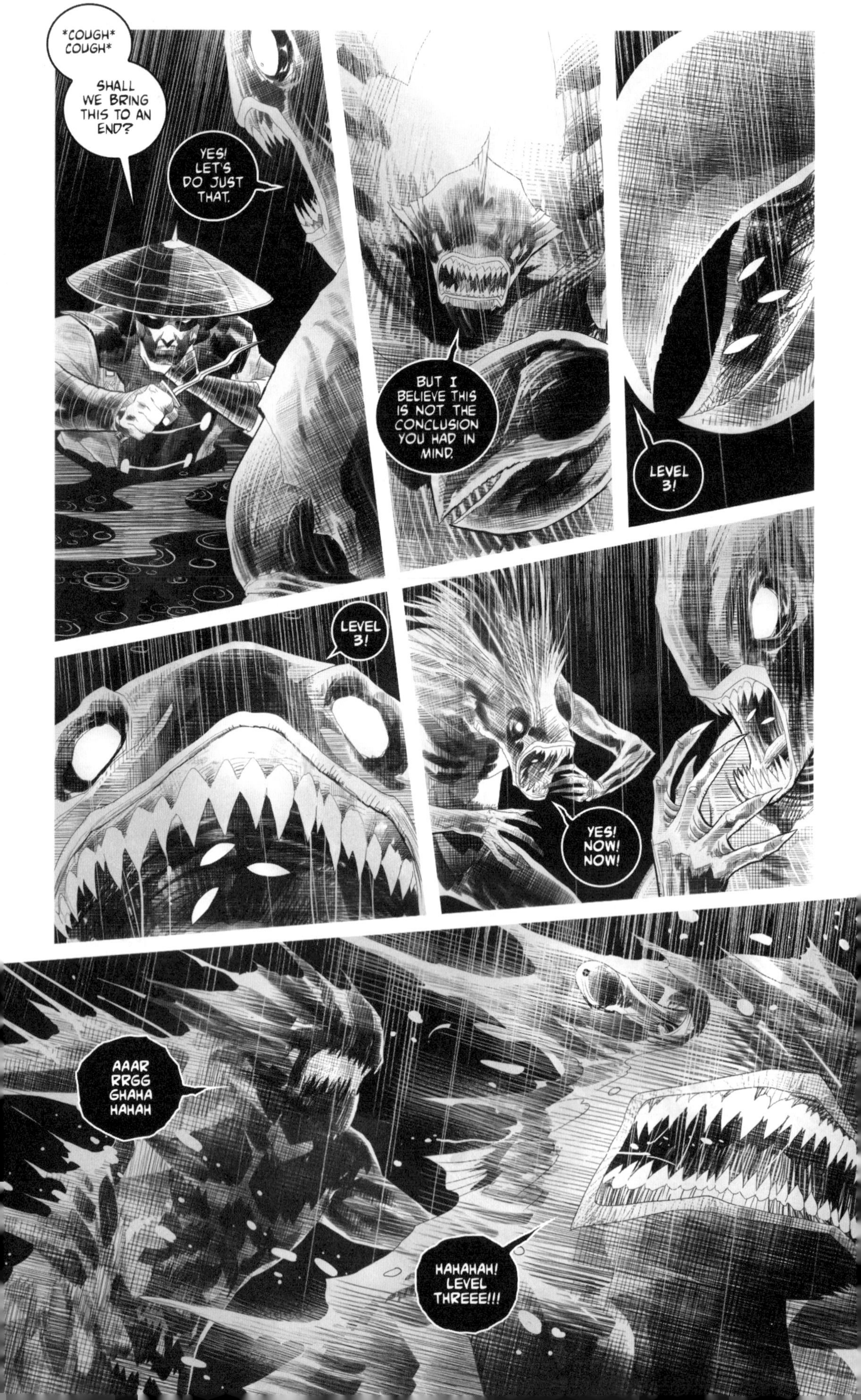
COUGH COUGH*
SHALL WE BRING THIS TO AN END?
YES! LET'S DO JUST THAT.
BUT I BELIEVE THIS IS NOT THE CONCLUSION YOU HAD IN MIND.
LEVEL 3!
LEVEL 3!
YES! NOW! NOW!
AAAR RRGG GHAHA HAHAH
HAHAHAH! LEVEL THREEE!!!

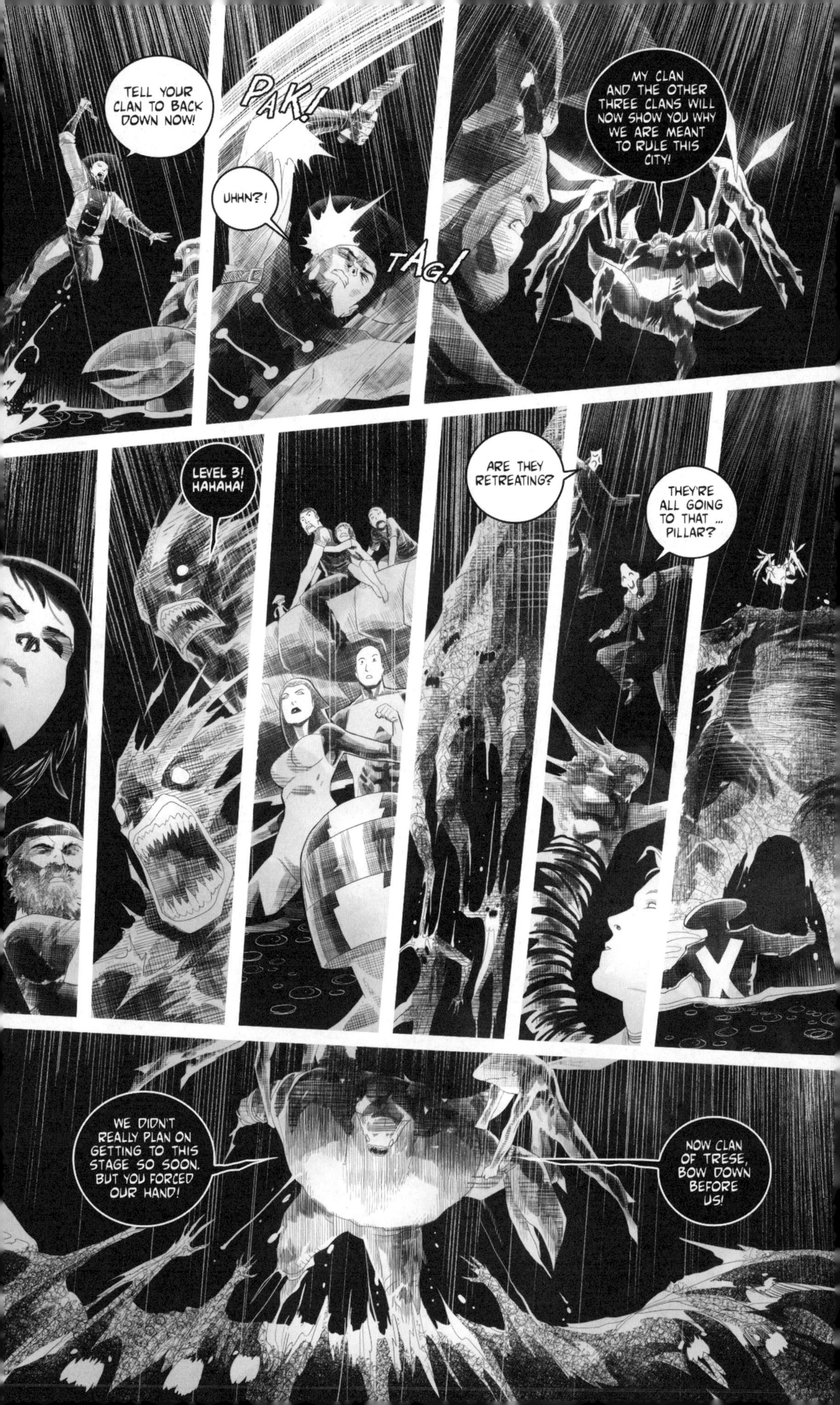
TELL YOUR CLAN TO BACK DOWN NOW!
PAK!
UHHN?!
TAG!
MY CLAN AND THE OTHER THREE CLANS WILL NOW SHOW YOU WHY WE ARE MEANT TO RULE THIS CITY!
LEVEL 3! HAHAHA!
ARE THEY RETREATING?
THEY'RE ALL GOING TO THAT ... PILLAR?
WE DIDN'T REALLY PLAN ON GETTING TO THIS STAGE SO SOON. BUT YOU FORCED OUR HAND!
NOW CLAN OF TRESE, BOW DOWN BEFORE US!

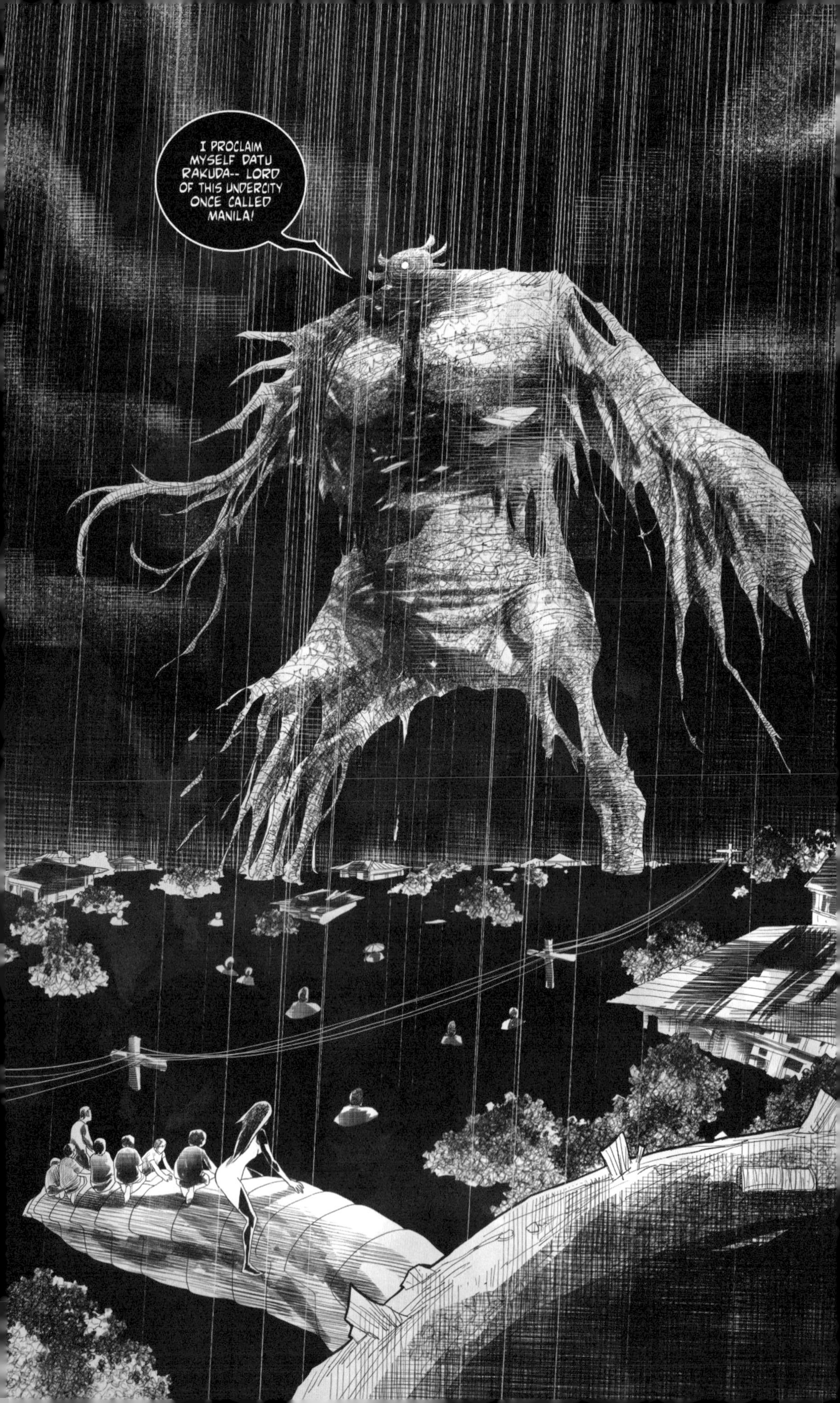
I PROCLAIM MYSELF DATU RAKUDA-- LORD OF THIS UNDERCITY ONCE CALLED MANILA!

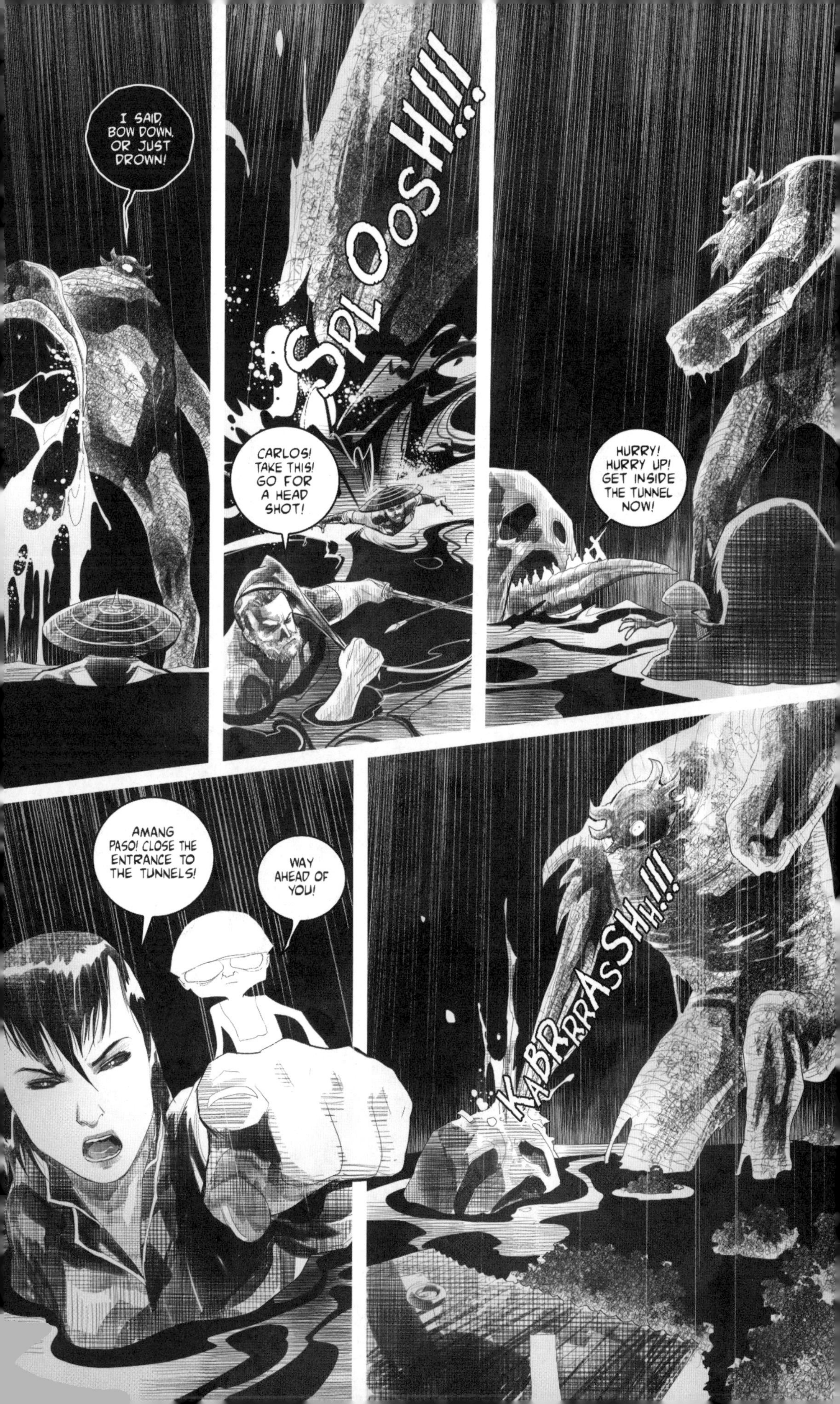

I SAID, BOW DOWN, OR JUST DROWN!
SPLOOSH!!!!
CARLOS! TAKE THIS! GO FOR A HEAD SHOT!
HURRY! HURRY UP! GET INSIDE THE TUNNEL NOW!
AMANG PASO! CLOSE THE ENTRANCE TO THE TUNNELS!
WAY AHEAD OF YOU!
KABRRRASSHH!!!

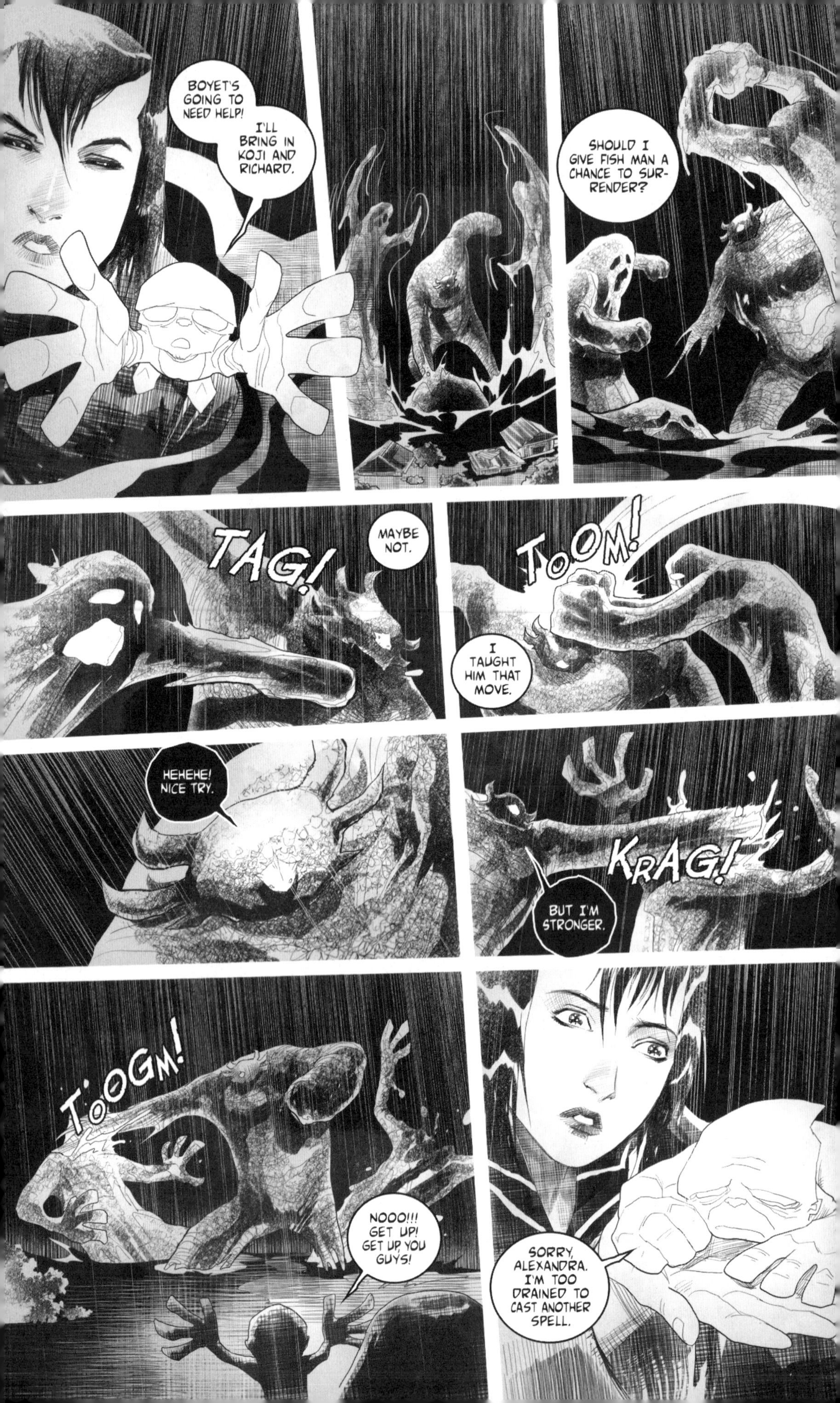
BOYET'S GOING TO NEED HELP!
I'LL BRING IN KOJI AND RICHARD.
SHOULD I GIVE FISH MAN A CHANCE TO SUR-RENDER?
TAG!
MAYBE NOT.
TOOM!
I TAUGHT HIM THAT MOVE.
HEHEHE! NICE TRY.
KRAG!
BUT I'M STRONGER.
TOOGM!
NOOO!!! GET UP! GET UP, YOU GUYS!
SORRY, ALEXANDRA. I'M TOO DRAINED TO CAST ANOTHER SPELL.

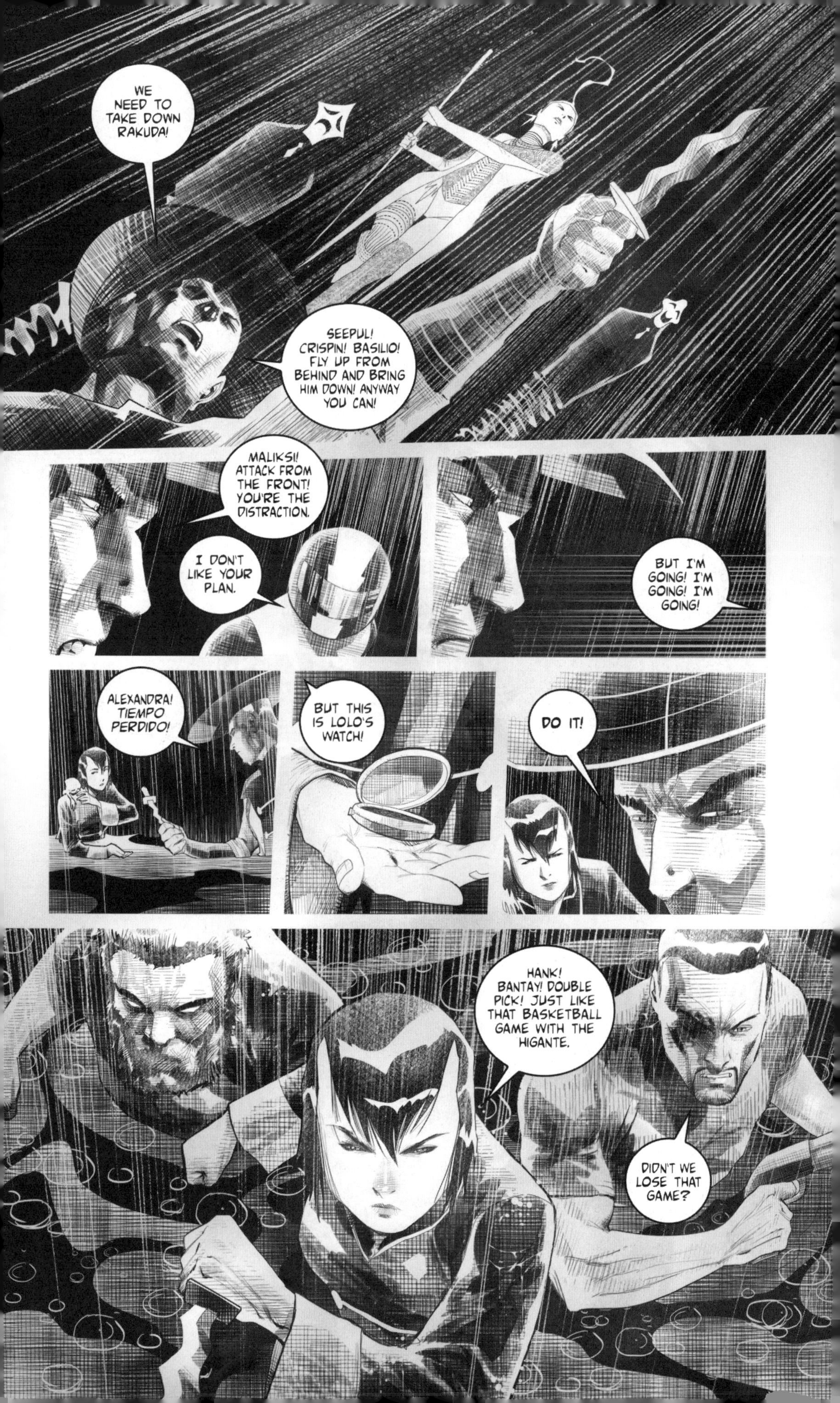

WE NEED TO TAKE DOWN RAKUDA!
SEEPUL! CRISPIN! BASILIO! FLY UP FROM BEHIND AND BRING HIM DOWN! ANYWAY YOU CAN!
MALIKSI! ATTACK FROM THE FRONT! YOU'RE THE DISTRACTION.
I DON'T LIKE YOUR PLAN.
BUT I'M GOING! I'M GOING! I'M GOING!
ALEXANDRA! TIEMPO PERDIDO!
BUT THIS IS LOLO'S WATCH!
DO IT!
HANK! BANTAY! DOUBLE PICK! JUST LIKE THAT BASKETBALL GAME WITH THE HIGANTE.
DIDN'T WE LOSE THAT GAME?

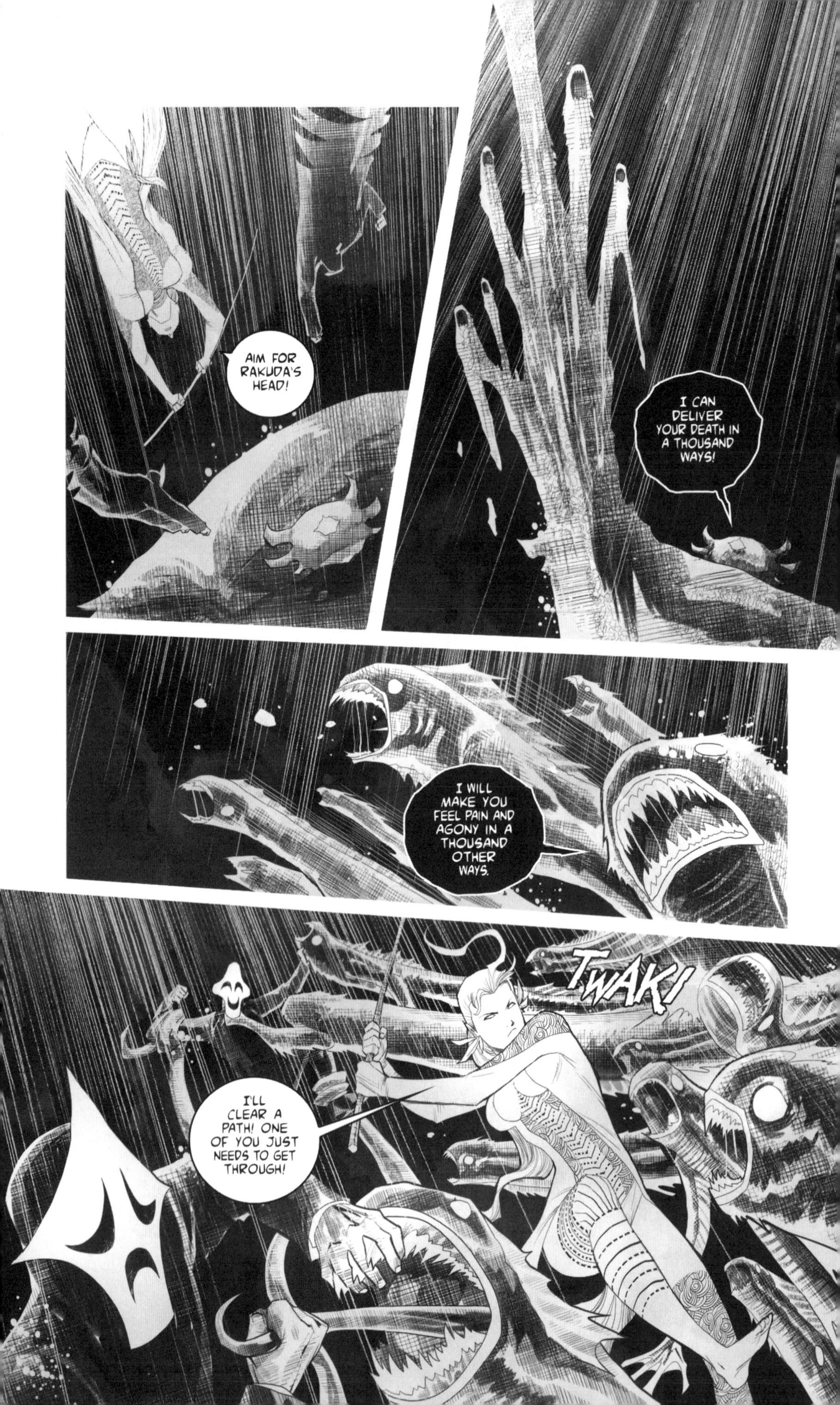
AIM FOR RAKUDA'S HEAD!
I CAN DELIVER YOUR DEATH IN A THOUSAND WAYS!
I WILL MAKE YOU FEEL PAIN AND AGONY IN A THOUSAND OTHER WAYS.
TWAK!
I'LL CLEAR A PATH! ONE OF YOU JUST NEEDS TO GET THROUGH!

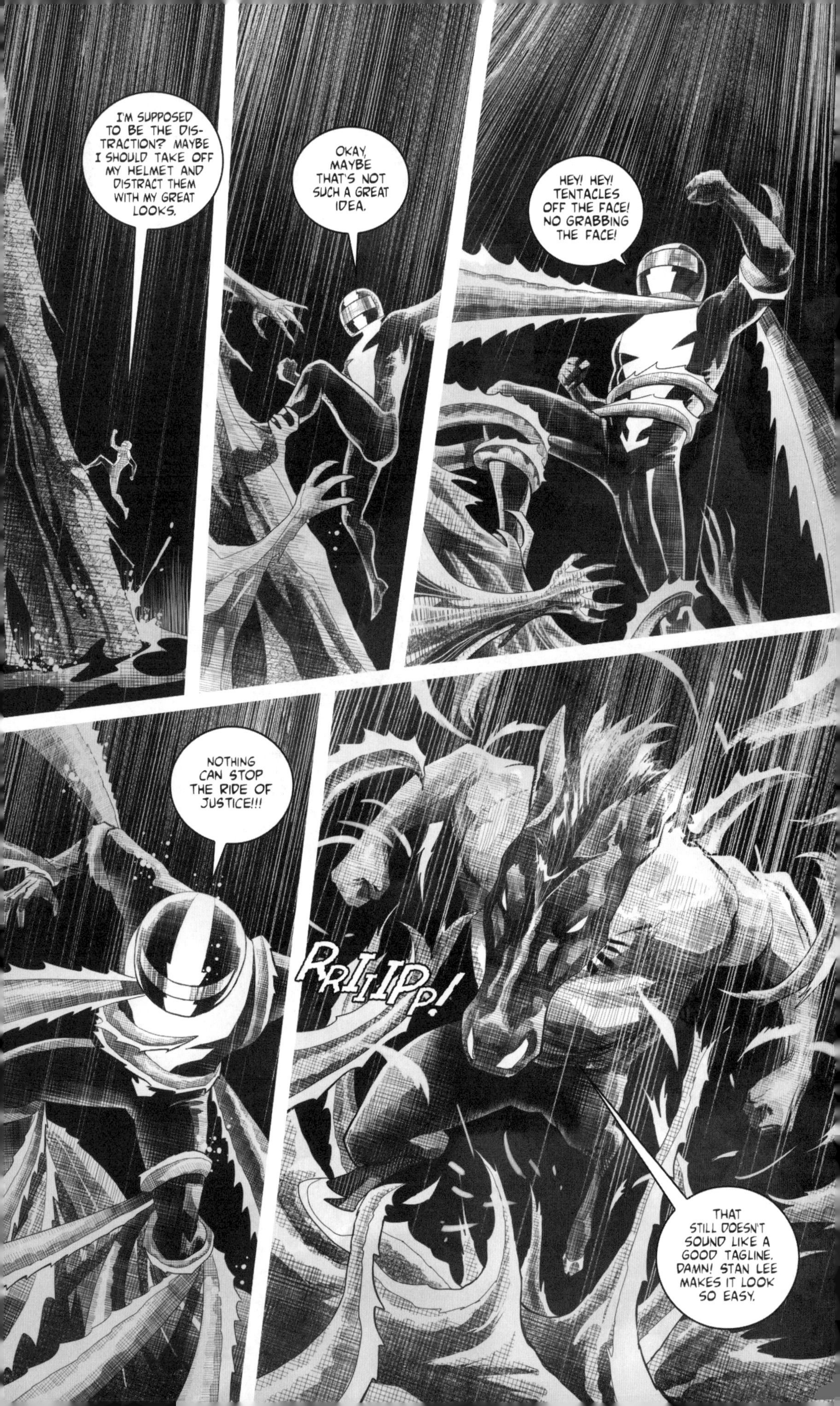
I'M SUPPOSED TO BE THE DIS-TRACTION? MAYBE I SHOULD TAKE OFF MY HELMET AND DISTRACT THEM WITH MY GREAT LOOKS.
OKAY, MAYBE THAT'S NOT SUCH A GREAT IDEA.
HEY! HEY! TENTACLES OFF THE FACE! NO GRABBING THE FACE!
NOTHING CAN STOP THE RIDE OF JUSTICE!!!
RRIIIPPP!
THAT STILL DOESN'T SOUND LIKE A GOOD TAGLINE. DAMN! STAN LEE MAKES IT LOOK SO EASY.

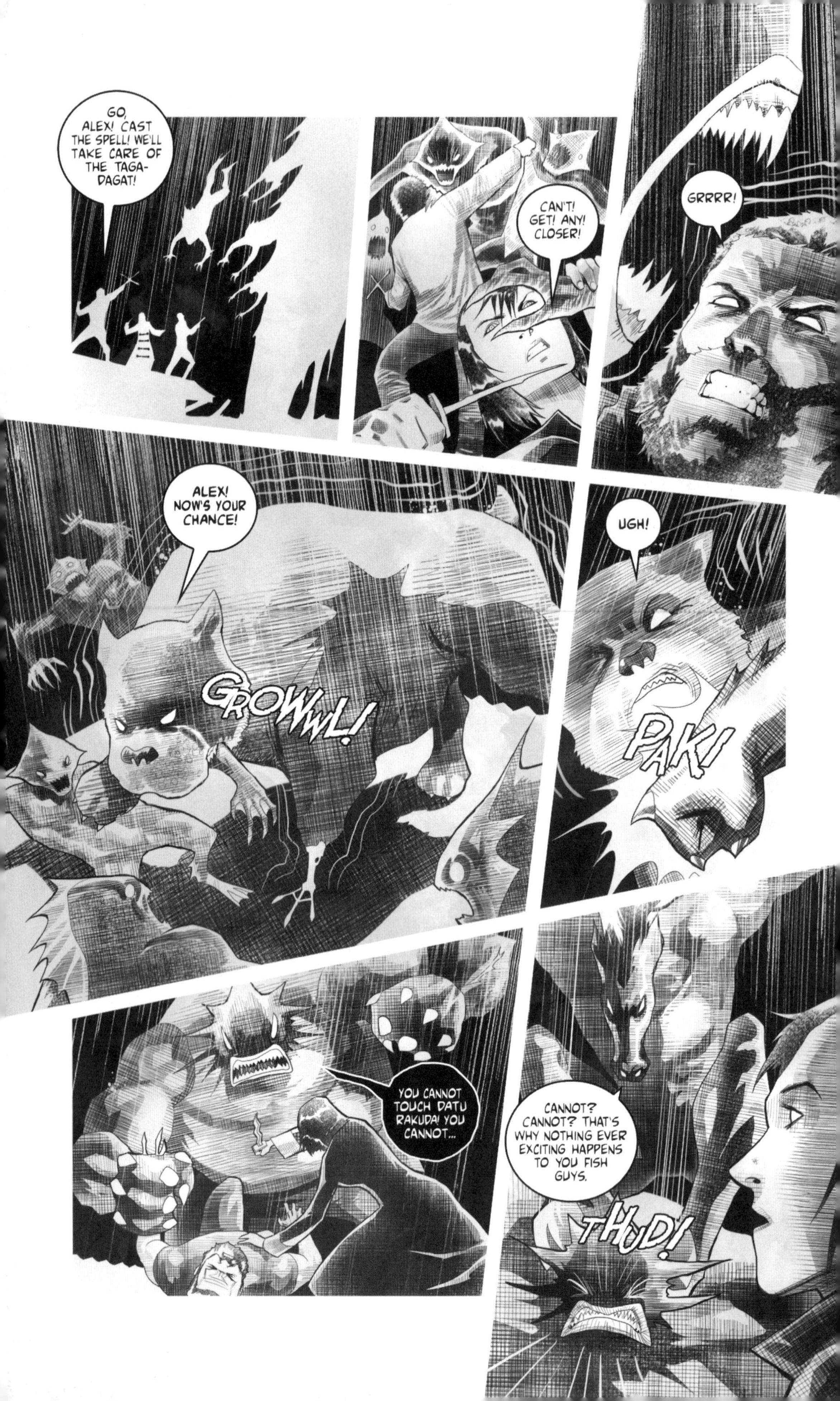
GO, ALEX! CAST THE SPELL! WE'LL TAKE CARE OF THE TAGA-DAGAT!
CAN'T! GET! ANY! CLOSER!
GRRRR!
ALEX! NOW'S YOUR CHANCE!
GROWWL!
UGH!
PAK!
YOU CANNOT TOUCH DATU RAKUDA! YOU CANNOT...
CANNOT? CANNOT? THAT'S WHY NOTHING EVER EXCITING HAPPENS TO YOU FISH GUYS.
THUD!

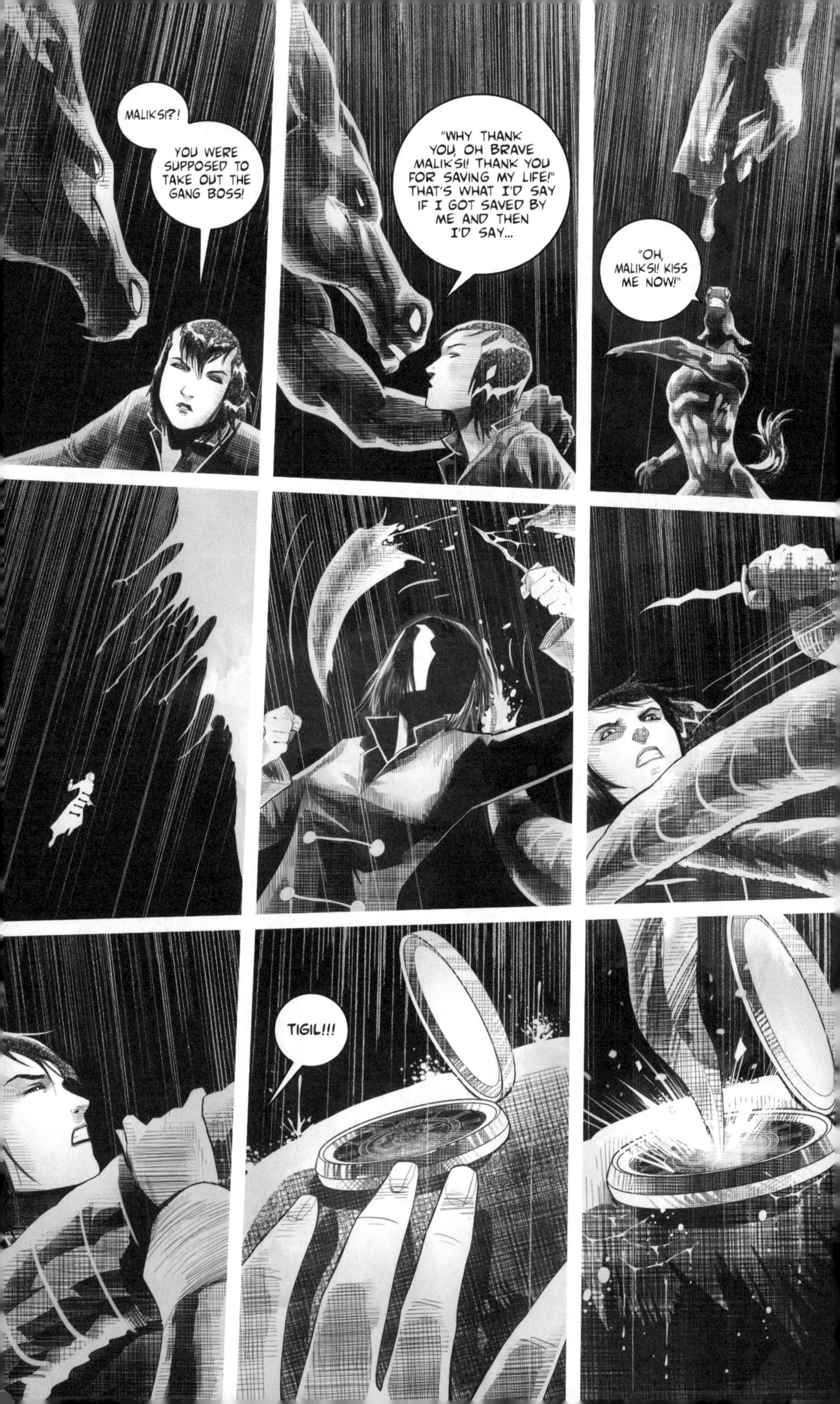
MALIKSI?!
YOU WERE SUPPOSED TO TAKE OUT THE GANG BOSS!
"WHY THANK YOU, OH BRAVE MALIKSI! THANK YOU FOR SAVING MY LIFE!" THAT'S WHAT I'D SAY IF I GOT SAVED BY ME AND THEN I'D SAY...
"OH, MALIKSI! KISS ME NOW!"
TIGIL!!!

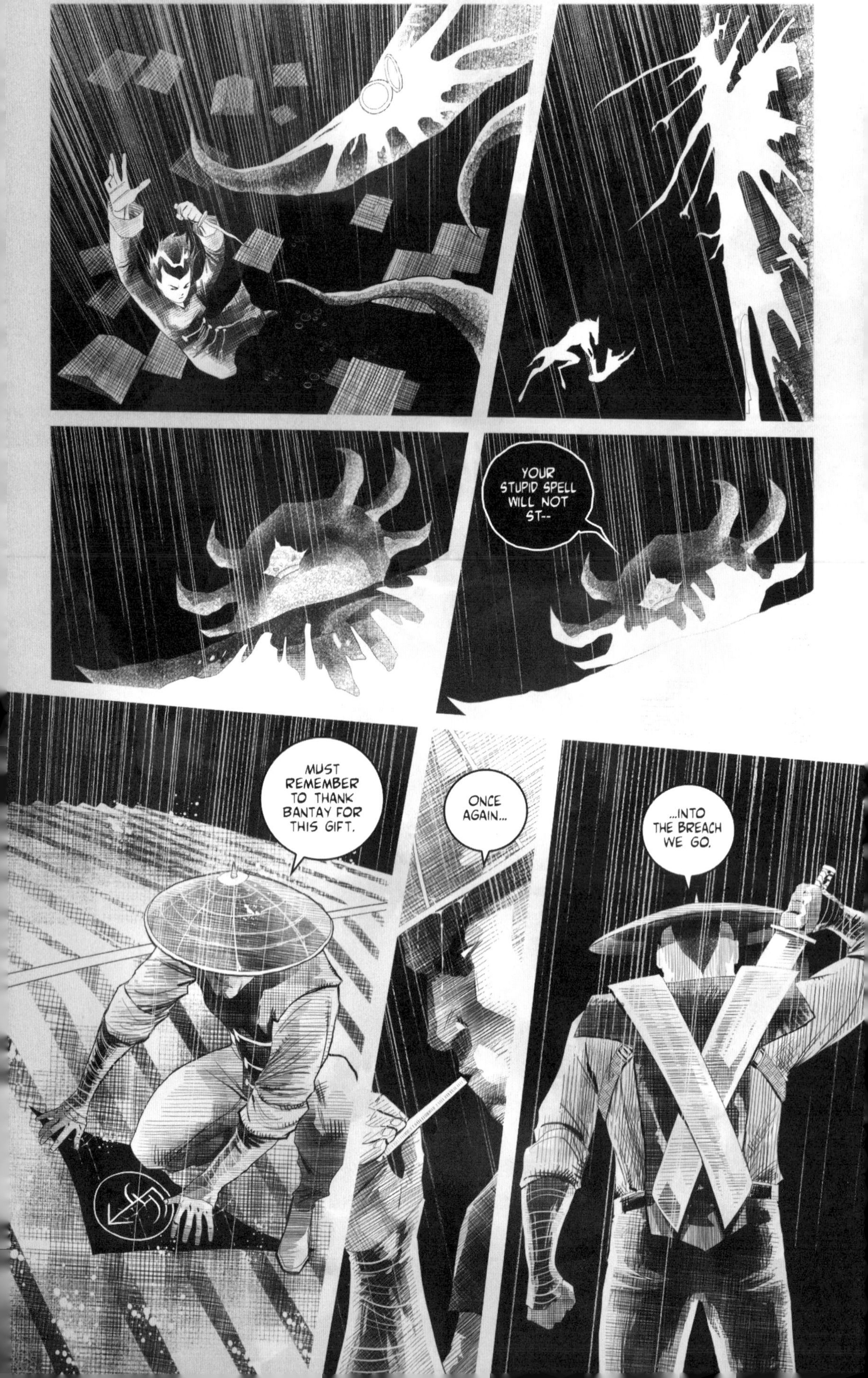
YOUR STUPID SPELL WILL NOT ST--
MUST REMEMBER TO THANK BANTAY FOR THIS GIFT.
ONCE AGAIN...
...INTO THE BREACH WE GO.

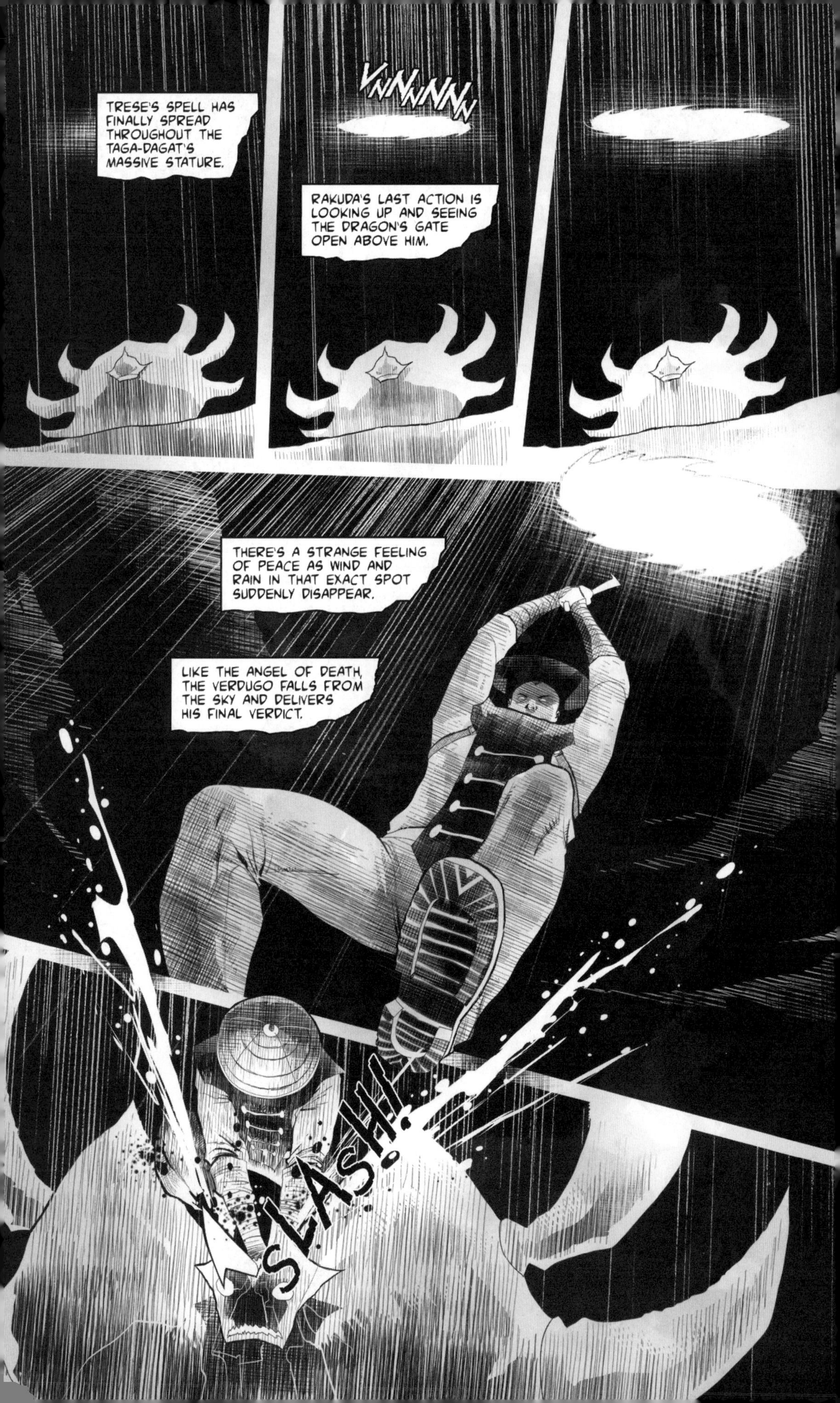
TRESE'S SPELL HAS FINALLY SPREAD THROUGHOUT THE TAGA-DAGAT'S MASSIVE STATURE.
VNNNNNN
RAKUDA'S LAST ACTION IS LOOKING UP AND SEEING THE DRAGON'S GATE OPEN ABOVE HIM.
THERE'S A STRANGE FEELING OF PEACE AS WIND AND RAIN IN THAT EXACT SPOT SUDDENLY DISAPPEAR.
LIKE THE ANGEL OF DEATH, THE VERDUGO FALLS FROM THE SKY AND DELIVERS HIS FINAL VERDICT.
SLASH!!

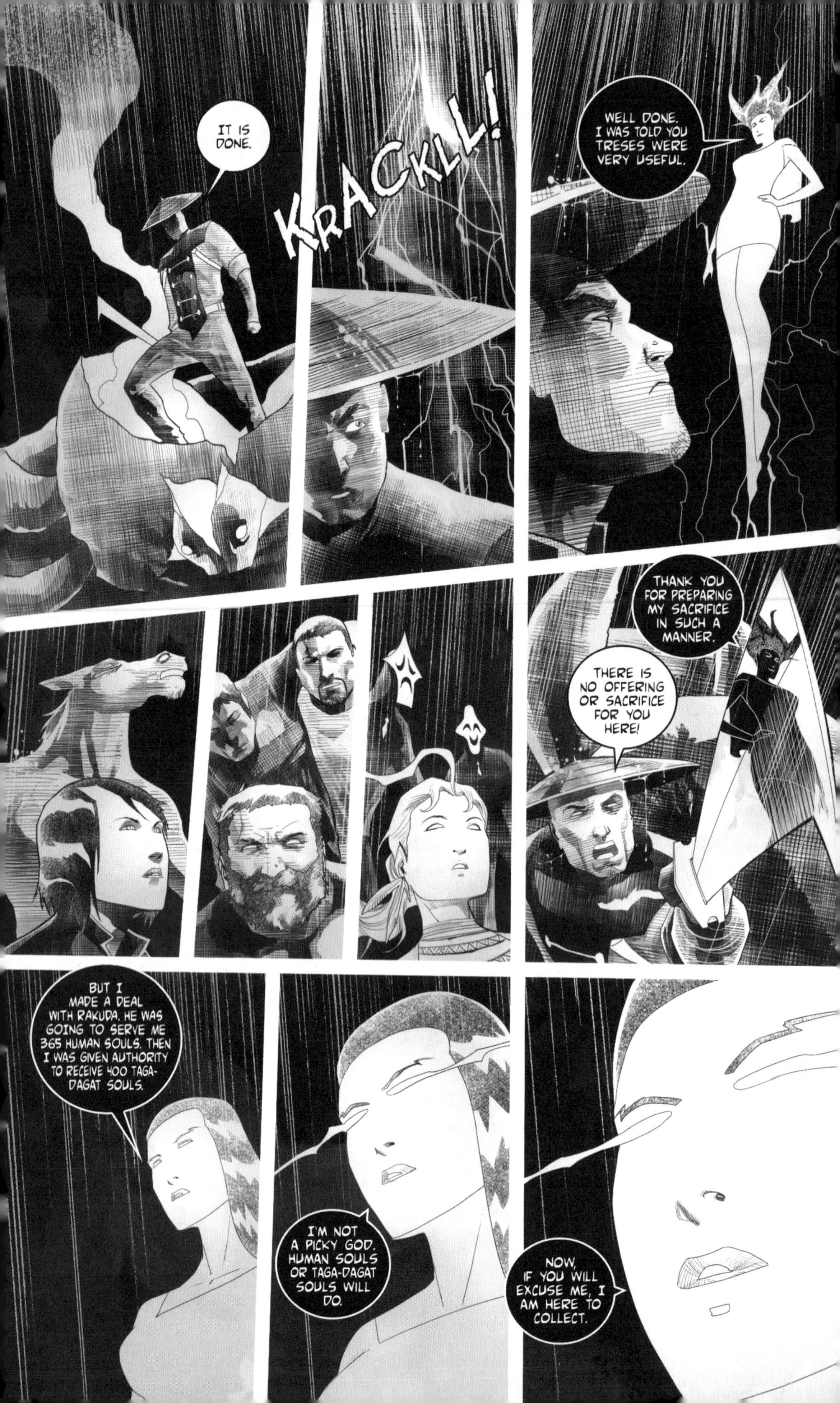
IT IS DONE.
KRACKLL!
WELL DONE. I WAS TOLD YOU TRESES WERE VERY USEFUL.
THANK YOU FOR PREPARING MY SACRIFICE IN SUCH A MANNER.
THERE IS NO OFFERING OR SACRIFICE FOR YOU HERE!
BUT I MADE A DEAL WITH RAKUDA. HE WAS GOING TO SERVE ME 365 HUMAN SOULS. THEN I WAS GIVEN AUTHORITY TO RECEIVE 400 TAGA-DAGAT SOULS.
I'M NOT A PICKY GOD. HUMAN SOULS OR TAGA-DAGAT SOULS WILL DO.
NOW, IF YOU WILL EXCUSE ME, I AM HERE TO COLLECT.

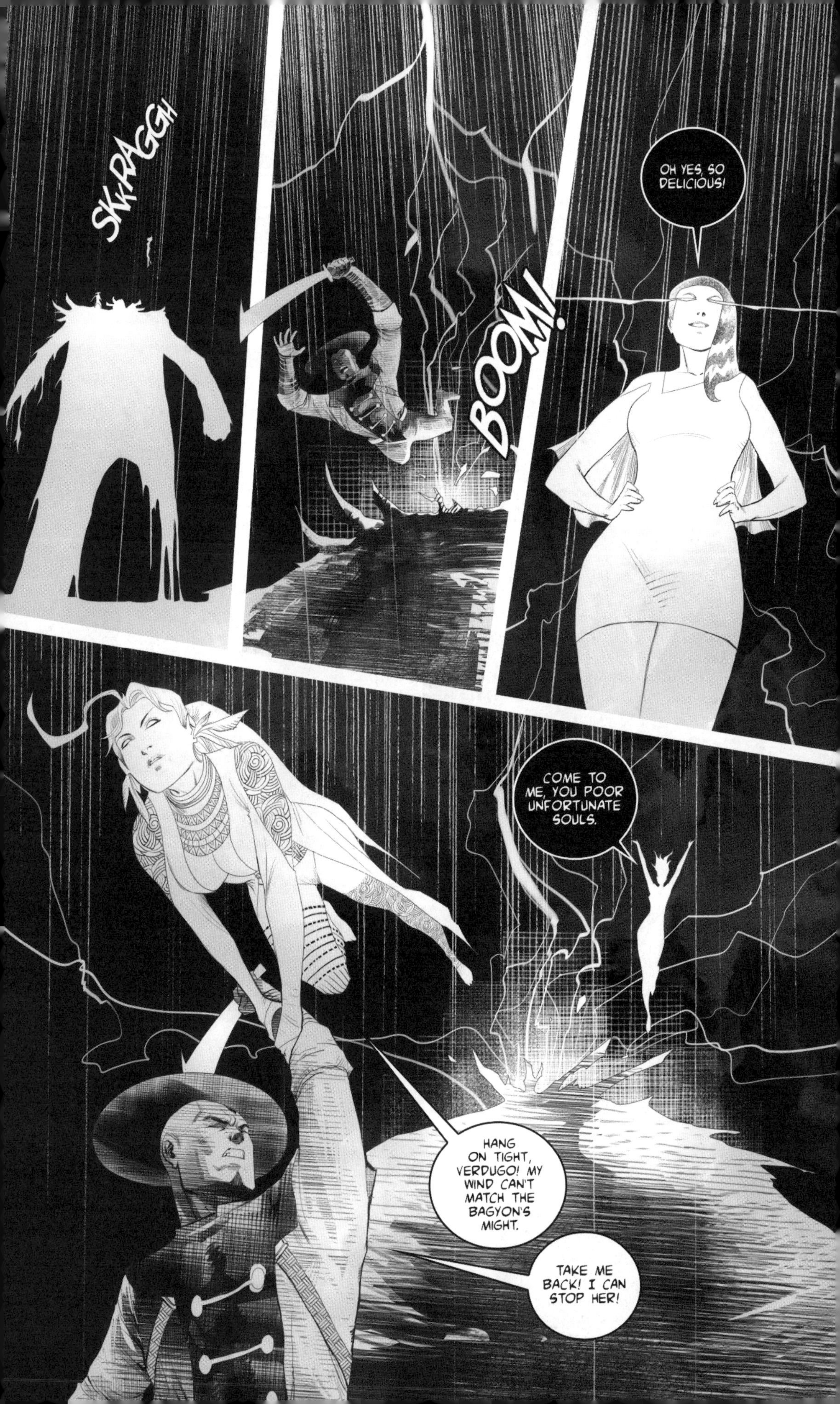
SKKRAGGH
BOOM!
OH YES, SO DELICIOUS!
COME TO ME, YOU POOR UNFORTUNATE SOULS.
HANG ON TIGHT, VERDUGO! MY WIND CAN'T MATCH THE BAGYON'S MIGHT.
TAKE ME BACK! I CAN STOP HER!

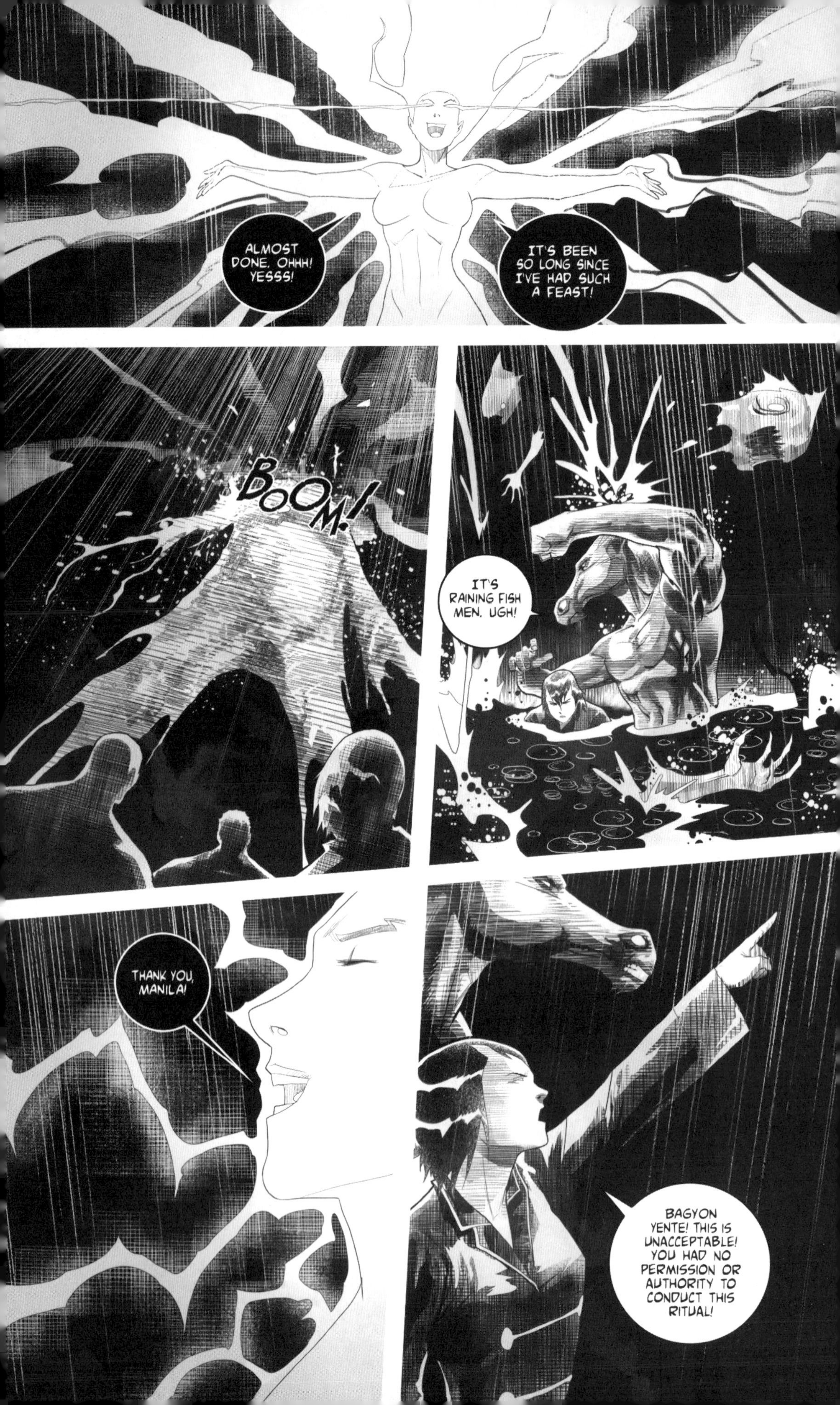
ALMOST DONE. OHHH! YESSS!
IT'S BEEN SO LONG SINCE I'VE HAD SUCH A FEAST!
BOOM!
IT'S RAINING FISH MEN. UGH!
THANK YOU, MANILA!
BAGYON YENTE! THIS IS UNACCEPTABLE! YOU HAD NO PERMISSION OR AUTHORITY TO CONDUCT THIS RITUAL!

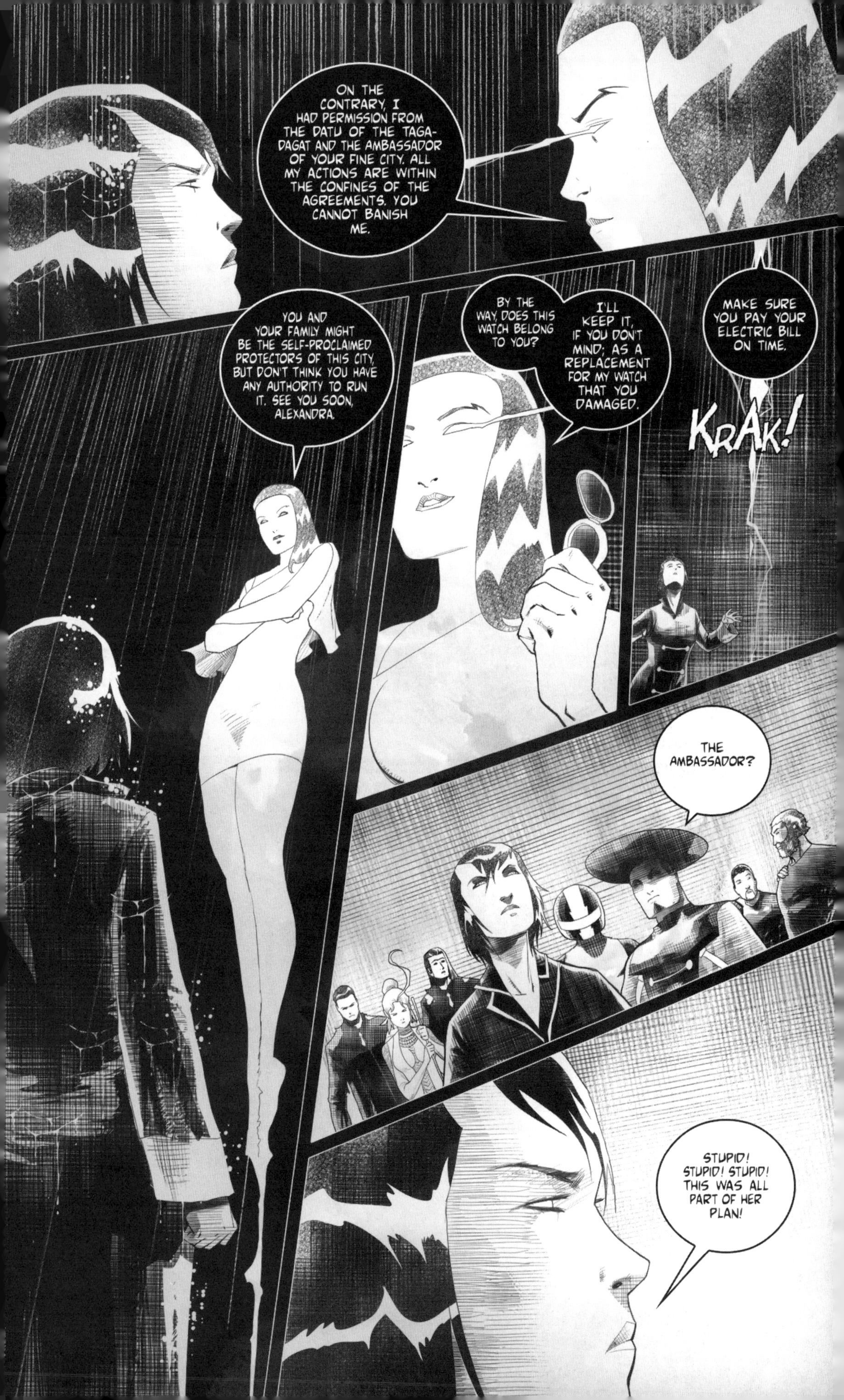
ON THE CONTRARY, I HAD PERMISSION FROM THE DATU OF THE TAGA-DAGAT AND THE AMBASSADOR OF YOUR FINE CITY. ALL MY ACTIONS ARE WITHIN THE CONFINES OF THE AGREEMENTS. YOU CANNOT BANISH ME.
YOU AND YOUR FAMILY MIGHT BE THE SELF-PROCLAIMED PROTECTORS OF THIS CITY, BUT DON'T THINK YOU HAVE ANY AUTHORITY TO RUN IT. SEE YOU SOON, ALEXANDRA.
BY THE WAY, DOES THIS WATCH BELONG TO YOU?
I'LL KEEP IT, IF YOU DON'T MIND; AS A REPLACEMENT FOR MY WATCH THAT YOU DAMAGED.
MAKE SURE YOU PAY YOUR ELECTRIC BILL ON TIME.
KRAK!
THE AMBASSADOR?
STUPID! STUPID! STUPID! THIS WAS ALL PART OF HER PLAN!

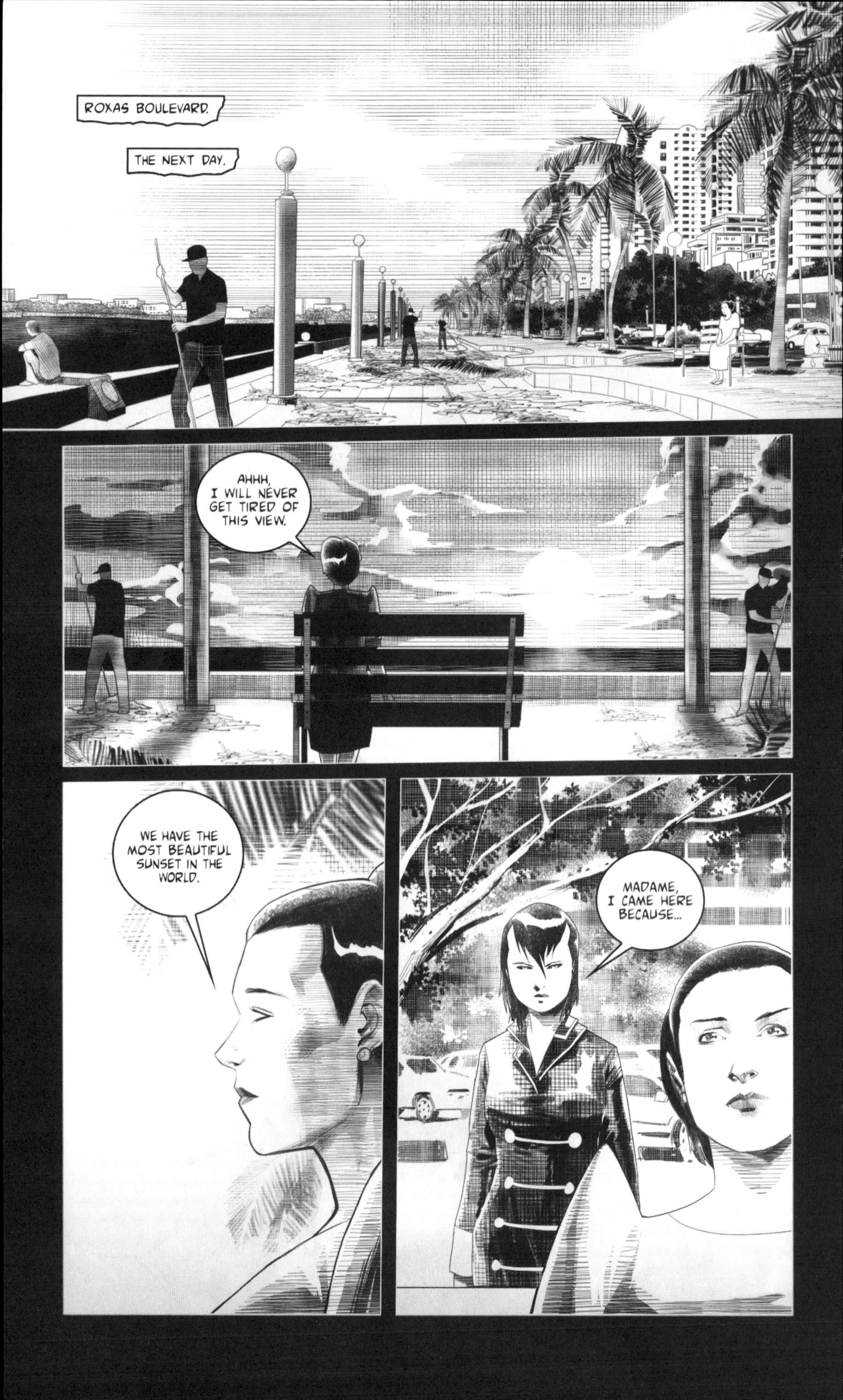
ROXAS BOULEVARD.
THE NEXT DAY.
AHHH, I WILL NEVER GET TIRED OF THIS VIEW.
WE HAVE THE MOST BEAUTIFUL SUNSET IN THE WORLD.
MADAME, I CAME HERE BECAUSE...

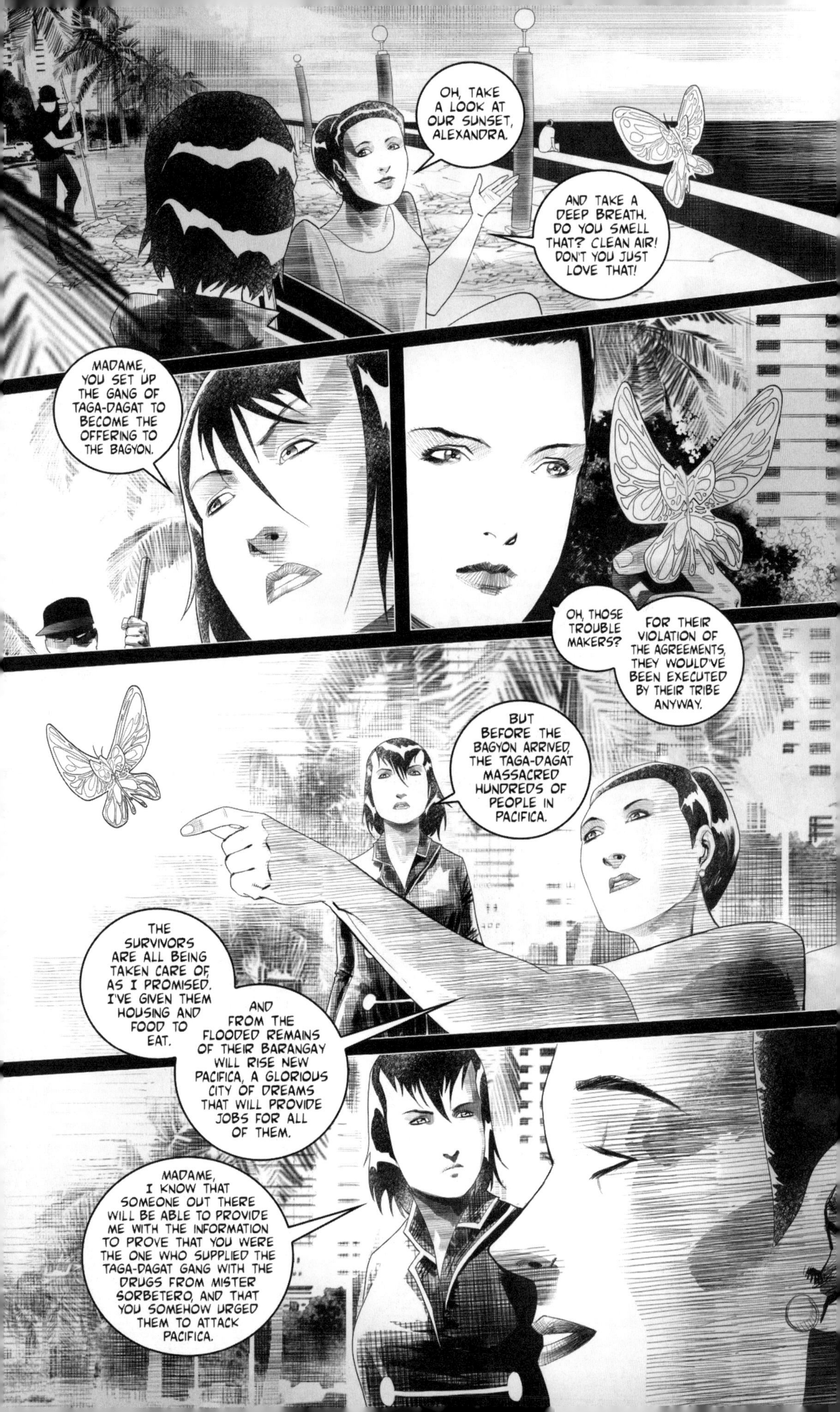
OH, TAKE A LOOK AT OUR SUNSET, ALEXANDRA.
AND TAKE A DEEP BREATH. DO YOU SMELL THAT? CLEAN AIR! DON'T YOU JUST LOVE THAT!
MADAME, YOU SET UP THE GANG OF TAGA-DAGAT TO BECOME THE OFFERING TO THE BAGYON.
OH, THOSE TROUBLE MAKERS?
FOR THEIR VIOLATION OF THE AGREEMENTS, THEY WOULD'VE BEEN EXECUTED BY THEIR TRIBE ANYWAY.
BUT BEFORE THE BAGYON ARRIVED, THE TAGA-DAGAT MASSACRED HUNDREDS OF PEOPLE IN PACIFICA.
THE SURVIVORS ARE ALL BEING TAKEN CARE OF, AS I PROMISED. I'VE GIVEN THEM HOUSING AND FOOD TO EAT.
AND FROM THE FLOODED REMAINS OF THEIR BARANGAY WILL RISE NEW PACIFICA, A GLORIOUS CITY OF DREAMS THAT WILL PROVIDE JOBS FOR ALL OF THEM.
MADAME, I KNOW THAT SOMEONE OUT THERE WILL BE ABLE TO PROVIDE ME WITH THE INFORMATION TO PROVE THAT YOU WERE THE ONE WHO SUPPLIED THE TAGA-DAGAT GANG WITH THE DRUGS FROM MISTER SORBETERO, AND THAT YOU SOMEHOW URGED THEM TO ATTACK PACIFICA.

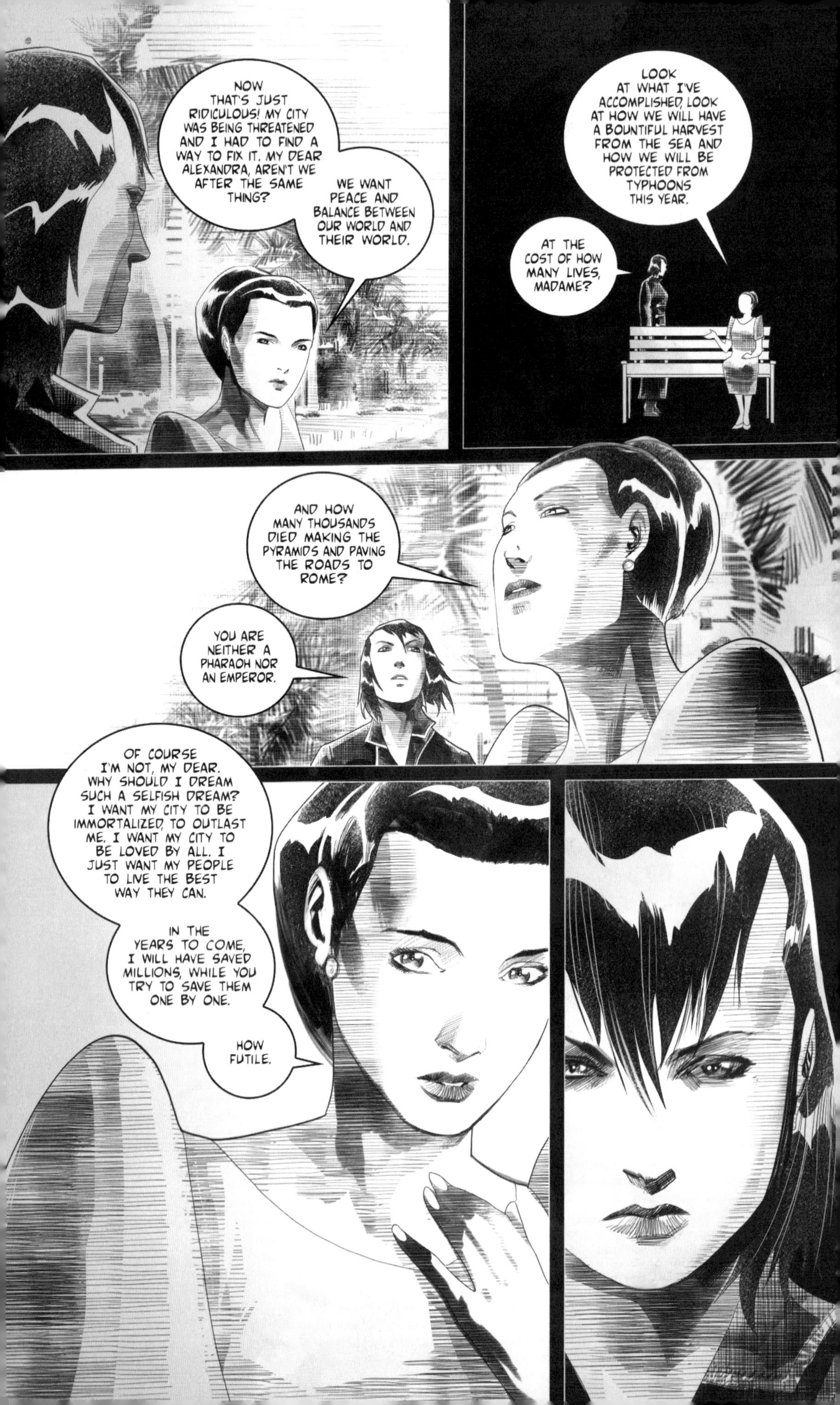
NOW THAT'S JUST RIDICULOUS! MY CITY WAS BEING THREATENED AND I HAD TO FIND A WAY TO FIX IT. MY DEAR ALEXANDRA, AREN'T WE AFTER THE SAME THING?
WE WANT PEACE AND BALANCE BETWEEN OUR WORLD AND THEIR WORLD.
LOOK AT WHAT I'VE ACCOMPLISHED, LOOK AT HOW WE WILL HAVE A BOUNTIFUL HARVEST FROM THE SEA AND HOW WE WILL BE PROTECTED FROM TYPHOONS THIS YEAR.
AT THE COST OF HOW MANY LIVES, MADAME?
AND HOW MANY THOUSANDS DIED MAKING THE PYRAMIDS AND PAVING THE ROADS TO ROME?
YOU ARE NEITHER A PHARAOH NOR AN EMPEROR.
OF COURSE I'M NOT, MY DEAR. WHY SHOULD I DREAM SUCH A SELFISH DREAM? I WANT MY CITY TO BE IMMORTALIZED, TO OUTLAST ME. I WANT MY CITY TO BE LOVED BY ALL. I JUST WANT MY PEOPLE TO LIVE THE BEST WAY THEY CAN.
IN THE YEARS TO COME, I WILL HAVE SAVED MILLIONS, WHILE YOU TRY TO SAVE THEM ONE BY ONE.
HOW FUTILE.

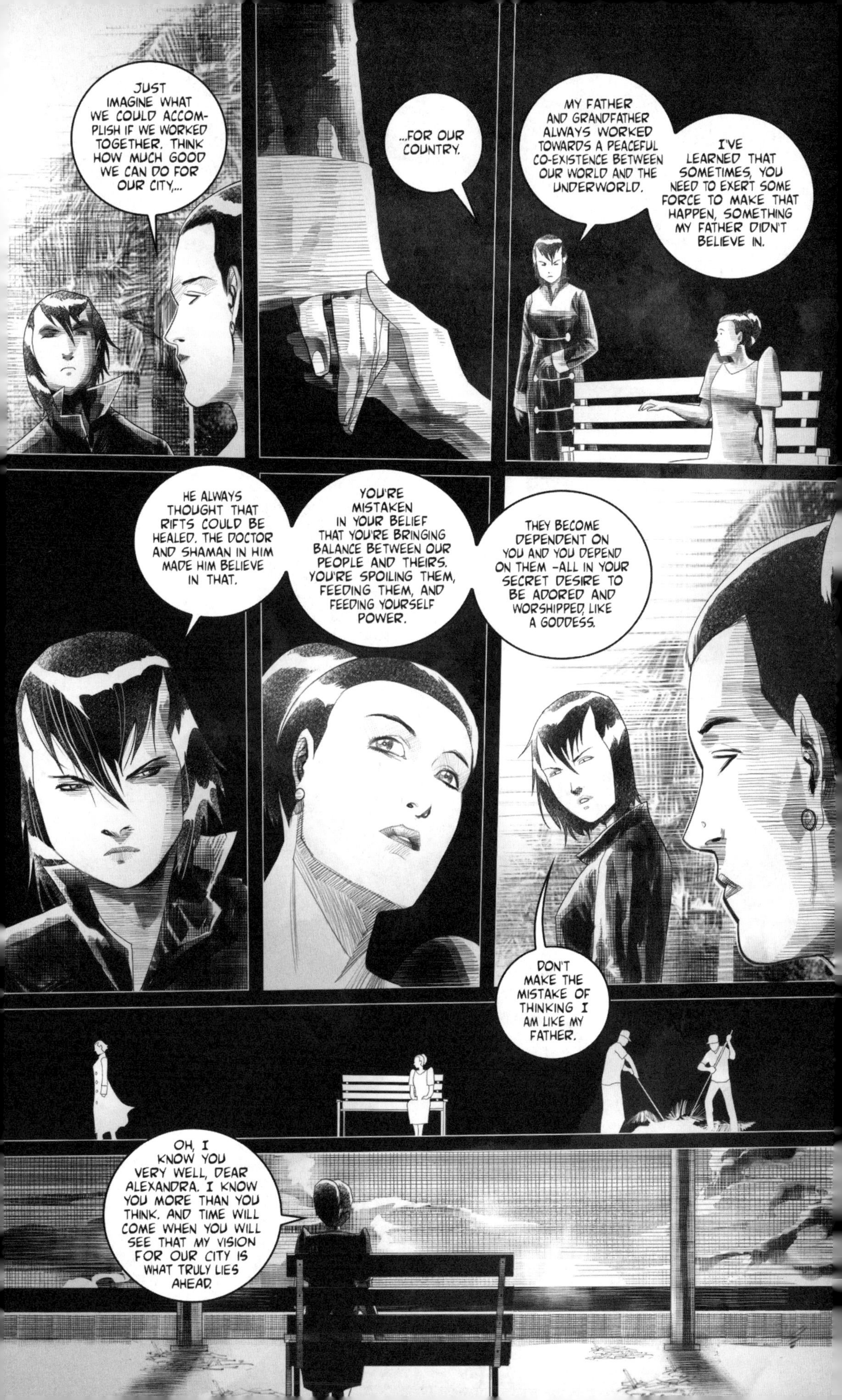
JUST IMAGINE WHAT WE COULD ACCOMPLISH IF WE WORKED TOGETHER. THINK HOW MUCH GOOD WE CAN DO FOR OUR CITY,...
...FOR OUR COUNTRY.
MY FATHER AND GRANDFATHER ALWAYS WORKED TOWARDS A PEACEFUL CO-EXISTENCE BETWEEN OUR WORLD AND THE UNDERWORLD.
I'VE LEARNED THAT SOMETIMES, YOU NEED TO EXERT SOME FORCE TO MAKE THAT HAPPEN, SOMETHING MY FATHER DIDN'T BELIEVE IN.
HE ALWAYS THOUGHT THAT RIFTS COULD BE HEALED. THE DOCTOR AND SHAMAN IN HIM MADE HIM BELIEVE IN THAT.
YOU'RE MISTAKEN IN YOUR BELIEF THAT YOU'RE BRINGING BALANCE BETWEEN OUR PEOPLE AND THEIRS. YOU'RE SPOILING THEM, FEEDING THEM, AND FEEDING YOURSELF POWER.
THEY BECOME DEPENDENT ON YOU AND YOU DEPEND ON THEM -ALL IN YOUR SECRET DESIRE TO BE ADORED AND WORSHIPPED, LIKE A GODDESS.
DON'T MAKE THE MISTAKE OF THINKING I AM LIKE MY FATHER.
OH, I KNOW YOU VERY WELL, DEAR ALEXANDRA. I KNOW YOU MORE THAN YOU THINK. AND TIME WILL COME WHEN YOU WILL SEE THAT MY VISION FOR OUR CITY IS WHAT TRULY LIES AHEAD.

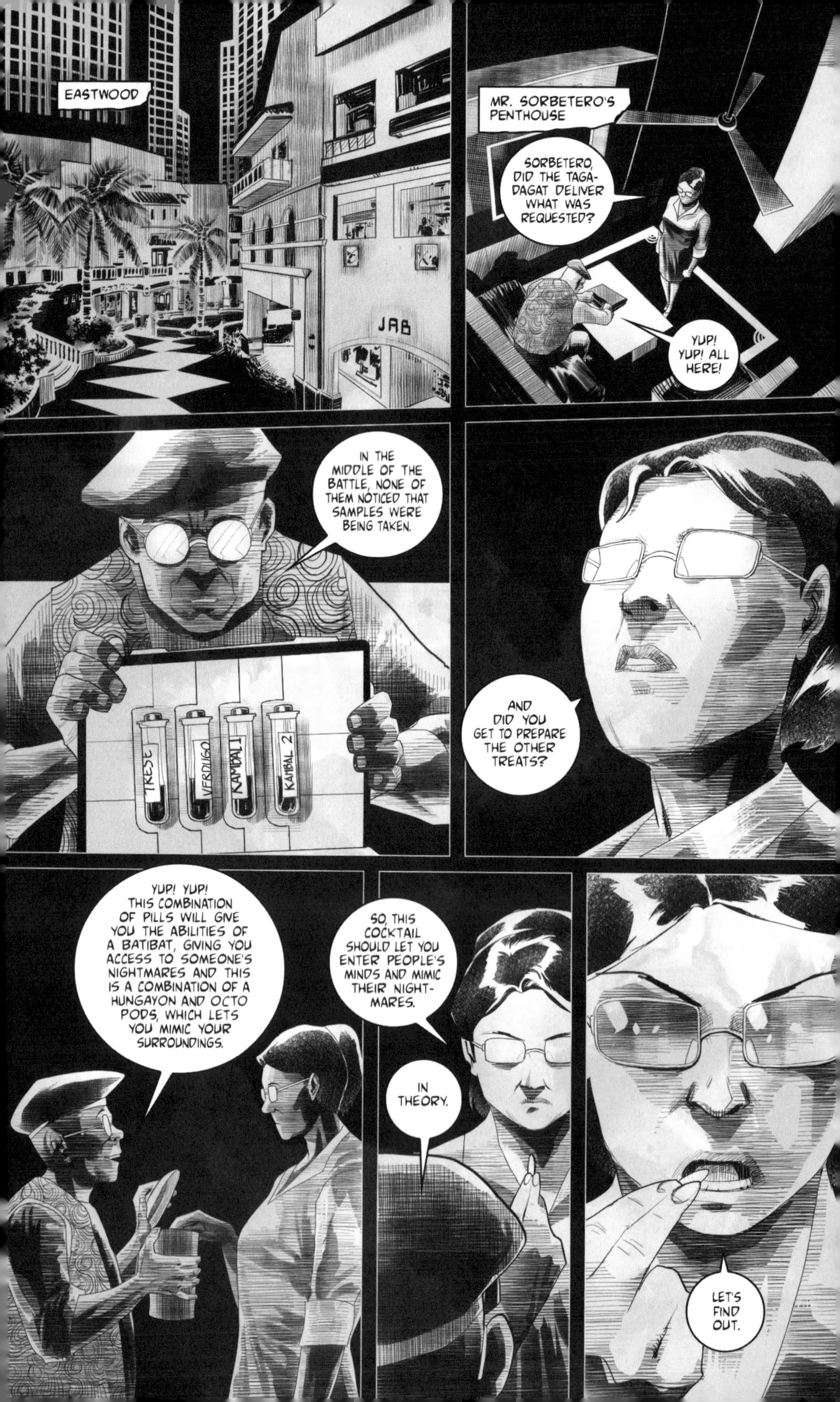

EASTWOOD
JAB
MR. SORBETERO'S PENTHOUSE
SORBETERO, DID THE TAGA-DAGAT DELIVER WHAT WAS REQUESTED?
YUP! YUP! ALL HERE!
IN THE MIDDLE OF THE BATTLE, NONE OF THEM NOTICED THAT SAMPLES WERE BEING TAKEN.
TIKESE
VERDUGO
KAMBAL 1
KAMBAL 2
AND DID YOU GET TO PREPARE THE OTHER TREATS?
YUP! YUP! THIS COMBINATION OF PILLS WILL GIVE YOU THE ABILITIES OF A BATIBAT, GIVING YOU ACCESS TO SOMEONE'S NIGHTMARES AND THIS IS A COMBINATION OF A HUNGAYON AND OCTO PODS, WHICH LETS YOU MIMIC YOUR SURROUNDINGS.
SO, THIS COCKTAIL SHOULD LET YOU ENTER PEOPLE'S MINDS AND MIMIC THEIR NIGHT-MARES.
IN THEORY.
LET'S FIND OUT.

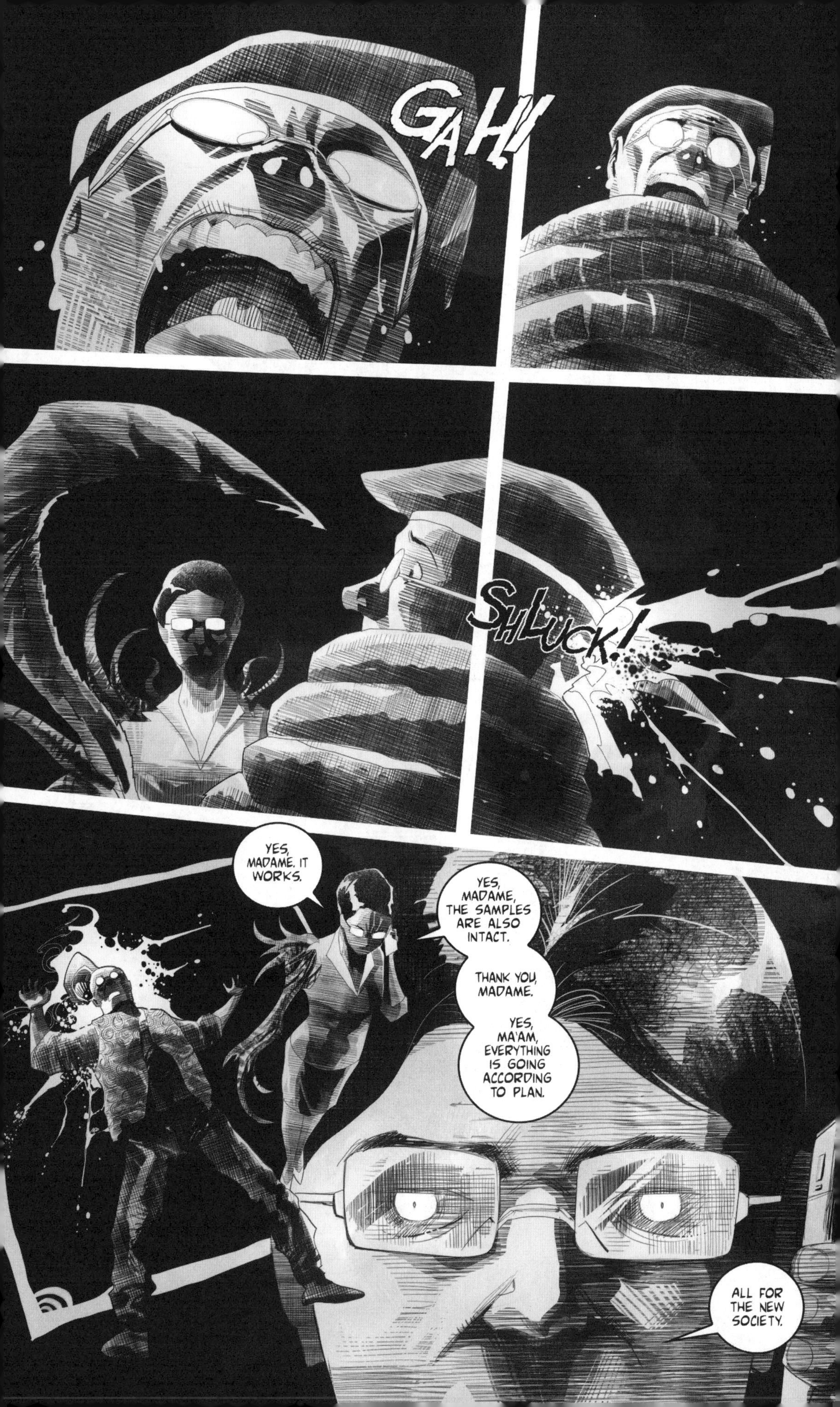
GAH!
SHLUCK!
YES, MADAME. IT WORKS.
YES, MADAME, THE SAMPLES ARE ALSO INTACT.
THANK YOU, MADAME.
YES, MA'AM, EVERYTHING IS GOING ACCORDING TO PLAN.
ALL FOR THE NEW SOCIETY.

THE DIABOLICAL.

I DON'T NORMALLY DO THIS, BUT HANK INSISTED THAT WE GATHER FOR A MEAL.

OH, I JUST WANTED AN EXCUSE TO SEE YOU KIDS ALL TOGETHER AGAIN.

AND OF COURSE, WE MUST THANK ALEXANDRA FOR CASTING THAT HEALING SPELL AND MAKING US READY FOR THE NEXT BATTLE!

IT WAS SO MUCH FUN! CARLOS, WHEN ARE WE GOING TO DO THIS AGAIN?

AGAIN? WELL... I GUESS WHENEVER WE NEED TO HANDLE ANOTHER MAJOR THREAT.

LOVELY! THEN WE SHOULD HAVE A NAME.

LIKE A TEAM? LIKE A SUPER TEAM?

WELL, SINCE IT WAS OUR DEAR FRIEND WHO GATHERED ALL OF US, MAYBE WE SHOULD BE CALLED...

VERDUGO'S SIX... UMMM...

SEVEN! WAIT... WHERE'S BANTAY?

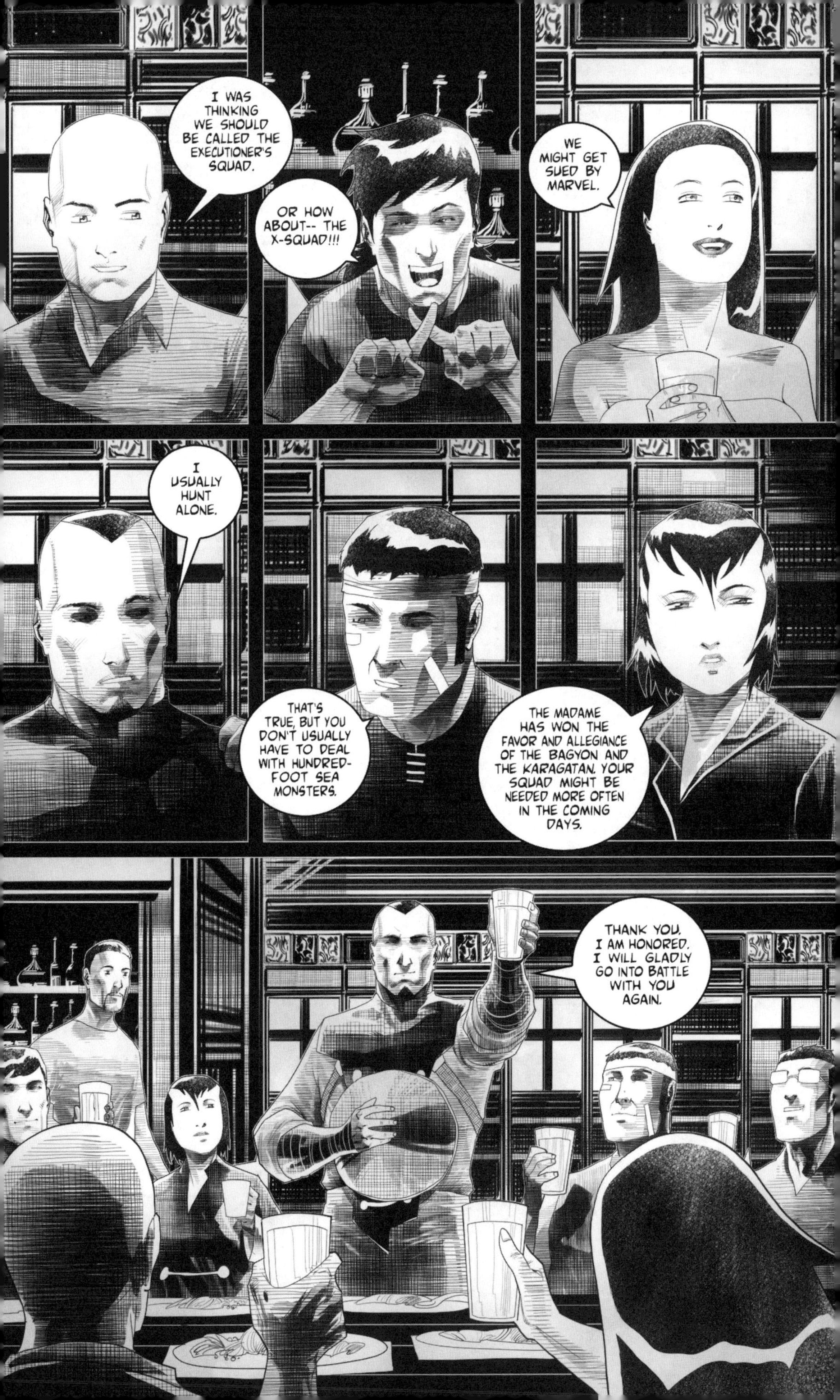
I WAS THINKING WE SHOULD BE CALLED THE EXECUTIONER'S SQUAD.
OR HOW ABOUT-- THE X-SQUAD!!!
WE MIGHT GET SUED BY MARVEL.
I USUALLY HUNT ALONE.
THAT'S TRUE, BUT YOU DON'T USUALLY HAVE TO DEAL WITH HUNDRED-FOOT SEA MONSTERS.
THE MADAME HAS WON THE FAVOR AND ALLEGIANCE OF THE BAGYON AND THE KARAGATAN. YOUR SQUAD MIGHT BE NEEDED MORE OFTEN IN THE COMING DAYS.
THANK YOU. I AM HONORED. I WILL GLADLY GO INTO BATTLE WITH YOU AGAIN.

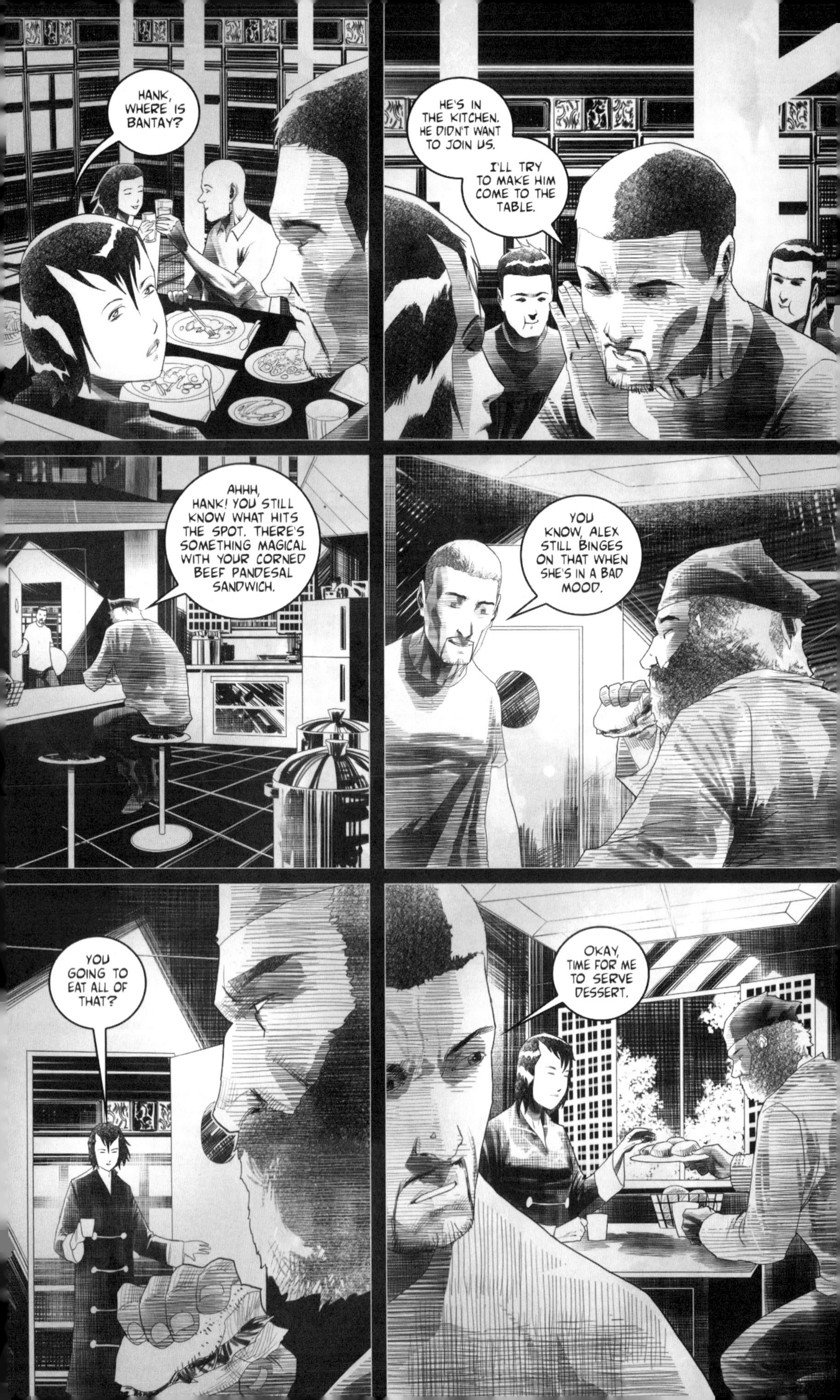
HANK, WHERE IS BANTAY?
HE'S IN THE KITCHEN. HE DIDN'T WANT TO JOIN US.
I'LL TRY TO MAKE HIM COME TO THE TABLE.
AHHH, HANK! YOU STILL KNOW WHAT HITS THE SPOT. THERE'S SOMETHING MAGICAL WITH YOUR CORNED BEEF PANDESAL SANDWICH.
YOU KNOW, ALEX STILL BINGES ON THAT WHEN SHE'S IN A BAD MOOD.
YOU GOING TO EAT ALL OF THAT?
OKAY, TIME FOR ME TO SERVE DESSERT.

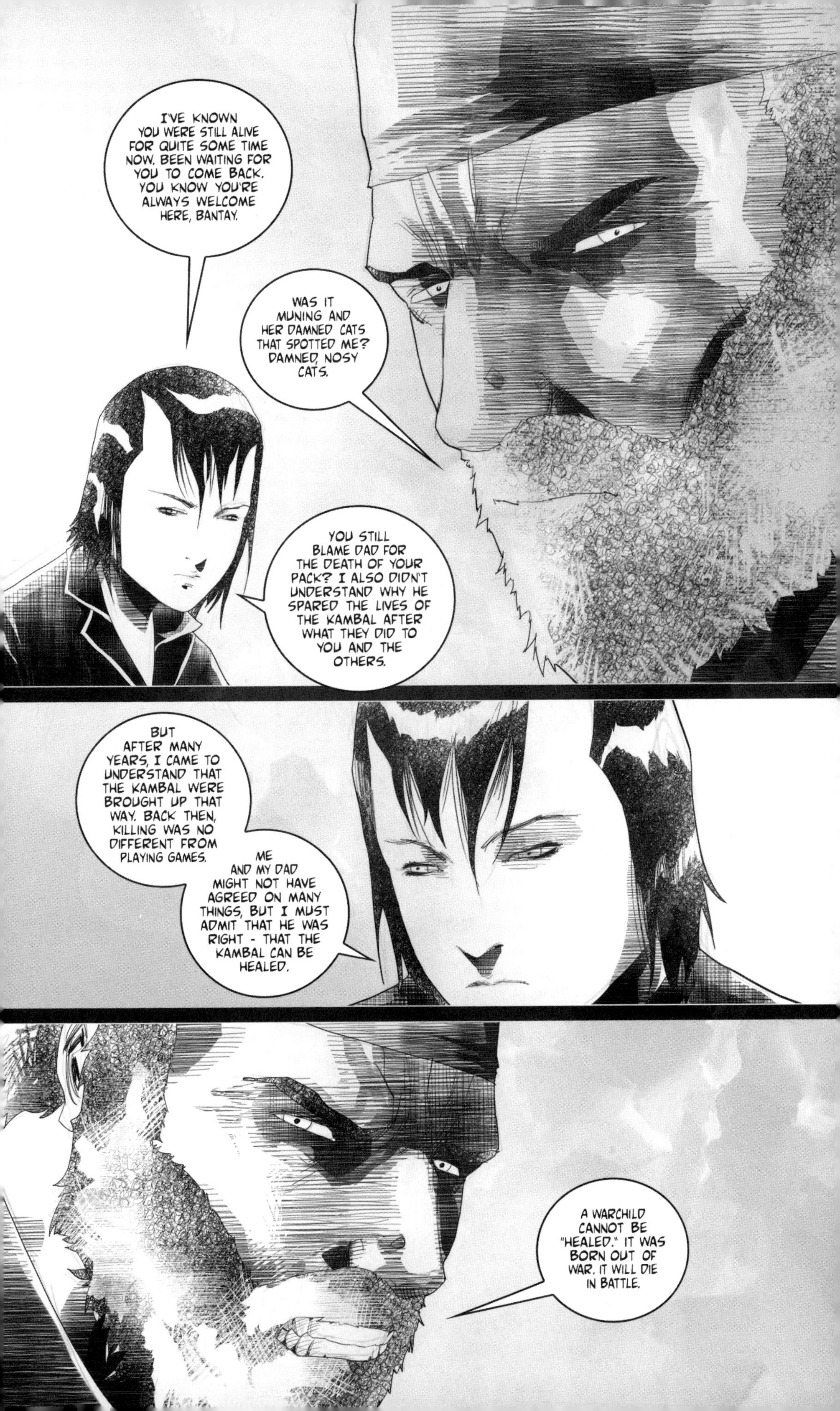
I'VE KNOWN YOU WERE STILL ALIVE FOR QUITE SOME TIME NOW. BEEN WAITING FOR YOU TO COME BACK. YOU KNOW YOU'RE ALWAYS WELCOME HERE, BANTAY.
WAS IT MUNING AND HER DAMNED CATS THAT SPOTTED ME? DAMNED, NOSY CATS.
YOU STILL BLAME DAD FOR THE DEATH OF YOUR PACK? I ALSO DIDN'T UNDERSTAND WHY HE SPARED THE LIVES OF THE KAMBAL AFTER WHAT THEY DID TO YOU AND THE OTHERS.
BUT AFTER MANY YEARS, I CAME TO UNDERSTAND THAT THE KAMBAL WERE BROUGHT UP THAT WAY. BACK THEN, KILLING WAS NO DIFFERENT FROM PLAYING GAMES.
ME AND MY DAD MIGHT NOT HAVE AGREED ON MANY THINGS, BUT I MUST ADMIT THAT HE WAS RIGHT - THAT THE KAMBAL CAN BE HEALED.
A WARCHILD CANNOT BE "HEALED." IT WAS BORN OUT OF WAR. IT WILL DIE IN BATTLE.

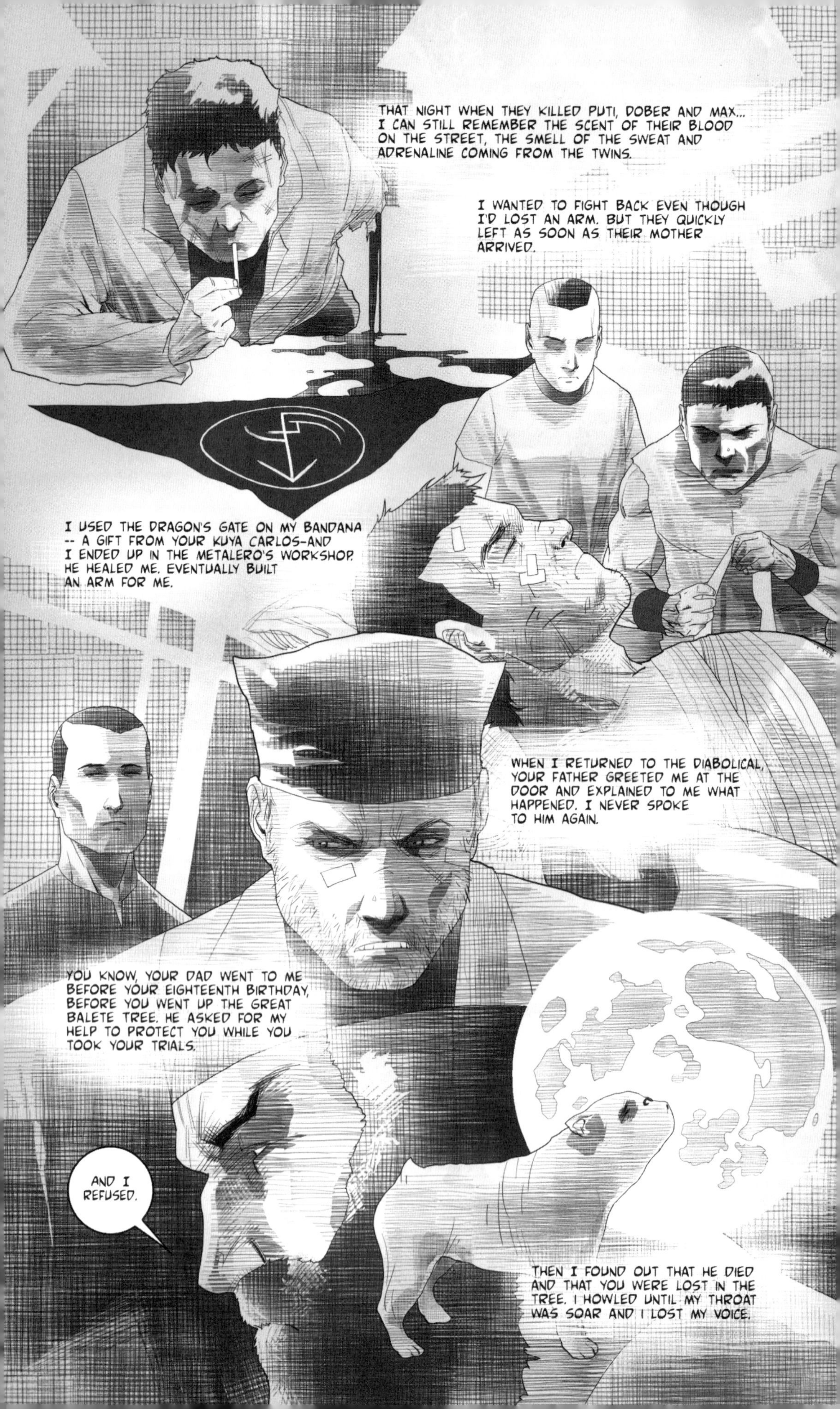
THAT NIGHT WHEN THEY KILLED PUTI, DOBER AND MAX... I CAN STILL REMEMBER THE SCENT OF THEIR BLOOD ON THE STREET, THE SMELL OF THE SWEAT AND ADRENALINE COMING FROM THE TWINS.
I WANTED TO FIGHT BACK EVEN THOUGH I'D LOST AN ARM. BUT THEY QUICKLY LEFT AS SOON AS THEIR MOTHER ARRIVED.
I USED THE DRAGON'S GATE ON MY BANDANA -- A GIFT FROM YOUR KUYA CARLOS-AND I ENDED UP IN THE METALERO'S WORKSHOP. HE HEALED ME. EVENTUALLY BUILT AN ARM FOR ME.
WHEN I RETURNED TO THE DIABOLICAL, YOUR FATHER GREETED ME AT THE DOOR AND EXPLAINED TO ME WHAT HAPPENED. I NEVER SPOKE TO HIM AGAIN.
YOU KNOW, YOUR DAD WENT TO ME BEFORE YOUR EIGHTEENTH BIRTHDAY, BEFORE YOU WENT UP THE GREAT BALETE TREE. HE ASKED FOR MY HELP TO PROTECT YOU WHILE YOU TOOK YOUR TRIALS.
AND I REFUSED.
THEN I FOUND OUT THAT HE DIED AND THAT YOU WERE LOST IN THE TREE. I HOWLED UNTIL MY THROAT WAS SOAR AND I LOST MY VOICE.

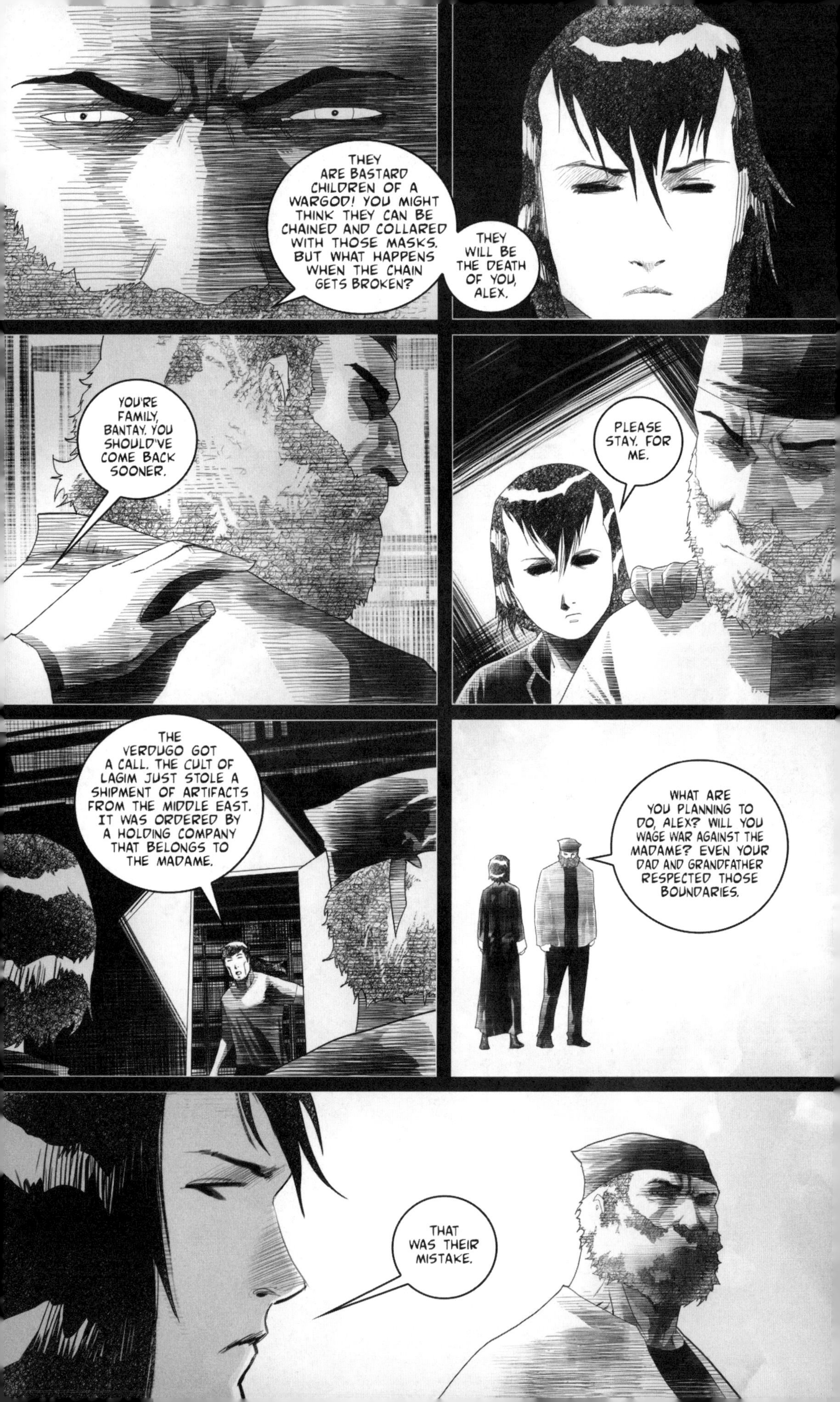
THEY ARE BASTARD CHILDREN OF A WARGOD! YOU MIGHT THINK THEY CAN BE CHAINED AND COLLARED WITH THOSE MASKS. BUT WHAT HAPPENS WHEN THE CHAIN GETS BROKEN?
THEY WILL BE THE DEATH OF YOU, ALEX.
YOU'RE FAMILY, BANTAY. YOU SHOULD'VE COME BACK SOONER.
PLEASE STAY. FOR ME.
THE VERDUGO GOT A CALL. THE CULT OF LAGIM JUST STOLE A SHIPMENT OF ARTIFACTS FROM THE MIDDLE EAST. IT WAS ORDERED BY A HOLDING COMPANY THAT BELONGS TO THE MADAME.
WHAT ARE YOU PLANNING TO DO, ALEX? WILL YOU WAGE WAR AGAINST THE MADAME? EVEN YOUR DAD AND GRANDFATHER RESPECTED THOSE BOUNDARIES.
THAT WAS THEIR MISTAKE.

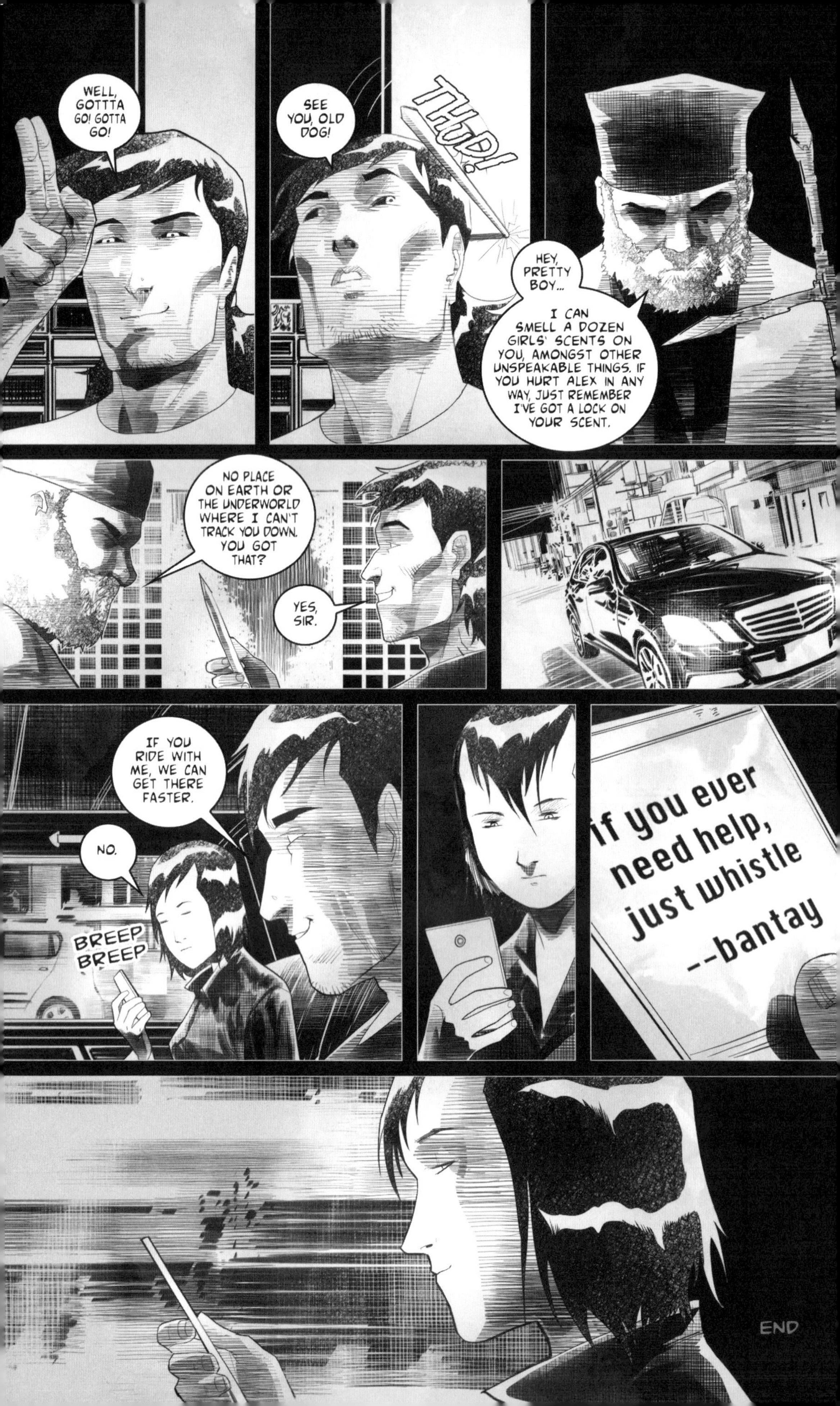

WELL, GOTTTA GO! GOTTA GO!
SEE YOU, OLD DOG!
THUD!
HEY, PRETTY BOY...
I CAN SMELL A DOZEN GIRLS' SCENTS ON YOU, AMONGST OTHER UNSPEAKABLE THINGS. IF YOU HURT ALEX IN ANY WAY, JUST REMEMBER I'VE GOT A LOCK ON YOUR SCENT.
NO PLACE ON EARTH OR THE UNDERWORLD WHERE I CAN'T TRACK YOU DOWN. YOU GOT THAT?
YES, SIR.
IF YOU RIDE WITH ME, WE CAN GET THERE FASTER.
NO.
BREEP BREEP
if you ever need help, just whistle --bantay
END

ABOUT THE AUTHORS

Budjette learned how to swim when his dad threw him in the deep end of the pool, which he how he learned most of life's most important lessons. In many occasions, he has jumped into / was pushed into projects that he thought he knew how to handle, only to realize that he had a lot to learn in order to finish it. Neil Gaiman once said, writing a serial comic book is like jumping off a plane while knitting your own parachute.

Kajo, like most people, admittedly or not, enjoys the feeling of sinking. He makes an effort, unconsciously, to hit the bottom whenever an opportunity presents itself. The pressure and the darkness underneath creates a certain drama that he craves from time to time. He enjoys the imaginary cheers and the victorious music playing in his mind's ear upon rising to the surface. His ego likes the sudden rush of oxygen as he prepares to sink again. He's addicted to this cycle.

But little by little, he's learning that drama is really unnecessary and just floating around is much more natural and fun.

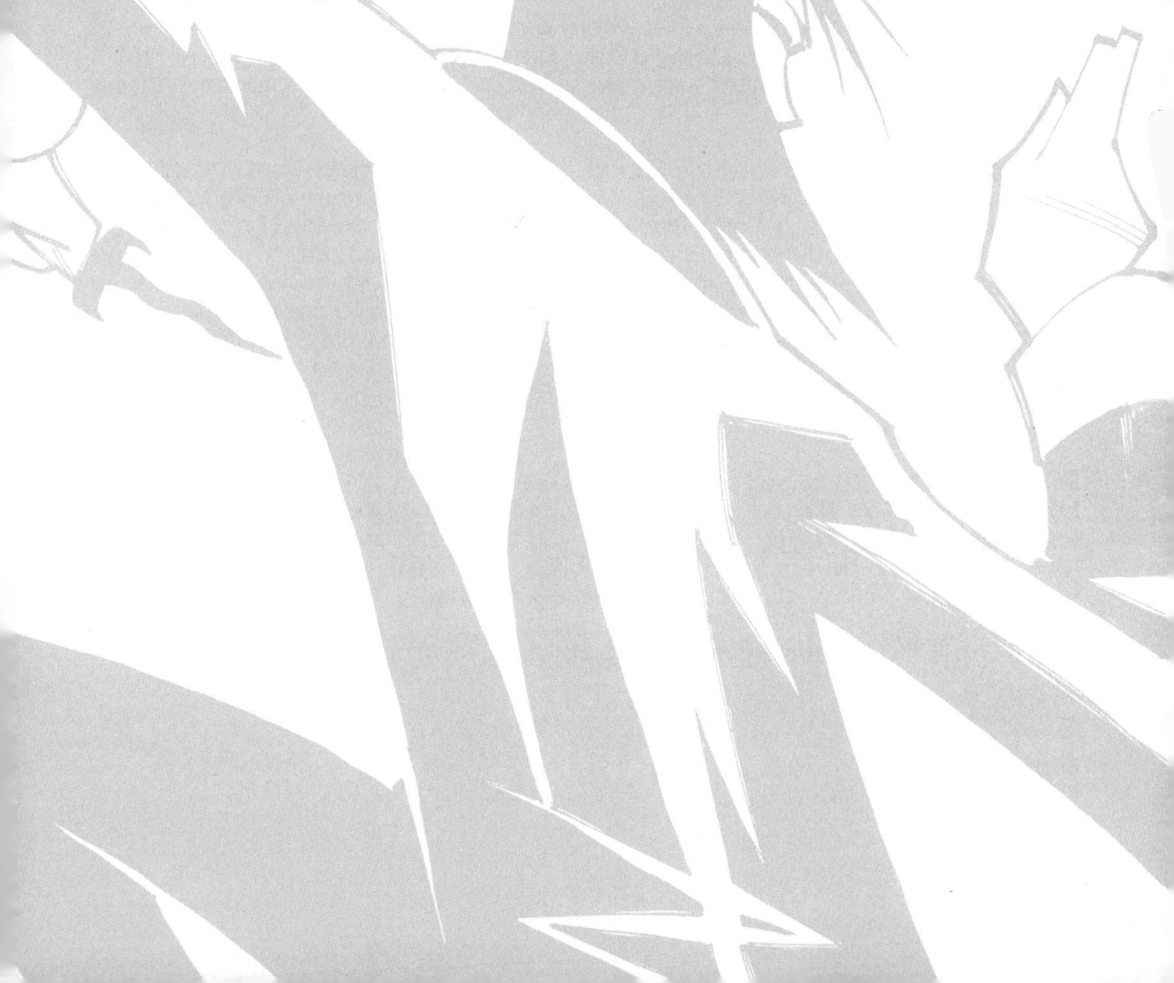

AFTERWORD

As most of you might already know, the name "Anton Trese" was the name of the fictional host we created for a radio show back in the 90s. The scripts were co-written/co-produced with my friend Mark Gatela, who thought up of the name Anton Trese.

One of our episodes was about a siokoy-type creature that hunted people in the city whenever it rained and the streets got flooded. I can't remember what I called the creature, but I definitely didn't want to call it a siokoy, since that elicited more giggles than screams. I have this vague memory of linking the creature's origins to the undersea city of Lemuria (probably because we were listening to too much Ernie Baron).

Years later, after Ondoy submerged the city, the idea of these undersea monsters came bubbling up to the surface of my brain. One of the images that got circulated on the net during that time was a certain part of the city that got surrounded by the flood waters, so it looked like a small island. That image reminded me of the comic book "30 Days of Night," where vampires discovered this town in Alaska that had to put up with a whole month without sunlight; which made it the perfect vacation spot for vampires.

So, I now had my setting and my main villains for the book. If Trese was going to go up against a whole tribe of Taga-Dagat, I thought she'd need a little help from her big brother. Ever since we introduced the four brothers in Book 3, we'd get the occasional question about them, which is why we decided to start bringing in the brothers one by one. Expect to see more of the Trese brothers in the next books!

We had a lot of fun with those scenes where Verdugo was recruiting the members of his Squad. I've always wanted to do a "recruitment sequence" similar to how Prof. X recruited the Uncanny X-Men, where we'd see a bit of each character and the Professor would come over.

Talking about the members of the Squad, we can already guess that you all have questions about the return of Bantay. Well, we had that planned all along, we just didn't know when we'd bring him back. (Okay, well, actually, Kajo had that planned all along – after we had finished Book 3, he pointed out to me that in the crime scene, there were only three bodies because he had meant for Bantay to somehow escape the Kambal after his arm got ripped off.) The original idea was for Bantay to hide under a nearby manhole, but as I started to write the script I thought that maybe he also had a vial of Dragon's Blood. It was Kajo who thought of putting the Dragon's Gate sigil on his bandana, which would give him easy access to the portal.

So, there you go kids, a look at how comics are made. It's not always mapped out, but most times, it's like a juggling routine between two people and you're just suddenly surprised that your partner threw you three balls and a chainsaw and you have to figure out how to keep the act going. If you do it right, then the audience will never know (unless you spill all your secrets, like this).

Once again, thank you very much for picking up, reading, and sharing our stories.

Budjette Tan
October 2014
Paranaque City